Watergirl

Cover Illustration: Juliann Whicker
Graphic Design: John H. Whicker

ISBN-13: 9781490445847
ISBN-10: 1490445846
Whicker Books, Athens, Ohio

For Charlotte and Evie, my own mermaids.

Chapter 1

It started like so many of my dreams, underwater. Everyone moved slowly through the halls of school, shadows of blue and green shading faces of people I knew so they looked different, special. I didn't notice the water we all moved through, didn't think anything about it until someone dropped a notebook and the papers fell up, spreading around me like a whirlpool had caught them. That's when I realized that I couldn't breathe. I batted the papers away from me when they clung to my face and arms, covering my nose and mouth as though the water wasn't enough.

When I gasped myself awake in my bed, still tangled in my daisy printed sheet and my night-shirt while I struggled to breathe, I counted to ten then started over when my heart wouldn't stop pounding, lungs straining to catch any oxygen they could. I didn't have asthma, nothing except a not entirely irrational fear of water and drowning.

It sucked that the nightmare woke me up so early on one of the last few mornings that I could sleep in before school started. Summer was winding down, but it didn't act like it with record highs hitting our small town in rural Ohio, damp heat competing with the rattling air conditioner that tried so hard to pump the cold upstairs where we slept.

That afternoon, the sun beat down and the humidity sucked away my will as I shoved our eco conscious push mower with my last reserves of strength. If I'd followed my dad's advice, his, "It's going to get hot today. You should mow before ten," then I wouldn't have nearly died of heat stroke and been a perspiring mess, but I wouldn't have

compiled my new favorite playlist to listen to while mow-
ing, either. My dad didn't exactly understand my priorities,
then again, sometimes I didn't either.

Later, before work, I almost skipped the shower. I
hated showers anyway, but haunted from remnants of my
dreams, the idea of voluntary immersion was almost too
much. I saw in my mind the contemptuous curl of Sheila's
mouth if I didn't take a shower. My coworker's disgust
would last my entire shift, far longer than the clawing fear
of a two minute dunk.

I survived the trauma then rode my rusty trusty bike
to work letting the sun and wind dry my boring brown
hair on the way through the winding culdesacs to down-
town, passing the smoothie place to pull up at the red
brick two story stuck between a Chinese restaurant and a
pet store.

The sign, 'Jupiter's Moon' as far as I could tell, had
nothing to do with the music shop that sold a little bit of
sheet music, mostly CD's and videos downstairs, while
upstairs housed the massive record collection.

After I clocked in, I stood sorting the new music, the
stuff that would sell from the ones I'd stick in a pile for
people who'd be willing to dig for it, when the bell on the
front door jangled.

I looked over at Sheila where she swayed with her iPod
completely oblivious to the front door, blond hair swirling
around her shoulders in a way that reminded me of my
dream. Sheila was the pretty girl, hired to lure customers.
I was the tough girl, hired to keep the customers from taking off with stock, at least that's what Tuba said. That's not
his real name, obviously, it's just what he's called, a morph
of his name from middle school when he was called Tubby.
He still was Tuba Tubby when he jostled one of the players,
you know, football.

"Can I help you?" I asked, hopefully loud enough that
Sheila would hear and notice that I had more going on
than she did, but as usual she was completely oblivious. I
could only see the top of the customer's blue hat with some
sport insignia on it until he looked up.

Cole. My gut dropped into the basement. Cole was in my store. My brain stuttered, stopped then went into overdrive. I hadn't seen him all summer since I'd been avoiding anywhere he might be like a plague, unlike the last five summers I'd spent semi-stalking him, and now all my work, my struggle to maintain sanity and distance was crushed when he came to my store, my turf and flashed his smile at me. Cole smiled at me. My brain shut off again.

"Hi. Do you have the new..." He named a generic almost death metal band while I nodded, blinked then lurched between the shelves of musicals towards the back wall. He followed close behind me. Not close enough that when I stopped he ran into me, but close enough that I could drop kick him if I wanted to. I wanted to. If I kicked him down, he'd sweep me right on top of him.

The warning tightness in my chest forced my eyes off his stomach, where I could practically see the muscles beneath the t-shirt. No thoughts of being on top of Cole. No martial arts or memories of any kind allowed to mess up my mind. I couldn't think of the time before he played football when we were sparring partners and best friends. I couldn't think of that first kiss by the lake and the way I'd never thought about another guy since.

"So, do you know when the next album comes out?"

How many times had he asked that? His face had that blank look he got when he realized that it was me in front of him, the one girl in the world who he couldn't see, like I became a ghost that day in seventh grade.

"They spew that crap out every eighteen months. They don't want to be replaced by another nameless, soulless moneymaker by actually taking the time to make something worth hearing." Had I said that out loud? It was an almost intelligent thing to say. Maybe my summer avoiding him wasn't wasted after all.

I veered around him, nearly running to the cashier desk where I could duck under the counter and take a deep breath before standing, not meeting Cole's gaze when he handed me the death metal album. I rang him up and was giving him his receipt when the bell jangled again. I didn't have to look up to know who the giggling wave of euphoric stupidity was. Apparently Cole needed some cheering from his cheerleader girlfriend to help him with his bad music purchase.

"Watergirl, have you got anything good for when we go to Ceramic Lake today?" Sharky's tone was two octaves higher than mine, sweet enough it was almost forgivable when she giggled for no apparent reason. Seventh grade I'd fallen into the manatee pool on the school field trip and come out with a new name. Only in middle school would they use a near death experience against you.

I ignored her as I handed Cole his bag then grabbed an invoice sheet to stare at like I'd found a new religion. Her name was Sharly, but everyone I knew called her Sharky, just not to her face. It's called self-preservation. I'd been composing something memorable for the last day of high school, but I still had two long years to work on it.

I tried as hard as I could not to notice the way she draped herself over Cole named after Cole Porter who he actually used to listen to, but now he was lost to whiny metallic, kill, die, torture, music. It probably soothed Sharky. I smiled, looking up at the two of them with a smirk on my face.

"Have a nice day," I said with as much fake cheer as possible while Cole frowned, narrowing his eyes at me like he saw me, like he wondered what my smile hid, but of course that was giving him credit for more intellectual curiosity than he deserved. I ducked under the counter and marched myself into the New Age section to lose myself imposing order on chaos.

Chapter 2

I had all day stocking shelves and listening to customers, not thinking about Cole with Sharky at the lake, listening to that hideous music. All summer I'd avoided knowing where he'd be in case I accidentally found a desperate reason to be there too. Obsession was fun to read about, less great to actually experience. Four years of obsessing and I was ready to move on—at least part of me was. Only one of the horrible things about when school started on Monday was that it would be impossible to avoid him entirely.

After work, I met Flop and Junie for smoothies, barely not taking an extremely long way past Ceramic lake. They talked about school while I slumped in front of my berry cherry blast. Junie shoved her almost black, waist long hair back behind her ears then leaned forward, gazing at us intensely as she gave her spiel about how much she hated the institutionalized setting where people were primed to become the next generation of consumers. During the breaks of Junie's lecture Flop talked about boys. Flop always talked about boys.

Junie said, "It's crazy the way that people with real congealing brains in their skulls can walk around like automatons. It's sick."

Flop responded by leaning forward in her chair with an elbow on the stained wood table, beachy waves surrounding her adorable heart shaped face. "I saw Derek at the market the other day with his mom. He is getting totally hot even if he is short."

That was my cue to say, "Cole came to the store today."

Junie and Flop both looked at me, Junie with a scowl and Flop with sympathy in her warm gray-blue eyes. Junie said, "Do you think he uses airesol, or mousse for his hair? Either way I can't see how you could find a guy who is so socially irresponsible attractive."

Flop raised her eyebrows at me speculatively. "Was he wearing his gray t-shirt with the bloody monkey on it? I love how his arms look in that one."

I shrugged and shoved my spoon around in my purple smoothie hating that I couldn't look at him objectively, to notice what he wore and dissect it the way Flop could, or hold him in contempt the way Junie did. I always loved the way his arms looked, felt, were, and who cared what was in his hair as long as I could run my fingers through it? They accepted my personal obsession, sort-of, but it was time for me to get over him, to stop thinking that some day he'd walk up to me and take up where we left off. Intellectually I knew that I didn't respect him as a person, not when all his humanity had been sucked out of him by his teammates, and Sharky of course. I couldn't pretend he wasn't hot, but there were other hot guys, just ask Flop. I had to get over him… somehow.

"Who's the hottest guy in school?" I asked, forcing myself to think about someone, anyone else.

"Hot in what way?" Junie asked while Flop got a serious look on her face. "I mean, some guys are geeky hot, and other guys are just bodies."

"Just bodies," Flop and I said in unison then smiled at each other.

"If we're talking strictly superficial, I'd have to go with The Captain," Junie said with a slight smile.

I nodded reluctantly. While I couldn't stand the guy and Cole was the only person I felt anything about, no one could objectively deny that the swim captain wasn't streamlined perfection when he slid through the water showing off a chest that had attained legendary status. Girls went to meets to ogle him. I didn't, not when meets had to do with water, but I'd seen the photo of the swim team beside the rows of trophies every time I'd walked past the office for the past two years.

"Maybe this year he'll ask me out," Flop said, shoving her beachy blond locks over her shoulder with a sigh that was only part melodrama.

"You want to date someone who thinks that life is competitions and grades? The Captain doesn't ask girls out," I said scowling into my smoothie. "He's possibly nastier than Sharky."

Junie humphed. "Too many people waste high school wandering around completely unfocused."

"We're supposed to be unfocused, otherwise we'd have no chance to experiment with what we want before we're tied down to a career and kids," Flop said, scooping up the remains of her smoothie.

Junie got a gleam in her eye, the same gleam she got any time someone disagreed with her. "It's not like you can't figure out what you want in life and actually make progress towards your goals. Look at Watergirl. She has a job that is linked to her career goals while she's performing in choir and making the most out of the music our limited high school has. She has a plan."

"I do?"

Most of my planning had to do with ways to 'accidentally' run into Cole. I'd always hung out at the music store; it seemed a natural to get a job there when I'd turned sixteen. As for choir, it frustrated me as often as I enjoyed it. I'd get anxious and my lungs wouldn't work quite right. I composed, but nothing good. As for my future, who knew what I'd do with the rest of my life other than stalk Cole and wish I were Sharky?

"I have a plan," Flop said with a smile. "I'm going to move back to the beach and marry a gorgeous surfer god who loves me as much as he loves the waves. It wasn't my idea to move into landlocked Ohio where the water and bugs both smell. Not that I regret meeting you guys," she added while I rolled my eyes.

"Ha. We both know you'd ditch us in a second for the beach."

"Like you'd ditch us if Cole decided he wanted you and

how Junie'd ditch us for a really good conservation rally."

"It's responsible to care about our environment," Junie began, but I lost the rest.

For a few minutes I'd forgotten about school, about the fact that summer had ended and I'd be back in the same halls as Cole, seeing him when he didn't see me, wanting things to be the way they'd been so much that I couldn't breathe. Would I always feel like that: half of a person without him? At least I didn't have to sit alone. I had Junie, Flop, Tuba, what more could I want? They were real. They didn't judge me, at least not more than I judged myself.

Chapter 3

It was an average first day of school with slamming lockers, screaming students, and the general chaos and havoc that comes with cramming a million teenagers into one big box. Before class started I stood beside Flop's locker talking to her about her schedule and how likely it was that the cute geeky guy from last year was in her math class again when there was a kind of swell in the sound level, a rise and drop that made everyone look up to see what was going on.

I caught my breath. Cole wore his bloody monkey shirt. He didn't have cheerleaders with him. He walked surrounded by other football players, his linemen flanking him like he was on his way to score a goal. I stared at him for a moment, feeling the familiar drop in my stomach while my heart thumped and mouth went dry. I'd nearly gathered enough self-control to turn away when Flop dug her nails into my arm and whisper screamed. I hadn't noticed Junie until she leaned over me, looking past Cole.

"Hmmm," she said, quirking an eyebrow, managing to look intellectual in her beret and flowing skirt. I followed her gaze and Flop's, but I didn't see what the big deal was. The Captain walked by and while he was gorgeous, all blond, tan, chiseled cheekbones and pouty mouth, he knew it, and there wasn't anything interesting about that. I went back to staring at Cole's retreating figure and ignored Flop's nails until he was out of sight.

I exhaled, not sighed, because sighing at the sight of a guy was more pathetic than I could handle being on the first day of school. Together we started for class, fighting our way through the teeming hordes.

"Did you see his eyes?" Flop asked dreamily. "Like diamond emeralds. I've never seen him before. Who is he?"

"I heard Sean is hosting an exchange student this year. That must have been him," Junie said airily. Sean? Since when did we call The Captain Sean? It made him sound practically human. I studied her, at the way she smiled like she had a secret, and Junie didn't do secrets. Part of why she hung out with us, the less than mainstream, was her hatred for popularity in general. To admire someone who epitomized popularity wasn't her. She hadn't chased a guy since the time she told Dean in eighth grade that she liked him. He announced it to the school, humiliating her, so she'd decided she was done with boys right before she beat him up. Sometimes her convictions got in the way of her pacifism. Dean spent most of his class periods doing enterprising business behind the bleachers. Anyway, she felt for me and my unrequited love for Cole.

"I'm impressed with Sean being interested in foreign relations." Junie said which got Flop's attention too. She called him Sean again. She didn't say nice things about cute guys as a rule. When she noticed the way we were staring at her she lifted her chin a little bit. "It's surprising to see a jock act practically humane," she added but it still seemed suspicious.

"I'm totally interested in foreign relations," Flop said with a dreamy sigh while I rolled my eyes. How hot could the exchange student have been? And what, exactly, did diamond emeralds look like?

At lunch we met at the 'weird' table, Tuba's grand name for our half hidden table where it lurked behind potted plants on the corner of the commons.

At the table there was Flop, Junie and me plus Sandra who was new and was sitting with us because Flop had invited her and she didn't know any better, yet, and a skinny geek called Dill who had spent a few months in Germany over the summer and therefore Junie had thought would know something about geo something waves that caused cancer. He didn't, and after ten minutes of Junie's hopeful conversation we drifted into silence. Dill wouldn't be invited back, and Sandra finished eating in record time and took off.

"Why don't you invite anyone to eat with us?" Junie asked me after we were alone.

Flop leaned back in her chair with her eyes closed like she was tanning at a beach. I stared at Junie's hands while she folded her napkin into an intricate origami shape.

"I don't like people," I said, mashing the leftovers on my tray into grayish-orange sludge.

"You might if you talked to them." Junie said in that tone of voice, the one she used when she decided it was her job to fix somebody. "What about the new guy, the exchange student? He's cute."

"Hey, I liked him first," Flop said lazily, but didn't bother opening her eyes. She was in the zone.

"We're going to tryouts after school," Junie announced.

"The only thing trying out today is the swim team." I stared at Junie with dawning horror. I'd seen posters all over the place; apparently someone had been bored over the summer.

"Swim team?" Flop sat up and stared at Junie. The zone had officially closed. "You mean the water swimming team?"

Junie nodded with determination that made my heart sink and my head kind of light.

"I have choir after school," I said sounding far away even to myself.

"Choir will only meet for ten minutes today for you and the other non-newbies. Come on," she said rolling her eyes. "I'll go with you and then afterwards we can swing by the pool and see how the swim tryouts are going."

"That might be a bad idea," Flop said in a way that came across more like, have you gone crazy woman? But Junie didn't seem to mind. When people questioned her authority, she either enjoyed fighting or completely ignored them.

"I think," she said, looking from me to Flop with an intensity that made the hairs on my arms stand up, "That

this should be a year of facing fears. I am afraid of relationships, and therefore am determined to have one. Flop, you
are afraid of functionality and therefore I challenge you to
become more weather conscious. Watergirl, you have two
things you need to overcome, your fear of water, and your
whole hooked on Cole thing. Swim team is a double dose
of what you need. Come on, lunch is over." She marched
off while Flop stared at her then at me sympathetically. I
looked down at her sandals then up at her.

"I think you have great style," I said.

Of course she had great style but it was more suitable
for sitting at the beach somewhere. She had been known
to come to school in a tank top, short shorts and sandals in
the snow.

"Do you think she's serious about having a relationship?" We both stared at Junie where she left a wake of
those with weaker wills behind her. I could only shrug and
pity the fool.

Chapter 4

It took ten minutes of Junie talking and pulling me while Flop looked concerned before I walked through the doors to the pool.

I had a relationship with water that wasn't entirely mutual. Water loved me. Just that day as I'd walked past the drinking fountain, the water had sprayed up in the exact place where my face would be because it was a living force that wanted to make me miserable. I knew that was impossible, and the guy drinking from the fountain had something about the fountain having bad pressure, but it was hard not to be superstitious and consider myself cursed when bad water stuff happened to me way more than probability dictated.

It wasn't all the time, no, just often enough for me to get careless then water came out and grabbed me. If there was a problem with the plumbing I always ended up soaked. Both times that I'd been to the pool I had to be fished out, once by Flop who could swim from her days training to be a lifeguard before she realized you had to sit in the sun with your eyes open, and once by Bernice, a girl who had been our friend until she'd joined the swim team and got a new group. Her defection bothered Flop much more than Junie and me; we were already used to that kind of thing. It was actually Flop's concern that made me walk through those doors more than Junie's pushing. I wanted to prove that there was nothing wrong with me, that I wasn't cursed, that I was normal.

It was fine. We sat on the balcony far away from the water. Flop relaxed into her analyzing the various guys and the way they filled out their jammers while Junie stayed silent, only once complaining about how many people the price of the pool would have fed.

In spite of my nervousness it fascinated me to see people cut through the water like that, people as comfortable in the water as out. I felt jealous of Bernice and the easy way she treaded water while laughing with her friends. Who could laugh when they were busy screaming?

"See? Nothing bad happened," Junie said after the tryouts were over and the bleachers were clearing. She was in no hurry to move, and Flop was in her zone, so we stayed where we were for a few minutes. Junie finally stood up and started for the doors which was my cue to poke Flop.

I stood up and heard a giggle. All right, you hear giggles a lot in high school, but not from Junie. I looked over and saw Junie taking the steps two at a time to hurry down to intercept The Captain. His normally golden hair looked dark when it was wet but other than that he looked like he'd never been in the water. I stared openly at Junie as I trailed her down the steps, Flop snickering beside me. Junie did not giggle. She did not flirt. The Captain gave her a cool smile. I couldn't help but think that if she wanted a real relationship she might want to try one with someone who actually had a beating heart. Maybe spending so much time in jammers around girls in swimsuits had something to do with it. Maybe it took the edge off teen hormones to be immersed in so much near nudity. At any rate, he'd never shown more interest in anyone than the cold indifference he gave Junie.

The rest of the team gathered around The Captain while he stared above her left shoulder, and Junie gushed about how much potential the team had that year and blah, blah, blah, nothing about politics. Flop smiled up at a guy who was kind of cute and he smiled back at her.

I, absorbed by the site of Junie flirting, forgot that I was within fifty feet of wet. A girl came up to the group squealing and bouncing about her place on the team. She knocked a guy back who stumbled right into me. I stood at the edge of the crowd separated from Flop and Junie when with arms flailing I felt the edge of the pool under my heels.

For a moment I hung there, struggling with my balance, but the inevitable pull of water dragged me backwards. I knew not to panic, intellectually, but they don't call it a panic when you can be intellectual about something. I hit the water, enveloped in its deathly embrace as I sank rapidly however I beat my arms.

I felt someone wrap an arm around me in the water, pulling me to the surface as he tried to save me, but that didn't stop me from flailing and breathing water, choking and coughing, then sinking again when I accidentally elbowed the rescuer in his very hard head.

"Hold still," I heard someone shout at me when my head came up for a moment, but I couldn't hold still when I was sinking in water. That's the whole problem with water: the sinking.

Someone grabbed me by the back of the shirt and heaved me out, someone with icy blue eyes, perfect tan, and the muscles that made hauling me out look like nothing. He didn't put me down right away, My shirt dug into my armpits while I dangled, him holding me out away from him like he feared whatever I had might be catching.

"Tryout is over," The Captain announced to the room in a voice as icy as his eyes. When he set me down, the only people left were heading out the doors, never looking back because their master had spoken. He folded his arms over his chest while he glared down at me, soaked, gasping, shaking so hard I thought maybe I'd vibrate myself right back into the pool.

"Hey, are you okay?" The accented voice came from behind The Captain where he stood blocking the pool.

"She's fine. Get changed," The Captain commanded. "Actually," he said, cocking his head but staring right at me, into me. "Are you all right? It looked like she might have knocked you out for a second." The accusation in his voice made me shrink in my skin.

"I'm sorry," I muttered, but glared at him. If he'd been worried about one of his swimmers then he should have saved him instead of standing on the side glaring at me.

"I'm fine. Didn't see that elbow coming though," the guy with the sexy accent said with a laugh. I shoved my hair out of my eyes and looked down at the damage. I was soaked, and of course, wearing a white t-shirt so that my hot pink bra was completely visible. Nice. I pulled down the shirt where it had hiked around my armpits, sighing when I saw a ripped seam.

The captain muttered under his breath before he reached up, sliding his shirt over his shoulders to reveal a chest that blocked out the rest of the world.

Wow.

It took me a second to register the hand holding the shirt out at me with a disgusted look on his face. Right. The captain didn't show off his hotness like other guys would, therefore my staring would be insulting. Apparently. Oh. He was still waiting for me to take the shirt.

I snagged it then he grabbed my shoulders, spinning me around before he proceeded to push me towards the girl's locker room. The whole process was completely rational but at the same time he didn't have to push me around.

"Bring it back as soon as you can," he ordered before opening the door and shoving me through, closing it firmly behind me.

I stood there in the dim light shivering until, with a thump and a flare, all the lights came on, Flop and Junie burst through the door, not the one by the pool, the one leading to the main hall.

"Are you okay?" Flop asked, the concern etched across her face. Her big gray-blue eyes looked ready to weep for me.

I rolled my own as I turned, pulling off my soaked shirt and my bra with my back to them. I put on the captain's shirt, ignoring the weird scent of it as I pulled it over my head. "Fine. I'm used to it."

"So, the foreigner saved you, right?" Junie asked, looking nothing close to contrite about dragging me into danger.

"The Captain hauled me out like a stinky fish," I said,

enjoying the way her face fell. Had she thought that I'd hit it off with a guy for rescuing me? Was that the reason she'd dragged me to the try-outs: to make me look helpless and stupid so someone would like me? Where was the Junie we all knew and loved who hated arrogant men and weak women? "I knocked the exchange student out with my elbow."

I definitely enjoyed Junie's expression when she heard that. I sighed as I wadded up my shirt, hiding my bra in its depths as I left the locker room. I hated walking in wet jeans, not to mention my soaked sneakers, squelching with every step. Junie and Flop followed, racing to keep up with me. I wasn't really mad at them, not when I could have refused and acted like my own person instead of letting Junie have her way, the way I always let her get her way.

"Do you want to…" Flop began but I cut her off.

"I'm going straight home to change. I don't want to do anything but listen to music for the rest of the day."

"Watergirl," Junie began, but I slammed through the doors to outside, glad the sun was hot, that my bike hadn't gotten jacked, and left them both behind.

Chapter 5

I didn't go home. I wanted to cry and scream, and the walls of my house were too thin for that, not if I didn't want a pep talk from my dad.

Stinky Lake was two and a half miles from town, less if you had wings, but I didn't, just a bike. The road there wasn't much of a road, more an indentation with the remainder of long ago gravel. Stinky Lake was smaller than most of the ones around my small town, Ceramic Lake being the largest and most popular lake that actually had a white imported beach and a dock. I preferred Stinky, even if it was covered in algae and toxic seaweed half the time. I liked that it wasn't on maps as a tourist destination. There was only one place boats could launch but usually didn't because the mud was so bad that they usually got stuck.

I spent most of my life avoiding water, but for some reason, this out of the way lake where the herons swooped and the wind licked the water into curls was the only place I could relax. I could breathe there.

I ditched my bike on the bank of the road, following a deer trail through the brush, avoiding poison ivy and rugosa until my hands brushed the strands of willow that hung to the ground like a curtain. Inside, once the strands had fallen back, leaving the rest of the world behind me, I felt the knot in my chest loosen a little.

I felt safe beneath the green strands that touch the ground on one side and the water on the other. I pulled my notebook out of its place among the roots and curled up against the trunk, opening up to a blank page.

I bit the end of my pen before I wrote:

Junie's been reading romance novels or has turned evil. Her scheme involved me, water, and a cute guy rescuing me. Unfortunately I knocked out the cute guy and ended up being saved by The Captain, or Sean as Junie is now calling him. What's with him? Like I wanted to fall into the water? It's not rational to think that every time I get close to water I'll fall in. He looked at me like I should know better, like I did it on purpose. And Junie. She would deserve him for what she did to me, but no one deserves being with someone who's so perfect that every one of your flaws is etched permanently across the sky. Not that Junie has flaws. See, they're perfect for each other.

I scribbled violently on the page until I felt silly then laughed as I threw down the notebook. The wind rustled the branches but inside, underneath the green arc the wind, the sun felt far away until there was nothing but muted sound: water lapping, leaves rustling, birds calling. I closed my eyes and let the tension ease out of me, forgetting about everything, even my wet shoes. I let myself drift and float while the water lapped beside me with a regularity that soothed, reminding me of my mother.

I didn't remember very much, flashes of sunlight on water, bright, but not as bright as her laughter, the warmth of her arms wrapping around me, the press of her kiss in my hair, and of course, the singing.

I opened my eyes and realized that the light beneath the tree was dim. Soon there would be lightning bugs and I'd feel the pull, the need to go to my rock. I waited with my arms wrapped around my knees until the golden sky faded to dusky blue before I pushed up from the ground and stepped out into the night. I walked through the grass following the curves of the lake. When I reached my rock, I climbed up the side, feeling the crumbling moss under my fingers until I'd made the top and lay on my stomach looking down over the darkly glistening water.

A strange stillness spread over the world, not even the birds or frogs making a sound. I felt the song swell in my throat starting out like a sigh, a breath, a breeze. The words made no sense to me except in a dream way, words my mother sang to me about the pretty birds, the pretty sky, while the sweet fish swim. The sound grew until I felt it was my breath, my voice rustling the water below me, stirring it into curls and ebbs.

I sang until my throat tightened and my breath came short. My song faded into a whisper as I rested my cheek against the still warm stone until my heart beat evenly and my breath became a regular in and out, in and out. Then I could go home.

Chapter 6

When I pulled up at my house, coasting to a stop, I stared at the front window where a light burned. My dad was up, waiting for me. My pants weren't soaked at that point, mostly damp. Maybe he wouldn't notice. He didn't pay very much attention to things like clothes, but The Captain's shirt was way too big for me. If I'd laid out my shirt when I was at the lake it would have been dry, but I hadn't thought about it.

I hesitated a few more minutes before dropping my bike and clomping up the front steps, the wood sagging beneath me as I crossed the porch.

I was going to kill him. Not my dad, The Captain.

My father flung open the door for me, stopping me dead as that look on his face made his brown eyes flat, angry, the eyes of a stranger.

He gestured to the ragged brown couch then stood waiting, tall above me as he crossed his arms over his chest, reminding me of The Captain. My dad usually had a smile and a gentle pacifistic outlook, even when he was breaking boards and teaching some cocky kid humility in the dojo, but at that moment, he looked different, like a stranger as he asked me questions for an hour until he finally let me eat cold mac and cheese then go to bed. He didn't usually ask so many questions, but he wanted to know where I'd been, because he'd called Junie and Flop and knew I wasn't with either of them, what I'd been do-ing, no, hanging out was not an acceptable answer, and all because the fantastic leader of the swim team had come over for his stupid shirt. Yeah.

The Captain had come to my house and told my dad all about how I'd fallen into the pool at school then gone on about how I should take swimming lessons.

The questions weren't as bad as the guilt stuff. No, not guilt tripping me, but himself.

See, my mother drowned.

She drowned but he wouldn't let me learn how to swim. My mother knew how to swim, was a fantastic swimmer, but it didn't save her, so he figured it wouldn't save me either, best I stayed away.

Finally, my dad swiped a hand over his forehead, pushing back his brown hair to reveal the worry lines I'd put there. "I know things are hard for you and that sometimes you need your privacy, but I can't help but worry about you. I need to know where you are. If you can't be responsible and let me know, so I don't have to worry, we'll have to sell your computer so you can get a cell phone then I can call you and make sure you're safe."

The computer had my music on it, not an amazing program, but good enough that I could make something with the software, something that gave me dreams of composition classes in college someday, if I got that far. It wasn't that I didn't want a cell phone, but I needed the computer.

I felt worse and worse as he talked, knowing he'd have an aneurism if he knew where I'd been—high on a rock over the lake when I couldn't swim. He never yelled which only made it worse.

The next morning I rode my bike to school early, Sean's shirt in the top of my backpack. I waited in front of his locker, feeling like an idiot but refusing to notice the looks people gave me: look, there's weird Watergirl, now stalking the captain of the swim team instead of the star quarterback.

He finally showed up, blinking at me with a frown while I shoved his shirt at him.

"Here's your precious shirt. I'd hate for you to spend another moment of your life without it." I hadn't meant to say anything but the words came out before I could stop them. I spun around to leave but he fell in beside me, having no trouble keeping up with my near run.

"Weren't you going to thank me?"

I stopped, shocked as I turned to stare up at him. "Thank you?"

"You're welcome," he said with an odious grin as he turned, sauntering back to his locker.

"Thank you?" I hissed at his back, following him. "You talked to my dad. He was worried out of his mind because you had to tell him that I fell into the pool and then I came home late. He's irrationally overprotective enough as it is that I don't need you to make him even more worried about me. You should have kept your shirt if you couldn't handle it being out of your sight for five minutes."

"I drove to your house because I was going to give you a ride," he said, pulling books out of his locker, frowning at the cover of his physics book. "I didn't see your bike on the way, but I thought maybe you took a longer way home, although why you'd take a scenic byway in wet jeans, I have no idea."

"You didn't have to talk to my dad."

He glanced at me, but this time there was no amusement, only the ice cold that made me stop, think, realizing that I'd been yelling at the captain, and he was not the type to sit back and take it.

"You're irresponsible. Whatever you were doing was stupid, wasn't it?" I blinked and took a step back, but he shut his locker then filled the space between us, leaving me no room. "Your dad worries about you and I worry about my shirt. Luckily neither one was hurt." He stepped around me and left me standing there, feeling like…I didn't even know what I felt like. Dizzy, but not the dizzy I felt around Cole. Angry, but more than that: guilty. How dare he make me feel guilty, like my dad didn't fulfill the role of guilt doler? It was none of his business what I did. I should have 'accidentally' stained his shirt with mud or something.

"Don't you have a class to go to, Watergirl?" he called over his shoulder, his voice cutting through the noise, making everyone stare at me, someone who'd been addressed by The Captain, even if he hadn't been looking at me at the time.

Chapter 7

"So," Flop said when I made it back to my locker. It took me until I was pulling out my books to realize that I didn't do my writing assignment for my first period class. I pulled out a paper and started scribbling about an epiphany I'd had during the summer. I had two sentences on bike tire pressure written before I said hey to Flop, shoving my backpack in before slamming the locker shut and continued about the tire thing. I'd had an unnaturally vast amount of bike tire problems over the summer. Yes, I had my license, and yes, I lived over two miles from school, but being friends with Junie required a little more investment in the environment than carpooling.

"I'm sorry about yesterday. I had no idea Junie was playing matchmaker. How weird is that? Kind of makes sense though, I mean, you're not going to go out of your way to find a guy."

I rolled my eyes as we started walking, putting away my lame assignment. "I have to stop listening to Junie. She's going to get me killed one of these days."

"Your dad called last night. I thought you were going straight home." I didn't say anything, only frowned at my paper and noticed that I'd forgotten a comma. "Did you go to the lake?"

I'd accidentally told her once that I went there when I couldn't cope. She didn't usually mention it, only looked at me sympathetically.

"Yeah. My dad worries too much."

"I guess."

"He's threatening to trade my computer in for a

phone." I bit my lip. "I didn't mean to make him worry. Maybe I should get rid of the computer. It's a lousy program anyway. I think maybe they're going to put new computers into the school budget. I keep hearing about that."

"That's only Miss Winter's wishful thinking," Flop said with a shrug. "So, what did you think of him?"

"Who?"

"The guy with the sexy accent. Do you like him? He's really cute."

I stared at her wondering where she had been for the last four years. I didn't like guys. I liked guy. "I haven't actually seen him, but I liked his accent."

Flop sighed.

"He tried to save you. I think that said a lot," Junie said coming up to me while she adjusted her crochet flower blouse. It looked like something my granny had over the back of her couch, all orange and yellow acrylic.

"That is the ugliest shirt I've ever seen," I said, then clenched my teeth because I didn't say things like that. I didn't notice things like that. "So how's the relationship thing going, Junie?"

"I've decided who to have one with, so that's good," Junie said as we walked along acting like I hadn't insulted her clothes. Maybe she hadn't heard me. If yesterday's giggling was any indication I had a suspicion that she'd decided on someone I never wanted to see again. They would be perfect for each other.

"Um, is it Jim, the male cheerleader?" Flop asked sweetly. "He is kind of cute."

"Ha!" Junie said then swept her hair out of her eyes. I noticed that she left it down flowing over half her face in a way that made her look mysterious and girly, not pulled back in her regular aggressively functional pony tail. Down two days in a row—something was up.

"Did I hear you say that Junie thinks Jim is cute?" Tuba said scooting in beside Flop. There was something weird about him, well, besides the obvious tuba case that he had on one shoulder. He seemed taller and almost, hmm, dare I say it, muscular.

"Hey Tubes," Junie said with a smile.

I shuddered. At least Junie didn't call me Tubes.

Junie continued. "I didn't see you yesterday. You must not have been back from your summer trip yet. You'll have to tell me all about it. No, Flop," she said turning back to Flop. "It's Sean. He's the ideal candidate for my foray into a relationship."

Tuba kind of blanched, which made his freckles stand out in spite of the tan he'd managed to get over the summer.

"And Watergirl is getting over her fear of water and she's going to date this total water god," Flop said, filling him in without going into my big splash.

"And you," Junie reminded her, "Will wear a pair of winter boots when it snows before you catch another pneumonia."

"What about me," Tuba asked shifting his tuba to his other shoulder.

"You?" Junie asked looking surprised. "You're fine the way you are."

"And we're not?" I asked, but she didn't seem to hear me.

That day I had to rush to work after my choir rehearsal, which was fine because otherwise I would have had to argue for a very long time with Junie who wanted me to come with her to another swim thing. By the pool. With water. Yeah. She apparently was serious about Sean. When Tuba suggested that she join the swim team she actually thought about it for a minute. Maybe Junie was abducted by aliens who made her an evil, popularity craving human, or something.

Chapter 8

The next morning I felt a little sniffly, maybe allergies, maybe a cold, when Flop started talking the second she saw me. The exchange student, who's name was Oliver, or Olivier, she couldn't remember, had asked about me. I sort of pretended to be excited about the guy I'd never actually seen, but really, I wanted a guy to like me when I wasn't falling into pools, the way Cole used to like me back when he liked me. Maybe Oliver wanted details for when he shared with all of his cool foreign friends online how hilarious and idiotic the local Americans were.

I wanted to forget about it, but Tuba, who hadn't heard the story yet, had to be told in gory, graphic Flop detail full of dramatic pauses. That morning in the lull when the football players walked by, Flop gripped my arm tightly looking over them to see the new guy. For the first time in I don't know how long, I didn't see Cole. I didn't have the emotional space to feel a jerk of misery while I was busy feeling humiliation as I looked for the foreigner.

My first clear shot wasn't bad. He wore normal jeans and t-shirt but somehow he looked better than most of the guys around him. Maybe it was the way he stood so straight, or maybe it was the way he grinned over at The Captain who didn't look like he'd ever heard a joke in his life, much less made one, but Oliver, or Olivier was laughing like he had. He had nice white teeth and his black hair was a little bit curly, messy looking. His eyes, green and glistening were hard to look away from.

I stared the way I usually stared at Cole when he looked back at me, right into my eyes. I dropped my gaze to the floor and hoped he didn't realize I'd been staring at him, although why I wouldn't stare when Flop kept pointing at him, I didn't know. I waited long enough for them to have walked away before I looked up, and there he stood, not three feet in front of me.

"Hi. We didn't get a chance to be introduced yesterday. I'm Oliver," he said stretching out his hand to me.

"Did you say Oliver, or Olivier," I asked stupidly putting my hand gingerly in his to shake it. He kissed the back of my hand, like a prince in a fairytale. I immediately felt my hands get clammy.

"Whichever one you like better," he said in that accent that made me want him to recite the Alphabet for me. And then the Constitution.

"Ah," I said, needing to wipe my hand on my pants before he felt the sweat.

"I will see you later, Genevieve," he murmured before he turned to catch up to The Captain who hadn't bothered to notice me at all.

"Mmm," I said when he'd moved out of earshot then shut my locker door into my forehead. "Ouch."

"I take it that's the water god," Tuba said looking about as shocked as I felt. "He's shorter than I thought he'd be."

"He didn't seem short to me," I said still dazed from the hand kissing, the fact that he hadn't once mentioned anything water related, or maybe just my locker door where my head throbbed. He'd even called me by my name, the one my mother had given me. I didn't think anyone at school even knew my name.

In my classes, I listened to my teachers, but every once in a while I'd glance down at my normal, tan hand and remember the press of the foreigner's lips. At lunch I sat down across from Flop, opened my lunchbox then froze over my hummus artichoke sandwich when the captain and Oliver showed up, at least Oliver smiling and sitting down like no one could possibly object to his magnificent presence.

"Sit down," Junie said, beaming at The Captain where he stood behind Oliver's shoulder, his face expressionless.

"I was just telling Watergirl about what an amazing season you guys are going to have this year. We're all excited to see the new member of the swim team compete."

"Why do you call her Watergirl?" Oliver asked, leaning across the table to look at me, not at Junie. I felt like a rare exhibit on display.

"Didn't I tell you that she can't swim and has an addiction to near death experiences?" The Captain said, pulling out the seat between Junie and Oliver then thumped his fingers lightly on the table. It probably meant something, secret man code for, 'do we have to be here', but Oliver ignored him while he stared at me.

"You really can't swim?" Oliver asked, staring into my eyes until I felt like the only person in the world, caught in his magical green gaze. The moment shattered when Junie gave a strangled giggle. I looked up at her.

"You should teach her how to swim."

Flop gasped beside me while I stared, feeling like this was one of the dreams where the room was about to fill up with water and no one would notice until it was too late. Tuba muttered something under his breath.

"Hey, I need lessons for English, and you need lessons for swimming. I think it would be a good trade," Oliver said then put a hand on my shoulder, giving me the full attention of those mystical green eyes.

I shook my head and forced myself to take a bite. I took my time chewing and swallowing. "If you need help with English I guess I could help you, but I'm okay with my current non swim status. We can't all be half fish."

"She's right, she's fine without your lessons," Sean said before he shoved back from the table. "Why would someone who's constantly almost drowning want to know how to swim? It would take all of the excitement out of it. It's best if she stays away from water and the half fish."

I stared at him then looked away when I caught the full weight of his glare.

Note to self: Do not ever do anything to really piss off The Captain. Not swimming was bad enough.

Chapter 9

The rest of the week fell into an unusual pattern for me, starting with the morning when my brain fought over which guy to stare at, or in The Captain's case, avoid completely. Every time I saw his frown I felt guilty, like he knew that while I still saw Cole and the world stopped, I'd been having notes floating through my brain that I had to scribble down, notes that matched Oliver and his green eyes. The Captain's look seemed to warn me against being an idiot about Oliver the way I still was for Cole. Or maybe it was my overactive imagination.

I closed my eyes and leaned my head on the locker, blocking out any and all guys while Flop clutched my arm, unable to look away from so much hotness. When her grip loosened, I put my books in my locker and shut the door.

Lunches settled back to normal, only I didn't usually see anything because of the notes, the ones that wrapped around me and carried me away that I had to record, to write in my notebook, scratching them out and starting over again and again while Flop commented on movies or guys and Junie pined for her Sean. Tuba watched Junie with a weird expression on his face, amused, but kind of disgusted too. Not that there was anything disgusting about The Captain. I glanced from Tuba's face to the swimmer's table and saw him, sitting like a king while his subjects amused and entertained him.

His eyes flicked to me for a second, icy blue eyes making me feel guilty, like he knew what I was writing, knew what I was thinking. I stared at my paper, taking a few minutes for my focus to come back before I could remember the strain I'd been trying to capture.

I wondered if Oliver and The Captain sitting at our table been a hazing tradition for the new team member—but The Captain wouldn't have time for that kind of nonsense. I didn't mind. I preferred to study Oliver from a distance, dissecting his voice, his hand gestures instead of trying to talk to him and sound rational. I wished I could transfer all of my obsession from Cole to Oliver, but my heart still went crazy when I was anywhere close to Cole, and that Thursday he'd bumped into me and I hadn't been able to think for the rest of the day while my arm throbbed.

On the positive side, I made it all the way to Friday without having to change my clothes from water accidents. After school, I felt like celebrating and wondered if Flop wanted to go get a smoothie with me. Coming through the hall towards me was The Captain and his fans, Junie trailing along behind them. They passed by me except that Oliver stopped, standing in front of me until I looked directly at him.

"Hey Genevieve. I haven't seen you around very often. Such a tragedy."

"Did you go selectively blind? I've been around every single day."

I blinked then frowned down the hall where Flop would be coming.

"I have seen you, of course, but trying to get ready for the swim meet, trying to understand all my assignments, I suppose it's left me too distracted from the things I would really enjoy."

I felt my heart pound while I looked up at him, trying to gauge how much of what he said was sincere. "You said you needed English lessons. If you were serious, I could help. Although, honestly, Flop is better at English than I am."

He smiled, a smile that showed his perfect white teeth against his tan skin. "There will be a party tonight at Ceramic Lake. You should come with me."

My mouth opened then shut. "Excuse me?" I asked

staring at him where he leaned against the locker beside mine, looking relaxed. "I'm not invited."

I felt my skin prickle at the thought of going to the party where Sharky and Cole would be reigning queen and king, while The Captain and his troops would show up, march around, then leave. My freshman year I'd gone, watched through the bushes, staring at Cole, the way he relaxed, laughed, looked as warm and beautiful as sunshine, then watched as Sharky hit on him until I had to leave before I got sick. Oliver had no idea what he had just asked me to. He would be fine there: athlete, hot guy, maybe give Cole and Sean some competition. Maybe he meant that maybe he'd see me there, you know, like you saw people at the grocery store.

"It's supposed to be a nice lake with a good beach. Do you know it?"

"Um," I tried to think of a non-humiliating way to bring up my unpopularity. "We have a movie party at Flop's house. It's going to be beachy." I exhaled, relieved that I'd managed to avoid the whole I'm a loser thing.

"We'd love to go," Junie said coming from nowhere with Flop at her heels.

I stared at her feeling hugely embarrassed. Junie was out of her mind if she thought I was going to crash a popular party. All week she had been acting weird, but was she suicidal?

"What about movie night?" Flop asked giving Junie a hurt look.

"We have movie night every Friday night. Come on."

Just then Cole and his friends came down the hall throwing their ball around. A guy got knocked into his locker but no one stopped to help him out. I stared at Cole and kind of missed the rest of the conversation. That was unfortunate because when I tuned in Oliver was raising his black eyebrows at me and smiling slyly.

"What?" I asked.

Oliver just waved with a, "See you at nine," over his shoulder.

"What just happened?" I demanded feeling slightly

hysterical.

"He offered to pick you up, and when you were all, Coling out, Junie said no problem, you'd drive and meet him there and that would be better so you're all fixed up. Seriously Watergirl, could you pick a worse time to be obsessing?" Flop said with a sigh.

I closed my eyes and hit my locker with the back of my head. It didn't help. "So he wanted to take me? Like a date? Why?"

"Because he can see value," Junie said, linking her arm in mine and pulling me away from my locker. "This will be great for you to be with Oliver who is a real live person instead of drooling over Cole who's a figment of your fantasy. It's healthy."

"Try not to drool over Cole at the party," Flop added.

I groaned as I shook off Junie's hand and started down the hall towards my bike with my overpacked backpack. "There's no way my dad will let me go to a party where there's teen drinking and where the chance of fighting and sex are pretty much the only reason people go." Except that maybe he would. He gave me lectures about 'getting involved' that went on for what seemed like forever. Getting asked out by a boy was a big deal.

"You could say you were at the movie party with Flop," Junie offered. I stared at her until she started blushing. She was not into deception and hypocrisy as a rule. Her efforts to have a relationship were totally messing with her.

"So ask your dad, and if he lets you go, you'll go, otherwise, it's 'The Little Mermaid' at my house at eight!" Flop and Junie grabbed their bikes and we were off, much to the ridicule of Sharky and her friends in her red car with the top down.

The bike ride wasn't long enough. I pulled up at my house, a little white house with such thin walls that you could hear the rocking washing machine from the street, still wondering why he'd asked me. I shook it off as I dismounted and dumped my bike on the grass by the front porch with twisty metal railings. My dad would never let me go. It wasn't possible.

I was wrong. I told my dad while he sat in his favorite chair flipping through television channels. It went like this.

"A guy asked me to go to the lake with him."

"Tonight?" He put down the remote to sit up and look at him, the surprise evident on his face.

I rolled my eyes. "Yeah. Tonight."

"All right, don't stay out too late." He shifted his attention back to the television, but his gaze kept flicking back at me.

I stood there staring at him, refusing to believe what he'd just said. "There will be drinking, and probably some fights, and it will be at the lake. You know, the big wet thing that you would never introduce me to."

He shrugged and barely glanced at me. "You're getting all grown up. I can't protect you forever."

I stared at the guy who refused to ever let me have swimming lessons out of irrational fear that I'd drown, the guy who has instilled safety first into me every morning of school up until a year before, the guy who always read the obituaries of all the teens who died in motor accidents while under the influence to me during breakfast.

"But that's irresponsible for you to let me go to something that could end up being really dangerous. Besides that, I'll have to take the car."

He looked up at me, and I noticed how tired he looked behind his sad smile. "I've been thinking about it. I think I raised you with too much fear. I don't want you to think that you're not strong enough to take care of yourself. I've raised you up as well as I know how, but I can't baby you forever. Kids do stupid things sometimes, but maybe doing things when you're young and you have less to lose isn't the worst idea."

We stared at each other and then I went to my room with nothing else to say. What do you say when you dad betrays you? Where had this guy been when I was supposed to take swimming lessons? Seriously!

Chapter 10

I picked up Junie and drove to Ceramic Lake, listening to Junie flip through stations, none of which she wanted. I had to park at the end of a line of cars, lots of cars, next to the long grass. I wished Flop had come.

I could hear the music float over the air as soon as I got out of the car. It wasn't even bad music. I slammed the door and started towards the beach. It was still light but the sun would be down soon enough.

"This is going to be so fun!" Junie said bouncing along beside me.

I didn't look at her. I missed the old Junie who would bring a bagful of sacks to pick up the trash and organize whoever she could into saving the world one messy lake at a time. She didn't even have a bag. I shoved my keys in my pocket and walked faster, trying to get the humiliation over with so that I could go home.

There were already bonfires lit with flames licking the sky while people laughed and looked alien in the flickering light. I stayed rooted at the edge of the group unable to move forward into the happy crowd, including Sharky and Cole where they sat in the middle of their group.

"There you are," Oliver said coming up unexpectedly since I'd been staring at Cole. "I was worried you wouldn't make it."

"I'll see you guys later," Junie said taking off towards the bonfire where The Captain sat looking all cold and distant.

"So," Oliver said from my side when I still hadn't moved. "Do you want to sit down, or would you like to dance?"

"Dance?" I stared at him, and he laughed at my expression, which should have made me want to run away, but it wasn't at all a mean laugh. "The truth is that I can't dance either. Let's sit."

He took my hand and tugged me just enough to get me going towards a fire, somewhere between the football team and the swim team, where other people had come to party. It was so weird to have him holding my hand while Cole sat just on the other side of the clearing. He probably wasn't watching me. I couldn't check while I was with Oliver; I knew that much. I sat down and he sat beside me, letting go of my hand. I wiped my palm on my jeans wishing I wasn't so nervous. He picked a perfect spot where we could watch the sun set on the lake without being able to see Cole.

"How do you like it here?" I asked after a few awkward moments of silence.

"It's strange."

I looked up at him wondering if he was going to say anything else, but he kept quietly watching the lake.

"Your English is really good."

"Do you really not know how to swim?" he asked, turning to stare at me. His eyes picked up the last lines of sun and were brilliantly green.

I mutely shook my head and stared down at the sand. A weed stubbornly grew in the sand where it didn't belong.

"There is so much water here," he said quietly, "Lakes, pools, you would think that you would at least know how not to drown."

I shrugged and muttered, "Knowing didn't help my mother."

It didn't seem possible that he heard me, but he asked, "Your mother drowned?"

I took a deep breath before I nodded slowly. "She was a great swimmer but one day," I shook my head. "Anyway, so my dad just wanted to keep me away from water. Now it seems like he doesn't care, but I don't know. It's a lifetime of being freaked out about it."

"You're afraid of water?"

I shrugged feeling stupid.

"Water is dangerous," he said, almost like he was thinking out loud. "I'm going to get something to drink. What would you like?"

I said coke, not because I liked coke, but because it was the first thing that I thought of. I watched him walk away from me to the pile of coolers to fish something out and almost forgot that I was at the lake with Cole behind me.

"Look, it's Watergirl." Sharky's really annoying voice made me flinch. "What are you doing here? Probably going to cause a tidal wave or something." She laughed like that was sooo funny. Her cheerleader friends all giggled with her. I didn't want to, but I looked up to see if Cole was watching. He was. His frown showed how he felt about me invading his world, a world he'd thought safe from me and my kind.

I stared down at the ground and hoped they would go away, but apparently that was the wrong move to deal with aggressive animals, because Sharky came closer.

"You know what? You look so pathetic, I'm tempted to pay Cole to give you a good time just because it's the only way he'd ever look at you twice."

I looked up, shocked that she would talk about Cole like that, when she flipped open the can she'd apparently been shaking and hit me right in the face with the moldy mop smelling cheap beer.

"Oh no! It looks like you need a bath." Her eyes were all big and innocent even as she reached out to grab me.

I pulled away gasping for breath, struggling to get the beer out of my eyes. I didn't see the guys come up behind until it was too late. They lifted me into the air, upside down. I had a weird upside shot of Cole's face while he drank from his can watching me with a smile. His smile paralyzed me while Sharky laughed. The players spun me around until Cole disappeared, their hands grabbing my body, squeezing my flesh while I struggled, fought, screamed and kicked, but there were too many of them. Bodies pressed against mine until I felt crushed, suffocated, unable to fight or even move.

I heard shouting then got the wind knocked out of me when one of the players fell over on top of me. My head felt crushed until I was left alone on the sand, unable to breathe or move while my mouth opened and shut like a fish out of water. I gasped as my breath came back, rolled over, and promptly got tripped over by two guys tangled together, too close for their punches to do any damage. I scrambled up, staring around at the scene of mindless violence, bodies filled with one desire, one need to destroy, to hurt, to win. I ran across the sand, ducking around people I barely recognized the music mixed with screams and shouts. I stumbled out of the firelight, leaving the beach as I spat sand out of my mouth and wiped beer out of my eyes with my shirt. I turned and stared for a moment. Cole and The Captain circled each other, both of them smiling before they moved in with shameless brutality that made me sick, or maybe my stomach still churned from being crushed by a linebacker.

The night was filled with the screams of Cheerleaders as they scratched and pulled hair, swimmers against the football players while everyone else chose a side or left the way I had. Junie stood at the edge of the sand yelling about the futility of violence while the football players and swim team rolled dangerously close to the fires, punched, and in general acted like a perfect example of why my dad should never have let me come out there. There were splashes as the fighting moved to the lake.

I turned and left it all behind, but I couldn't stop feeling the sand under my shirt or the handprints on my skin that burned with the same heat that had my chest on fire.

I made it to the car and slumped in the driver's seat with my head against the wheel trying to keep it together. Never in my entire life had I felt so completely stupid. I'd spent four years wanting to be with the biggest jerk at school. It was like being love-sick over someone I didn't even know. What was wrong with me? I felt swamped and bloated with humiliation; it clogged the back of my throat until I thought I was going to throw up.

The door opened and Junie got in, slamming it behind her.

"I can't believe I thought he wasn't completely lame!" Junie began.

I laughed, a kind of choked sound. How could I ever have seen Cole as anything but just another jerk? I swallowed and got my keys out to start the car. My hands were so shaky; it took four tries to get it in the ignition.

"Sean didn't want to save you; he would have let them dump you in the lake if it wasn't for Oliver."

I shrugged. I deserved to be drowned in the lake for being so stupid.

"He said, and I quote, 'let them put her in the lake, you can fish her out.' But Oliver insisted, and finally Sean gave the word and all the swimmers jumped on the football players. Did you see Bernice punch Sharky? I have to admit seeing that makes me feel torn about my stand on violence."

"Junie?" My voice was quiet, still choked. "Could you just shut up? I don't want to talk about it. I don't want to talk about anything."

She nodded and let the drive pass in the silence I asked for. How could I have been so stupid to waste so much of my life on a guy like Cole? Maybe there were good guys out there, but he wasn't one of them. The only thing Junie was ever really right about was telling Dean off and being about her cause instead of focusing on guys. At least Flop gave them all equal interest that only lasted as long as they were in front of her. She was a little bit like a guy come to think of it.

I drove, glad that I brought the car, that I hadn't felt like just because Junie judged anyone who had too large a carbon footprint that I should ride my bike even as far as Ceramic Lake. I liked the feeling of being behind the wheel, of steering and being in control of something.

Chapter 11

When I burst through the front door into the living room, my dad said, "Isn't it a little early..." then trailed off when he got a good look at my beer and sand soaked self. "Genevieve," he said, abandoning his recliner to stand up, reaching a hand towards me like he wanted to say something. I stood there waiting until the hand fell to his side at the same time he exhaled, brows coming together in a worried line.

"I'm tired." I felt a surge of guilt as I left him there, in the dim light of the living room, a foreign martial arts movie playing in the background as his only company. It wasn't his fault I'd become obsessed with the first guy I kissed, that Sharky had it out for me almost as much as water did, and that mom had died and left both of us. Then again, it wasn't mine either.

I went right to bed after my thorough shower and although I expected to stay up all night reliving the magic, I fell right to sleep.

The next day at work, Sheila told me all about the party that had apparently been so phenomenally violent, it had reached college circles.

I rolled my eyes and moved away to catalogue music. If excessive violence was what cool college people were into, then maybe it was a good thing that my college future was iffy at best. I was glad that it was busy enough that I didn't have time to think too much, what with goths wanting to rate bands by grades of darkness and stuff.

I heard a bell jangle somewhere, but I was with a customer looking at show tunes so I didn't see who came in until he touched my elbow. I jerked away before I froze, feeling my blood drain from my extremities.

"Hey, Vee," Cole said then coughed and cleared his throat.

It had to be a dream. Any minute the music store would fill up with water and drown me.

After a few heartbeats waiting to wake up I managed, "Can I help you?" I turned away from him, clenching my fists so that my nails dug into my skin. My nails felt real.

"Can we talk for a second?"

He was still cute, but when I glanced over at him I wasn't paralyzed the same way. I couldn't help but see his smile while he let his friends torture me. He'd never been cruel before.

"Sorry, but I'm helping this customer. You can ask the other sales associate."

"Right, I just wanted to apologize for last night. Sharly got carried away. I swear I didn't know what she was up to, and on behalf of the entire football team, I'm really sorry."

I spun around to search his face for actual penitence, but he wasn't the guy I'd used to know. I couldn't read the stranger staring back at me at all. I didn't know who this football player was. I never had.

"Why?"

He gave me a blank look that jocks seemed so good at.

"Why are you here apologizing to me?"

He shrugged and looked sheepish. "Sean had me in a headlock in the water. Man, do not mess with him in water. On land, I could take him, but there was no way…"

"Sean made you come here and apologize?"

He shrugged. "He gets a kick out of humiliating his opponents. Too bad he doesn't do football. We would completely dominate."

I stumbled away from him shaking my head. "Get out. Four years of wanting you to be my friend and now The Captain says the word and you're here begging my forgiveness? Just get out."

He frowned and opened his mouth to say something, but I was done. I gave Sheila a frantic wave as I ran for the bathroom, climbing the narrow stairs to the second floor past the stacks of vintage records. At least Cole didn't follow me.

I leaned on the sink and watched the water run, swirling down the drain while my head pounded so hard I thought maybe it would explode. I got dizzy, black spots filling my vision until with a gasp I realized I hadn't been breathing. Not a good thing.

I felt dazed for the rest of the day by the most exciting discovery I'd ever had in my life: I didn't like Cole.

After work I hung out with Flop at her house where she was laying out in her backyard with her feet in a blow up pool. I collapsed in the lawn chair beside her, pulled off my tennis shoes, stuck my feet in the pool and did some really good breathing.

"How did last night go? Did you fall in the lake?" she asked when she realized I was there.

"Nope."

She opened her eyes and squinted at me, staring for a long time and looking surprised, but that may have been because her last eyebrow plucking was a little extreme. "Do you think Tuba's getting hot?"

"Yeah, I kinda do," I said which surprised her again.

But all she said was, "I hope he's not changing for a girl."

I didn't tell her about Cole. I didn't want to talk or think about that four-letter-word ever again. In spite of everything, feeling this vast amount of dislike was one of the best things that ever happened to me. All things considered, my life was actually looking up.

Chapter 12

I went shopping with Flop. Not Junie because, obviously, she'd complain the entire time about China and corporate America instead of focusing on cuteness. Yeah, me, cute, I know, but I was ready for a change. I got my hair done too, highlights with tons of chemicals. I used the same guy who always fixed Flop's 'beach blonde goddess' hair so I left feeling like a princess, my hair just right instead of its usual boring brown.

"I can't remember the last time you spent your money on something besides music and smoothies."

I opened my eyes wide at her. "Oh no! Well, we'd better grab smoothies before we go back to your house and download a new album."

She rolled her eyes then smiled, her luscious lip gloss reminding me of my lips, eyes, all of me, sparkling like her. I felt like sparkling, tossing my hair and checking out cute guys—guys in the plural.

On Monday I drove my dad's car to school after I picked up Flop.

As I stepped out of the car in my high heels, not too high since I didn't want to fall over, I felt like a new person—someone with super long legs and a short skirt. I slammed my car door and that was it. I was at school wearing girly clothes like a girly person with Flop in her summer dress beside me. We kind of matched. Weird. But hey, I could do weird, had been doing it my whole life.

Tuba rode up on his bike panting with his tuba. I felt a wave of irritation at Junie for insisting that everyone think the same way she did. She didn't have a tuba. Of course it might have been a reason that he lost so much weight.

"Hey," I said waiting for him as I held a door open, letting other people go by.

"Hey," a guy said that I hadn't actually met, a guy who smiled at me in a way that made me stare at him before I blushed and looked away. Flop got smiles all the time. It was fine. I just had to smile while tallying up his hotness and then forget about him. That's what she did, but since I was new at it, I just silently urged Tuba to come faster.

"Water…"

I cut him off before he said it. "It's Gen, or Genevieve. So, how was your weekend, Aaron?"

Tuba, er Aaron stared at me and Flop snickered. She thought Tuba's reaction was more interesting than the cute rocker guy who walked by and checked me out. I could practically feel him checking me out. I followed Tuba through the door, edging closer to him so that I was between him and the wall.

"Um, good?" He tried to twist around to talk to my face, but it was really better if he was slightly in front of me.

"Stay right there," I said putting a hand on his shoulder.

"You're trying to be visible," Flop reminded me. "Come on," she coaxed like I was a kitten she was trying to lure out from under the car.

I rolled my eyes and stepped away from Tuba, straightening up like I was proud of who I was. Well, I was.

"I'm fine," I said and strangely enough, I actually was. The looks weren't really worse than they'd always been, and without having to constantly look for Cole, I could focus on things like listening in class and talking to people. I wasn't up to inviting anyone to sit with us at lunch, but when my pen ran out in class and I actually wanted to take notes, I asked a girl if she'd loan me one and she said yes like that was normal, and it was.

It was so weird being normal.

It was all fine until lunch when I was walking through the cafeteria on high alert. Not because I was on the lookout for Cole, but because I knew that Sharky or someone was not going to let me get away with my new outlook unchallenged. This was high school, after all.

I used to do martial arts with my dad and Cole. When some jerk said, 'Hey, look, it's Watergirl,' and pulled the lid off his drink to dump it on my head I was already moving so my hand hit the bottom of the cup and it went into his face. Okay, it wasn't exactly martial arts, but it turned out that my reflexes weren't half bad when I wasn't obsessing over someone.

I said, "It's Gen, or Genevieve. Get a clue," before I walked to my table as snotty as Sharky ever was. It kind of shut down the cafeteria for a few minutes. It was like, silence for the passing of Watergirl. Of course it wasn't over, no, that would have been too easy, but the thing was, I kind of liked the challenge. I liked fighting back. The only reason I'd never done it before was because I was completely paralyzed by Cole not liking me.

"I thought we were all about nonviolence?" Junie said when I sat down.

I was all, "Really? Where have you been?" And she didn't say anything else because that was the first time she noticed my shoes, hair, and skirt, and her mouth flapped while nothing came out.

Tuba snickered until I smiled at him, then he choked and Junie had to thump him on the back. That's when Oliver showed up.

Okay. Oliver was nice and cute. But still. I wasn't about to start crushing on any guy. Not happening.

"I'm sorry about the party. I didn't realize it would be so..." he trailed off and winced.

"No problem. Hey, if you want to make up for it, I could use some swimming lessons."

Okay, now the whole table was in shock, and I was a little freaked out too, but apparently I was doing more than turning over a new leaf. Anyway, he nodded his head and I told him to meet me at Stinky Lake at five, when choir was over.

Everyone stared at me while I focused on not hyperventilating. It had been way too easy to sign my own death warrant.

"Wow," Tuba finally said while I exhaled shakily.

"Apparently," I said.

Flop patted my shoulder encouragingly. "It's going to be great. You can borrow one of my bikinis."

I put my head on the table.

"Perfect. At least something's going according to plan," Junie said, sounding irritable.

I looked up. She should be doing a cheer. "What's with you?" Her mouth got tight. "What happened at the lake, before the fight?"

"What fight?" Flop and Tuba both wanted to know, but I didn't look away from Junie.

"Sean told me that I seem like a really smart girl, so he can't understand what I'm doing acting like such an idiot about him."

"He didn't," Flop said with a gasp while I stood up, shoving my chair back.

The Captain wasn't sitting at his table anymore. When I looked around the cafeteria I saw him heading through a door into the hall. I avoided both idiots who tried to trip me as I walked, focused on Sean. My blood pounded in my head and I felt more alert, prepared to take him down however gorgeous/popular/whatever he was.

I caught up to him at his locker where he took his time spinning the dial.

"What is your problem?"

"Sorry?" he asked, looking up at me with piercing blue eyes that would have stopped a charging wild animal. Didn't stop me though.

"You're so good at apologies. Why don't you teach everyone else here how to apologize so they can be just like you? Oh, right. You already have."

"And here I thought you'd be ecstatic that Cole was acknowledging your existence. My mistake. The next time I have him in the lake, I'll just drown him."

"Oh, you saved him for me? How thoughtful. Why were you such a jerk to Junie?"

He smiled, and I had to keep myself from kicking him.

"Tell me, judging by what you know of your friend, do you think she's the type to take a subtle hint, a kind rejection?" I blinked at him. "What I've seen of her," he continued, folding his arms across his chest, probably to show off his muscles, only no, because he didn't do that. "Is that it takes serious force to change her trajectory. I don't lead girls on."

"No, you just leave them to drown whenever it's convenient."

"Do I? And here I thought that I dragged you out of the pool..."

"You told Oliver to let them throw me in. You have no idea how terrifying it was being..." My throat tightened and I swallowed shaking my head. "You have no sense of compassion."

"And you have no sense of perspective." He lifted up his shirt which left me blinking in confusion until I saw the bruise spreading across his ribs. I recognized that bruise. I'd had it twice before when I'd sparred with Cole.

"Cole kicked you. He has a really good kick."

"Yes. That was before I dragged him into the lake. Personally, I enjoy fighting as a sport, but," he said hiding his fascinating abdominals when he dropped his shirt. "My swimmers are my responsibility. Bernice has a sprained wrist. Not only is that tragic for our next competition, it's pain that she has because I authorized violence on your behalf." He stepped forward, shoving a finger in my face. His icy eyes burned into me. "Do you understand? When you went there, you knew what would happen. You can't challenge the status quo without backlash. You acted regardless of consequences, as usual. Maybe I should line up everyone injured fighting for you so that you can see and understand."

"I understand," I muttered, pulling away from him. "You're still a jerk." He was right though. When Oliver had asked me, I'd known it was a bad idea. When Junie had pushed me, I'd gone along with it. My dad had no idea what it was like for me on the outside. I should have made my own choice and stuck with it.

"And you're an idiot."

I glared at him, but then asked him because he seemed to have a really good sense of natural consequences. It was time to use his malicious intelligence for the greater good. "I asked Oliver to teach me how to swim. Do you think that's a bad idea?"

"Don't ask me what I think. You are perfectly capable of doing your own thinking."

I rolled my eyes. He sounded like my dad only more of a jerk. "Thanks for that vote of confidence. And here I thought you saw me as a complete idiot. I wonder where I could have gotten that. I think that with the way I am with water, it's stupid to not have some defense against it." I made it sound like an enemy. I thought he'd mock me but he only shrugged.

"It sounds like you've made your choice, Watergirl."

"Please," I said, curling my lip. "It's Gen or Genevieve."

"Really?" he asked, looking thoughtful. "Which one, Gen or Genevieve?"

I shook my head. "Either one."

"Maybe both? GenGenevieve? Or GenevieveGen."

I rolled my eyes and turned away from him wondering why he sounded amused. "Gen. Call me Gen unless you find a sexy foreign accent somewhere, then you can call me whatever you want."

I blushed as I walked away when I realized that had sounded like flirting. I didn't flirt at all, certainly not with The Captain.

After school I borrowed one of Flop's many bikinis and headed to stinky lake with her in tow. She had her chair in the back of the car, and we got set up on the muddy bank where I tried to stay cool. You know, not run screaming at the lap, lap sound of the water kicked up by a motorboat out there on the lake. For some reason as I sat on the edge in my borrowed bikini, challenging the lake, I did not feel relaxed. I knew it was no big deal to swim. Other people did it all the time. Flop started giving me some instructions, like, keep your eyes open and relax, it's all about breathing, that kind of thing, but talking about breathing made me want to hyperventilate.

It was five and I was all ready to pack up and go, but then I heard the sound of a car and then the top of Oliver's curly black hair was visible, then his eyes and smile as he climbed the embankment. He really was cute, and he wasn't wearing his jammers, instead he had some flowery trunks on and his shirt while he urged me into the water.

I nodded but it took me ten minutes to move from the water's edge to knee deep.

"Good," he said putting his warm hands on my arms. I nodded like I agreed, but suddenly I wasn't just worried about the water but about fish hooks in the mud that I was probably going to step on. He had his sandals on, and I wore flip flops, but still, one of those things could go right through the sole, and then I'd be in a hospital gown getting a tetanus shot in my butt.

He smiled at me, kind of close up, and I forced myself to follow him into the water past my knees, then to my hips until I was up to my ribs. At that point I stopped and blinked, wondering how I'd gotten that far without freaking out. He moved his hands to demonstrate cupping the water, and I got to do that and feel like a two year old. He demonstrated floating, kicking, and blowing bubbles, but it seemed like getting me in that far was all he wanted for that day. After an hour or so he said it was time to get out. I felt, well, kind of disappointed. I hadn't gotten any water up my nose or fallen and had him rescue me or anything. Huh.

Chapter 13

I hated to admit it, but The Captain's harshness was
exactly what Junie needed to give up on the whole relationship with Sean thing. As far as I could tell, Flop still wasn't
interested in any footwear requiring socks, but me, I was
different. It wasn't only my swimming efforts either. I felt
the difference every day in everything I did. Whether it
was getting dressed for school, refusing to work Sheila's
schedule, or driving my dad's car to school on days I didn't
feel like biking, it was different. I still recycled and stuff,
but I didn't feel like I had to do what Junie told me to do.
At first she didn't get it, but then everything was fine. Best
of all, she got over the Sean thing with hardly any bump to
her awesome self-esteem.

I met Oliver at the lake every day that week besides
Tuesday and Thursday when I had to work until dark, and
by Friday I actually swam. It was kind of pathetic, pretty
much dog paddling, but I kept my head above water, and
Oliver didn't have to grab me or anything. He was actually
a great teacher, not the flirty foreigner, but someone quiet
and watchful, paying attention to every detail while at
the same time smiling his approval when I did something
right. I couldn't imagine The Captain ever giving approval
to anyone.

He soothed me almost as much as the sounds of the
lake. At the end of the next week I kicked without splashing every time. Pretty amazing, I know. Anyway, by then
it was getting cold for swimming outdoors and Oliver said
we should meet early at school.

I agreed but I hadn't realized how different it would
be. It was fine at first, I mean, I felt kind of lame in Flop's

bikini in school, and it took me a few minutes to get over the no clothes at school nightmare feeling while the smell of chlorine made me miss Stinky Lake. The weird part was actually Oliver. We had been going over strokes and stuff for a half hour or so, when the rest of the swim team came in. Oliver wrapped up our lesson in a rush, and then he ripped off his shirt and shorts to join his team. He moved too fast for me say good-bye much less check out his near nudity. He was an unidentifiable fish, one with the team.

The Captain walked in, late, but no doubt he had a good reason. He saw me in the pool and frowned at me. I don't know why I'd hoped for something like a nod or a smile from him. He'd given me his approval though, to learn to swim, so why the glare?

He started giving orders while I climbed out, tugging Flop's suit in place to make sure nothing was going to fall out. I kept wanting to turn around as I walked to the dressing room, to see if Oliver would wave or something, but the way he left me at the edge made me pretty sure he wouldn't.

I washed my hair for a long time to get the chlorine out. It reminded me of Cole, the way Oliver had left as soon as the team showed up, like he didn't want to be seen with me. It made me realize that while we had been spending lots of time together for the last week or two, he still acted the same around me at school, I mean, as friendly and nice to me as he was to everyone else. I felt glum as I walk through the halls to class. I didn't even see Cole until he bumped into me. He stopped to apologize, like I want another apology from him. I shrugged and walked on. I got to my locker and Flop was there, looking like a beach girl.

"So, Cole was watching you."

"What an idiot," I said as I fished in my locker for my books.

She stared at me until I stood up, waiting.

"I guess you're really over him. Usually people go through a stage of anger, but you seem kind of okay."

I leaned against my locker. "Yeah. It's about time, don't

you think? This morning I did swimming with Oliver here and it was weird."

"Oliver? Is the sexy foreigner helping with transition?"

I shook my head. "I don't think The Captain likes me." I hadn't meant to say that. Why had Sean looked at me like that, like I was invading his pool with my non swimmer ways that might rub off on his team?

She blinked losing the smile she reserved for thoughts about sexy foreigners. "He doesn't like anyone," she said dismissively, munching on the edge of her muffin.

"I don't mean likes me likes me, I mean likes me to breathe in the same school as he does."

"Oh, Captain Hotness probably doesn't really care, he's just thinking about something deep, like semi-finals or something. You should talk to Oliver about it if it's worrying you."

I shrugged. No way I was going to ask Oliver about anything not related to swimming. He'd pretty clearly defined the boundaries of our relationship.

The next morning I met Oliver at the pool fifteen minutes earlier than the day before, which made it an ungodly, 5:30 a.m., but apparently I was truly dedicated. Anyway, we were by the edge. I was concentrating on keeping my hands cupped and my feet pointed while Oliver floated on his back beside me, murmuring every now and then about my technique which he couldn't possibly know because he wasn't actually looking at me.

"How can you tell my feet aren't pointed?" I asked then choked when I forgot to cup my hands. I should know better than to talk and swim at the same time.

"The sound is wrong," he said flipping down so he could demonstrate the difference, which I didn't get, but whatever.

I took the opportunity to rest on the edge of the pool. "So, does Sean hate everyone who doesn't swim very well?"

He raised an eyebrow. "Where did that come from?" He had no problems with talking and swimming at the same time.

I felt jealous for a second.

"Why else would he hate me so much?"

"Sean?" He smiled like I'd said something hilarious. "Sean does not hate people. Even people who can't swim."

"If you say so," I muttered.

"Sean doesn't like dating in school. He thinks it's a waste of time and energy to focus on one person when you should be worried about your life goals." That sounded like Junie but it made no sense. I wasn't trying to date Sean; I was learning how to swim the way he'd suggested to my dad.

"I'm not dating anyone. He should like that I'm learning to swim even if I am encroaching on the sanctity of his precious pool."

He glanced at me with a slight frown. "Maybe he thinks that my teaching you to swim is a little bit like dating."

I rolled my eyes while I clutched the edge. "I think dates should be less life or death, more movies." I braved my way from the side while I kicked my legs as fast as I could to keep from sinking.

"You don't think this is more than a friend helping a friend?"

His accent was so adorable.

"No, of course not. We're swimming. What could be less romantic than that?"

He mumbled something and dove deep into the water. I got nervous for a second without him there to make sure I wouldn't drown. I opened my mouth to call him, realized he wouldn't hear me because he was under water, and then had to spit when water got in my mouth. Gross, spitting in the pool. No wonder Sean didn't want me in there. I made it a point to keep my mouth shut from that point on, but I kept thinking about what Oliver had said. Did he think this was more than friendly? Maybe he was sacrificing his early morning sleep because he liked me. The thought had me moving towards the edge, forgetting about technique until I was out of the pool and in the dressing room before the swim team came out. I stopped inside the door when I saw Bernice and her friends in the locker room.

"Nice suit," she said before she went out. Her smile was not mocking and I was going to tell her that hers was too, but it was a navy blue, speedy suit that flattered no body.

By the end of that week, I was swimming pretty well. I blamed Oliver's teaching, and told him so. He smiled like he was flattered, but he didn't say much. It didn't seem like he ever talked much in the water. He was busy using his fishy senses instead.

"I think you can swim," Oliver said as we climbed out of the pool. I stared at him, uncertain as he pulled off his shirt and revealed his very naked chest. Usually as soon as I got out I bailed for the locker room before I had to go through the weird him in jammers part. I was much more comfortable with him in more clothes.

"Thanks. You're a great teacher," I said lamely, edging towards the locker room.

"I don't think you'll drown," he said and then I noticed the frown on his face. I stopped and stared at him until I got it, until things clicked and I knew what he meant.

"So you think I'm as good as I'm going to get and that I shouldn't waste your time?" I didn't mean for it to come out so blunt, but he only smiled ruefully.

"It's not a waste of my time. Floating in the water isn't exactly difficult for me. But you are really capable, and maybe your time is a little more valuable, particularly early in the morning."

So he was saying that he didn't want to hang out with me anymore. It hurt, I'm not going to say it didn't, but it was doable. I took a deep breath, forging through the pain, and stuck out my hand to him.

"Thanks so much for teaching me. You really are awesome. I'll see you around."

I didn't freak out or anything. In the locker room I felt a little bit stunned and kind of sick, but then I saw Bernice, and I did what any normal person would do.

"Hey Bernice. I know this isn't really your thing, but do you think you could teach me a few pointers on swimming some time?"

She stared at me, and then sat on the bench next to me while the rest of the team filed out. "I thought Oliver was teaching you. While that's cool, it really pissed off Sean."

"Yeah, well, Oliver's done a good job at making sure I don't die, but I want to be better than that. I want to swim kind of pretty, you know? Is that stupid?"

She laughed. "You're asking me? I live for swimming. There's no end to technique. Sean is an incredible swimmer, but he's gotten even better since Oliver came. Oliver gives Sean the competition he needs."

I shrugged. "I don't know what's up with Sean. I don't really care. I just want to keep swimming."

"So that's really all there was between you two?" Bernice asked giving me a sly glance.

I stared at her trying to figure out what was between me and The Captain. Oh. She meant Oliver. I shrugged. "He says hi to me in the hall. Sometimes I thought he might have liked me, but he's hard to read. Maybe it's his accent." Bernice kept looking at me, not entirely convinced and I felt uncomfortable. "Oliver's nice. I asked him to teach me how to swim, so he did. Now, you're nice, and so I'm asking you to take over where Oliver left off. What do you say?"

She thought about it for a second then nodded. "Why not? See you tomorrow, five thirty?" And that was it. No problem, but I still felt, I don't know, kind of let down by Oliver. I thought I looked kind of cute in Flop's bikini, but whatever. I guess it was the jammers thing; you just didn't notice bikini cuteness after a while.

Chapter 14

It was kind of lame not seeing Oliver very often. He was still super nice and stuff in the hall, but I missed hanging out without other people even if he didn't talk very much. It relaxed me the same way going to the lake did. I liked Bernice, liked the fact that I never felt weird in whatever I wore, and when she loaned me her old suit so I wouldn't have to adjust Flop's bikini every five minutes. I didn't have to worry about ulterior motives or if she really liked me. But learning to swim with her was less relaxing, more work.

Oliver came into the music store once while I was there, and it was kind of funny, kind of not funny, because Sheila saw him and zeroed in on him while he was asking me if I'd heard of a foreign band that we definitely didn't stock. She started flirting and asking him where he was from, what college he went to, and it was sooooo embarrassing. He didn't seem to notice. He gave her his nice smile and said something in his sexy accent that made her laugh. I felt invisible, like with Cole all over again and left him with her since he apparently wasn't there to see me. He left pretty soon, and I went home and looked up the band. Anyway, other than that it was the same old, "Hello Oliver, yeah, good, see ya later."

That year Flop was hosting the anti-Homecoming thing the same way she did every year, and she had decided that we were going to have a themed party where we dressed as our deepest innermost being. It was kind of fun to decorate and plan with Flop. She was always relaxed, and she had a great deck where we were going to hang lights and have music, like a real kind of fancy thing. Normally she'd do fancy and everyone else would do something else, but now that I had embraced my pretty, it would be at least two of us.

I was at the pool, finishing my lesson with Bernice one extremely early Monday morning when I climbed out and there was Oliver handing me a towel. I stared at him, glad I didn't have to worry about suit placement in Bernice's old speedo one piece for girls, which while it was really streamlined was not cute at all. So he handed me a towel and I took it with a smile while Bernice kept lapping. I noticed that he was wearing clothes while he followed me to the door of the locker room.

"How have you been?" he asked.

I nodded like that was an answer, but he waited and looked at me until I said something amazing like, um, fine.

"I haven't seen you around much. Your swimming looks really good."

I nodded. "Bernice is great. How have you been?"

He frowned and then he tried to smile, but I already saw that he had something on his mind. "There's a dance coming up. It's kind of formal. I'm wondering if…" was he going to ask me? "How serious would a girl think I was if I asked her because I'm a little interested in going, but I don't want to make the wrong impression. It's not that I don't like girls, but I am only here for one year, so I don't want to get into anything deep and cause anyone pain. Do you understand?" He asked with such a nice frown.

I patted his arm and got it damp because I forgot that I was standing in a swimming suit.

"Yeah, I think if you ask a girl then she'll think you're serious. That's kind of the point of Homecoming." I shrugged and edged around him.

"But if I asked you, when you understand how I feel…"

"I'm not going to Homecoming," I interrupted. "I'm going to an anti-Homecoming as my secret self. It's tradition to not go. I'd hate to break tradition."

"Oh," he said and sounded kind of bummed.

"You can come if you want," I offered. I didn't usually invite people but I felt kind of generous and like I could be as good with his whole, casual with the opposite sex thing, as he was.

He looked at me then he turned his head. I followed his gaze and saw Sean come into the pool in his jammers. He dove in without looking around. Watching Sean dive, a cut-out of muscular perfection, made me feel weird, inadequate or something. I would never be able to do that.

"Yeah, I think that would be good," Oliver said, but he sounded distracted.

"Cool," I said and finally made it into the locker room. Of course he wouldn't actually go to Flop's party, but it had been noble of me to invite him. Yeah like he needed my pity.

The next morning Bernice couldn't wait to ask me what Oliver talked to me about. When I saw the look of expectation on her face I was tempted to elaborate to give her a better story.

"So, he asked you to Homecoming?" she demanded.

"No, he asked if a girl would take him seriously if he asked her to Homecoming, and I told him that she would so he decided not to go. I invited him to Flop's party, so he might come to that, but I doubt it."

"Don't you like him?" Bernice asked, this time a little resentfully.

I thought about it. "He's cute and nice, but he doesn't like me. I think I'm done liking boys who don't like me more than I like them."

She looked at me, and of course she knew all about the whole Cole thing, but she didn't say anything, just put on her suit. In the pool we swam and kicked in time. She showed me a new trick to keep water out of my nose when I paddled backwards. It didn't sound like much but it reminded me how much I'd liked her before she became a swimmer. It was great that people could be nice and swimmers too. Too bad The Captain didn't know that.

Finally it was the night of Homecoming, or Flop's party anyway. I wore her old mermaid fin and put my hair in curlers with tons of mousse so it was all wild and stuff. I wore a skimpy top that I'd wrapped tons of seaweed around. I tucked all kinds of seaweed in the taffeta skirt tail thing too, for authenticity. I figured I may as well celebrate the mermaid in me that I'd worked so hard to awaken.

While I got ready, shaving my pits actually, I noticed my old scars at the top of both sides of my ribs were raised, like bumpy welts. Maybe it had something to do with all the chlorine or the speedo straps. I swabbed them with antibiotics and finished getting dressed.

My favorite part was picking music. It was my thing. For my song I'd narrowed my choices down to a nice ocean harmonic and a modern mermaid movie main theme. Tuba confided that he was coming as a Jedi. Not really a shocker since he always came as a Jedi if Flop made him dress up, so his music was a cinch. I'd come to the conclusion that Oliver wasn't coming since he hadn't mentioned anything about it.

I stood beside the stereo system on the deck beneath the twinkling lights and flower garlands when he came in wearing jeans and a t-shirt. He kind of stared at me, I mean, he really stared at me. I checked to make sure my top hadn't fallen off or something. I was intact, but he didn't stop staring.

"What are you?" he asked when he got close enough.

I swished my fin and kind of gave him an, 'isn't it obvious,' look. "I'm a mermaid, because now, Watergirl really is Watergirl. Thanks to you, so, thanks. Look, Bernice is here." I waved her over. She wore a cute skirt and top, but that was as far as she went. Tuba came in with his Yoda head and looked adorably Jedi. Junie in her hippie lady outfit got a kick out of it and kept pulling down his ears to kiss him on the top. I turned to Oliver to nod and laugh at them, but he was still staring at me.

"They're cute," I said and he finally looked away, nodding at my friends before he looked back at me.

"You look different," he said, edging closer like he wanted to check my hair for extensions.

"It's the seaweed. I'm surprised you came."

"Of course I came. It would break tradition to go to

Homecoming since I've never been either. Do you want to dance?"

I opened my mouth and remembered the beach, and the awfulness of that whole thing. "No. I do music. I get the person's theme on for them. Junie has Peter, Paul and Mary." I fiddled with the music and soon The Spinning Song came on. Junie started spinning around while everyone else cleared the floor. There were more people than the last time I'd looked. Apparently Flop had been busy inviting anyone who didn't have a date, as usual. "So what's your theme," I asked Oliver while he watched Junie bring it down with a kind of awe.

"Um, I don't have one."

"I have something just in case you showed up," I said as Junie's song wound down and we all cheered for her. I found my favorite song from the foreign band he'd mentioned that day he'd come into the shop and smiled at him while the sound floated through the air. It was hard with a steady beat, but there was musicality too. The singer, who of course I couldn't understand, sang like a dream, her voice rising above the harsh thumping and cruel guitars, somehow matching them with her contrast.

He smiled at me then took the floor, confident and easy as he proceeded to breakdance… or at least it might have been a breakdance if he hadn't been so incredibly awful. Tuba joined in and with Yoda and Oliver breaking out to this foreign techno metallic stuff it was overall the most hilarious thing I'd ever seen. I laughed so hard my stomach hurt.

It was a great party. Everyone had a great time, even Junie until she got backfisted by Flop when she did her uber cool diver moves. Tuba followed Junie into the kitchen while Flop felt bad and I tried to wait until Junie was off the deck before I broke into inappropriate giggles.

"You're good at this music stuff," Oliver said, handing me a little plastic plate full of chips and dip.

"Thanks. You're good at the…" I gestured to the floor, twisting my hands around. "Dancing stuff."

He laughed. "Oh, you're impressed by that? You should

see me slow dance. Where's your music Genevieve?"

I stammered for a second while he leaned behind me, flipping through the song list until he found the one with my name. He hit play and the deck filled with the sound of waves crashing, hearts thumping and a woman crooning, sounding a little bit like the wind at first.

"Come on," he said as he grabbed my hand and pulled me onto the floor. He put his hands on my waist while I stood there, not sure what to do until he pulled my hands around his neck then resumed his position on my waist. "We could stand here but it might get boring. Maybe we should move."

"I think you're supposed to move first and then I follow you. Unless you'd rather I…"

He spun us around, tightening his hands on my waist, pulling me against his body. I grew dizzy, half from the spinning and half from forgetting to breathe. The feel of him was different than I remembered with Cole. His body was filled out, strong, and his skin smelled salty, probably from sweat but with the magic sea music playing it made me think of saltwater, dancing underwater, me a mermaid and maybe him an unfortunate sailor I was dragging to his death, or something even more exciting. His cheek grazed my forehead and I felt a shock that had me holding very still, standing there with my heart thumping against his until the music stopped and I could step away from him as though a spell had broken.

I went back to the music, not looking at him for the rest of the party.

After it was late and most everyone had drifted off on waves of laughter, I was getting ready to go home. I had some stuff to carry, dip trays and some extra folding chairs I had to haul home. Oliver stepped up as I balanced a chair precariously, lifting half of them easily.

"Thanks," I said, blushing. I'd thought that he'd already left.

"This was different," he said smiling at me as we walked outside, down the porch steps and crossed the lawn to my dad's old rusty wagon.

"Yeah, Flop has some interesting ideas." I struggled for a minute with the key in the trunk.

"Can I help?" he asked then took the key and made the trunk open up with its familiar groan. "I had a lot of fun. Thank you for inviting me."

I nodded and shrugged, very aware of how close his arm was to my shoulder, scant inches from touching mine. "I'm glad you made it. Your break dancing was inspiring, and Tuba probably liked having another guy here."

He nodded then smiled at me but his smile seemed a little stiff. "I'm glad I could add to the testosterone level." His smile faded as he reached out and brushed one of my now frizzy strands out of my face. "There's something about you, something special."

I felt my heart pound in my chest while his hand lingered near my face. Was he going to kiss me? For a second he leaned forward a little but then he shook his head and turned away, stashing the chairs in the depths of the trunk before closing it with a thud.

"Good night," he said before he turned and walked off. I stood there for a while feeling part disappointed and part relieved before I got in my car and drove home. He'd really looked like he wanted to kiss me though. Huh.

Chapter 15

So that was Friday, and the next day I worked. Everything was fine, but I had that feeling in my stomach all day. The kind that made me glad that things were busy and I didn't have time to think. I hated going home for dinner where my dad was sitting there with a chocolate birthday cake for me. Yeah, my birthday was on the very same fantastic day my mother died. My dad tried, but I wished he wouldn't. I took one look at the cake and went to my room. I barely had time to throw myself on my bed with buds in my ears when my dad knocked on the door.

"I'm not celebrating my birthday anymore," I informed him without pulling the buds from my ears. I didn't have to speak loudly to be heard through the flimsy wood.

"Can we talk about it?" he asked.

"I think mom's death day cancels out my birthday. I don't want to think about it much less talk. Okay?"

There was silence for a long time then he sighed. I hated it when he sighed. I'd much rather have a lecture. I knew what to do with those. "All right. We'll figure out another day that's better to celebrate," he said and left me alone in my room with my iPod. I listened to Oliver's song on repeat almost wishing I had a Cole to be obsessed about so I wouldn't have to think about my mother.

That night after the house was quiet I biked myself out to Stinky Lake. I wore a sweater over my nightshirt and leggings because it was getting pretty cold. I hadn't been to the lake since I'd started swimming in the pool. I felt the strangeness of sneaking out to a lake, but it didn't matter. I had to go and remember however much I'd rather have buried myself in rapid drum beats.

I found my rock and sat there for a while, letting the darkness and night wind soak into my skin. It wasn't that dark; I could see the lights of the town and the millions of stars up above my head. It was quiet and solemn, a moment that stretched out forever until I needed to add my voice to the darkness.

The song swelled out of me like a moan, low and whispering until I found myself on my feet singing like I knew I shouldn't, but I didn't pass out right away, and my voice sounded good to me, right with the wind wrapping around me and my hair tangling in my face. The lullaby had the beat of my heart to keep it in time, a rapid beat that grew louder along with my voice. I sang for her, for me, for the becoming of who I almost was until I felt a gasp, the loss of oxygen. My voice whispered away as I fell into darkness.

I woke up with someone pulling me, holding me above water where I sputtered and coughed, thrashing until Oliver's voice in my ear calmed me down. I relaxed, limp and let him drag me to shore. He threw me onto a muddy bank before he climbed out and dropped down beside me. He started rubbing my sides, turning me so I could cough and spit out whatever stinky lake I drank until my throat ached while tears trailed down my cheeks. I breathed, relieved that I could breathe, that I hadn't drowned, feeling a growing horror at the stupidity of what I'd done. I could swim, but not when I was unconscious and I usually lost consciousness when I sang to my mother. I couldn't help it, but I could help standing up on the rock as though I didn't already know exactly what would happen. Sean was right. I was an idiot.

I pushed away Oliver and tried to sit up. I leaned my forehead on my knees and focused on the breathing, on the feeling of my wet clothes dragging around me and the night wind piercing through the fibers of my wet sweater. I shivered and Oliver put his hands around me, pulling me against his warm chest, warm in spite of his near nudity and still wet skin.

I shuddered, too aware of him without being able to

find the distance, the reason why I shouldn't relax against him and let the sound of his heart beat away all my other thoughts. I thought of Sean again, saw his cold eyes mocking me and pulled away from Oliver, rubbing my arms while I tried to stand up.

"Thanks for the swim. I've got to get home," I mumbled and tried to see in the dark where my bike would be. Were we on the muddy bank to the left or right of the rock?

"I saw you floating in the lake. You looked..." Oliver grabbed my hand while he wrapped an arm around my waist. "You were so still until I got close, and then you sank. It was like something held you up until I could get to you." He started smoothing my wet hair away from my face. "It was like a fairytale, a sleeping princess floating on the water, bathed in moonlight."

"That sounds pretty," I said with my hoarse voice while my head reeled. "What are you doing here?"

"I like it here. It's a good place to think," he said, leading me away from the lake as though he wasn't wearing nothing but underwear.

"Where are your clothes?" I asked, stumbling over something in the dark.

"I'll get them later," he said, wrapping his arm tighter around me.

I shivered and said through chattering teeth, "How are you not cold?"

"I don't know, adrenaline? I've swam through ice floes so this isn't very cold water to me."

"Ice floes. Huh. I have no idea what those are. Where are we going? I have my bike..."

"I can't let you ride home in this condition. You could get hypothermia."

"Hypothermia. How did I not die in the lake?"

"Can you remember what happened?"

I shook my head then shrugged. "I fell off the rock. I don't remember anything after that. Why are you here, again?"

We came out of the bushes onto the road right beside my bike. He let go of me so he could push my bike down the road a little ways to where he'd parked his car. I followed, shivering while my feet squelched in my sneakers. He stuck my bike in the trunk then he opened my door and left me to climb in while he went around to start the car and turn the heater on high.

I shivered and trembled as I held my hands over the hot air. I felt awkward when I realized that he was staring at me, but then he said, "I'll be right back," and he left me with the heater on while he went back into the dark and cold.

I couldn't help but notice that my wet clothes were soaking the nice leather seat and I'd gotten mud all over the floor. I stayed perched on the edge, trying to not make more of a mess than I already had.

Oliver came back quickly, sliding in and setting a t-shirt on the dash in front of me.

"You should probably change into my clothes," he said gesturing at it. I blinked, staring at the small innocent looking bundle and remembered the last time I'd put on a guy's shirt.

I shook my head. "I'm fine. If you take me home then I can take a shower and get into some clean clothes. Like this I'd only soak them anyway. I just want to go home."

"If you insist," he said but sounded disappointed.

I felt oddly guilty for not taking his shirt, but then he grabbed his shirt and pulled it over his chest. I felt much better after that. He wasn't Sean, leaner and shorter, but still solidly muscular in a way that fascinated me too much. He finally put the car into gear and after a drive during which he seemed to go too slow, he pulled up at my house.

"How did you know where I lived?"

"I think Sean mentioned it. I live with him you know. He's going to give me a lecture when he sees the upholstery on his car."

Sean's car? Of course. Oliver was an exchange student. He wouldn't have his own car.

"Great. Well, tell Sean I'm sorry, and thanks for saving me, Oliver." I got out of the car before I had to look at him again, but stood beside it, shivering as I waited for him to drive away.

He rolled down the window. "Next time you go out to the lake you should take someone with you for safety."

"Are you offering?"

He nodded, his face lit weirdly by the green neon of the car's radio. "Of course. I'm not joking Genevieve. The lake isn't safe. Something held you up, and I don't think it was human."

I stared at him. He didn't sound nearly as freaked out as he should have been for someone who thought there was some thing in the lake. "Like the Lochness monster, only, in Ohio?"

He smiled a little bit, his eyes looking black instead of emerald where he sat in shadows. "Dolphins save humans sometimes. Maybe someone released one of them into the lake."

"Oh, that makes sense." I rolled my eyes. "Good night." Nothing was going to make sense until I took a hot shower.

"Just stay away from the lake for a while. Promise?" he asked. I nodded although it was the same promise I'd made and broken to my dad a dozen times.

"Sure. Don't worry about me. See you later."

He nodded then said as the window began rolling up, "Good night then."

"Night," I said still waiting for him to drive away so that I could climb onto the porch and through my window so that my dad didn't freak out on me. I only realized after I'd showered until I stopped shivering that I'd left my bike in his, no Sean's trunk. Awesome.

Chapter 16

The next day my dad and I ate cake for breakfast. And lunch. And dinner. I couldn't stand chocolate cake, I mean, I think I liked it when I was four, but then for my birthday my mom was dead and I was trying to eat cake. It became torture to smile at my dad and swallow it down. I couldn't tell my dad though. It was tradition, and he was trying. I had to give him something normal to do.

I wanted to call Oliver, to get my bike back, but I couldn't bring myself to do it. First, I'd have to ask around for his number, and Junie probably had Sean's, and that's where he lived but Sean... well, I could wait until Monday.

Bernice wasn't there at the pool in the morning, but The Captain was. At first I thought he was going to yell at me for getting his car muddy but instead he walked right up to me and began talking about basic water safety. His voice was dead serious, cold, but it didn't stop him from being impossibly gorgeous with those piercing blue eyes and glaring six-pack. I felt completely disoriented. In my wildest dreams I never would have asked him to help me with swimming. I wasn't entirely sure he wouldn't let me drown. No, of course he wouldn't let me drown. It only felt like I'd rather drown than see him stare at me, making me more clumsy and accident prone than I usually was.

"Your form isn't bad, but you need to work on elongating your limbs."

I inhaled water and coughed and choked for a few minutes while he waited, like a floating statue, patient and so cold.

"Try again."

No comments about the choking incident, actually,

there was nothing cruel about anything he said or did at all, but the way he watched me was so unnerving. I kept expecting him to mention the mud in his car, but he never said anything about that, only grabbed my wrist to show me how to hold them right then guided my hand through the water. I could feel the difference, but when he let go I couldn't do it the right way.

When the swim team came in he ignored them completely, keeping his gaze locked on mine while he finished up my lesson. The technique I'd almost learned drowned a quick death since I was distracted by Oliver and Bernice. They were laughing at something another guy said, apparently taking the chance to mess around while their fearless leader was occupied.

"Focus." Sean's sharp voice grabbed my attention and his eyes kept it. "You know what panic feels like. Even experienced swimmers can panic, get turned around and make a lethal mistake. If you can't focus you could die. Control your body, control your mind; show me what I know you've learned."

For a few minutes the rest of the world disappeared and it was only me and my body moving while Sean's voice guided me.

His arm brushed mine beneath the water and the rhythm and concentration evaporated. I gasped and would have inhaled water if Sean didn't have his hands on my shoulders, holding me in place.

"Concentrate."

With him keeping me up, I closed my eyes and shoved the worry about drowning down. Instead I thought about my body, kicking, breathing, so many things to think about but somehow possible without the fear of sinking occupying so much space.

"Good," he said.

I opened my eyes and realized that he had moved me to the edge of the pool. "Good?" I didn't expect him to say something positive.

"Adequate," he said with a flicker of a smile. "That's it for today."

I nodded and he stayed there treading water, staring at me until I pulled myself out of the pool and headed to the locker room, shivering. I should have asked him if my bike was still in his trunk, but then I would have to admit that I'd gotten mud on the seat and all the idiocy that had happened before that. I liked him saying 'good' much better than his usual comments.

At lunch Oliver sat at the table with the swim team with Sean. He had a girl beside him who wasn't on the swim team, a cute brunette who I thought might be a sophomore. He draped his arm around the back of her chair while smiling at everyone at the table. I had to get my bike, but I couldn't make myself intrude. I'd thought there was something with him at Flop's party, and then at the lake… but no. Apparently not.

I had choir practice for the big concert coming up with work afterwards, then the long walk home. The next morning I wished I'd been able to at least talk to Bernice and find out if Sean would be in the pool with me again. I could sleep in for Sean however productive I was with him. I went to the pool, almost hoping it would be empty and I could practice by myself. Bernice was already there.

"So Sean yesterday… that was weird," I said.

"Oh yeah. I meant to call you, but I don't have your number," she said, and then we had to trade numbers. She programmed her phone while I scribbled her number on my hand. Techno me. After that we were ready for swimming.

"I had fun at the anti-Homecoming," she said before we got in the pool.

"Oh, yeah, it was fun." I didn't sound as enthusiastic as I would have before I'd seen Oliver with that girl. She definitely was a sophomore. "Wasn't Aaron a great Yoda?"

She nodded.

"So, why weren't you here yesterday morning?" I asked.

Bernice kind of blushed. "Sean wanted to make sure that you were getting the basics down. He's certified and stuff to teach swimming and I'm really not. He wanted to make sure that you weren't getting trained all wrong so you'd end up dead, and the blame would fall on the team. He's kind of annoying like that."

"Ah. So, did you pass?"

She beamed at me. "Yeah. He said you're coming along great, and that I'm doing an adequate job. From him that's serious praise."

"Adequate?" For some reason I had to fight down the snicker. "Yeah, from him that is serious. He could be a little less hard on people." Then I wouldn't have to fear asking him about my bike.

She shrugged. "Maybe, but when he finally does tell you it's good, you know that it really is. So, do you want to come to the party at Sean's house this weekend?"

I stared at her as she slid into the pool. "Sean of adequate fame? I think he'd kick me out."

"No he wouldn't. I can bring a friend or a date. I asked specifically because the last time I went I felt stupid, so I wasn't going to go unless I had someone to talk to. In the water I'm one of them but out of the water... I'm more comfortable with my old friends."

I took my time getting in, testing the water with my feet before plunging in completely over my head. When I came up she was waiting for my answer.

"Football players and cheerleaders?" The expression on her face answered that question. I had to get my bike, and I wanted to be her friend, maybe not the way we'd used to be, but still friends. "Yeah, I guess. If you're sure no one will mind, that would be cool."

Her squeal banished most of my reservations.

That day after school and choir practice I went to Stinky Lake. I'd told Oliver I wouldn't go without taking him, but he'd been with a different girl at lunch, blond this time, Kate who was in choir with me. It didn't matter. It was fine except that I didn't have my bike and I couldn't stop thinking about what would have happened if he hadn't come along. Maybe nothing. Maybe I would have floated until I'd come to and been able to swim to shore on my own.

I drove the car, which was nice because it had been drizzling steadily all day not to mention the fact that I hadn't gotten my bike back yet. I walked through the wet grass in my slicker watching the rain come down and down. At the rock I was careful; I didn't climb on it because it was slippery and falling was not on my to-do list.

I heard a motor on the lake and wondered who would be crazy enough to fish in that weather. The sound of the engine came closer. It wasn't a fishing boat. It was bigger and louder with nets, hooks, pulleys and other weird gear rigged around it. I saw lots of people on board, but I couldn't really tell what they were doing from that distance.

The vibe I got was all wrong. Instead of relaxed I got more and more keyed up until I shook my head and returned to my car. Once there I turned the heater up while the sound of the radio blocked the rain.

Finally I put the car in gear and drove home to call Junie about it. I didn't call Junie very often, not to just talk because that's not what she does, but if anyone knew what was going on at the lake, she would. I would also get Sean's number. I needed my bike.

She didn't know Sean's number. She had his address though. When I asked her about the lake she said that it had been closed because some kind of toxic bacteria had gotten in it that they were trying to treat before winter. Then she went on about the eco system of the lake and the way that conservation was never effective when you had more and more people acting irresponsibly, anyway, I kind of tuned out at that point because it wasn't anything I hadn't heard before. I still thought it was weird that anyone cared that much about a little bit of bacteria at Stinky Lake. Hardly anyone ever went there anyway; that's why I liked it so much. After I hung up, I spent some time in my bathroom, staring into the mirror and wondering if I looked like a mutant from the toxic lake when I'd fallen in, but the same boring girl with boring brown eyes and brown hair stared back at me. I had Sean's address so I could go to his house and… No. I would wait until the party to get my bike.

Chapter 17

For the party there was the issue of what to wear, but Bernice said a swimming suit was the only requirement, no sweat. I still didn't actually own a suit so I headed over to Flop's to apologize about missing movie night and beg her for help in the suiting up arena. She of course had a cute topper thing to wear over the ruffly bikini she loaned me.

"You're awesome," I said, looking in the mirror. I looked kind of cute. "I wish you would come."

She made a face. "No thanks. Sean is supposed to have an incredible pool and the best parties, but you'd have to hang out with him. He's not a warm person. If you leave early, feel free to come back over to watch a movie."

I sighed and fiddled with my shoulder strap. "I feel like an idiot. I wish I knew what to do around guys like Sean and Oliver." I shook my head while Flop laughed.

"Sean's easy. He'll think you're an idiot no matter what you talk about, so you don't have to worry about making an impression. You can't. With Oliver, I don't know. He seems to be the opposite—easily pleased by everyone. Have you seen the parade of girls he's been going through? Who knows what he actually likes."

"Yeah." Apparently not me. Ah well. At least I wasn't obsessed with someone who liked other girls.

After I was as cute as possible, I got a ride with Bernice. She looked cool and sporty in the tunic she wore over her suit, so maybe I looked okay too, only more frilly and bright, since it was Flop's outfit after all.

"Thanks for inviting me," I started awkwardly.

"Thanks for coming. It'll be much nicer to have someone there besides the swim team. I kind of like this guy, Ben, but no one on the swim team will admit to liking anyone, because of Sean, you know. Just because he thinks that relationships are a distracting waste of time doesn't mean that other people can't think differently."

"Maybe you should tell him that."

She laughed. "Right. Well, I would be if I dated a guy on the team, wouldn't I?"

"Going up against The Captain? Bernice, you're the bravest person I've ever met."

"He's not that bad…"

I laughed while she rolled her eyes.

Sean's house was awesome, all glassy and architectural when we pulled up. I'd seen the house before, of course. Our town wasn't that big, but I'd never thought I'd actually go inside or know the people who lived there.

"Sean lives here?"

She nodded. I gave her a sympathetic glance because coming there when you didn't know people had to be hard. It almost made sense that I was there.

We were lucky to get a parking spot only half a block from the house. We followed the walk to the open front door then we were there. It was imposing enough from the front but inside was even more mind blowing. There was a pool in what would be the living room of a normal person's house. It went from inside the living room to outside in the backyard. It was the kind of thing that I would have fallen into within fifteen seconds before, but now that I could swim there didn't seem to be the same pull. On the balcony above the pool, beautiful people lounged around in really fancy looking swim tops, the kind that looked like real dresses, carrying fruity drinks and laughing. Every pretty person from high school and some from college seemed to be there with the notable exception of any and all cheerleaders.

So this was what a real party looked like. I felt gawky and stupid. I didn't belong there, but I could tell that Bernice felt the same way. It was good that I could make up some of those early morning swim lessons she'd given me.

"So what do we do?" I asked her as I dodged a laughing girl running away from a guy who splashed me when he tackled her into the pool.

She shrugged. "I don't really know. There is a lot of showing off, diving, in the water dancing, food, drinks, and cute guys to flirt with. Do you see that guy over there by the Aquarium?"

I looked over at the wall and what I'd first taken as an elaborate wall-paper job I now realized was an enormous aquarium that took up the entire wall beneath the balcony. It was impossibly cool. I blinked, trying to get over the shark behind glass, and saw the guy she was pointing at, a normal looking guy who I'd vaguely noticed on the swim team before.

"Yeah. He looks nice."

"Will you come over with me?" I nodded. There was no way I was going to stand there by myself.

"Oliver, there you are." I heard a voice, all sultry and cute and looked in the pool where a really pretty girl floated with a coral colored drink in her hand. Who could float and drink at the same time? I hated her at once. The girl gazed up at the balcony. When I looked up, I saw Oliver perched on the railing with his arms spread eagled. There was no way he would jump into the pool full of people. It would be suicide. It would be homicide, but there he went, headfirst in a series of rolls and twists that ended with him in the pool with hardly a splash.

"He's crazy," I muttered, and Bernice nodded.

"Sean's actually worse. Of course they live here so they probably practice all kinds of stupid all the time, but that doesn't stop the other guys from having to show off."

I nodded at her and we had a girl bonding moment where we acknowledged how stupid guys were then we walked around the pool to where the guy, Ben, stood with a drink while he talked animatedly with another guy who didn't look like he was from the team.

He greeted Bernice, said a very nice hi to me, and then he and she start talking about team stuff while I watched the fish and coral behind them, really, it was the coolest thing. Apparently that was my thing to do at the party. I would have stared at the aquarium, the pale pink and turquoise pulsing anemones as mesmerizing as the pearlescent fish that fluttered by them, all evening except that I heard Oliver's voice to my right. When I looked up, I saw him walk out of the living room.

A week without my bike was more than enough. I hurriedly told Bernice I had to use the bathroom and that I'd be right back. She nodded but didn't really hear me. She was really into Ben.

I followed Oliver; I had no choice. The him avoiding me thing, which I swore was what he had been doing, was getting really old. His shirt dripped as he walked. I followed the watermarks and felt all Nancy Drew when he was out of sight and I was walking down a hall with rows of doors until I finally came to one where the watermarks stopped.

I knocked and waited, nothing, then the door opened, kind of fast so it startled me, and there was Oliver without his shirt on with a towel around his waist. His eyes were really dark and full, moist looking with only a little bit of green around the edge of his pupils.

"Hi," he finally said and stepped back. I followed because there had been something I had to talk to him about. Right. My bike. Funny how seeing him in a towel made that seem less important.

"What are you doing here?" he asked me after he shut the door behind me. The click of the door kind of made me jump. Did I really want to be in his bedroom with the door shut when he only had a towel on? I'd never been in a boy's bedroom before. I couldn't help but give it a quick curious glance to see what marks of ownership he'd left on it. There was a pile of dirty laundry but other than that and some shells on a corner of the dresser, nothing really showed personality.

"I was invited," I said with a shrug.

Oliver frowned at me and I crossed my arms over my chest.

"I really need my bike back, but I haven't been able to talk to you all week."

His eyes get even darker, and the way he stared at me made me wonder if he could focus on all of me at one time.

"You're in my bedroom. Did you think I'd be sleeping with your bike?"

I fought the blush. He'd made it clear at school that he was not interested in me. That he thought I'd cornered him in his bedroom for something besides getting my bike had my teeth clenching together.

"I thought it might be better to talk about my bike and the lake without other people around. I'm not really excited about admitting that I'm stupid enough to fall into a lake. It seems like you've been avoiding me, which is fine except that I really need my bike."

He shrugged. "It must still be in the trunk. You'll have to ask Sean to get it for you."

"Seriously?"

He raised an eyebrow and for a second the smile slipped and he looked colder than Sean.

"Wow. Thanks for that."

I turned to the door but he stepped directly in front of me. "Sean isn't giving me access to his car anymore. Otherwise I would have brought it back some time during the week. He's being a jerk."

"He's being a jerk? All week you could have mentioned that to me. I saw how busy you were, but still, I need my bike."

"Sorry. I didn't see you very much." He smiled, but it was a twist of his mouth that didn't have anything to do with the rest of him. He didn't see me, but not because I wasn't there. I felt a wave of humiliation that had me crossing my arms over my chest.

"Whatever. I've got to get back to the party."

"Genevieve," he said in a soft voice while he reached out to stroke my cheek or something but I jerked back before he could touch me.

"The only thing I want from you is my bike. If you don't have it then there's no reason for me to be here with you in a towel," I said keeping my eyes firmly on his face.

"I want to be your friend, but sometimes friendship

gets complicated," he said while his fingers curled and uncurled. It reminded me of tentacles, squid or octopus, unconsciously flexing, searching for prey even in their sleep.

"No, friendship is simple. It means that even if you're dating other girls you still talk to me and let me know what's going on. Now move before I move you."

He smiled, cocking his head. "Is that a threat?" but he stepped aside as he said it, opening the door for me. "Sean's in the kitchen."

I scowled at him. "I would never have taken that ride if I'd known it was Sean's car."

"Why not? Sean has a good car."

"It's perfect, just like him. The problem is that he's really particular about his perfect things not coming in contact with me. Oh well. Thanks."

He raised an eyebrow. "I noticed his hands coming into close contact with you in the pool. It wasn't, how do you say it, professional?"

"He must have thought I needed help desperately." I scowled then forced myself to walk past him irritated instead of charmed by his smile, at least mostly.

"If you are you sure you don't want to take advantage of me, I suppose I'll see you after I put on some pants."

I shook my head but couldn't fight the blush as I went back the way I'd come. I really had pretty much stalked him. Muscles, tan, the perfect shoulder to hip ratio, it had been seriously hard not to notice that stuff. Good thing I had so much practice not noticing hot guys.

I wandered through the house until I found myself in an enormous kitchen, all hard edges, metal and glass, where Sean stood at the blender pureeing something.

He glanced up at me, and I felt half as cute as I'd felt right up to that point. Beside him was the girl, the one who could float and drink.

"Hi," she said offering me her hand. "I'm Brenda. I've never seen you at one of Sean's parties before."

I took the hand limply and felt crushed by her awesome grip. "I'm Gen. I came here with a friend."

"Oh?" she said in a way that made me feel like I shouldn't wander around without the friend in case I destroyed something. "Did you need something in here?"

"I wanted to talk to Sean."

She glanced up at him, inviting him to share her disbelief, but he was focused on shredding strawberries to a pulp.

"Go find Oliver, Brenda," he told her.

She raised her eyebrows, but just like everyone else, she obeyed The Captain and left the room. We stood there for a time, both of us staring at the whirring machine.

"You wanted to talk." It wasn't a question.

"I think my bike is in your trunk."

"And?"

I put my hands on my hips and glared at him. "And, I want it back, so if you could take a minute away from your awesome and way too cool for me party to get it, I'd be ever so grateful."

"How did it get in my trunk?" This time he flipped off the blender and looked at me, leaning against the counter in a way that I shouldn't have found threatening.

I shifted to crossing my arms over my chest. "Oliver gave me a ride. I'm sorry about the mud and the water on your seat."

"What happened?"

Exactly. I'd known he'd make me feel like an idiot. Of course he would. What else did he live for?

"I was an idiot. Big surprise, right? I went to the lake to sing, lost consciousness when I know that when I sing too loud I can't breathe, fell off the rock into the lake and then floated for however long until Oliver dragged me to shore. So, sorry about the mud. I would never have taken the ride however hypothermic I got if I'd known it was yours and I'd taint it. If you've finished humiliating me, can I get my bike back?"

He frowned the longer I talked until by the end he was scowling. "So that's why Oliver wanted my dad to drag the lake."

"Oliver... your dad..." I rubbed my hand over my

forehead and felt the beginnings of a headache. I was ready for Sean's contempt, braced for it, but he seemed interested in all the wrong parts. "So, your dad's was the boat I saw? Oliver said there was something in the lake." I laughed, more of a wheezy thing while Sean stared at me until the laughter choked and died. "I take it there was no toxic bacteria. What did your dad find?"

"The boat you saw?" Oliver's sexy accent sounded accusing. "You promised me that you wouldn't go back to the lake without me."

I jumped as I turned around, bumping into Sean in the process. He didn't budge. "Yeah, well, you were busy. I didn't even have your number. Also, it was a promise made in a moment of uncontrollable shivering weakness. Those don't count."

"Don't they?" Sean asked, looking down at me with his eyes of slivered chips of ice.

I swallowed as I stared up at him. He stood way too close for comfort.

"Good to know." He shifted his attention to Oliver, which was a huge relief. "What did you see?"

Oliver shrugged casually as he moved to take an apple from the fruit bowl that had been perfectly symmetrical. "I didn't see anything. Your dad hasn't found anything either. For all we know, Genevieve is able to float while unconscious."

"But you think there's something there." Again, not a question.

Oliver shrugged again. "I think a lot of things. Genevieve, this song is very good. You should dance with me." He abandoned his apple and reached for my hand.

"I don't dance," I mumbled as he pulled me away from Sean and across the kitchen.

Sean frowned after me.

"Wait I need..."

"I'll bring your bike to your house tomorrow," Sean said giving me a cool nod. "Enjoy my too cool for you party for as long as you like."

I pulled away from Oliver as soon as we'd left the

kitchen. "Seriously, Oliver, I'm not going to dance with you."

"Why not? I didn't think you were so bad the other night," he said, moving his hips back and forth while he leaned towards me. After all the other girls, I still found his smile utterly charming. It was a good thing that he'd reminded me of the week before when I'd thought he'd actually liked me. I did not need more heartache.

"If I dance with you then other people will think we're serious."

"One dance? Come on. Who cares what other people think?"

"Not you, apparently," I said, trying to ignore the innocent confusion in his eyes. "You lead girls on, Oliver, and it isn't nice. Every time you sit with a girl at lunch she thinks she's special, that you like her."

"I do like her. I like lots of people."

I glared at him, but how could I hold onto a glare when he looked so bewildered and adorable with a black curl falling over his forehead. "Everybody can't be special, or that's not special, it's something else. I don't dance with anyone, ever. If other people see me dancing with you they'll think something serious is up. They'll think you're my boyfriend."

He frowned. "Would that be so bad?"

I was saved from answering when Brenda came up and threw her arms around him to give him a hug. When he turned to smile at her, I slipped away. Maybe it wouldn't be bad for him but it would certainly suck for me. I shrugged it off and found Bernice who was still talking to Ben.

I stood beside her for a few seconds until Oliver came into sight, dancing with Brenda like he was having the time of his life. It felt good to know how quickly I could be replaced.

"Bernice, I'm going to walk home."

She looked up at me as if surprised I was still there. "Oh. If you want to go, I'll drive you."

"It's early still," Ben said, putting a hand on her arm. She blushed and I stepped away.

"No, you have fun. I like walking, and it's not far."

"You can't walk in your suit. It's too cold out."

"Can I come?" Ben asked.

She beamed at him. We piled into her car with Ben in the backseat leaning up to talk to Bernice and me by default. I changed at my house then headed to Flop's where I could watch the last half of a horrible movie with a hideously happy ending. I didn't have to tell her about Oliver and what a jerk he was, not like I'd have had to tell her about Cole, so maybe my obsessive tendencies were fading in my old age. One could hope.

Chapter 18

Work the next day was good. I was organizing the meditation music—I always found that extremely meditative—when Tuba, er, Aaron came in to talk about the likelihood of the tuba becoming the new alternative instrument. I had no idea what he was talking about, but I nodded my head.

He turned to go then stopped and looked at me, kind of nervous. "Do you think Junie would go out with me?"

After a few shocked seconds I forced my mouth to shut. "I have no idea. She went after The Captain for no rational reason so who knows? She should though. I mean, any girl would be lucky to date you."

He nodded but his face kind of fell.

I nudged him. "You could date me if you wanted some practice first."

He smiled but shook his head, kind of sad. Why did Junie have to be so… like her? If she got it into her head to date him, then nothing other than complete annihilation of her ego would stop her. Then again she could take up with Jim, the male cheerleader. Who knew?

Not me.

The long trek home after work made me even more angry at Junie for no rational reason. When I made it to the walk, there parked beside the porch was my bike. At least I thought it was my bike. While it was still rusty, it had what looked like new brakes, and the tire pressure was perfect in the brand new tires. I stood there staring at my bike as giddiness built. I had to see how she rode.

I hopped on then glided down the street, checking out the gear shifts, so smooth, like she was brand new. My bike was bought second hand and the gears had never worked right. I found myself on the familiar road out to the lake, pushing the pedals as hard as I could, I felt the wind whip my hair away from my face, so fast and free like I was flying. I stopped at the lake, standing with one foot on the pedal while I thought about whether to go back home or go check out my tree. I smiled as I pedaled my bike through the weeds, finding my new tires awesome the way they gripped the earth. I made it to the tree, huffing and out of breath. I collapsed beneath the willow fronds, glad that I couldn't hear a motor on the lake to disturb my peace.

I closed my eyes while I thought about my bike, my amazing thing then stopped smiling quite so much when I thought about where it had come from. Sean. I didn't like owing him. I'd been saving up for a new music program, maybe it would be enough to pay for the bike. With that semi-bitter taste in my mouth, I listened to the water while the wind blew the long willow strands around me.

I fell asleep. I must have fallen asleep because when I opened my eyes I thought there was a face with black, moist, alien eyes gazing down at me, but after a blink it was just me, alone under the tree. I must have dreamed it. I heard a rustle but before I could sit up, the strands parted and there was Oliver, eyebrows drawn together while he stared at me.

"What are you doing here?" We both said it at the same time.

I shook my head while he looked past me, towards the water where it lapped against the bank.

"Did you see something?" he asked, stepping over me and crouching down to peer into the water.

"I was just... why are you here? You're always here when I'm here. Are you following me?"

He glanced at me, and I felt like an idiot. He didn't have his nice guy smile on so it was only his apathetic hot-ness I was faced with. "I should be. I think it's attracted to you. I've been trying to see something, and it only comes when you do."

"What comes? What are you talking about? There's nothing there."

"Not now," he said nodding.

I got slowly to my feet, following him out from beneath the tree. "What do you think is in the lake? What did you see?"

I stumbled over my bike. I picked it up, pushing it after Oliver where he walked quickly away from me.

"Oliver, what's going on? I mean, the floating in the lake thing was weird, but there wasn't anything there, not really, was there? Oliver, stop walking, I'm talking to you."

He stopped, his back to me for a few seconds before he turned around. His smile was back on his face, his easy smile that made him seem accessible.

"Genevieve, such a beautiful name." He ran a hand over my handlebars like a caress with his strong fingers. "It isn't what I've seen so much as sensed. I feel a presence; don't you? What draws you to the lake? Something pulls you here, puts you under its spell." His voice was soft, compelling. "A little bit like you, the way I feel drawn to you. You're not like the other girls."

I swallowed as his fingers followed the lines of my bike until they slid over my hands where I gripped the handlebars. His hands felt cool on my skin making goosebumps pop up on my arms.

"If you mean that I'm as susceptible to your foreign accent as other girls, I'm afraid I'm exactly the same. Are you trying to distract me?"

His smile turned mischievous as his hands followed my goosebumps up my arms to my shoulders. "Not exactly. I have a lot of curiosity. You, the lake, they are things which seem worth pursuing."

I shivered as his hands moved back down my arms. "Until the next sparkly thing comes along, yes I know. Tell Sean thanks for the bike. I'd better go home before I fall into the lake or something."

I pulled away, but it was harder than it should have been, like he was right about there being a pull between us, holding us together.

"He gave it back to you; that's hardly something that requires gratitude."

I shook my head, smiling as I patted my bike. "No, he did an incredible job; it's as good as new, better than new. I guess he couldn't bear to see something that bad so he had to fix it, but whatever his reason…"

Oliver moved around the bike so he was right beside me. He took my hand, gripped it firmly in his then leaned forward, as though he were going to kiss me.

I pulled back at the last second, turning away while I tried to breathe.

"Oliver, no. I can't kiss you, or anyone. I'm not like other girls. I get obsessive about guys. Believe me; you do not want me to obsess about you. It's not pretty. It's not that I don't want to kiss you, and if I could be one of those people who kiss different guys and compare technique, that would rock, but I'm not, and I can't."

"Ah, Genevieve," he whispered as he slid a hand through my hair, pushing it back, away from my face, "I'm afraid it's inevitable. We keep running into each other, here, alone. I was meant to taste your lips."

I turned to him, whispered, "No", as his lips came over mine, soft at first, but then something changed, the softness became hard, the taste became bitter, wild, fierce and uncontrollable. His mouth, dominating me brought me awake, aware of the strangeness of him, his taste, scent, motives, all unknown and foreign to me.

I shoved against him, scraping his mouth with my teeth until I tasted his blood, felt him topple backwards, pressing against his mouth until he couldn't breathe, until he struggled for air, for release.

I rolled off him, gasping in the grass, poked by dead weeds while the lake rustled angrily behind me.

"What was that?" I demanded, glaring at him, daring him to have a reason for kissing me when I'd made it perfectly clear that I didn't want it.

He was still laying where I'd left him, staring at the sky with his eyes wide open, but his pupils, so dilated that I couldn't see any green at all, only black.

"Oliver? Oliver?"

I shoved his shoulder, and his hand caught my wrist as his head turned, his eyes boring into me.

"What are you? What did you do?" His voice was an accusing whisper.

"What did I do? Are you crazy?"

He dropped my wrist and rolled over to his knees, leaning over them like he was going to throw up.

"Basium furoris: the kiss of madness." He laughed—a sound that chilled me with its instability. "Caught with my own snare, how fitting. Sean would approve." He looked at me, his eyes still terrifyingly black.

His eyes. I felt a gnawing in my stomach that had me gasping for breath as need crawled out of the pit of my heart and filled my veins with poison. I closed my eyes as nausea wracked me, not the kind that made you throw up, the kind that made you wish that you could throw up, or die, something to make it stop.

I forced myself to stand, leaning against my bike as I pushed through the weeds. I had to get away from Oliver while I still could. I could feel the sickness grow, changing into a throbbing ache that needed me to turn around, to find the originator of the pain so that it would stop. I moved faster. It took forever until I finally stumbled onto the pavement. I wobbled so badly I thought I would crash, but my instincts kicked in until I was flying over the road, scattering gravel behind me as I flew, as if the monster in the lake were coming after me.

Chapter 19

I slept, tossing and turning, as though I were in a fever, my dad's voice coming and going until I finally woke up, unblinking in the dark.

I looked at the clock, the 4:57 in luminescent green. At first I was mostly numb, but when I rolled over, when I pushed myself up in my bed, it all came back: the wracked agony that made me want to scream into my pillow. I knew that pain. That was the pain of watching Cole smile at someone else, the pain of knowing his eyes were on another, only it wasn't Cole. It was Oliver, as though I was back in 7th grade, twisting apart with no idea what I'd done to make the one person I needed leave me. Had Cole been my friend for a while after the kiss? A week, maybe, before he got weirded out by the staring, the calls, the constant need I had to see, hear, and touch him.

I rubbed my face, trying to shake off the madness. It didn't work, but that was okay, well, it would be okay in four years when I could finally look at another guy. Hopefully I could avoid kissing at that point though. I gritted my teeth and my eyes watered as my heart pounded. I went to the bathroom, leaning over the sink while I washed my face. When I looked up, there was something off, wrong. My pupils weren't as dilated as Oliver's had been, but they were larger than I was used to.

There was no point trying to sleep so I made a playlist. I tried to make a playlist, but no song fit. The hard Euro stuff wasn't weird enough. Maybe if it had been a blend of New Age, water sounding… I worked, trying to blend a couple of things together, which is where my dad found me when he came into my room.

"Yeah?" I asked pulling off my headphones.

"Are you going to school today?"

I stared at him. Wasn't it Sunday? Had I slept almost two days? My stomach twisted. Maybe that was real hunger instead of obsessive I-want-Oliver-right-now hunger. I smiled at him.

"School, yeah, thanks."

I didn't bother looking cute. It was enough to shove my books in my bag knowing that I hadn't done my homework and that I might see Oliver in the halls and have a complete breakdown.

No breakdown. Oliver didn't show that day, but other interesting things happened, like getting sent to detention for fighting. It was kind of funny because I'd been under attack by Sharky for so long and no one ever sent her to detention. Kind of funny because she thought that she could torment me forever without me actually breaking her nose. Well, it wasn't that great a nose.

It was in the cafeteria. Of course it was. All bad things happened there. I'd been on my guard for the last few weeks so no one had been able to really get me, but that day, I was so distracted looking for Oliver that when Sharky tripped me then dumped her coke on my head when I was down, I grabbed her chair and jerked it out so that she hit her chin on the edge of the table. I punched her. Okay, I hit her a few times. She was going to be ugly for a couple of days at least.

I wasn't proud of what I did. At least not entirely but I could have done serious damage to her kidneys, broken a bone, done something that would require life flight, you know, bad stuff. I didn't hurt her that bad, so when everyone freaked out about it, I didn't get it. Junie was there yelling at me, following me to the office after the teacher dragged me off Sharky, Ghandi quotes the whole way. Seriously. They wouldn't let Junie into the office which was a relief. I still had coke dripping down the back of my neck. I needed a shower. Obviously, looking at me, I wasn't the one who started anything, but since I'd done so much damage, whether I started it or not...

Well, I got a chance to have a shower. For the rest of the week I had the chance to hang out at my house taking as many showers as the hot water heater could support, all because of one little nose bleed. And a cracked jaw. Okay, maybe a loose tooth, but nothing serious. I didn't understand why my dad of all people would be so freaked. He had to come home early from work, which his boss would not appreciate, to pick me up at school. He rode his bike, actually my bike, the one Sean had made so nice. It reminded me of Oliver, and for some reason the anger flared up again, throbbing in my veins with the imbecilic need I had to find him, to know where he was, what he was doing and make sure that it was all about me. I wished Sharky was around so that I had an excuse to pound someone but of course she wasn't. She was already at the hospital.

My dad stayed home with me on Tuesday and made me quote the whole peace, duty, respect crap in Japanese over and over and over until I wanted to kill someone. He was worse than Junie. Not what I'd call effective. I wasn't even allowed to work. My manager would have given me a hard time but my dad didn't give him a chance.

While my dad spouted the whole peace, duty, respect crap, people took one look at his steely gaze and backed off. No one messed with him. Sheila would hassle me for making her pull my shift. Off work for a week. No school, no work, no friends, no tv, no internet, no iPod, nothing but me and the shaking.

When I closed my eyes, Oliver's looked back at me. I saw all the different expressions from sweet and funny, to serious, cold and accusing. Who was he? Not that it mattered. There was no chance he'd want to be with me, that he'd be able to focus on one person for any amount of time, no way that being with him was an option, but it felt like the only possibility, the only reality that I could possibly survive. It was like drug withdrawal. The shakes, the outbreaks of irrational anger, the inability to stay still while I grew more and more exhausted. I ate, because my experience with Cole told me that not eating would only make it worse. I did homework badly. I couldn't focus on anything, not when the world was coming to an end at any moment, when it felt like it already had. The only thing that saved me was knowing that it would end. Four years was a long time, but maybe it wouldn't be so long if I could play it smart, avoid starting a stalker cycle, nipping the obsession in the bud before it could really bloom. I certainly couldn't stalk anyone cut off from the rest of the world.

On Thursday I broke my dad's house arrest and rode my bike to the lake. Oliver would be in school. Oliver had to be in school. If Oliver came, who knew what stupidity I might attempt. I might try to kill him, or kiss him instead. My mouth watered at the thought. How pathetic.

I sat on the rock, perfectly aware that I could fall in, but I didn't care. I wanted there to be a monster who might drag me under until I stopped seeing Oliver, stupid Oliver every time I closed my eyes. It made me want to stare unblinking, but my eyes watered and there was Oliver. I wondered what he was doing, then shook my head, staring down at the reflection. I was a blurry blob, not particularly human looking, more like an outcropping on the rock than a person. I felt so tired, so stupid, so crazy and just out of control. I started to cry, you know, graceful quiet crying like all the heroines on movies did. Yeah right. Blubbering, howling, messy, snotty crying that felt really good when I'd worn myself out. I laid there like a soggy dishrag trying to breathe. At least I felt better than I had since the moment when Oliver decided to kiss me. I felt my heart settle a little, not as though the pain were lessening, but as though I had accepted it, and it were somehow less potent after that.

I lay there listening to the wind rustle through the dry grass and reeds, to the lap of water on the shore and another sound, a whistling hiss that must have been the wind. This last sound was so soothing that I fell asleep, drained, numb and weirdly content.

Chapter 20

Monday, I was back in school. Awesome. Everyone stared at me, voices kind of hushed and nervous when I passed, like I was dangerous or something. Dean and a bunch of people from his group nodded at me like we were friends. Junie completely ignored me, and at lunch when I sat down, got up and left. I barely noticed because I was trying hard not to stare at the swimmer's table and see if Oliver was there.

"Hey Gen," Tuba said, smiling at me. "Don't mind Junie. She's having a mild crisis."

Flop shook her head. "So Gen's supposed to be cool with Junie's freak-outs, but where's Junie's support when Gen goes nuts? It's not fair."

I forced myself to focus on the conversation but decided I didn't want to talk about going nuts.

"How is Sharky doing? I didn't seriously hurt her, did I?"

Flop shrugged. "You know people like her. She'd rather have a broken leg than a messed up face. I think she's staying low until the swelling is all gone. I've heard a rumor that she's taken this chance to get a nose job."

"Awesome." I bit my lip then the name came out unbidden. "Have you seen Oliver? I had to tell him something, but I haven't seen him all week. You know, house arrest and all that."

"Sure. He came back to school Thursday, but he was out for a while. With the flu, I think." She turned her head to look at the swimmer's table. The table I hadn't looked at yet. "He's sitting there eating. Maybe he still feels sick. He's not talking to anyone." She turned back to look at me, frowning a little bit. "He's right there. Why didn't you see him?"

The look on my face before I focused on my sandwich must have given me away because she gasped making Tuba ask her if she was choking.

"It's a long story," I said before she got a chance to ask. Of course she'd ask, and I'd tell her, and she'd want to know how good a kisser he was, and I'd have no idea because even though I could still taste him, I had nothing to compare him to besides Cole.

Somehow I made it through lunch without glancing at the swim table. I bolted, ducking out the door. After school I went to Flop's house. I didn't have time to go into details before I had to go to work, but I told her enough that she knew what she'd already guessed: I was obsessed.

"Maybe it would work out with you guys though. You know?" she said.

I tried to keep my heart from hoping. "No. You know what he's like. He has a new girl every day."

"Not since he had the flu. Maybe he's a changed man."

I thought about it for a second then shook my head. "I don't know. Maybe it would be nice to be obsessed with someone who was obsessed with me back, but maybe it would be even worse. Cole did me a favor by leaving me."

"Really? Wow. You sound so mature."

I rolled my eyes and then I had to ride my bike really hard to work where Sheila did give me a hard time.

By Wednesday Junie decided to talk to me. What she said wasn't particularly soothing, but it was probably good for me to hear about the ways in which violence had brought about every evil in the world. No one bothered me. It wasn't quite the relief I'd hoped for. In my choir group, no one wanted to stand by me. In the halls I got tired of glares and stares. I'd figured it would go away, that people would get bored with it and move on, but by Friday I was still big news. I probably would be until Sharky came back to school.

Flop rolled her eyes when she noticed people whispering about me. "Seriously, did they think that anyone could be so nasty and not get it in the end? It's karma."

Tuba nodded and patted my shoulder. Junie started with her new thing that would save me. I needed to take up meditation. She was convinced that chanting to New Age would bring me back to myself, whoever that was. I found fliers and pamphlets in my locker every time I opened it. So, not relaxing.

I took to eating my lunch as fast as possible then ducking outside the school where I'd wander around until it was time to go to class. That day, Friday, Cole came up to me during lunch while I hung out with a brick wall.

"Hey, what's going on?" he asked leaning beside me.

I stared at him with my mouth open before I shook my head and glared at him. "And you care why? How's your girlfriend?"

He shrugged. "She's fine. She's coming back Monday. She's plotting all kinds of revenge so you should probably watch out."

I waited for him to leave after he'd finished with her threats but he didn't move. "Thanks for the warning. I'll have to practice my knife hands."

He smiled, and I almost remembered the kid I used to really like. "You should. Do you want to spar?"

I stared at him while he shifted into a defensive position. He was actually serious. I was weirdly tempted—it would feel good to flatten somebody—but I wasn't going there with Cole. I wasn't going anywhere with him ever again.

"Do you seriously think that's a good idea considering how big a jerk I think you are?"

He smiled and cocked his head. "You quit training. I seriously doubt you can beat me up these days. Check it out." He flexed his muscles. I rolled my eyes and looked away but not quite able to choke back the laugh. It should have been borderline creepy to have Cole messing around with me, but it felt almost normal.

"Yeah. Very, um, nice. So you're trying to beat me up to get back at me for making your girlfriend's face match her soul?"

He gave me a long suffering sigh. "Sharly's fine. You didn't even break her nose. Apparently you're out of shape."

I shook my head and turned to walk into the building. If we kept talking like that, I'd forget that we were enemies.

"Hey," he called after me. I stopped but didn't turn around. "You should watch your step. Sharly's seriously pissed."

I turned and glared at him. "After five years of wishing you'd talk to me, now you won't shut up. Sharky's always hated me. I'll cope."

He chewed on his bottom lip then shrugged. "It's nice that you're back to normal. I'd like for us to be friends again. I asked your dad what I should do when you started acting weird; he told me to give you space, time, that it would pass. He was my sensei, not like I could say no."

I stared at him feeling like my feet were coated in oil and I was sliding somewhere down down down really fast. "My dad?"

He nodded. "He'd noticed some changes in you too."

I turned and kept walking into the building. I concentrated on the feeling of the metal handle in my death grip as I shoved through the glass doors, walking into the hall that smelled like industrial carpet, dried sugar and sweaty teenagers. I wanted to bury my thoughts in that smell, the sound of people talking and laughing like there was something possibly funny in this world. My dad and Cole decided that him treating me like I didn't exist was the best thing for me. I shook my head and was glad no one talked to me, that people stayed away. I didn't feel up to fighting, all I wanted to do was curl up and die.

I stopped abruptly as a chest materialized in front of me. I blinked at it, hoping it would go away, but the muscular arms folded over it and I knew he wasn't going anywhere.

"Sean."

"How are you doing?"

It took a ridiculous amount of effort to raise my eyes to his face, chiseled jaw, ice blue eyes. "Crap, crap, crap. You?"

He frowned at me like he was studying me for signs of weakness and fear. "You stopped swimming with Bernice. You haven't answered her phone calls."

"Oh, right," I muttered and wished someone would kill me. "I slept in on Monday, not really, but you can tell Bernice that, then I've been in detention all last week for almost breaking Sharky's nose. I wasn't allowed to see or talk to anyone. I guess I didn't really think about it this week; with everything being so messed."

"She thinks you're avoiding her. She feels like she deserves it for not being a good friend to you for so long, that she offended you at my party. She cried on me, got my shirt wet."

I rolled my eyes. "Seriously? You have to get over your shirts. They're washable. Getting wet and dirty is what they do, other than cover your body, which half of the female students resent your shirts for anyway. I'm sorry that I hurt Bernice's feelings. Honestly. I wasn't thinking about her at all. I'm just trying to keep breathing. Do you know where she is right now? I can clear all of this up and you won't have to confront me about your shirts ever again."

"She'd be at her locker," he said finally stepping away from me so I could pass. He kept walking with me though, apparently feeling the need to escort me to her so I wouldn't hurt her feelings so she messed up another one of his shirts.

I stopped when I saw her standing close to Oliver, talking to him in a low intense voice while she used her hands to gesture something.

"Bernice," I said, sounding like a robot. "Can we talk for a minute?"

She turned from me, and I saw Oliver grab her hand. My stomach dropped like a rock as I saw that touch, felt like my heart had been ripped out of my chest. I turned and started walking. I had to get away from her, from him, from them.

"Hey, wait up," she said, catching up to me.

I kept walking until I ducked into a girl's bathroom where I ran the water in the sink then splashed my face a few times.

"I'm sorry," I said when I finally had it enough together that I didn't think I would try to strangle her when I faced her. "I haven't been feeling very well. That's not a good excuse. I really appreciated all the time you spent teaching me how to swim, the early mornings, being my friend. I'm sorry that you felt like I didn't care. I do care."

Her eyes were all big and vulnerable. "So, you're not mad about me talking to Ben and ignoring you the whole time at the party? I only realized I did that afterwards. I felt so bad."

I shook my head. "No. He seems really nice, and I thought he liked you, but if you like him so much, why were you holding Oliver's hand?"

She frowned at me, confused for a moment then waved my question away. "I think he was getting my attention, wanted to say something but then Sean and you came. I'm really glad you came."

She hugged me. I stiffened up at first, but then, after a few seconds, I hugged her back, kind of delicately. I wasn't really a hugging person, but maybe I should have been, because after she pulled away I felt a teeny bit better.

"So you haven't been feeling well? You're not the only one," she said, checking her teeth in the mirror. "Sean is incredibly pissy and Oliver..." She shook her head pityingly. "He broods like he's homesick or something."

"Sean?" I sighed as I remembered the bike thing, the him fixing my bike thing and me not even bothering to say thank-you. I had to stop letting everything else disappear because some idiot boy kissed me. I liked hearing that Oliver wasn't still flirting with every girl though. I liked it way more than I should have.

I had to rush to class after that, but after school I hunted Sean down, waiting at the edge of his pack of groupies.

"Gen," he finally said after the crowd had cleared.

"What were you autographing?" I asked, watching the last girl walk away still staring at Sean with a struck look on her face.

"Is that a request? I'll have to decline; I only give autographs to true fans. What do you want?"

I blinked at him then reminded myself that I did want something, and it was to be nice and sound grateful. It would not be easy. "I want to know how much I owe you for working on my bike. I came up with a list, but I'm not sure I can pay it all right away because…"

"Fixing stuff is a hobby of mine," he said turning to his locker as though he were finished with the conversation.

I was trying to sound grateful. "That's a nice hobby, I guess, but doesn't it get expensive? I'd love to pay you, at least for parts."

"I only used stuff lying around. I have no idea what anything costs, but even if I did, there's no way I'm taking money from you."

I stared at him, bewildered when he glared at me, like I'd insulted him. "But I want to. I love my bike. You made her fly, better than new, I can't imagine the time, effort, money, at least I can pay you for one of those."

His eyes got even icier as he said, "You've been to my house and I've been to yours. You can't afford me while to me the expense is nothing. You're insulting me when you assume that my time and energy can be bought."

I threw my hands up in the air. "Fine. I'm sorry I insulted you, thanks for fixing my bike, good-bye."

I stopped when he grabbed my arm. "You're welcome." I was going to jerk my arm away, but he let go before I got the chance. We stared at each other until he cocked his head to the side and looked me up and down. I looked at what he saw, and realized I was wearing the same clothes I'd been wearing all week. Why hadn't I noticed that sooner?

"Nice," I muttered.

"There's something you can do for me," Sean said bringing my attention back to his face. "Something I can't buy. If you'd really like to," his mouth twisted, "Pay me back."

"Um, sure." I did, didn't I? It would be nice to feel good about my music program and my bike. "What can I do?"

I saw myself hand-washing and ironing his shirts for a

week, but surely he could pay for someone to do that.

"I'll pick you up tonight, six-thirty. Do you have work?"

I shook my head. "What exactly are we talking about? I have to know what to wear."

He looked at my clothes again while I sighed. "You can wear whatever you want," he said. I got the idea he wanted to leave but instead he added, "I suppose I should warn you. I want you to be a human shield."

"A human shield. So, armor? At least a bullet proof vest?" My dad actually had one of those in the shed.

He shook his head. "I have to go to dinner with my mother. You know how my personality comes across as slightly cool and reserved?"

I stared at him. "You mean arctic and an arrogant jerk?"

"That," he agreed not even slightly bothered by my description. "My mother makes me look like a wriggling puppy."

I examined him, perfectly still, a statue type person if ever there was one, with the features that always looked disapproving. I smiled as I imagined him bouncing around on his hands and knees with his tongue hanging out of his mouth, drooling on my shoes.

"I may never look at you the same way again."

"I'll survive. Do you agree to come?"

"I already agreed. If you really need someone to take potato shrapnel for you, I'm your man."

He almost smiled. Not that his face changed at all, but I could sense that. Not really, but he should have cracked a smile. Anyone else would have.

"Six-thirty," he said, turning away.

"I need your number."

He raised an eyebrow.

"In case something comes up and I have to cancel, or if I want us to match, or if I have sudden allergies you should know about, you know, things like that."

He still looked skeptical.

"Also so that I can call you and hang up on you at three o'clock in the morning fifteen times."

"In that case," he said, and pulled out my notebook.

His writing was as precise as his swimming technique. I couldn't stand people with perfect handwriting, except when writing notation. Music was something you shouldn't mess around with. He wrote his number on the top of my page above something I'd been working on, a song that had come to me the last time I'd been at the lake, something dissonant and circular. He hummed it, so quietly that I could barely hear him, or maybe it was just in my head. He handed my notebook back then turned on his heel without another word, obviously finished with our business.

Whatever. As I walked away from him I felt a wave of misery that made me stop, blinking back tears. Blink. Oliver. Blink. Oliver. Blink. My dad and Cole planning my ultimate humiliation.

"Flop," I said as soon as I saw her. "Can I stay at your house for the rest of my life?"

She raised her eyebrows and shrugged. "Okay. I was going to do a shirtless hot guy marathon this weekend."

I nodded. "Great. That sounds really fantastic."

"You okay?" she asked as we walked outside towards our bikes. I smoothed my hands over the bars, wishing I could rip the stupid thing apart and burn it in Sean's yard. I patted it, offering an unspoken apology. I would never hurt her. "Turns out my dad told Cole to stop talking to me back in the day."

She stopped walking and her eyes kind got all freaky looking. "Seriously? Wow. You must be seriously... what are you?"

I shrugged. "I don't know. It's like my whole existence doesn't make sense. Oliver—it's like a knife twisting every time I think of him, and Cole wants to be my friend, and Sean asked me on a date with his mother. The only thing that makes sense is Sharky. She wants to kill me."

Flop shrugged. "I guess it's good that some things never change. Wait. What was that part in the middle, about a date with Sean?"

I shrugged uncomfortably. "Dinner tonight at six-thirty

where I'm a human shield between him and his mother. I think he wants me to wear the same clothes I've been wearing all week."

She shook her head. "You have to dress nice or the waiters will treat you like crap. I take it you're going somewhere nice."

I gave her a helpful blank look.

"I can't see what I think of as Sean's mother going somewhere they serve hamburgers."

"He said that she's kind of mean."

"Mean and rich. Why are you doing this? I mean, Sean's hotness will never be debated, but for your very first date ever, you'd think you'd go somewhere fun with someone you kind of liked."

I waved away her concern. "I don't like guys; I am irrationally obsessed with them. While Sean's a jerk, he's honest about it. He's not really that bad, anyway. He did rescue me from the pool."

"And loaned you his shirt," she added.

I rolled my eyes. "Yeah, the guy knows how to sacrifice. And he fixed my bike."

"Sean fixed your bike?" She frowned at it, unable to see the wonder behind the still rusty frame and peeling paint.

"New tires, brakes, fixed the timing on my gear shifters, seriously. The guy knows bikes."

"Why don't I know about this?" She turned her frown on me. "Captain hotness fixed your bike and then asked you on a date? We could have been squealing for days."

I took a deep breath as I saw Oliver in my head, his dark eyes closing while his hair brushed my forehead. "Oliver kissed me and I forgot about my bike."

She blinked at me. "When did he kiss you? You never said anything about a kiss. All you said was that you were obsessed. He kissed you? Where? What was it like?"

I scowled at my bike, kicking rocks. "He smelled weird. He said crap about how we were destined to kiss, and I said, nope, not interested, and then he kissed me anyway, and I did not break his arm, I just stood there and let him kiss me. Then I knocked him over onto the grass."

"Hot," she murmured appreciatively.

"Not hot, itchy because the weeds were all poking my head, and I was mad, mostly at myself because, honestly, what is wrong with me? The last time I kissed a guy, the Cole obsession happened. This time, it's Oliver. I do not need this. I'm so distracted, I forget to change my clothes and didn't notice Sharky until it was too late, and Bernice, completely blew her off. I like Sean." That last bit surprised both of us. "I don't think about Oliver very much around Sean; I'm too busy feeling humiliated and disgustingly idiotic. Believe me, that's better for me. I am so sick of being obsessed." I leaned over my handlebars while my stomach tightened until I was that close to throwing up.

"You know," Flop said thoughtfully, "This might be Sean's first date too. Whatever else happens, you're going to look good."

Looking good would be nice, but no one looked good mid-vomit.

Chapter 21

Sean picked me up at Flop's house. I was waiting on the front porch so her parents wouldn't have to feel like surrogates. I wore Flop's cousin's old dress. Her cousin bought a lot of clothes then passed them on to Flop in spite of Flop being too short and slim to fit into most of it. The dress pinched me a little bit in the waist and I'd had to use a push-up bra to fill out the top, but for someone else's dress, it wasn't too bad. I kind of liked it, silvery blue with a little gathering at the V-neck, as Flop said, sexy but not slutty. She'd said the same thing about the mid-thigh length.

I fiddled with the choker Flop had tied around my neck as I perched on the edge of Sean's white leather seat. Ropes of freshwater pearls twisted around to meet the large glistening shell in the middle. It itched. My hands moved to the comb holding one half of my hair away from my face. Flop had convinced me that messy was a good look for me, so I'd just left it down.

Sean hadn't said anything yet, only grunted when I opened the passenger door and slid in. I should have worn my jacket over the dress, but it really didn't go. He wore a button-down shirt and nice slacks, but he didn't look any better than he usually did.

"You did a good job getting the mud out," I said, mostly for something to say.

"Leather wipes down easily. The mats are hoseable."

Wow. What a fun conversation. "Nice. So, where are we going?"

"Le Pisces."

"The fancy French seafood place on the lake where the cheapest plate's thirty bucks? I might stick with the water."

He glanced at me with his familiar frown. "The water starts at forty bucks a glass. They import vintage bottles. There's nothing like aged water." He actually rolled his eyes. "I'm paying for anything you want to eat. The jobs I get in the summer make actual money. You should try it sometime. What's with the dress?"

"What?" I looked down at myself and noticed that the V-neck was a little deeper than it had been at Flop's house. Hm. I'd have to watch that. "You said to wear what I wanted."

"You wanted to wear that? I don't think Flop's dress fits you very well."

"Well it's too late now, unless you want to trade. Maybe it would look better on you than on me. You do have a freakishly narrow waist."

"There are very few things in this life that I can't improve, but I'm afraid that dress is one of them."

"Shut up. I look good. Flop wouldn't have let me leave if I didn't."

"So Flop's the one I'll have to thank."

I shrugged. "I guess so. Make sure your thanks are your typical lavish ones."

"Like your thank-you? The one where you tried to buy me off?"

"Exactly like that. Offer her money to dress me again. She'd be able to invest in some matching heels. You know what your problem is, Sean?" He face showed no expression. "You have no idea what being imperfect is like."

He smiled at me, only a flash but it was stunning. "I'm afraid you're going to have to work a little harder if you're trying to insult me. That came across as a compliment."

I rolled my eyes and sank against the seat. However hard I tried wouldn't be good enough, therefore, there was no point in being anything other than myself. If I messed up his car, shirt, whatever, so be it. He wouldn't be surprised.

When we walked into the restaurant, the woman I guessed was Sean's mother was already at our table as we approached. She looked nothing like Sean with her dark hair and darker eyes except that she dressed and moved as flawlessly as he did.

"You're late," she murmured without standing. Her tan skin picked up the light from the lake, giving her face a glistening sheen, or maybe that was some age-defying lotion or something.

"This is Gen," Sean said coldly.

"Hi." I waved stupidly while she gave me a cold stare that gave me goosebumps, or maybe that was my lack of jacket. I pulled out my chair and sat down so that I could pick up the menu and hold it up between us. I put it down when I realized that it was all in French. Awesome.

"What's good?" I asked the general air between Sean and his mother. There was a lot of air between them since he'd scooted his chair closer to me. Should I be afraid?

"I already ordered," she said coldly. She said something in French that I didn't catch as she examined me, like I was a bug she was about to dissect.

"That sounds per..."

Sean cut me off. "I hope you got breaded calamari to go with the raw eel."

"Raw eel?" My voice squeaked.

His mother glanced at him, indifferently. "Of course."

She turned to me, and I forced myself to smile brightly, like when facing the librarian with a water damaged library book.

"You're that girl whose mother was brutally murdered before her body was thrown in the lake. It wasn't this lake, was it?"

I stared at her. My voice finally came out, choked sounding. "It was an accident."

"Was it? Really? How do you know? Who told you it was an accident? Your father, I suppose. Tell me then, what did happen?"

I shook my head tightly. "I don't want to talk about my mother."

She raised an eyebrow, the only shift on her emotionless face. "Does it hurt? Thinking that someone you loved so much will never come back to you?"

Yes, it hurt. My heart pounded as I stared at her, her eyes like chips of black ice in her smooth skin. "I suppose I'm lucky that my mother didn't choose to abandon me and only see me once a year."

I stopped breathing for a moment as my words hung above the table, while her eyes narrowed.

"You're right. If I had not left Sean with his father, he wouldn't be the weak creature he is, incapable of going against his father's wishes, destined to remain the ambitionless, worthless flesh you see before you. He could have been so much more," the words were harsh but she said it in the same emotionless monotone. There was something worse about that. She looked away from us, out the window at the lake.

The waiter came, bringing plates she must have ordered, some steaming, some on ice. I was almost tempted to take something black and gooey looking on ice. I'd probably get food poisoning so we would have to go to the hospital instead of staying there with her. It wasn't quite tempting enough. Instead I chewed on a breadstick.

"What do you do?" I forced myself to ask as I stared at something in a red sauce that may or may not have just moved.

"I make certain that business runs smoothly. What do you do?"

I blinked at her. "I…"

I glanced at Sean for help. What did I do other than become obsessive about stuff? If she found Captain Sean less than perfect there was nothing about me and my life that she'd like.

"Um, I ride my bike."

She didn't seem to hear me as her focus shifted to Sean. "You have one last chance to make the right choice. If you come to Florence this summer, I'll train you to become something you can barely imagine. Otherwise, you'll be considered negligible." She wiped her mouth on her napkin and stood. I had a moment of fear as she gazed down at me before she walked to Sean, putting her hands on his shoulders. It wasn't a maternal gesture, no, it made me think how delicate his throat looked and how easily she could crush his windpipe.

"Consider well. Your choices may impact the lives of others." She looked at me with her fathomless black eyes and I shivered but couldn't look away.

She finally left, her movements fluid and precise at the same time, like a dancer. She didn't look back. Once she was out of sight I sank my head on the table, narrowly missing a slimy brown thing.

I stayed like that for a long time.

"Did you fall asleep?" Sean sounded amused.

I raised my head wearily. He was amused. He was actually smiling at me, me who felt like I'd been through a war and back.

"Why me? Junie would have been better."

"Junie would have giggled and flirted with me."

That was true. "So. I'm feeling like you might have taken advantage of my gratitude. I think you owe me food I can actually eat. Raw eel?" I shuddered. "Not that I would have been able to eat anything even if it was one of Rosie's steak and onion blossom specials. Who can eat under pressure?" I examined his plate. "You didn't eat anything either."

He shrugged. "No, I don't eat around my mother. Even if she didn't have them poison the food, which I can't guarantee, being around her gives me too much adrenaline. Fight, flight, not eat."

I stood up, feeling exhausted. The waiter who came to our table didn't glance at me. I'd become invisible at some point. So much for looking nice.

He stood up, dropping bills on the table. "Rosie's steaks and onion blossom sounds good."

I shook my head. "All I need is a drive through. Burgers, fries…"

"Not drive through. Don't you care what's in your body?"

I stared at him, at his chiseled jaw and the mouth that looked little bit pouty, then at the table and the bits and pieces of who knew what, some of which looked like enormous slugs. "Not really. Especially if Junie isn't around to tell me what chemical is in the bite and what the slaughter yard smells like."

"No drive through. There's no way I'm allowing the scent of fast food to permeate my upholstery."

"Ugh. Sean, you are seriously messed up."

"You met my mother."

I looked up at him where we stood right outside the door waiting for the valet to bring his car around. He didn't look vulnerable, but I had met his mother. She'd called him a worthless loser right in front of him. No one living in reality could call Sean anything other than a motivated, disciplined perfectionist in everything he did.

The car pulled up and he went around, ducking in while I stared at perfect Sean in his perfect car. No one had a perfect life, not even him. I didn't feel any better about him not being perfect; I felt sad instead. I climbed in then leaned over and gave him a hug. He stiffened like I'd tazered him.

"What are you doing?"

"It's called a hug. They make people feel better."

"You feel better now?"

"I'm going to sit here until you hug me back. I'm not really a hugger either, but it does make you feel better."

"I could force you off of me."

"But you might mess up your upholstery. It's a hug Sean. Go with it."

He slowly raised his arms on either side of me. They hovered a couple inches away from me. "This is creepy."

"Yeah, that's because you're acting like an idiot. Hah. Captain Hotness doesn't know how to hug." I squeezed him tighter, enjoying the way he stiffened up even more. Apparently I had a teeny sadistic streak.

He exhaled and grabbed me, crushing me against him in a sudden movement that compressed my lungs so that I couldn't breathe. Before I could pass out he let go, pushing me back into my seat. He proceeded to buckle me in, making sure I was firmly in my seat and didn't try any more 'creepy' hugging stuff.

I giggled.

"Don't make that noise."

I giggled again, with the added attractiveness of snorting at the end.

He sighed. "Don't tell me that you've succumbed to my charms."

"Ha. I was picturing you as a wriggling puppy. I'm safely ensconced in an obsession with someone else, so you don't have to worry about me hugging you with ulterior motives."

"You are?" He glanced over at me with a frown. "So that's why you stopped changing your clothes."

"Thanks for noticing."

"What's it like?"

"Hm? Smelly, I guess. Also itchy."

"Being obsessed. What is that like?"

I shrugged and turned on the radio. His sound system was amazing and the tunes playing? I'd never heard them before but it was like a score off an awesome movie, something dark, brooding, but with moments of perfect tone and harmony that made me want to cry. I'd meant to find any stupid love song and say, 'like that,' but instead I listened to the music, sinking back into the leather while the sound crashed around me and he drove through the encroaching shadows, precise driving that matched the music.

He pulled up outside Rosie's Steakhouse with the car idling while he waited for the sound to swell then dissipate into nothing. He shut off the engine and got out, spare movements that never used more energy than necessary. My dad would have liked to train him.

"Do you have a sensei?" I asked when I got out, looking at him over the top of the car.

"Hm?" He frowned at me.

"You move like a... well, an athlete I guess. Never mind."

"You're watching me move? Maybe I am your new obsession."

I rolled my eyes as I went around the car to him, then

happened to glance down and saw how low my dress had plunged while my skirt was way higher than mid-thigh. "Hold on." I yanked on it while he stared at me until everything was back inside my dress. "This dress migrates towards my waist. Like I need extra fabric there. Okay. I'm good."

He was still staring at me.

"What? Did I miss something?" I twisted around to see the back while he made a choking noise that after a moment I realized was laughter. "Sean? Are you okay? I hate to tell you this, but you actually laughed. Out loud. You might need to be committed if this happens again."

"I apologize. It won't happen again. Unless you do that…"

"What?" I frowned up at him. "Seriously, what?"

He shook his head and walked inside. I followed, trying to see my reflection in the window, but I looked fine. Once inside the smell of steak wafting through the air made my mouth water and my eyes droop in expected fulfillment.

It was late for dinner so we didn't have to wait for a table, either that or one look at Sean and the hostess forgot who the reserved table was for. As we walked through the room, I felt the hair on the back of my neck rise. Football players apparently loved steak on a Friday night. I edged closer and closer to Sean the deeper into the throng we went.

Cole was at a table with a bunch of guys since Sharky was still out of commission. Oh how I almost felt guilty about not feeling guilty. The waitress seated us two tables down from them, far enough I didn't have to worry about a coke on my head, not far enough to block out their conversation, if you could call grunting and chanting conversation.

Sean ordered for both of us before the waitress could leave to get our waters. He was a paragon of efficiency.

"Is it one of them?" he asked as he slid into the booth, gesturing behind him at the group.

"One of what?"

"Is your new obsession another football player? Like your last obsession."

I rolled my eyes. "Is my obsession your obsession? What would you call that?" Actually, I hadn't thought much about it, or Oliver during the drive or dinner with his mother. "No. That you don't know is a good sign. Apparently I'm getting better at..."

"Someone at the swim table."

I frowned at him. "Why would you say that?"

"You used to look at us, wave at Bernice, but you don't anymore."

"I don't look at anyone during lunch anymore. I have better things to do."

"Like stare at your lunch. You didn't deny it. It is someone at the swim table, but not me." I rolled my eyes. "Is it Ben? That might be why you've been so distant from Bernice..."

"Oliver. It's Oliver, okay? Why do you keep asking me? It's none of your business. So, I let him kiss me even though I knew it was phenomenally stupid. Thanks for reminding me, by the way. The only good thing about being with you is that I don't think about him."

He tightened his jaw, the muscle twitching as he glared at me. "You let him kiss you. Why am I surprised?"

I blinked at him. I wasn't prepared for the contempt that dripped from his voice. "I don't know. You're always telling me how stupid I am. I'd think that you'd expect it."

Our steaks came and I dug in as eager to end the conversation as I was to eat. I didn't notice him for awhile but eventually realized that he'd stopped eating and was pushing his potatoes around his plate instead.

"Hey, Vee," Cole said leaning over the back of my booth to hover over me. He probably didn't mean to come across as threatening, but he was right above my head. "So, you and Sean on a date. Nice."

I stiffened. "Cole. How's Sharky?"

"Good. She's coming to school on Monday. Don't forget what I told you, and Vee, if you want to come over tomorrow morning to spar, you know you could use the practice." I twisted my head up and to the side so I could get a good look at him. He smiled, a nice smile that I didn't expect. "And," he added, dropping his gaze, "If you wear that dress, I'll let you beat me."

The dress. I didn't do anything while he strolled away from me, laughing at his friends loudly so that everyone in the restaurant looked up at him. Once he was out of sight I pulled up the dangerously low front while I tugged down the skirt.

Sean spoke quietly. "Cole seemed friendly. Maybe he misses having a pathetic girl trailing him around."

I glared at him. "Maybe. Or maybe he wants to pick up where we left off."

He leaned forward, narrowing his eyes at me. "Did you let him kiss you? You did, didn't you? So, how long were you obsessed?"

"None of your business."

"You were friends though, maybe you liked him, maybe you thought you loved him before you kissed. That's an emotional bond. With Oliver, what did you have? You were interested, but not emotionally involved. Otherwise you would have been jealous instead of disinterested the more girls he collected."

"Great. I really love talking about my obsessions. It's so helpful when I'm trying to forget about them. Well, you know what? It's your turn. Why don't you have a girl-friend, Sean? Think how convenient it would be to have only one girl instead of a whole crowd. You would waste so much less time trying to deal with infatuated people. Think of the shirts that got wrinkled as girls pressed against you. One girl, that's all you'd need, but no. Is it really because you can't deal with a distraction? You seem pretty capable of balancing plenty of things at once. Why not? Oh, maybe she'd get close to you, hug you. Maybe she'd hurt you, break your heart, but no, that's not the is-sue, because you don't have a heart."

He raised an eyebrow and I noticed his scowl had faded slightly. "You think that having someone else at-tached to me would solve anything? It would only be one more person who wants something from me, who felt that I owed them. You wouldn't know what that was like. No one expects anything of you. You're so passive, you don't choose anything; everything in your life is circumstantial. The only thing I've ever seen you choose against someone else's will was when you disobeyed your father and learned how to swim. You probably didn't tell him though. You wouldn't like the conflict. The only reason you go to the lake when everyone wants you to stay away isn't because you choose it, but because it draws you there, compels you. Your will is weaker than a body of water. I don't understand how you can be so passive about your own life. It's the only one you have."

"Maybe I am passive, but you're such a perfectionist that you won't let anyone close enough to you that would compromise your vision of the perfect little world. You're never going to be happy until you…"

"I don't want to be happy. I want to be free. I will live my own life, whatever my mother, father, Oliver, or teachers, think. My life. My choice." His voice was as icy as his eyes, brilliantly gazing into, through me. His jaw was tight, his mouth a thin line as he glared. He looked ridiculously perfect.

"What does Oliver want from you?"

He blinked and looked disoriented for a second before he looked at me with a stubborn set to his mouth. "Oliver wants my loyalty and obedience, but I'm sure he has other things in mind for me. His scope has never been small. Oliver has reasons for everything he does. Everything."

"So why did he kiss me?"

His jaw tightened again. I shouldn't have brought that back up. "I wasn't there. I don't know the circumstances around the magical moment."

"So you're concerned that my obsessions might have an impact on your personal space?"

"I hardly see you becoming obsessed with me any time soon."

"I mean, why else are you being such a jerk about the kiss? Maybe you're right about me; I'm perfectly aware that it was incredibly stupid to let him kiss me, but it's not nice to talk to me like that. Why would you even bother? You've accepted that I'm whatever, so why would you act like it's a problem for you?"

"I like to fix things. Maybe you're the most broken person at school and I think…"

"What did you say?" I stood up, having lost my appetite a while before.

"Maybe I think…"

"You said I'm broken. I'm broken and you can fix me by telling me what an idiot I am? Unbelievable." I walked away from the table, almost surprised when he came with me.

"Maybe drive-through would have been better," he mumbled.

"I'm not talking to you," I said, talking to him which kind of defeated it, but I wanted to be clear.

"Fine with me."

I rolled my eyes, biting back my own, 'fine with me,' because that would be childish and talking to him.

I didn't start for the parking lot. I wasn't going to spend any more time with him than necessary.

"Where are we going?" he asked, an enormous presence as he walked a little bit behind me on the side of the road.

I clenched my jaws to keep from saying anything. I was going home; he'd figure that out when we got there. I wrapped my arms around myself as the chilly autumn wind blew through my stupid dress. It was dark, dark enough that I felt nervous on the edge of the road as cars and trucks whizzed past. Maybe someone I knew would stop and offer a ride. Sean would eventually give up and leave. A hundred steps later he still walked behind me, humming under his breath in the most annoying way possible: not loud enough to hear, not quiet enough to ignore.

"I didn't expect you to look so nice."

I stopped walking, startled. I actually turned around to see if he was mocking me. His face was shadowy, but he seemed serious. "You think I look nice?"

He frowned. "I wanted to bring someone my mother wouldn't notice, someone she could immediately dismiss that would keep her conversation less... Anyway. I didn't think you'd show up looking like an actual date."

"Flop said the waiters would treat me like crap unless I dressed up."

"So you dressed for the waiters."

I nodded then realized that I'd forgotten that we weren't talking. I tripped, yelping as my ankle twisted in the heels I wasn't really used to running around in—in the dark. I sat on the side of the road staring at nothing while he crouched beside me. I fought back stupid tears although everything seemed mildly hilarious at the same time.

"How bad is it?" he asked. When I didn't answer he pulled off my heel and ran his hands over my foot. I jerked away but that only hurt it more.

"Don't touch me."

"You've left me no choice. You won't make it home before morning crawling, and you're not walking on that foot tonight. Now, I have to carry you." He didn't sound happy about it, which was probably why I let him lift me off the ground without a struggle. He began carrying me back to the distant lights of Rosie's Grill holding me away from his body.

"You're not going to fight me," he said in an already strained voice, "You're too passive for that, besides which, if I dropped you, it would hurt."

He was right. I wouldn't fight him. Was I really that passive, letting him carry me when he wanted to? Not that he really wanted to. No. I didn't have to fight to make a choice. I could choose something else, something he'd really hate.

I leaned against him, wrapping my arms around his neck while I nestled my cheek against his throat. I could feel him swallow down his discomfort or nausea at having me so close. I smiled.

"Oh, Sean, you're so big and strong to carry me all the way back to your car. I don't know how I'd survive with a less hot date. I can't live without you. Every moment away from your manly chest makes me burn."

"I think you're supposed to burn when you're touching my manly chest," he said dryly.

"I burn all the time, with you, without you, the burning won't stop."

"How uncomfortable. Have you thought of going to a doctor?"

I choked back a laugh. No. This was serious. "I don't need a doctor. I need a mechanic, someone who knows how to fix things, someone who can put me back together."

"You're not broken. I didn't mean it that way. I was just being a jerk. I'm sorry I made your thing with Oliver worse for you. You don't need that." His apology was mumbled under his breath, but he did say it out loud.

I didn't know what to say. An apology? Maybe I shouldn't torture him. I eased away from him, but he seemed to have most of my weight against his chest. It was probably easier for him to carry me while I hung onto him.

The lights of the grill didn't seem to get any closer and I felt weird as every footstep traveled through my body, as the memory of Oliver, of the kiss fought with the reality of Sean's arms around me, the feel of his muscular chest against my body. I didn't burn exactly, but it was weird. I was very aware of him, of every movement and the tension in his arms. I could feel the tightness in his arms, shoulders, chest grow the longer he carried me.

Finally, we were at his car, in the dark, and he lowered me onto the hood while he stretched out, filling the whole world with the breadth of his arms.

"Sean?" My voice came out small. He grunted. "It was stupid of me to walk off in the dark."

"You would have made it home, no problem if you hadn't twisted your ankle."

I smiled a little bit as he opened the door then picked me up again before he lowered me into the car. After I was in, it took him a second with his face inches from mine while he got his arms out from under me.

"Sean, your hands are shaking."

"You're heavy," he said with a slight twist of his lips

that left me unsure if he were mocking me or himself.

Chapter 22

After icing my ankle all weekend, on Monday at school, I barely limped when Dean and his friends nodded at me as I walked into the building. I nodded back at them instead of glaring, you know, kind of like I'd given up caring about who I liked or didn't like, it was too much to keep straight. I was busy focusing on wearing clean clothes. Go me.

Oliver walked by as I stood at my locker. I made a point to say hi to him and not notice when he looked through me like he couldn't see me. I saw Sharky with a group of her friends as I walked to class with Flop. I smiled at her and said "hi". Okay, it wasn't hard to smile, not when I could tell she still had a little bruising around her jaw that she tried to cover with makeup.

She looked at me. I felt sick when she looked away scared. I wasn't scary; I wasn't the evil person who made people suffer. Except to her, I was. Huh. Anyway, I felt slimy and sorry. I opened my mouth to say so, but we were past her, and there was Cole. He said hi to me first, so I said hi back. He was still the jerk who watched me get a face full of beer, but he wasn't really evil. Probably.

At lunch I had no appetite, not when my subconscious kept bringing up Sharky's fear and Oliver's kiss. Worse were the rumors that Flop told me all about, rumors that I was dating Sean. No one believed it, of course, but a rumor like that made people stare at me, dissecting everything I did, every bite I took, every single glance I gave to the swim table. I avoided the cafeteria completely. Instead, I stood outside watching crunchy leaves swirl around in the cold wind, glad that it was warm against the bricks where

I leaned.

I felt a light touch on my shoulder, sliding my hair back. I couldn't move, breathe, or think. My heart pounded when I felt his breath on the skin of my neck the moment before the pressure of his mouth. I gasped as his teeth gripped my skin, sliding down to my shoulder while he tasted me with his tongue. It hurt as the bite deepened, and I knew it would leave a mark.

Oliver was there, finally. I turned, wrapping my arms around him, pressing my body against his, feeling the pounding in my chest, the ache that finally disappeared, the agony of unfulfilled obsession gone as I leaned against him, slid my hand up his neck and into his hair, digging my fingers into his scalp.

He stiffened, freezing as I curled around him. He had to want me. He hadn't started kissing my neck for no reason. Sean said that Oliver always had a reason, so why had he kissed me, made me crazy if he didn't want me to touch him, didn't actually want me?

He pulled away, and I stared at him, the dark eyes with only a ring of emerald, the way his lips trembled, and he held his hands in fists.

I'd embraced him, not because I wanted him but because my obsession demanded it. He didn't want me to affect him, no, he only wanted me to want him. At least that was the only thing that made any sense.

"Why did you kiss me at the lake?"

He blinked and then his smile was there, the easy flirty smile that was so easy to swallow. "It seemed like the thing to do."

"Why? We were talking about…" I'd told him about Sean fixing my bike. Sean said that Oliver wanted him, had plans for him. I shook my head because it made no sense, but at the same time, why was Oliver there, sucking on my neck when he'd made a point to avoid me for the past two weeks? Was it Sean? Was it the fact that I'd been seen on a date with Sean and now everyone was gossiping about us being together?

"Don't do that again," I said in a shaky voice.

"Do what?" he asked with a charming smile as he leaned forward, too close.

I stepped away, needing to run away or throw myself at him. It was incredibly hard to stand there, to look at Oliver and study his reaction. "You're really nice, but you should know that I'm seeing someone else. I can't go around behind his back; it wouldn't be right."

His mouth tightened just a little bit. "So, you're really dating Sean?"

I shrugged and let myself blush. "It's kind of crazy, but something about him is exactly what I want. The other night after I twisted my ankle and he had to carry me home, well, later we... you don't want to hear details, but after that, I couldn't possibly mess around with you, however cute your accent is."

I stood there staring at him with that almost-lie between us. He studied me as carefully as I studied him. I didn't expect it when he took two steps, pinning me against the wall, pressing against me the way I'd wanted him to do a few minutes earlier.

It was so obvious, so blatantly his reaction to me being with Sean that made him want me to want him. It pissed me off.

"Get away from me." My voice came out quiet, but dark, rich, the way my voice came when I sang to the lake. He blinked but didn't move. "Get away from me!" This time my voice was a roar that came from the pit in my stomach where all my obsession had coalesced into fury.

He took three stumbling steps backwards while he stared at me then turned and disappeared.

I slid down the wall while black spots flecked my vision. I put my head between my knees because maybe that would keep me conscious, but then there were voices I heard in and out, but nothing to see, and then Sean's voice, saying things I couldn't make out, and then his hands were on me, putting my body on the ground like a corpse before I felt his breath, his mouth over mine.

His breath filled my lungs, his hands on my chest in a precise rhythm, his mouth cool against mine and tasting of oatmeal cookies. Cookies one of his groupies probably baked for him. It would have worked for me. Someone should seduce me with cookies. Not Oliver. Not Oliver who hated me with Sean but didn't want me. Sean who was completely right about me being a passive idiot about my own life. Sean who had his mouth on mine and therefore was a likely candidate for my next obsession.

I shoved him away from me, relieved when he sat back on his heels. A large crowd had gathered around us. "Get away from me. How could you..."

I sputtered and heard the mutters around me, the disgusted looks of people who saw me get CPR from Sean and then treat him like a jerk. It didn't matter though, not if I was about to feel the madness, the obsession, but I didn't. He stood, looking down at me, amused while I breathed on my own, still panting but sure that I wouldn't pass out again. After a few seconds I knew that it wasn't going to happen. Maybe I could only be obsessed with one person at a time.

I reached up for his hands, pulling myself up then kept rising on my tiptoes towards him. He raised an eyebrow but didn't leap away from me even as he watched me coming. I brushed his cheek with my lips before I stood straight, still holding onto his hands, very aware of the crowd around us.

"I'm sorry I freaked out, Sean. Thanks for saving me." I sounded remarkably close to how Sharky sounded when she talked to Cole. Gag.

He slid an arm around my waist when I stumbled as we walked into the building.

"So... why did you give me CPR and how did you know I needed it? Not that I actually needed it. I would have been fine eventually." He still had his arm around me, his big hand secure and strong on my ribs.

"People have a crazy idea that we're dating," he said with a shrug. "I blame the dress."

I stared up at him, at the angle where I got a clear shot of his nostrils. So, who else in the world had perfect nostrils?

"Oliver doesn't seem too thrilled with that," he said sounding thoughtful.

"No, he isn't," I agreed then shook my head and tried to pull away. He didn't seem to notice and without biting him or stomping on his foot, I was sort of stuck close to him. "I actually told him that it was true."

"Technically, we did date."

"Sean, your mother was there. I don't think it counts as a date if you bring parents."

"The dress counteracted the parent," he argued, nodding as he passed a girl who greeted him with a shriek of excitement before she turned a look of loathing on me. "So, you told Oliver that we're dating, and most of the school has heard rumors that we're together. One of my team came to get me when you passed out. What do you want to do about it?"

I stared straight in front of me feeling nauseous while I tried to block out the stares and whispers.

"Um, I think it's time for us to see other people. What does Oliver want with you? Are you guys secretly gay?"

His smile mocked me. "If I were secretly gay, would I tell my girlfriend that?"

"Girlfriend?" I stopped walking, staring at him while I felt my toes go numb. "No one said anything about being your girlfriend."

"You did. Last night. It made sense, sort of. At any rate, I'm curious what would happen if people thought that I was involved with someone. It might cut down on some annoying issues."

"You didn't tell me what Oliver wanted from you."

"I thought we agreed that we were both secretly gay."

"I'm not gay, oh, you and Oliver. Well, as far as I can tell, gay guys don't usually bite other girl's necks, however much they want her boyfriend." I winced as the word came out of my mouth. Sean was not my boyfriend. The idea was too ridiculous to comprehend. It was so laughable, why weren't more people laughing? "Not that you're my boyfriend, anyway, you'd better drop me off at my locker, you know, and remove your arm from my person before you go on your oatmeal cookie eating way."

"You're tasting me? Would you prefer raw eel?"

"Ooh, how did you guess?"

Why did I feel like blushing? He was the one who put his mouth on top of mine. I was just lucky I hadn't become obsessed with him. I wasn't, was I? No, I didn't think so.

"Sean, seriously, the next time you see me passed out, please just leave me alone. I'll recover eventually and thinking that I was going to be obsessed with you was not fun. Obsession sucks."

He smiled, showing a gleam of white teeth that made him even less accessible than his usual ice cold gaze. "I'm immune to obsessive love. It's the only pleasant trait I inherited from my mother."

I frowned at him. "You're immune? Are you joking? No, I don't think you are. So, you think that if I kissed someone else I'd be obsessed?"

He shrugged and pulled a cookie out of his backpack. He offered it to me, and I took it, incapable of saying no when I'd skipped lunch.

"You could try it and find out, but as your boyfriend, I don't recommend it."

I rolled my eyes. Like I'd ever be Captain Perfection's girlfriend, like anyone would ever be good enough for him.

"You're not… it's just what I told Oliver."

"Either way, I'm grateful that you started our relationship in clean clothes."

"Yeah, well, that's how deeply I feel for you. You're seriously going to let people think that you're dating me? If you are actually going to get a girlfriend then you should get one that's in the same sphere as you."

"I did date you. It's part of public record at this point. What sphere is mine?"

"You're one of the smart people and the swim captain, so a brainy class president type or an athletic type would make sense for you."

"But she'd have to be someone who didn't giggle, or want to sink her hooks into my non-beating heart and turn me into her drone. What about you? Am I too much of a

frigid jerk for you? Are you worried I'll ruin your reputation as obsessed girl who only likes boys who don't like
her?"

I did mind, but when he put it like that, wasn't it a
good thing that people saw me dating Sean? It definitely
dragged me out of my obsessive mode. Every time I talked,
well, argued with him, I forgot about Oliver.

"You're so hot, how could I possibly say no? Oh Sean, I
feel a giggle coming on. You'd better go before it comes out
or I do some creepy hugging."

He finally let me go as he stepped back, shaking his
head as he looked down at my shoulder.

"He ripped your shirt. Does he respect nothing?"

I pulled the shoulder up, shrugging as I started for
class. "He's a foreigner, what do you expect? Probably runs
around in a loincloth or something, doesn't understand the
sanctity of shirtness."

"So few people do."

I nodded sadly. "It's like people think they're just
things, to wear and throw away."

I saw a flash of grin before he turned, moving into the
crowd. He still stood out, taller, bigger than everyone else,
and fifty times hotter. Yeah, I watched him walk away. As
his official but not actual girlfriend, I was supposed to do
that. Yeah.

That was the last I saw of him that day. My shoulder
throbbed as I sat in my science class, trying to focus on the
teacher, but seriously, nothing like molecular biology to
bring a girl's head out of the clouds. Not.

After school Bernice stood next to Tuba by my locker,
talking about music. Tuba looked glad to see me because
he didn't know why Bernice was talking to him. She
smiled when she saw me because it was really unlikely
that she wanted to talk about music, particularly marching
bands. It wasn't even Tuba's thing and he was in one.

"So, I wondered if you could give me a ride. I noticed
that you drove today."

I nodded, sure, but I was totally prepared when she
brought up Oliver and Sean as soon as we were buckled.

"This is so weird," she started off. "I heard that you were dating Sean and that Oliver attacked you during lunch."

"Crazy."

"I mean, not that Sean wouldn't date you because you're nice and cute, but he doesn't date anybody. And Oliver attacking you? He's like a sweet little boy, you know? You can't take his flirting seriously, but he'd never hurt anyone."

I sighed. "It's hard to explain with me and Sean. He took me to dinner on Friday, but there hasn't been any kind of commitment, you know? As for Oliver..." No way I was going to talk about the kiss of madness. "He kind of ran into me during lunch. That's it."

She gasped. "Sean really asked you out? I kind of thought that they were gay."

"It crossed my mind. Maybe they are. Maybe Sean just took me out so that no one would know."

"Right." She frowned. "So, he didn't kiss you or anything?"

"Who, Sean?" That was a little bit personal. Not like curiosity about kissing Sean wasn't perfectly healthy, but it seemed weird for her to ask like that. "Not really." I bit my lip as I remembered her talking to Oliver, the way that they'd leaned in close and looked like best friends. She would probably tell Oliver whatever I told her. For the sake of keeping him thinking that I was with Sean, I said, "I think everything's going to go really slow. We don't want to rush a good thing, you know?" That was a line from a song, the last song which had played on the radio. Hopefully she didn't pick up on things like that.

I leaned forward to change the station and my shirt flopped open where Oliver had ripped it. Bernice gasped and grabbed my shoulder, staring at the mark I could still feel.

"That doesn't look very slow to me. Wow." She stared at it for a long time before she looked up at me with something like envy in her eyes. "Sean is the best. You are so lucky."

"Yeah. He's awesome." If you wanted to be with someone who made you feel like an imbecile every five seconds.

"I thought you liked Oliver, but hey, if you can get Sean…" she shrugged like the rest was obvious.

"So what about you and Ben?" Wow, letting Sean take credit for the bite was really weird. I should have asked his permission, but it wasn't like I'd told Bernice that he was the one who bit me.

She stared at the window while she answered. "He hasn't asked me out."

"Well, maybe you could ask him to a movie or something."

She turned to look at me and a slight smile crossed her face. "Maybe now that Sean's dating you, Ben won't feel like he's betraying the swim team if he dates me. Maybe I could ask him, although," she added with a frown, "I should at least get him to think that he's asking me."

"Sure," I said but felt out of my depth. Flop would know what she was talking about. "I think he really likes you."

"You do?" Her eyes lit up. I got to spend the rest of the drive listening to how amazing Ben was. I dropped her off and then headed home, because that's where I went for spaghetti on a Monday night.

School was okay. I went back to swimming with Bernice in the morning before swim team and felt more and more comfortable in the water. Actually, when I was swimming under the surface with nothing but bubbles for company was the only time I didn't feel alone. It was almost as good as going to the lake.

I liked having Bernice back even if Junie wasn't quite sure about her. Bernice sat at our table a few times a week. Flop and Bernice talked about Ben because Flop always knew what to say about guys. She could handle the obsessive guy talk for hours. After all, my personal Cole obsession hadn't bothered Flop for years.

"So," Flop began one lunchtime as we sat around the table. "Who would you be most likely to make out with alive, dead, whatever."

"Dead? Gross!" Tuba said wrinkling his nose. He was usually pretty good with the girly stuff, but apparently this was too much, because he threw his fries down and left, when he never went without finishing his fries.

"I don't mean dead..." Flop began, but Bernice interrupted her with a totally gooey, star struck look.

"Ben. If Sean ever lets him date."

"Gandhi," Junie said, making Flop pout.

"Gandhi? Seriously? Gandhi makes you want to get naked?"

"You didn't say naked, you said make out. I don't think physical relationships should be about superficial things like appearance and age, it should be about souls uniting who truly are in sync with each other and the universe."

Flop rolled her eyes. "Prince, before he got saved. I mean, those boots of his are so sensual."

"Boots?" we all asked in a chorus then broke out laughing because Flop was definitely changing if she found boots attractive.

"What about you, Gen?" Bernice asked, and I could tell by the look in her eye that she was remembering my shoulder and thinking about Sean. The truth was, I hadn't really seen Sean for a week. Being his pseudo girlfriend was a lot like being nothing at all. Not that I minded, but awareness of Oliver kept creeping up on me, insidious tentacles that crawled through my brain. Having conversations with Sean that didn't mean anything kept Oliver out. I looked up and met Oliver's eyes across the room. I couldn't think of anything else.

"Oliver." I said in an unfortunate lull after the laughter died. His name was too loud on my lips, too sure for someone who was supposed to be dating someone else.

"He's hot," Flop said easily, but Bernice made a choking sound. Before I could get a look at her face, she'd left the table, not looking back.

"Well, so much for that," Junie said, watching Bernice leave. "She's here physically but her soul belongs to the team, and The Captain. For someone who's supposed to

be your boyfriend, he's not really around you very often."
I shrugged but Junie wasn't done. "I can't believe I used
to think that being his girlfriend would work. He really
doesn't care about people very much. You care too much,
especially about Oliver who I can tell is your obsession,
even if you've managed to keep pretty cool about it."

"I didn't really mean..."

Flop rolled her eyes. "So what if she's obsessed with
someone besides Sean. It's probably part of their dynamic."

"Yeah. Sean's the only guy in school that prefers a
girlfriend who likes someone else better." Junie shrugged.
"He doesn't act very into Gen, but what do I know? He's
still as cold-blooded as ever. He'll never be real boyfriend
material."

It was true—which was why he was so perfect for me
as my not real boyfriend. It was confusing though. For me
and the rest of the student body.

Everything was fine; work was good with no one annoying coming in, a slow night really, and then I went
home, riding on my bike with the perfect gear shifters and
peeling teal paint. It was better like that, more me. Who
wanted perfection when they could have character? Right.

Next day, swimming with Bernice was fine, except that
she seemed more tense than usual and suggested we wrap
up early.

"Is something wrong?" I asked, treading water.

She glanced at me and then away. "I've been hearing a
lot of weird rumors. You said that you were dating Sean,
but someone said they saw you hooking up with Oliver
during lunch, one of those losers and who believes them,
but anyway, it's weird because Sean's the captain, you
know? Oliver's my friend and we're pretty close, but I don't
want to see Sean get hurt."

"I guess that makes sense. Actually, Sean hasn't talked
to me for a few days, so maybe it wasn't really a thing after
all. I don't know about Oliver; I never know about Oliver. I
don't want to hurt Sean either. Really, I don't think I could.
He's got crazy strong walls that keep everyone out, you
know?"

She nodded but still looked worried. I rolled my eyes as I pulled myself out of the pool. "I'll talk to Sean after school."

She gave me a weak smile, but somehow it didn't make me feel better. My shoulder still ached. Lunch was weird because half of the student body wasn't there.

"Field trip?" I asked Flop when she finally sat down beside me.

She shrugged then went into the importance of pedicures.

Junie and Tuba showed up at the same time before Bernice came over, kind of nervous looking.

"Hey, Gen?" she said, quiet.

"Bernice always has a good pedicure, which is so great because being on the swim team, people are always staring at your feet," Flop said.

"Hey, ladies," Dean said from behind her, looking eagerly at me, like I was about to hand him a big bundle of something illegal. We all stared at him as he slid into the empty seat beside me and tapped the table with his fingertips. "So, you got with the foreigner? If you're into different guys, I could hook you up with some fine..." Junie backfisted him before I had the chance to do anything other than stare.

He got up, sputtering mad, and then quieted down when he saw Junie in her goddessy fury.

"What do you think you're doing, Dean?" She glared down at him and he shrank beneath her gaze.

"If she didn't sleep with him, then it's too bad that Sean's going to rip him apart," he muttered, stumbling away from the table.

"Who? What..." I sputtered, staring after him when Bernice put a hand on my arm.

"Sean's fighting Oliver in the back parking lot. Apparently Dean heard the same rumors I did."

I sat there for a second, confused, shaking my head. "Sean wouldn't fight Oliver for me. It makes no sense."

She frowned at me, like I should have been doing something instead of sitting there. I got up and ran with my friends beside me, through the halls to the parking lot behind the shop building. Bernice and Dean were right. A huge crowd jeered and fist pumped like the idiots they were. I shoved through the crowd until I was held back by the ring of guys who kept the circle with their outstretched arms. The guys were mostly swimmers, but a few other guys I didn't really know were there too.

I watched while Sean and Oliver circled each other, both of them without shirts. Of course Sean wouldn't want to get it wrinkled or bloody. Oliver wasn't as tall as Sean, but he looked no less capable as he took his time before moving with lighting speed to place two punches on Sean's body before moving out of range.

Sean was not nearly as graceful out of water and slower than Oliver, but when Sean finally landed a blow to his face, it knocked Oliver back, snapping his head back. I was used to sparring, to watching feats of violence, but this wasn't the same. These weren't fighting for an award on clean technique, they wanted to hurt each other. For me? It made no sense because Sean had made it clear that was the last thing on his mind, and Oliver had avoided me since the wall incident.

"So, now what?" Junie asked beside me.

"Can we just watch? They're both really hot," Flop said from my other side.

"I feel something really stupid coming on," I muttered before I ducked under the outstretched arms and moved into the ring.

I had to dodge to avoid Oliver's backswing before I stepped in front of him and right into a direct punch from Sean.

Ow. I opened my eyes and saw the sky with two dark shadows bending over me. I made a gurgling sound as I tried to breathe around the spreading awareness I felt in my ribs. At least he hadn't hit my face. I probably wouldn't have a face.

Someone yelled something, and the crowd chanted, 'teachers, teachers.' Cole pulled me up by the armpits and started dragging me towards the building.

"Hey, Vee," he whispered in my ear. "Nice move."

I gasped. "Thanks. Years of training kicking in."

He snorted. The walk was a blur until he left me on a wooden bench in a locker room. I leaned over my knees, working on the breathing, aware that my ribs might never be the same again. I took a deep breath and was about to check the damage when I heard Oliver's voice and froze. Oh, it would be so easy to forget that I'd ever wanted anything other than to lean against him when he sat beside me.

"Are you okay?" he asked.

I managed to glare at him. "I'm great. Thanks for asking. Now go away."

He smiled like I'd said something funny, his green eyes shining brilliantly as he settled a first aid kit on his knees. "I'm good at helping with injuries," he said pulling out a tube of something. "Let me check it out."

"Um, no. I've done my stupid thing for the day, now I'm just going to go home. I'm not letting you touch me. You certainly won't let me touch you."

He shrugged then handed me the tube. "Well, you stopped the fight, even if you had to pay for it. What if I wanted you to touch me?"

I shook my head. "Why? Why would you ever let me make you vulnerable?" I took the tube and realized it was an analgesic. I could use some numbing. I rubbed some of the goop on my ribs.

When I handed it back, I made the mistake of looking straight at him. He sat closer than he had a moment before. He took the tube while I froze, feeling my heart race and my stomach clench. "My vulnerability for yours. It's a fair trade. And," he said, handing me an ice pack, "I can't stop thinking about you, remembering the feel of you, your taste. I'm already too vulnerable, what's the harm in tasting a little satisfaction?"

I reached up and grabbed his shirt in my fist. He didn't move, but I saw him swallow. He blinked when I ripped it, the shirt, showing his shoulder. "I'm going to bite you." He still never moved while his eyes grew darker by the second. On his neck I could see the pulse beating beneath the skin. So close, so incredibly close, and he hadn't moved away from me, if anything he leaned closer.

I lost track of reality. It started with my mouth on his shoulder in a nice bite, the kind he'd left me, but then his hands were in my hair, and he was murmuring my name in my ear, and things got hazy. The relief was so incredible, touching him the kind of high they warn you against with drugs. There was a lot of mouth to mouth resuscitation, only less breathing, more tongue, and then I jerked away from him when I realized his hands were sliding beneath the waistband of my pants.

"What are you doing?" I asked then realized how tangled up we were, that his shirt was half off of him.

He stared at my mouth then forced his eyes to meet mine. "I'm sorry, was I not allowed to kiss you back? I'm afraid I got distracted." He gave me his crooked smile. I wanted to kiss it off his face but instead I got to my feet, wincing when I tried to straighten my ribs. I'd completely forgotten about Sean's punch.

"That's what we call groping, not kissing. You didn't say anything about that," I muttered as I smoothed down my shirt and shoved my hair away from my face. I'd meant to get revenge, not make out with him in the locker room—the boy's locker room. Gross.

I winced my way across the floor, just glad that no one had walked in on us. Who knew? Maybe someone had come in. I wouldn't have noticed a tsunami. It was lucky that I noticed groping.

I walked out the doors and into a way too familiar chest. At least it wasn't his fist. Again.

"Sean." I was as tired as I sounded, and leaving Oliver, moving away from him had me fighting the nausea and the bits of my brain that were screaming at me to stop being a lunatic and go back in the locker room and grope him back.

"Funny, I don't remember punching you in the face."

"Huh?" I looked up at him, and saw his icy eyes staring down at me, cutting through me.

"Your mouth is swollen."

I put a hand to my lips and remembered the pressure of Oliver. Oh, I really was going to throw up. I grabbed onto Sean, trying to stay upright and not vomit on his shoes, or worse, shirt. After a moment it passed and I leaned against the wall instead of him.

"Yeah, it all started with revenge, but I think it's a slippery slope. It's best to forgive and move on. Otherwise..." I shook my head. "Ripping his shirt wasn't nearly as satisfying as I'd thought it would be. So, what are you doing here?"

He gave me a flat look. "I'm debating whether to apologize for punching you, or inform you that it's not very bright to step into the middle of a fight."

"You could do both. Or better yet, neither. You're right, it was stupid, but I couldn't let you guys hurt each other over me."

"Over you? Seriously?" The look he gave me was so humiliating.

I blushed as I edged away from him. "My mistake. Sorry. Bernice and Dean said... But I should have known because you told me you wouldn't fight anyone for me. So, why were you fighting?"

He shrugged. "It was a bet. He bet me that for all my size and strength, he could still beat me up. If we hadn't wanted an interruption then we shouldn't have fought at school."

"That's it? You wanted to prove that you were tougher than him? You both looked so bloodthirsty."

"You met my mother."

"So, she makes bets with people that she can beat them up?"

"No, she kills them."

I stared at him while he stared back, and I felt something weird happen inside my head.

"So she's in the mafia or something?"

"Something."

"She wants you to go to Florence so she can teach you to kill people?"

"Yes."

I closed my eyes and started giggling. It hurt to laugh with my ribs, but that didn't stop me from wheezing for way too long. I clutched my ribs while Sean frowned at me. I couldn't help it.

"Sean, can you give me a hug? I know I'm an idiot but..." I was going to tell him I was about to hyperventilate and have a mental breakdown thinking about the raw eel and dinner with the assassin, but I didn't have to because he held out his arms.

I didn't cry, so he wouldn't have his shirt to complain about. He didn't crush my lungs that time, either. Finally I pulled away, amazed that he would have let me invade his personal space for that long.

"Thanks," I muttered without looking at him directly. I did feel better.

"It wasn't as bad that time," he said, sounding surprised.

I looked up at him and he met my eyes.

"Not as creepy."

I rolled my eyes and started my agonizing way down the hall towards my next class. "You, with your family, can call hugging creepy? What else do you find creepy, peanut butter sandwiches? Dryer lint? Oh, I know. Wrinkled shirts."

"Hey," he said, catching the back of my shirt so I had to stop with a jerk. That hurt. "Are you okay?" He looked concerned when he looked at me, his frown more worried than disapproving. "It was a very solid hit."

"I'm fine. I used to spar. I've taken worse. After a couple of days I'll be able to breathe normally and everything. How about you? Oliver seemed to do some damage."

"He won technically, because you took that last punch."

"What did he win? Does he get to drive your car and get it as muddy as he wants? Maybe you have to wash and iron all his shirts, or better yet, he gets to wear yours."

He looked at me, and the frown grew a little deeper as he moved away. "He gets to take me to meet his family during Christmas break."

I stared at him. "Huh." I frowned. "Are you sure you guys aren't gay?"

He gestured towards my mouth. "You tell me."

"Um, okay. But, why does he want to take you home with him?"

He shook his head. "I'm sure he has his reasons."

"Why did he let me bite him?"

He shrugged and started walking faster. "I don't know that any more than why you're not still in there, bruising your mouth on him."

"He groped me."

Sean raised an eyebrow, and I blushed.

"Not that it's any of your business, but I'm not used to that kind of physical contact. Like you and hugging, you know?"

He frowned thoughtfully. "Interesting."

"Isn't it though?"

He shook his head. "Get to class, Gen."

Right, like there was some point to going to class when you could barely sit up and were dizzy from kissing some idiot foreigner. Ah well. Attendance counted for something.

After school Junie waited by my locker with a worried expression on her face. No lecture, just a sympathy shoulder pat while she said nothing. Junie didn't usually say nothing.

"What's up, Junie?"

She scowled suddenly furious, black eyes flashing, so I stepped back. "I'm such a hypocrite. All my talk about pacifism gone the second that idiot showed up. I judged you so harsh, but man, it felt good to shut Dean up. Not that it was right, of course it wasn't, but…" Her shoulders slumped.

"Junie, it's all good. No one's perfect, not you, not The Captain; you have to allow yourself to really relish these opportunities for self-realization. It's not every day your inner psyche comes out and punches someone. You have to figure out what it means and let it help you become a better, stronger person." I had no idea what I was talking about, but it was the sort of thing she would have said to me. "Maybe you should take up meditation. We could do it together," I added which made her brighten up even while I inwardly groaned.

Chapter 23

I was hanging out in Flop's Bermuda theme room with my feet in the purple foam filled pool when she brought up Oliver.

"He's totally stalking you." Words that always got my attention. "Not obviously if you didn't know to look for the signs, but he totally plans his route, passing right behind you so he can watch you without you seeing him. Very deja vous with how you were with Cole. So glad you're not into Cole anymore. Not that he wasn't hot, but crushes should end a natural death."

"Yeah, on to a bigger better obsession."

She rolled her eyes. "So, everyone's saying that you cheated on Sean with Oliver. Do you want to do damage control or ignore the whole rest of the student population?"

I stared at her. "Someone thinks it would be conceivable to cheat on Sean? It's kind of stunning how ridiculous all of this is, don't you think? That people believe I was with him in the first place, me and The Captain," I shook my head. "I would have been laughing hysterically before all of this went down." I closed my eyes and sank deeper into the foam. "I'm trying to not obsess about Oliver, you know, I think I'm almost good at the not obsessing thing, but the Sean thing, or the not really Sean thing makes everything more complicated, or not really, but people think it is. He knows about everything with Oliver. So, why do I feel guilty?"

"Guilty? You feel guilty?" She sat up flinging purple foam all over the room.

"What? It's a guilt complex. I'm entitled to those, aren't I?"

She narrowed her eyes on me with focus she usually reserved for seriously cute guys. "You like him."

"Who? Sean? No. He's... I mean, I can't like one guy and obsess about another one. He's The Captain. He doesn't like me."

She cocked her head thoughtfully. "We'll see."

No matter what I said after that, she wouldn't lose her annoyingly smug look. She thought she knew what was up, and Flop, well, she wasn't usually wrong, but this time, she was. You didn't take someone you liked to dinner with your killer mother. I shuddered thinking about it.

When I got home my dad had a message for me from Bernice. She wouldn't be able to meet me for swimming. My heart pounded as I stood there feeling that twist in my stomach, the guilt but also plain anger. Junie was right. Her soul belonged to the swim team.

The next morning I was at the pool, at 5 a.m. because then I could be in and out without anyone knowing I was there.

The day was particularly cold, cold enough that a rim of ice was on the edges of the puddles I splashed through on my still peeling bike in the predawn air. I got my suit on in the frigid dressing room then padded barefoot over the cold tile to the pool.

I stepped out of the dressing room then caught my breath as I saw Sean perched on the edge of the diving board, like a bird as he stretched his arms then catapulted off, twisting and flipping in the air until with barely a splash, he slid into the water.

I felt weird, my stomach twisting while my heart pounded. It was probably because I expected to be alone, nothing to do with the sight of Sean performing like an Olympian to an empty room. I sat with my knees to my chest while I waited for him to come up. Was he waiting for me so that he could give me more pointers? Why did that make me smile? I hadn't seen him in so little clothes for so long; I'd almost forgotten how beautiful he was.

The seconds stretched out into minutes until I realized with a shock that he should have come up by then. My mind froze as I sat there then stumbled up, sliding on the tile so my dive into the pool was crooked. I held my breath, fighting down the panic as I searched the pool. When I saw the dark form floating across from me I swam to him in quick, sure strokes, my heart normalizing as I focused, the way you did in kata.

I was almost to him, ready to grab him under the armpits and drag him to the surface when he looked up with his blue eyes, but they seemed dark and strange in the shadows beneath the water. I reached for him, wrapping my arms around his chest while I kicked up, struggling to lift his weight and mine. The surface seemed miles away as I hauled his limp, incredibly heavy body up, lungs bursting, forcing myself to stay calm until finally, I broke the surface, sucking in lungfuls of air as I blinked water out of my eyes. Sean floated on his back while I swam, dragging him to the nearest side. What I would do when I got there, I had no idea.

"Sean," I gasped, hardly with enough breath for words once I had the edge under my hand.

"Hm?" he asked, sounding curious.

"Are you dead?"

"I don't know. I've never been dead so I'm not sure what it would be like. I object if this is heaven. If this is hell… it's about right."

I hit him in the shoulder, hard enough that he should have winced but he just looked at me with curiosity in his ice blue eyes.

"You were under the water too long. You should have drowned." I pulled myself out of the pool and collapsed on the tile, glad that it was cold, that I could shiver and lay there limp, although I kept my eye on Sean to make sure he didn't sink again.

He pulled himself out in an easy motion that contracted the muscles in his arms and chest. His muscles were absolutely impressive, and getting such a close view was really fascinating. His abdominals… who had muscles like that?

He hid them when he sat beside me, leaning forward

so he could frown at me. "So that was you rescuing me?"

I blinked at him. "I wasn't doing anything else."

"How long were you up here, watching me?"

"I wasn't watching you, it's not like I haven't been coming to the pool every morning for over a month. I just saw you do those flip things and then nothing. For how long? Ten minutes?"

His piercing eyes narrowed at me. He opened his mouth to say something scathing when Oliver's accent bounced off the tile. "You didn't see what you thought you saw."

I turned my head and felt the overwhelming need to be one with him. Ugh. "Thanks for that, Oliver. Actually, I did see what I saw, but thanks for the vote of confidence. Sean should be dead."

"Is that what you want?" Oliver asked, in a low voice with his sparkling green eyes focused on me.

I stared at him, at a loss for a second. "Yeah. That's why I dragged him out, so he'd be dead. Way to use deductive reasoning. Are you on drugs, or what?"

"Drugs. Definitely drugs," Sean said decidedly.

I frowned at him as I finally sat up, body protesting. Of course, my ribs still had serious damage, so that wasn't a surprise. I had no idea what he was talking about. "I'm feeling a little bit like I fell down a rabbit hole. What is with you guys? What are you doing here so early? I came early just so that I could swim without running into anyone."

"You shouldn't do that," Oliver said, walking closer. It wasn't fair that he was fully clothed. It made me feel more vulnerable. "You might have an accident, drown, and then where would you be?"

"At the bottom of the pool, unless I floated when I was dead the way I do when I'm unconscious," I responded automatically. "Whatever," I said, standing up. "Apparently this pool is not a place for people like me."

"Where are you going?" Oliver asked, but it wasn't a question, not when he was looking over my shoulder at Sean.

"Gen," Sean said, making me turn around and look at

him where he sat, comfortably on the frigid tile. Of course he would be comfortable; they were probably the same temperature. "How long do you think that people can hold their breath?"

I blinked. "Four, five minutes? Why?"

"I've got good lungs. I'm wondering if you happened to check the time so you could tell me approximately how long I was under the water. I might have broken a record."

I shook my head as I tried to remember. It had been a little before five when I got there, the clock in the dressing room had shown that, but now, when I looked on the wall at the clock, I noticed that the second hand didn't move. "I'm sorry, I really couldn't say. It seemed like ten minutes, but I wasn't counting, so I don't know. It was a really long time."

Sean stared at me with his blue eyes until he finally nodded then looked past me at Oliver. "I think we're good here. Gen," he added, standing up. "I think that with the whole me punching you thing, it would probably be best if we were no longer together. Do you understand?"

I took a step back before I shook my head. "What, you're not going to ask me what a smart girl like me is doing acting like an idiot over you?"

He smiled, a stunning smile that was really wasted on me. He should have found someone he liked. Maybe he had. "That would be calling you smart. Since when do I do that?"

I rolled my eyes and turned to leave, stopping abruptly when I realized Oliver had been right behind me. "Excuse me, I'm going to leave before I burst into tears from Sean breaking my delicate heart."

Oliver stared at me for a long time, a strange look that felt like he was weighing something before he stepped aside.

"I'll see you later," he said, quietly.

I ignored the goosebumps his voice gave me. Who could distinguish a few goosebumps from the shivering? "Not if I see you first."

The sound of his laughter followed me out of the room.

I stood under the hot water from the shower for a long time, hating that I could only warm up half of my body at a time. That had been really weird. If Sean hadn't been drowning, it was horrible of him to make me drag him up, not that him being horrible was weird, it was afterwards with Oliver. He'd acted like I was trying to drown Sean. That was a mind-boggling idea: me taking on Sean in the water. Sean had told me, not me really, but Oliver, that we weren't going out. It had seemed like there was a lot of communicating between them that I wasn't getting, but whatever. I slammed off the water. If Sean didn't want to date me, if he'd found someone better, more perfect like him, then I was happy for him. More than happy, ecstatic. I dressed hurriedly then hurt my wrist shoving open the door. Oh well. It would go with my ribs.

I spent the rest of my time before class sitting in front of my locker doing homework. My teachers would be so impressed. I was putting my extra books in when Cole came by. In the old days I would have stared at him while he looked through me, but now he put a hand on my shoulder, making me drop a book.

"So, Vee, how's it going with Sean?"

"It's not," I muttered, picking up the book from the bottom of my locker and putting it back on the top shelf. "We aren't seeing each other anymore."

"Because he hit you? You wouldn't take that personally. So why?"

"How is this your business?"

He leaned against the next locker, apparently not going anywhere soon. "I liked you with him. He's a good guy."

I stared at him. He was still hot, gorgeous really. Why was I surrounded by hot guys now, none of whom liked me? Torture. That's what it was. I had done something evil in a former life, so this was my punishment. I shrugged. "I don't really know. I think it had to do with…"

"The girl on his team? Are you jealous?" I stared at him. "Bernice, right? She's cute, but not really…" he wrinkled his nose. "He likes her, but not seriously. Like us, you know?"

My eyeballs were going to dry out and drop out of my head if I didn't blink at some point. I blinked. "Yeah. Like us. So, was there a mass hallucination I missed? I have no idea what you're talking about. We're like, nothing. And Sean and Bernice are like family. Swim family. You ditched me when I needed you most. Sean would never ditch one of his own, not if they needed him."

He nodded. "Yeah. Like I said, he's a good guy. But that girl, she's not like him, or you. She's like me." He gave me a half smile. "I'm not the only one who bailed on you. I'm just the hottest."

And on that note, he left me alone to fight the need to bash my head into my locker.

Chapter 24

I made it through the rest of the day, but I didn't feel so well, probably from the freezing cold tile. The way other girls looked at me didn't help. There was so much, 'hah, like you thought you were good enough for Sean but you're still the freak, Watergirl,' that I could barely take it. At home, after wandering around the house for awhile, it was time to go to the lake. Just me, my notebook and my super sore ribs. I wore my warmest parka, the one I'd stolen from my dad, military surplus or something. The ride was hard because breathing hurt. Stupid Sean. I parked my bike and found the willow looking naked with stringy branches hanging down, stripped of green. Oh well. I slipped under them anyway. My music and poetry weren't really coming but the questions were.

1-How long was Sean under the water, anyway?
2-Why did he not drown?
3-What does his ideal girlfriend look like?
4-What's with Oliver?
5-What's with Cole and what he said about Bernice?
6-Were they really fighting over going away for Christmas?
7-Why do I feel like I have to come to the lake?
8-What about what Oliver saw at the lake, no, not saw but thought he saw?
9-Why do I have to be obsessed with anyone I kiss anyway? Will I never be allowed to have a normal boyfriend and stuff?

I put away my notebook because I was tired of trying to make sense of stuff. It would be better to forget. That's what I'd come to the lake for—to forget. The wind sighed around me, a song that made me feel more lonely.

I needed to sing. I fought it, but the pressure built up in my chest until an awful sound came out, a choked, bleeding sound that surprised me. Did I really feel like that? I tried to close my mouth but the sound kept coming and with it, tears.

I sang until the sound ended, cut off with a sob as I curled in the parka and rested my head against the bark of the tree. I heard a splash and jerked up because it was probably Oliver, but no. When I looked up, I saw nothing until I looked over at the water inside the circle of willow fronds. A bulbous head with two dark eyes stared at me while strands of seaweed trailed down between them, seaweed that didn't grow in my freshwater lake. The eyes lifted and the lips drew back in a snarl while a horrible hiss came from its throat. It was probably ten feet away from me when it lunged for me with its claws.

I scrambled away, ducking out from beneath the tree, feet pounding as I ran, pound, pound, to my bike, lame bike, I needed a car! Then I was pedaling clumsily away. I pushed, faster, faster, until I was back in town but I didn't slow down until I realized I was at Sean's house. I dropped my bike and ran up his sidewalk to bang on the tall front door.

I had my mouth open to scream, 'there's something in the lake!' when the door opened and Bernice looked out at me with a frown. Nothing came out of my mouth. I shut it.

"Gen, what are you doing here? I didn't know you were coming to Oliver's going away party."

"I… Oliver's going away?"

She nodded and I thought I saw a flicker of satisfaction on her face. "It's too bad the team will lose such a good swimmer, but he had an emergency at home he has to leave for."

"Oh." I stared at her and she stared back.

"Do you want to come in, or maybe I could get Oliver…" She frowned. "Unless you were looking for Sean, but I heard you guys weren't together anymore."

"Yeah. I had something of his I wanted to give back, but you know, I don't want to bother him at his party. I'll just see him tomorrow." If I wasn't killed in my bed by the monster. I shuddered.

"Are you okay? You don't look very well." Her concern was kind of annoying.

"I think I might be coming down with a cold or something. Anyway, I'll see you later."

"What's up?" Sean's voice came from behind Bernice.

"Nothing," we both said at the same time.

Sean stepped close behind Bernice so that I could watch him rest a hand on her shoulder while he leaned close to her ear.

"You're missing the party," he said in a low voice.

She nodded and looked up at him with luminous eyes and a stunning smile. Wow. She really liked him.

"I was just going," I said, backing up and almost falling off the steps.

"Didn't you need to give something to Sean?" Bernice said turning a puzzled frown in my direction.

"It'll just take a sec," Sean said, stepping past Bernice, and waiting until she backed off to close the door on her.

"I don't have anything for you. It's stupid. Didn't really happen. I'm just having a hallucination, like the other stuff going on, like you not drowning, and the Cole thing. It's all good. I think it's the flu, you know?"

He frowned at me. I realized then why I'd come to Sean's house. I wanted a hug. Why would I have come all this way for a hug from Sean? It made no sense.

"I'll walk you home."

I blinked at him. "I have a bike."

"I can keep up."

I shook my head. "You have a party. It's nothing. I was stupid to come here, you know, like I usually am."

"I'm coming with you."

I sighed. I couldn't argue. I didn't want to argue, not when the monster clawing… and then there was the other thing, the Oliver leaving thing. It was one thing to fight an obsession, it was another to know that he wouldn't be there, that he'd be gone and part of me would be ripped out along with him.

I sneezed.

"Bless you."

We started down the sidewalk, me pushing my bike with him on the other side. "Why are you coming with me?"

"I don't like parties."

I looked up at him. "Then you shouldn't have them."

"I'm The Captain."

I rolled my eyes then shuddered as I had a memory of the monster, the hissing. He put a hand on my shoulder. For a second I felt better until I remembered him putting his hand on Bernice's shoulder and pulled away from him.

"What is it?" he asked, his voice authoritative and commanding. Who wouldn't tell him when he used that voice?

"You're not my captain. You're not my pretend boyfriend, you're not my anything, so why am I here, with you? It makes no sense. We have nothing in common, you can't stand me, and really, I don't exactly enjoy the way you make me feel, but here I am." I shook my head.

"That's it?"

I stared at him levelly, taking in his chiseled cheekbones and general perfection. "No. It's not. What it is, is none of your business. I really should have gone to Oliver, but I didn't think about it." He'd been sure there was something in the lake all along. He wouldn't think I was crazy. Wait. I kind of wanted to be crazy, to have been hallucinating. I did not want validation about monsters. I sighed. I wanted a hug.

"This isn't about this morning?"

I frowned at him. "So you can hold your breath for a long time. So what?"

"And about Cole?"

"No."

"But, it's about Oliver. Are you feeling... sick about him leaving?" His icy eyes felt accusing but at the same time, looked concerned—about me.

I swallowed. I was, but that wouldn't give me nightmares.

"That must be it." I stopped on the sidewalk. I was

done with this conversation, done with blocking him when I just wanted a stupid hug.

"Sean, will you please go away?" My voice came out small and vulnerable. Crap. Where was my powerful voice, the one that had made Oliver leave me alone, then again, also the one that made me faint? I tried again. "Otherwise, I think I'll cry on your shirt. I don't think you'd survive that, so..."

He reached over the bike and pulled me against him, for a second blocking out the monsters with his slow, steady heartbeat. "Go for it," he said, against my hair.

My heart sped up as I blinked completely dry eyes, then closed them, leaning against him. We stood like that for too long, until my legs were cold and he was probably freezing because he only wore a long sleeved shirt with his jeans.

A car drove by, the headlights startling me and making me pull away, feeling self-conscious. "Um, are you cold? We'll have to see if you can keep up," I said, climbing on my bike without looking at him.

I pushed off and he kept up with a steady jog, his feet pounding against the pavement beside me. We were a few blocks from my house, so after only a few minutes, we were there. I got off, then frowning, unzipped my dad's parka and handed it to him.

"Night," I said, leaving him there, holding my parka in his strong hand like he had no idea what it was. "Don't get mud on it," I called over my shoulder before I let the screen door close behind me.

Chapter 25

So that was that. Oliver was gone. The lake really had a monster. I really had to work overtime after Thanksgiving and the Holiday rush got crazy. I didn't have time to notice my stupid sick heart looking for Oliver every other second of every day. The other half I was looking for monsters. I was busy practicing Christmas chorale arrangements, hanging out with friends.

One thing that slowly got weirder and weirder until it was impossible to ignore was the fallout from having two of the hottest guys at school supposedly fight over me: I'd become someone guys wanted to date.

At first I stared at them in stunned silence when they asked me out, then I gave lame excuses about work and stuff, then I said yes. His name was Jack, and he was in choir with me so at least we had something in common. We went to a movie. He laughed too much. He touched my hand too much. The best part was when we were driving home and sang Christmas carols along with the radio and did parts. We sat in the car at my house, practicing our parts for the chorale when he lunged for me.

I felt really bad about hitting him in the face and told him so a lot of times, but he kept apologizing with his hand over his face dripping blood until I got out. I felt bad, but I would have felt worse if he actually had managed to kiss me and I became obsessed. Dates apparently, weren't for me.

When the first snow fell, I was still riding my bike to school, skidding at the corners, but alive and in one piece. When I got to school, I turned the corner of the hall, and there was Flop at her locker, right beside my locker, looking so unlike herself that for a second I thought she was someone else. She wore boots, pants, sweater, coat, scarf, the whole thing.

"Flop?" She turned and gave me a sunny smile, totally ignoring the way that me, and Junie who had just showed up, stared at her.

That day at lunch, while snow piled up outside, I looked at our table, at Tuba who didn't need fixing, Flop who looked ready for a ski resort, me, who knew how to swim and was officially over Cole. Junie's psychotic plan actually worked, except of course for her and her relationship thing.

A few days later, only a couple days before Christmas break and the Christmas concert that my teacher was freaking out about, like she did every year, a new guy came to school, shaking snow off his long blonde locks, looking only slightly out of place in his shorts and sandals as he walked through the hall, past Flop who stared, love-struck at first sight.

That day was reconnaissance, which meant that she talked to everyone she knew about who he was to find out what classes he was in and where he was from... that kind of thing, then she had two classes in a row with him, the last two, and she could flirt with him in person. The next day he showed up at our table, and the day after that, and the day after that, falling into our little group without any apparent effort.

Logan was from southern Cali and had a passion for all things sunshine. Flop was sunshine, so naturally they were in lockstep. They had these crazy conversations that didn't make any sense to anyone else, but they didn't seem to mind that there was anyone else, so that was fine. Right. He was totally nice, but sometimes I wanted to sit and talk about hot guys, not just one hot guy, Logan, who I wasn't allowed to think of as hot, anyway, although he was, not as hot as Sean or Oliver, but you know, pretty good.

Whatever. I was okay for Flop to be happy when I was miserable. At least I had Junie to be miserable with, at least I had Junie until the unthinkable happened.

First of all, New Year's parties should be banned. I mean, after Christmas break, why do people have to dress up and get confetti in their eyes anyway? Total overkill.

So it was a week after Christmas during the break when we were all hanging out at the coffee shop eating bagels and drinking hot chocolate—everyone was Junie, Flop, Logan, and Tuba. Sean came in, looking glistening from the snow melting in his short hair and eyelashes, looked around the room then came straight for our table.

I blinked at him when he pulled up a chair, as comfortable with us as though we were his team. We hadn't talked since Oliver's going away party, hadn't really looked at each other. He must have just returned from his Christmas break, with Oliver if he'd actually kept that bet.

"Hi," he said with a smile at all of us, a gleaming, toothy smile that made me think I must have chocolate on my nose or crumbs on my shirt.

"Hey," Logan said easily, shaking his hand like it wasn't so weird to see him there. The rest of us kind of nodded and stuff, except for Junie. She glared at him.

It was sick the way he did it, sick but impressive. He started with Junie, telling her about an internship with a conservation group that worked on some oil damaged beach trying to restore the ecological system, and how he could email her the information if she was interested, which, if the way she kept nodding and nodding and nodding were any indication, she was.

After that, he turned his attention to Flop and Logan, asked them if they'd gone swimming since he'd moved there, and invited them to his New Year's Eve party, and us when he looked around with an including smile, his eyes somehow less glinting than usual.

"I'd have Flop on the team any time if she were willing to do the early morning drills, but either way, you two should be there." His words and tone were so precisely flattering, I was left speechless. "All of you should come, unless of course you have your own plans. Anyway," he said, standing up. "I hope you can make it." He looked directly at Tuba when he said it.

Logan was ecstatic with the idea of bringing in New Year's Eve in a pool with Flop, and Junie said it would be interesting and educational, besides which, she could ask Sean about what other internships he knew about. Tuba, Flop and I exchanged skeptical looks.

"What do you think, Gen," Tuba asked me with concerned brown eyes. "You've gone to one of his parties before. Would we have a good time?"

I shrugged. "The music is good, the food is good, his house, well, it's incredible. There's this aquarium that takes up an entire wall in the living room, with sharks in it. The pool, also in the living room is huge, and everything's perfect. I guess you could have fun, if you wanted to go. The only thing I didn't like were the people. Everyone was so…" I shrugged and took a big bite of cookie.

"That's elitist," Junie said.

I sighed.

"Of course Sean attracts superficial, but he's deeper than that." Oh great. I really did not want her to start giggling again. "I say we go. A New year, a new experience…"

"Where we go doesn't matter as much as that we're all there," Flop said, frowning at Junie. "If Gen wouldn't be comfortable at Sean's party, then we won't go."

Logan frowned, wrinkling up his cute forehead. "Why wouldn't Gen be comfortable?"

Flop leaned a little closer to him so she could tell him under her breath about how I'd dated Sean and it hadn't worked out.

Logan nodded like that made sense. "Okay," he said. "The pool would be cool, but so long as I'm with Flop, I'm good."

Everyone stared at me. Flop and Tuba wouldn't care what we did, but Junie and Logan…

"Sure. Let's go. It'll be fun." Not like I could keep everyone from having a good time, and maybe it would be fun, I mean, how could it not be when I'd be there with my friends, my real friends?

I looked cute when Logan and Flop came by to pick me up. Logan even said so in the brief second he didn't devour

Flop with his eyes. Ugh. I hated happy people. We picked up Junie and Tuba, kind of crammed Logan's his little subi, but we liked each other so it was okay.

At the party Logan pulled off his shirt and dragged Flop into the pool right away. They were so at home in the water, paddling around, looking cute, faux splashing each other while their legs bumped. Me, Tuba and Junie stood around awkwardly while we listened to great music and watched the creatures in the aquarium.

Tuba cleared his throat. "Junie," he said. We both looked at him. His brown hair looked a little sweaty. "Do you want to dance? This is great music. Not as good as Gen..." he said giving me an apologetic look. "But maybe..."

"Sure," Junie said, grabbing his hand and pulling him away from me, towards the millions of other people, most of them ridiculously beautiful until they were out of sight.

That left me alone, well, alone with everyone else crowding around. I saw Bernice and waved when she noticed me because even though she ditched us, I could be better than her.

I stood there by myself, not because guys didn't ask me to dance, but because I didn't dance. It was fine to hang out beside the aquarium watching the shark and the stingrays, along with a motley of other beautiful fish play intricate games I couldn't follow. I could have watched them forever, at least until I heard someone clear their throat behind me. I turned around to tell whoever it was that I wasn't interested when I stopped, staring at Ben, Bernice's crush.

"Hey," he said with a sort-of nod.

"Ben. What's going on?"

"Do you want to dance?"

I stared at him. "I'm sorry. Shouldn't you be asking Bernice? I'm pretty sure she likes you."

He frowned, his face looking less sweet, more tormented. "Yeah, I thought she might like me, but when I kept asking her out and she always had a reason why we couldn't go, I finally realized that there's only one swimmer that she'll ever really see."

He turned around and I followed his gaze. Sean walked through the crowd with an unreadable expression, nodding at people who greeted him, making his way over to us.

"I'm glad you came," he said to me as he handed me a drink, then glanced at Ben with something like dismissal. Ben's cheeks got red as he turned away, leaving me with Sean.

I glared at him, at his blue ironed t-shirt that made his eyes even more brilliant.

"What is this?" I asked, lifting the orange drink with an umbrella in it.

"Orange juice, vanilla protein, bananas, ice, and an umbrella." He raised an eyebrow. "You looked like you could use something to do with your hands. At parties you shouldn't stand around looking bored. You might insult the host."

"I wasn't bored. I was talking to Ben. Now," I said, handing him back the drink, "I'm going to swim. See how much fun I'm having?"

I slipped off my clothes that were over my suit, awkwardly aware that Sean watched me while he sipped the drink instead of going away.

He waited until I was halfway in the pool before he said, "Sounds good," then peeled off his shirt, tossing it on top of mine. He dove in, narrowly missing people as I finished sliding into the water. I choked when he came up right beside me, treading water without any apparent effort.

I tried not to look at him, but I kept bumping against him as I struggled to stay afloat. Finally I swam back to the edge, pushing through bodies until I finally could pull myself out. I headed, dripping, for the pile of clothes beside the aquarium ready to change and bail.

"Leaving already?" He was right behind me. Did he not remember telling me that we weren't going to see each other anymore and then the past month and a half we hadn't, to our mutual happiness and joy? He sounded like the concerned host, but his eyes were mocking.

"What's your problem?" I was so done with his games.
"Problem?"

I glared at him. "Go play concerned host to somebody else. I know that you love to irritate me, but right now, I want to actually have a not horrible time for my New Year's Eve, okay? Why don't you go find Bernice and bring in the New Year together?"

"Bernice?" He looked confused as he bent down, retrieving the orange drink before he began drinking it again.

"Yeah, you know, the girl on your swim team that used to be a friend of mine. And what's with people who can swim and drink at the same time?"

He blinked at me. "I know Bernice, but I think she's interested in Ben. As for the other thing…" He shrugged. "It's a skill beyond me. Maybe we could practice together. We could start in the hot-tub, sitting instead of floating. What do you think?"

I stared at him. "I don't get you. Are you flirting with me?"

He looked at me with a frown. "Apparently not. I think that I was trying to flirt with you, but that's not the same thing." We frowned at each other for a few minutes, both of us dripping.

"Come to my room," he finally said. "I'll explain." His voice was different, softer but more dangerous.

I shivered as I crossed my arms over my chest. "You'll explain why you're trying to flirt with me? You could do that here."

He smiled at me, a smile that unfolded slowly.

"All right. This song, do you remember it?" I listened and smiled as the strange melody, the darkness and the intensity built. It was the music from his car during the date with his mother. "If you dance with me, I'll give you the entire album. It's not something you can download or find at your music store."

I hesitated too long. He took my hand, leading me not to the middle of the crowd, but into an alcove that was darker, less populated.

I felt weird when he put his hands on my hips with only the thin fabric of my wet swimming suit between us, weirder when I put my hands on his slick shoulders and we started moving more or less to the beat. I really wanted this music and a dance wouldn't kill me, even if my heart pounded and I had to remind myself to take even, calm breaths.

He reached up and pulled my hand down onto his hip, which was weird, but not too weird, I mean, hips were pretty safe places, relatively, at least I felt that way until the pressure of his hand pushed mine into his skin, through the place where skin should cover bone, but instead covered nothing. I jerked back while he watched my reaction.

"What the...Your shorts..." I could see the fabric folded behind his skin in a way that just wasn't normal. He casually pulled it out, like a hip wedgie then put his hands back on my hips and back to dancing like nothing had happened.

I stared at his face, the way he looked at me without any expression at all and I tried to act normal. Maybe he had a deformity that would explain everything about him, why he kept away from relationships, that sort of thing.

"What was that?" I asked, proud that my voice didn't shake, at least very much.

He cocked his head to the side. "Do you want to see?"

I shook my head quickly. "No, of course not. I'm just worried. Are you okay?"

He looked down, not answering my question.

"Sean?" I put a hand on his face and he looked up, quickly, reminding me of the time at the bottom of the pool. I swallowed and tried to pull away, but he had his hand over mine, keeping it there against his cheek.

"Come on, Gen. I think it's time."

I followed him as he led me through the crowds, up the stairs, down a hall and then into a room, shutting the door behind him.

Chapter 26

He leaned against the door while I stood there, feeling more idiotic than usual. It was his bedroom, I realized. If I'd thought about it at all, which I hadn't, at least much, I would have expected his room to be clean and cold like him, but instead it was a mess of laundry and books strewn around.

He put his hands on his waistband and began pushing his black swim shorts down, over his hips.

"Wait," I said, gripping his large hands in mine. "You don't have to do this. I mean, obviously, this is really personal and I don't think you're wearing anything under those shorts. I can't handle that much nudity. Okay? I don't want to insult you by freaking out, but I've never seen a naked guy, and I'm already pretty much freaking out."

"I actually noticed," he said with the faint smile that was probably genuine. "Hand me that towel. Would my towel covered body be too much for you?"

For someone with a disability, he really acted cocky. It was probably the chiseled cheekbones that made him such a jerk. I rolled my eyes and grabbed the towel, relieved when he didn't try to take anything off until he had it firmly tied around his narrow waist, narrow waist and exercise video abs, with arms and shoulders that looked capable of anything. I forced my eyes back to his face where he was shaking his head at me. Right. We all knew he was hot; I had to get over it.

"This is it," he said, turning to the side. The stretch of skin from his waist ended at three rows of slits where his skin should have been. I forgot about hotness as I slide my hand over the silky skin to touch the line, gasping when it opened and closed, fluttering like a butterfly, or something else insanely cool.

"It's like a gill," I whispered as I traced the lines with my fingers, feeling my breath catch in my throat as they ruffled under my hand.

"Very like, in fact, identical. Would you like to see the matching set?" I stared at him, leaving my fingers on his 'gills', feeling light-headed and dizzy.

"Matching set? Of gills?"

He sighed and pulled my hands to the other hip, placing it over his other 'gills', where they pulsed under my hand. My fingers accidentally slipped inside one of the gaps. I blinked as I felt the soft warmth and sliminess coat my fingers. I jerked my hand back.

"I'm sorry. Did that hurt?"

He didn't answer right away. I couldn't see his face because mine was right up to his muscular chest, so close that I could see the golden hairs sprinkled across the chest, with my hands on his naked hips and nothing but a towel, a towel that as far as I could see had nothing holding it up but me where I leaned against him.

"It's just weird," he said.

I almost laughed at that. Like me touching his gills was weirder for him than me. I ran my fingers along the edges, sliding inside them slightly probing but hopefully gentle enough that it didn't hurt him. They pulsed against my palms, like live creatures.

He put his hands on my legs, right below my swimming suit. I didn't mind, not when I was feeling so unsteady, like I might pass out at any moment, but then he slid his hands up, fingers finding their way beneath my suit that made me pull away.

"What are you doing?" It was like he was groping me, but this was Sean. He held the towel in front, but the rest was bare, bare from head to toe with tan, muscular perfection and gills in between. I fumbled backwards for a wall to lean on but found the bed instead. I flopped down on it still unable to take my eyes off of him, the gills, mostly the gills but also, holy hotness. The picture beside his trophy in school did not do him justice.

"So that explains it," I said, mostly to myself as I clenched my fists into his blue duvet. "You have this… thing, and it makes you feel like you're different, maybe like you are part fish, and that's why you won't let girls get close to you, and why Oliver wants you, to do experiments or put in a circus, something. It explains everything."

He blinked his blue eyes at me, the same color as the duvet. "Does it?"

"Some people are born with extra toes. You have these gills. You're not a freak, though," I said hurriedly, leaning forward to touch his arm, his tan arm, corded with muscles. "They're amazing. You're incredible. Don't let one small abnormality get in the way of the rest of your life."

"That's… touching. Honestly, Genevieve," he said with an icy look that had me pulling my fingers back. "I did not bring you here so that you can validate me in my insecurities."

I blinked at him, startled by his harsh tone. "Right. Sorry for thinking for a second that you might feel like an outsider from having non operable gills. My mistake." I stood up then sat back down when I got dizzy. I leaned on my knees, putting my head in my hands until I could get it together enough to get out of there. "So, why am I here?"

"I need to check you for gills."

I looked up, slowly. There was no way he'd said what I'd thought he'd said.

"I don't have gills."

He was standing over me with his massive arms crossed over his massive chest while a not so massive towel covered the bits right in front of my face. "Show me."

"No."

He smiled slightly. "I have another album that you would…"

"No," I said as I stood, still dizzy but managing to stand on my own. "You're not buying me with more music, however incredible it is, which I'm sure it is because your taste is… We're not talking about your music. I'm not taking off Bernice's swimsuit in your room."

He curled his lip. "You think that I'm trying to get you naked?" Oh, the contempt. "You're a crazy human, if that's what you are. You fit into that world less than I do."

"Oh, really?" I sputtered, but I had no idea what to do with this kind of attack. "Just because you have one small, okay two, gills, doesn't mean you're not human. Fine. I'll do it, but only if you rip one of your shirts up the sides so that I'm mostly…"

I didn't finish saying it when he grabbed a folded shirt from the top of a basket and ripped it with his teeth before he tore a strip from the hem up to the sleeve. He did the other side while I watched then handed it to me, turning his back to me while I stood, holding the ruined shirt in my fist. I'd never thought I'd live to see the day when Captain Sean ripped a shirt of his own free will.

"Go ahead then," he said in that cold voice that matched his eyes.

I gritted my teeth and yanked the shirt over my head before pulling off the swimming suit. When it was around my ankles he turned around again while I was sliding my hands through the sleeves. I forced myself to hold still while he touched my skin. If I'd thought it was weird touching him it was nothing compared to his hands, butterfly soft on my skin as he searched every inch from my ribs to my knees. He ran his hands over me again using a little more pressure while I bit my lip and clenched my fists, telling myself that it was fine, that nothing was going on there, he was just checking me for gills, then he used his nails. He didn't scratch my skin, but the feel gave me shivers and made me want to hang onto something.

He exhaled and I could feel his breath on my skin. When I looked, he was searching my skin with his eyes while his hands slid down, squeezing and pulling, a bit like a massage until his nose brushed my leg. I gasped then backed away from him, once more hitting the bed. This time when I went down, I landed on my back and couldn't get back up because he followed me down, his hands on either side of my face.

"My mother would kill you. Oliver would too, only

quicker." He frowned at me, so close that I could see the striations of his eyes.

"You're not them." I was too stunned to be freaking out. I'd freak out later when he wasn't on top of me.

He blinked at me while that slight smile flashed over his lips. His lips did not look cold and fish-like. "You have to promise that you won't reveal what you saw to anyone, ever, for as long as you live."

That pissed me off. "Like I was going to. Look, Captain Hotness is actually a psychotic fish boy. What would I get out of that?" I wiggled but he only leaned more of his weight on top of me. His weight included skin, lots and lots of bare skin. Not that I noticed. I was too busy being pissed. And breathing.

"Not to Flop, Junie, anyone."

I rolled my eyes. "Yeah, I got that was part of the anyone, ever for as long as I live."

He was too heavy. My breathing was becoming more and more shallow while familiar black spots danced on the edge of my vision.

"Or you can stay there and suffocate me, then you wouldn't have to worry about me running around and announcing you as the swim fraud you are. Don't you think it's unethical to be on a swim team when you have gills? Oh, right, they're non-functioning, aren't they? They kind of moved a lot to be non-functional. Does the chlorine bother them? What would you have done if I had gills?" My words came out in gasps until everything disappeared.

"I'm not that heavy," he said when I finally blinked my eyes open. I turned my head and found him lying beside me, leaning on one elbow while he looked down at me with one raised golden eyebrow.

"You are too," I said, poking him in the ribs. He still didn't have a shirt on and poking him in the ribs was a moot point since he had too many muscles for his ribs to be even slightly visible. That much muscle was freakish, come to think of it. It made total sense that he wasn't human.

"What was I saying? Oh, right. Your mother was going to kill me?"

He shook his head and sat up. "I didn't say that."

"Yes, you did," I said, sitting up and realizing that he'd put a blanket over me. Hopefully before he'd seen too much. "Does she have gills or is she afraid someone's going to lock you up and wants to protect you? That actually sounds more maternal than I'd given her credit for."

"She's Vashni. She, and those like her, have gills like mine. My father, a Soremni, was exiled after he removed the king's eye. It's a long story. Anyway, Oliver thought that you were Vashni, like my mother. He thought that you were trying to seduce me, to make sure that I wouldn't find my sympathies aligning more with the Soremni than the Vashni. Why else would we both find you so fascinating? Why else would the two of you be affected by the kiss of madness? We can't breed with humans. We don't look at them like that, at least not typically. You're different. There's a gravity to you, like the way you feel about the lake. But, you have no gills. Are you still breathing?"

I blinked and realized that no, I hadn't been breathing. I took big, gulping breaths as I tried to process.

"You're not human?"

He shrugged. "No."

"You can't breed with humans?"

He shook his head. My eyes wandered down to his towel, to the bit between his gills.

"So, how do you breed?'"

His laugh turned into a cough. "That's what you want to know?"

"Yes. No. I don't know. I finally convinced myself that the monster at the lake wasn't real, and now..." I stared at him. He looked human, except for his abundance of hotness. I should have known. So, if he wasn't human, why did all girls find him so hot? It really shouldn't only go one way.

"You saw something at the lake?"

His frown made me stop staring at his chest. Good thing.

"What? No. It was a hallucination. Didn't I say that?"

He sighed. "When did you have your hallucination?"

I scowled. "It wasn't memorable enough for me to say."

"You're really stubborn about this. It was…" He raised his golden eyebrows at me. "That's what you wanted to talk to me about the night of the party. Why didn't you?"

I shrugged. "I didn't want to keep you from Bernice. So, why do you touch her if humans are so repulsive to you?"

"I don't touch her."

"Yes you…"

"What did you see at the lake?" He stared at me with those eyes, so demanding, cold and emotionless.

We both heard the knock on the door right before Junie threw it open. She stared at us, while Bernice, Brenda and Flop stood behind her, staring with mouths open. Bernice's eyes flashed as she glared at me, like she would get me for my betrayal.

Junie said, "Sorry, I was going to find you and tell you I'm with Tuba. I'm his girlfriend. Right before the New Year so I can fulfill my whole list, no, that's not why I'm with him, but because he's… Anyway, you guys are busy so…" She slammed the door, leaving me with Sean. Me in his ripped shirt in his bed and him in a towel. Awesome.

I buried my head beneath his fluffy pillow, moaning and feeling like I was going to throw up. If I threw up in his bed that would completely serve him right. He wasn't even human. I would lose whatever reputation I had over a non-human who couldn't breed with me if he wanted to. Not that he wanted to. Who says breed anyway? Oh, non-humans apparently. Ugh. I was going to die or worse, not die and then what? Nothing, that's what. My life was over, ended, over, ended…

"It's not that bad," he said pulling the pillow off my head. "You're not going to die. We'll simply tell people we're back together and then…"

"No." I sat up, pushing against his ridiculously muscular chest for no apparent reason because he didn't budge. "I am not going to pretend to date you ever again. The next person I pretend to date is going to be human, okay? I need a drink. A serious drink without an umbrella. Don't pretend you care about your reputation. Now people will think you're human and that I'm a slut, so we can both be totally happy." I put my head in my hands. "I'm going to die."

"I'm getting you a drink and your clothes," he said, finally getting off the bed to pull on some pants beneath the towel. "Nothing with alcohol; I don't do alcohol. Try not to freak out too much while I'm gone."

He left me alone, in his bed. Like I was going to stay there. I grabbed a shirt to pull over the ripped one, long sleeve, button-up, and then grabbed a pair of soft pants, probably for exercise with a drawstring that I could tighten. Apparently in spite of how it looked, my waist was way narrower than Sean's. Small victories. I opened the window, shivering as the cold wind swirled into the room. Was I seriously going to sneak out of his room just so that I wouldn't have to walk through the party after Brenda and Bernice had done their damage?

I climbed out, eyeing the drop. I did it all the time, sneaking out of my house, but usually not in winter without shoes. Bare feet helped me grip the stone edging, and then it didn't, but I landed into some evergreens, poky, but no broken bones. The fence was easy enough to scale, but the outside was twice as high as the inside. Very high defense. Maybe they were worried about being attacked by more fish people. I dropped down, feeling like a spy, also like an idiot because landing jolted feeling through my feet, feet that wouldn't feel much after a few blocks. I sat down and made knots at the bottom of the way too long pants then I was ready to go.

I'd gone four blocks when Sean's car pulled up beside me. He drove along while I ignored him. He kept it up, driving right beside me without opening a window or anything. Finally I turned around with my arms crossed over his shirt. It was not a warm enough shirt. I could see his face, lit by the green of his radio, and could hear the pumping beat that came from his awesome stereo system.

He didn't move, didn't do anything while I stood there shivering until I walked around the car and pulled open the passenger door. It wasn't locked. I slid inside, embraced by marvelous warmth and music that sent a tingle up my spine. My clothes were neatly folded on the seat, my shoes and socks on the floor beneath them with my coat draped over the back. I closed the door behind me, sealing out the frigid air.

He didn't say anything, so I didn't either. Instead I began unbuttoning the shirt I'd stolen. He put a hand out to stop me.

"If you're too warm, I can turn off the heater."

I glared at him then sighed instead. "Yeah. Don't watch me change my clothes, not that you want to, since your kind find mine absolutely revolting. Go ahead. Look out your window." I shrugged when he kept watching me and kept unbuttoning his shirt. I still had the ripped one underneath it. "Whatever. I think I ruined your pants. You'll have to send me a bill, or just yell at me about it. Pants aren't really for walking on, but your shoes were crazy big on me. Maybe I should have taken them anyway. Maybe if you had slippers. Why don't you have slippers? Is it a gill thing? Do you sweat? Never mind. I'm not interested."

I slid the button up off my shoulders and felt the heater blow on my bare skin on my sides where the shirt was ripped. I ignored him as I took off his shirt and grabbed my bra, the hot pink one I'd brought in my coat pocket. I changed with my back to him so even if he was watching, which he probably wasn't cuz I didn't have gills, he wouldn't see much. I struggled for a second with the clasp behind my back before it snapped together. Then I had my shirt on, and did the rest of my changing into underwear and jeans under cover of my parka.

I turned to him, and he didn't seem to have looked away, still watching me with nothing on his face that I could read.

"Do you like it?"

I blinked at him. "What?"

He frowned. "Your pink bra. Your hideously garish underwear. Obviously I'm talking about that. The music. Do you like the music?"

I glanced at the radio. I hadn't paid as much attention
to it as I had to not flashing more than absolutely necessary. "It's brilliant. Is this what you were bribing me with
the second time?"

He nodded then turned up the volume. I leaned against
the seat and let the beat press against my skin, like a touch,
the notes and chords brilliantly wound together then
winding through me. I couldn't hear all the parts, there
were too many, but never too much. When he turned it off,
I blinked, halfway asleep.

"You're home."

"Oh. Thanks." I got out, holding his door open as I
stood looking back at him. "Do you want me to try and fix
your pants?"

He looked at me with more irritation than usual. "No.
Happy New Year."

I frowned at him then stepped back as he reached over
and pulled the door shut in my face before pulling out,
leaving me in front of my sad little house.

"Happy New Year," I muttered to the glowing taillights
before shaking my head, I went inside.

Chapter 27

It wasn't midnight when I walked in. I paced around the kitchen until I couldn't take it anymore. Sean had gills. There really was some kiss of madness that wasn't just me being all cracked up. What if Cole had gills too? Crazy. The music kept going through my head, the music from his car, far stranger than the first stuff, but deeper too. I knew there was a monster but it didn't seem to matter. Monsters, boys with gills, it was all good.

I left the kitchen, the house, letting the screen door click closed behind me. I rode my bike through the freezing air with a bright moon to ring in the New Year with the monster in the lake.

When I made it up to my rock, I stopped, feeling my heart sink. It wasn't empty. Cole of all people sat there with a six pack of beer, singing something by Barry Manilow. It made me smile until he saw me and stood, nearly falling off the rock. He did not care what he put in his body.

"Hey, Watergirl. Want a beer?"

"Hey Quarterback. Where's Sharky?" I sat down with a sigh as memories of him, me and the rock came back. We used to hang out there, back in the days when we hung out. I took the beer but didn't open it.

"She's with Sean."

"Hm. I don't think so."

"I mean," he said, leaning against me with his shoulder. "You and Sean aren't together, and neither am I and Sharky. We broke up. We're finished. On New Year's Eve."

"I'm sorry," I said, and I almost was. "You can find someone better."

He shook his head. "Yeah, maybe. Lots of fish in the

sea, right? How about you? I heard you went on a date and broke the guy's nose." He nudged me again, heavily that time. He was very sloshed. Unfortunately, reminding me of fish in the sea while I sat on the rock looking out at the lake reminded me of the monster.

"And monsters in the lake," I said, searching the glistening dark water for signs of the creature. "It was a bloody nose. He tried to kiss me. You know what happens."

He nodded. "Did you kiss Sean?"

I shook my head no. "Do you believe in monsters?"

"Sometimes. Not usually though, because I lack imagination. It's a good thing. Do you remember the nightmares I used to have? I told you about some of them; you probably forgot. Sean still likes you."

I groaned and put my head on my knees. I was ridiculously tempted to tell drunk Cole all about Sean and his gills. Instead I elbowed him.

"You should go home while you're still conscious. I hope you're not driving because you're wasted."

"You could drive me. Are you going to sing?" I stared at him, the only person I'd ever brought to the lake while I sang. "I'll sit here and listen," he said, leaning back on his elbows. He should have been cold in his jacket, but maybe the alcohol kept him warm.

"I can't..." but I could. I turned away from him, staring at the lake, at the pale reflection of the moon staring back at me. The song had threads of Sean's music, but something else, misery, but something exulting at the same time. Was it the wonder of gills, of something magical touching my life even if it came in the package of too cold Sean?

I didn't know, it didn't matter, nothing mattered but the music and the water where it stirred beneath me, rustling along with my song until my breath came short and I felt Cole's hand on my shoulder, surprisingly steady for how drunk he was.

I blinked until my vision cleared then gave him a slight smile. He pulled me over until I had my head against his shoulder and his arm went around my waist, familiar but really wrong at the same time.

I pulled away. He wasn't my best friend any more. He wasn't the person I went to when I needed to freak out. That was Sean. Why, I had no idea because he wasn't exactly pleasant or even the same species, but it was how it was.

"I've got to go."

"Yeah," he agreed, but he sounded disappointed.

He moved to get up, tripped, and ended up sprawled on top of me. My head hit the ground with a thud.

"You okay?" he asked in a wheezing whisper then started laughing. He couldn't get off me while he was laughing, and I couldn't get him off me because he was too heavy.

"Cole, seriously, you smell like cheap beer. Will you please get off me?" He only laughed louder, howling like the drunk idiot he was. "Cole!" I said, elbowing him somewhere in his body, but it didn't make a dent.

Behind me I heard something that made me very cold and very still. The hissing I'd had multiple nightmares about came from the lake, close behind me. It couldn't get me up on the rock though. The hissing came closer and closer while I felt my insides quiver with fear. I had to get Cole off of me. I twisted under him while I levered him up, ending up half on, half off him, just in time to see the claws scrabbling on the edge of the rock. Awesome. The bulbous head was next, black reflective eyes glittering at me until it came all the way up. It hissed, only slightly louder than the wind. It looked from me to Cole where he lay, still laughing, then made a move.

I pulled us both back, off the rock and into the weeds, but not before tendrils of what looked like seaweed lashed out at Cole, ripping the beer from his hands and leaving a bloody weal down his arm.

He finally saw the monster and with that, he was practically sober. The monster hesitated on the edge of the rock, over us while we backed away, tripping on uneven ground until we turned and ran, never looking back until we made it to the road, but even then, I didn't argue when Cole grabbed my bike and threw it into the back of his truck.

I grabbed his keys when he started for his door, and he climbed through, into the passenger side, while I put the truck in gear and peeled out, away from the lake and the monster.

It hadn't touched me but Cole held his hand to his arm where blood dripped down to his elbow.

Its eyes had bothered me most. Something about them was so human. If there were people walking around with gills, monsters swimming around in lakes, what other crap was there that I couldn't see? It was a question I wasn't ready to ask.

I pulled up in front of Cole's house then started out but he grabbed my shoulder.

"I wasn't drunk enough for us both to imagine that."

I took his hand off of me. "I am not talking about anything tonight. I'm going home." I handed him his keys and slammed the door.

Chapter 28

I spent the next day sleeping, that and trying to write the music from the night before, Sean's and the stuff I'd sung at the lake. I couldn't focus on the monster, on what it meant. The next day at school Cole nodded at me but didn't try to talk, which was fine because I still didn't want to deal with it. If I did, then I'd have to talk to Oliver or Sean, Sean who might know something about monsters in lakes, and I couldn't think about that.

It was bad enough walking through the halls and hearing the echo, 'slut' as I went. I went on one date, and I was a slut. Nice. Okay. I was in Sean's bed. I shook my head because that whole thing was beyond explanation. I didn't even understand how all of that went down.

At my locker, I stood there staring at the mess on the bottom, wondering if I'd actually left it that bad before break or if it had magically compounded. Flop put her arm around me.

"How are you doing Gen? I don't care what they say. I don't believe a word of it."

I sighed. "Well, you were sort of there, you can't not believe that I was in his bed." I shuddered.

"Yeah, but there was a reason for it, like you passed out or something. Probably hit your head at the bottom of the pool and he had to resuscitate you and then you went into shock so he had to get you warm. He was naked because... You have to help me out a little bit."

I grabbed her by the shoulders and stared into her beautiful, limpid grey blue eyes. "He asked me to dance, we danced then we went to his room and got naked. I'm a slut, what can I say?"

She blinked at me then cocked her head to the side. "Huh. So, are you obsessed with him, or what?"

I shook my head and stepped back from her. "You don't mind if I'm a slut? Flop, you rock. No, I'm not obsessed. I mean, it's Sean. What girl wouldn't get naked with him if given the opportunity."

Her eyes widened. "So, you actually saw him naked? Did you pass out? What was it like? I mean, before Junie had to tell you that she's together with Tuba? And how weird is that? But perfect because now we're all dating people."

I crouched in front of my locker and began pulling out papers that I should have turned in months ago. I could throw them away. Nice. "It was weird. It was definitely something worth seeing." I shook my head. "I didn't even think about Oliver with all of that going on. So, that was good. I guess. Yeah, weird about Tuba, but I kind of saw it coming, at least I knew that he liked her."

"I had no clue. So, are you and Sean together for real this time?"

I exhaled and opened my mouth to tell her no, absolutely not, but a CD case dropped on my pile of discards and I looked up to see Sean leaning against the locker beside mine, smiling at Flop. Smiling.

"What did she say?" he asked her like I wasn't right there.

She blushed and edged away from him. "Um, I'll see you guys later."

I glared at him while she took off. "You didn't have to scare her away."

"I brought you the music. Did you tell her I bribed you with music? She would understand that better than whatever else you told her."

"Who gets naked for music?"

"You, although you weren't technically..."

"Sean," Bernice's voice set my teeth on edge. I turned away from them, shoving everything back into my locker, except the CD, that I put into my bag.

"I'm busy," he said coldly to her then touched my hair.

No. I was not playing this game again. I stood up, turned around and was going to tell her, him and the rest of the world that we weren't together and wouldn't ever be, then saw who was with Bernice. I stopped breathing.

I didn't do anything when Sean wrapped his arm around my shoulders and pulled me against him while I stared at Oliver.

"Come on Gen," Sean said dragging my unresponsive body away from Bernice and Oliver. "We're going to be late for class."

I couldn't turn my head to stare at Oliver with the way Sean had me. I couldn't do anything but let Sean tow me to class. I leaned against him, glad he could block out the rest of the world, glad he was immune to obsession. I wouldn't have been able to resist Oliver, wouldn't have been able to do anything, not without time to prepare, even then, Oliver with his glossy black hair, diamond green eyes and warm smile had completely blown me away. I had to see him again. I had to touch him and make sure he was real. I had to…

I turned my face into Sean's chest and listened to his heart pound. After a few minutes of that I tuned into the rest of the world and pulled away from him, realizing that I'd just had a very public display of affection with Sean. Awesome.

"We're not dating," I told him as I took a step back and ran into the propped open door of my English class.

"No. We're not. If we were on a date, we wouldn't be in separate classes. See you later, Gen," he said, turning and walking off, leaving me with a class full of stares to deal with as I stumbled to my chair. Oliver was back. I did not want Oliver back. Five seconds of my seeing Oliver and everything with Sean imploded.

After first period I ran into Cole in the hallway. He stood in the middle of the hall, not moving while a stream of humanity trailed on either side of him.

"Cole?" I said when he didn't move or seem to notice me. I looked down and saw his books scattered around him while he held his arm, the one the monster had hurt.

"Cole?" I ducked around him so I could see his face, but when he looked up at me, I didn't feel any better. "Come on," I said, dragging him into the choir room right across the hall since no one would be there at that hour. He stumbled but didn't fall until I got him into a chair. I took a deep breath before I forced my shaky hands to roll up his sleeve. The sight of his swollen, red arm made me more nauseous than seeing Oliver had.

Oliver. He knew medical stuff and might know more about this than normal, human doctors.

"Cole, I'm going to go get help, okay?" His face was pale, and I could see traces of blue veins up his neck. It couldn't be a good sign.

I left the room, closing the door behind me. I ran through the halls to Oliver's locker then stopped when I saw Bernice, not him. She saw me, and the way she looked at me stunned me. When had she started really hating me? I spun around and saw Sean walking away from me. How had I missed him?

"Sean!" I raced after him then caught his hand in mine when he stopped.

He turned to me with a smile. "Finally playing your part with conviction? That's unexpected, Watergirl."

My part? Oh, as his girlfriend. I'd argue about that another time. I leaned up and took his face in my hands then whispered in his ear. "Cole's bad. The lake creature got him the other night. He's in the choir room. Oliver said he was good healing people, like you are with bikes. I don't know if he just said that to check me for gills, but Cole needs something. What do I do? It's swollen and he's turning blue."

His hand came around my back, pulling his body against mine. "Oliver's good. I'll bring him with me. You stay with Cole. Don't let anyone see him. Okay?"

I nodded, feeling the roughness of his face against my cheek before I pulled away, gave him what I hoped was an alluring smile, and took off, trying to look happy in spite of everything, in spite of Bernice's clenched teeth and not knowing what I'd find in the choir room.

Cole was still there, but his head lolled back in his chair while his arms had fallen limply at his sides. I closed the door behind me, leaning against it for just a second before I crossed the room to kneel in front of him. His eyes were closed and the blue veins had spread across his face.

I should have made him go to a doctor or told Sean about it, something. I hadn't wanted to think about it, to worry about it, to face the fact that there was something in the lake and something had to be done about it.

The door opened and Oliver entered followed closely by Sean. I pulled back from Cole when Oliver approached, opening his backpack as he crossed the floor. He checked Cole's vital statsitics while I hovered, fighting the need to be close to Oliver, like we needed that.

"Genevieve, I don't need any distractions while I help your friend. Could you give me some space?"

I nodded and made myself leave, finding Sean where he stood beside the door like a burly guard.

"I'm sorry. I was stupid. I should have told…"

"You're not stupid. You don't trust me. I'm sorry that you couldn't come to me before this."

He pulled me into a hug and the desperation for Oliver clogging my throat disappeared. I leaned against his chest while the fear and worry melted away.

"I need a jar or some kind of large container," Oliver said, his voice filling my brain for a second, confusing my body. Why would I hear Oliver and feel Sean?

Sean pulled a water bottle out of his pack and drank it until it was empty then threw it across the room to Oliver who caught it with barely a glance in our direction. I stayed where I was, with my back against Sean while I watched Oliver and Cole.

So, I was definitely not going to be a doctor. Oliver punched holes into Cole's arm then the blood came out, well, not blood because it was blue, and blood is red, well, once it hits oxygen it's red. Oliver started swabbing his arm all over with something that smelled like pumpkin pie. I would probably never eat it again. Cole started twitching, which I hoped was a good sign. It wasn't long after the arm hole punching that Cole's face started to look normal. He was sitting up, annoying Oliver who kept telling him to hold still.

I exhaled, realizing that I hadn't been breathing much and felt Sean's hands on my shoulders, squeezing out tension. So weird. After that Oliver helped Cole up, telling him that he would take him home.

That left me and Sean with seven minutes left until the next class. I stared at the clock for a few seconds, still standing closer to him than I had to.

"So, do you want to talk about it?" he said as I forced myself to edge away from him.

"New Year's Eve, after you dropped me off..."

"Actually, I meant about how you feel."

I turned to stare at him, but it was the same cold non-human with no possible interest in my feelings. "And you care, why?"

He raised an eyebrow. "You look like you're about to go into shock, cold clammy skin, pale, you mentioned that you'd rather I didn't give you CPR again."

I rolled my eyes. "I feel sick. Half from the blood, or whatever that blue stuff was, and half from Oliver. I wish I'd known he was coming back. If you hadn't come when you had... And Bernice hates me. But Cole. I feel so guilty about everything. I knew there was a monster in the lake, I saw it, but then, on New Year's Eve when he was on top of me and wouldn't get off, I heard the hissing." I had to stop so that I could take deep breaths. "It was a blob with these weird seaweed whips, and that's what got Cole. I should have taken him to the hospital or something. I didn't want to talk to you any more that night, not after everything... It was too much. The monster was too much. I kind of shut down and did nothing. Like usual. All day yesterday I stayed in bed and tried not to think. I didn't talk to anyone, not Flop, my dad, because what am I supposed to say? Either I'm crazy or the rest of the world is. So, yeah. I'm a little bit freaked out."

"Hmm," he said noncommittally.

"Do you know what's in the lake?" I asked, studying

his perfectly chiseled face for clues.

"To me the injury looked similar to a sting ray or jelly fish, something that attacks the nervous system. I suppose I might as well tell you, the Vashni have some creatures they've bred with tentacles that could do that kind of damage: ripping open the skin and injecting it with venom."

"Venom. Vashni. Your mother..." I would have fallen over if he hadn't grabbed me around the waist, holding me against his not at all cold body. "Your mother knew about my mother. What if she put the monster in the lake, or at least knew about it? What if the monster dragged my mother under the water?" My voice was barely audible with my face smashed against his chest between his pectorals.

"It's an interesting theory," Sean said. "It had to get there somehow. It didn't seem to be breathing air, did it?" I shook my head, still against his chest. "So the questions are, how long has it been there, who put it there and why, and of course, what exactly it is."

"So," I said, pushing away from him so I could be like him, rational, analytical, cold. "How do we find out?"

He frowned. "The easy way? Capture it and dissect it. The more difficult way would be to ask my dad."

"Your dad..."

"It's time for class, Gen. Do you want me to walk you?"

I opened my mouth to say no, but then shrugged instead. Not being his girlfriend at that point would be stupid, particularly when I still felt dizzy and stuff.

At lunch Sean sat beside me before anyone else joined my table. I stared at him, waiting for him to talk about his dad, or Cole, something like that.

"Have you heard of Messleraim?" I blinked at him while Junie sat down, trying to look like she was cool with Sean being at our table. He pulled out his iPod and slid it to me. "Most people hate it. It can get discordant."

I put his buds in my ears then slid mine over to him because you know, music manners were all about sharing, so long as you weren't file sharing, because that was unethical, like competing in swimming with gills. The music was something like metallic orchestra but had weird moments of other that sounded ambient, like underwater echoes before the screaming guitars took over again. It sounded like a battle, an epic fight with blood, gore, timpani, all underwater. It was long, but I didn't mind because I could stab my cauliflower in time to the swelling violence while Sean listened to my playlist.

Maybe it took fifteen minutes to finish the song, and then I hit pause and pulled out the buds.

"Wow, Sean. This is weird." I meant it as a compliment. He smiled, only a little bit but that probably meant it was genuine. Like I knew.

"Thanks. I liked your 'Egotistical Jerks' list. Everyone's got to have one of those."

I blinked at him while I tried not to blush. "Doesn't everyone?"

"It's almost as good as your, 'Stupidly Obsessed' list."

"I do not have a 'Stupidly Obsessed' list," I said, grabbing back my iPod. There, right above 'Egotistical Jerks' was 'Stupidly Obsessed', just like he'd said. I stared at him. "You made me a list."

"Everyone's got to have one of those." He smiled at me, a full smile that showed his teeth. For some reason it reminded me that he wasn't quite human and also that the rest of the table was listening to every word we said.

"So, what's on your too-weird-to-be-human list?" I asked him, forcing my own smile.

"The same thing that's on yours," he said easily, sitting back.

"Wow, you guys are so romantic," Flop said, staring at me like 'what are you doing?' "Matching playlists, huh? That's a fun idea, don't you think so, Logan?" She elbowed him and he nodded, like a puppet doll.

"Awesome."

"So, Sean," Junie said, ignoring the whole romantic playlist debate. "Thanks for that email. I applied for the internship. I've never heard of that company, but it's huge. I really hope that I get it."

Sean nodded.

"It's during band camp, right?" Tuba asked, looking a little nervous, like maybe he shouldn't bring up whether or not their schedules were compatible, like it would be too controlling or something.

She beamed at him and held his hand, knotting her fingers in his. "Yes. The session I signed up for is during your yearly trek to marching madness. Like I would miss spending the summer with you outside of the penitentiary, I mean, educational facility."

The way they smiled at each other, not obsessed, 'I need you or I'm going to die,' but just so freaking cute and perfect, like how did it take them so long to figure this out when it seemed obvious afterwards. I grabbed Sean's hand and squeezed. He squeezed back and I sat there, encased in cold steel that slowly eased all life out of my fingertips.

It wasn't the most pleasant lunch, but I didn't think about Oliver or Cole very much at all. Some things were more important than pleasant.

It was in the parking lot after school that I almost died. Sharky might have felt bad afterwards, but when it came to me on my bike, she simply ignored us, making me get out of the way. That was usually fine, but with the icy January weather, I barely got out of the way of her car, swerving then completely losing it, sliding across the ground with my bike on top of me.

Sean pulled up in his car while I sat there, trying to ignore the people staring at me. "Nice bike weather. I'm willing to give you both a ride home."

"You're willing? Wow. How could I possibly refuse such a generous offer?"

"I have no idea. It would probably take a stronger soul than you. Do you need help getting it in the trunk?" he asked the last bit with a kind of sigh.

I stared at him while the ice melted and soaked into my pants and underwear. If I sat in his car, I'd probably get it wet. I smiled at him and got up. "No, I'm fine. Just pop it open," I called shoving my bike towards the back. It took me a little bit of fiddling to get the whole thing in. Sean ended up coming to see what I was doing, and slipped it

in as easily as if he carried my bike around all the time.
Whatever. "Thanks," I said with as big a smile as would fit
on my face. "You're such an amazing boyfriend." I reached
up and put my hands around his neck, staring deeply into
his blue eyes. "I could stand here with you all day, but I'm
going to try and get at least some of my Biology homework
done tonight." At the thought of Biology, I couldn't fake my
bliss.

"Do you have work?" he asked as we got in. He didn't
try and open my door for me or anything. I settled back in
his seat, perfectly content with whatever mess I left behind.

"Tomorrow and Saturday. After Holidays are slow, not
much hours. Where is your music?" I asked after he pulled
out and there was still silence.

"You actually have an egotistical jerks playlist."

I frowned at him. Where had that come from? "You
want to listen to it in stereo? 'I'm too sexy' would definitely
get me in the mood for homework."

"Why do you have it?"

I felt myself blushing. "None of your business."

"You're saying that it doesn't refer specifically to me?"

I closed my eyes and tried to think how to say it. "Yes,
it does. Okay? You're the hot jerk, and I'm the weird idiot.
So, I made a playlist. It's what I do."

"I suppose since you allow me to be hot that I shouldn't
mind the jerk."

"I wouldn't think you'd care enough to mind anything
at all."

That shut him up for a few minutes. "Just because I
don't get close to humans doesn't mean I don't care."

"Then you should act like it. Maybe you are acting like
it." I shrugged. "So, Sean, what does caring look like to
you?"

His glance was a frown. "I think that the problem is
that the caring and being a jerk go together for me. I don't
tell other people that they're idiots. You should feel special.
I also don't let other people hug me."

"Let me hug you..." I sighed. "Right. I feel totally special. The only girl you've shown your gills to, or taken to

meet your mother, I mean, wow. I'm the specialest girl in the whole world."

He made that sound, the choking that was probably a laugh. "I'm not the only thing that finds you special." I got chills when he said that. When I looked over his face was serious. "The thing in the lake, it's you that it comes for."

"Can we go back to talking about how you're such a jerk?"

"How about we talk about how to keep you alive?"

"I'm open to ideas."

He nodded then pulled up to my house. My dad's car was in the driveway so he was home. "I could help you with your homework."

I froze mid door opening. "What? How would that keep me alive?"

"While working on that problem, I could help you pass your classes. Biology fascinates me. I might be able to explain things in a way that you found accessible."

"Don't you have things to do?"

He shrugged. "I have homework too."

We stared at each other until I realized that I had to say something. "Sure." I'd half expected myself to make excuses, but I felt kind of lame after the playlist. Lame enough to invite Sean into my cramped, messy house.

What I didn't expect was my dad freaking out. When he saw me and that I'd brought someone in, at first he smiled and was all, hi, how you doing, then he saw that it was Sean and it was like someone flipped on the lethal assassin button and my dad was stalking towards Sean like he was an armed intruder or something.

I jumped back, keeping between my dad and Sean.

"Hi, Mr. Castle," Sean said, extending his hand like my dad wasn't glaring at him.

My dad glared at the hand, then glanced at me. I mouthed, 'dad, what's with you,' and he kind of frowning took Sean's hand in a firm grip that he didn't release.

"You're father is Reeve Fielding. Aren't you a little old for my daughter?"

Sean blinked. Apparently being disliked by parents

was new for him. "I'm a senior and she's a junior, but it's hardly..."

"You're eighteen, and she's underage. It doesn't matter what grade she's in." I wanted somebody to kill me. First he was encouraging me to go partying, then he tried to bust Sean for accosting a minor. Awesome.

"Dad, we're going to do homework," I said, wrapping my hands around his arm. He had a lot of muscle for an old guy. "Next time, we'll go to his house, where you won't be able to supervise with your overprotective paranoia."

"Next time?"

"Sean is my boyfriend," I said, glaring at my dad. I wanted to glare at Sean too, but whatever. "That means that you'll be seeing a lot of him whether you like it or not."

Sean and my dad stared at me like I was the one with gills. My dad's face got red and his eyes looked like they were going to pop out of his head, but then with a deep breath, it was all gone and he smiled at Sean then stepped back without ripping Sean's arm out of its socket.

"Well, that changes things." My dad's voice was not friendly, not really in spite of the smile. He glanced at me. "I guess it's too late to forbid you to grow up and date."

I laughed, or tried to, but it came out like one of Sean's. "Yeah, so, we'll be in the kitchen," I said, dragging Sean with me.

Homework wasn't the world's most romantic thing, particularly at my house, at the kitchen table where there were still dishes from breakfast. Crap.

"We really should have done this at your house," I said shoving things into the dishwasher.

"You saw my room." He said while he helped with the dishes like there was nothing embarrassing about being a complete slob. He turned on the radio. The only stations that came in were cheesy country. We listened to it until the kitchen was as good as the peeling linoleum would let it be, and we could sit down to homework.

I opened my book and immediately wanted to shut it. He leaned over and started explaining stuff. At first it made no sense, but as he kept talking it was like that time in the pool, where the rest of the world drifted away and I could focus on his words. A few things clicked, which was good for me. After I had enough comprehension that I could do my assignment, we spent the next three hours in deep contemplative silence with the radio a low background noise.

My dad kept coming in, to get stuff, but how many drinks did he need? It was so embarrassing. On the positive side, I couldn't remember the last time I did all of my homework. Whatever else Sean was, human or not, he was definitely good for my grades.

Chapter 29

Days fell into a pattern, Sean in the morning, Sean at lunch, Sean in the evening, or earlier if I didn't have work or choir and he didn't have swim stuff. I had a really great time embracing him in public and feeling him stiffen up when he didn't expect it. I especially enjoyed calling him, 'baby'. He hated it more than anything, except for when I made him cookies. I didn't really cook, so my cookies were the kind from the frozen section where you stick them on a pan and into the oven. Sean forced himself to eat one when I brought him a stack. I didn't have to fake my joy when I gave him those.

The second time I did it, he took one with a sigh as other girls watched with obvious jealousy. Oh to be the girl who gave Sean cookies. "You might be taking this girl-friend thing a little too seriously."

"I guess I won't show you the tattoo I got last weekend then."

"When did you have time? If I have to sit through another beach movie this Friday, I'm going to tattoo my eyes shut."

"That might be a hard look to pull off, but if anyone can do it, you can. You're not looking forward to the Bette Midler movie? Maybe you'll remember some swim stuff you have to do."

"Maybe. Maybe I could make you dinner."

I grimaced. "Yeah. You can show me how it's done. Linguine with eel heads and raw clam soup."

He stepped forward, close enough that I stumbled back, feeling the locker behind me. His eyes were astonishingly blue, his body massive and impenetrable, blocking out the rest of the world.

"How do you do that?" I asked, shamelessly staring at him.

"I don't. Eel heads aren't in my repertoire. I would actually make a dinner that you would appreciate. That is the purpose of gifts, isn't it?"

"I mean block out everything else," I said, ignoring his jab as I held my plastic container of cookies between us. "Even my obsession isn't noticeable when you're so close. Do you think it has something to do with your immunity to…" I didn't say the kiss of madness because someone might have been listening to us. Not that it would mean anything to anyone, but it would be weird. Not like me baking cookies for Sean wasn't weird, or me and Sean standing so close… Anyway. No need to be weirder than necessary.

"Do I?" As he frowned down at me, I realized he was looking at my mouth. Of course it was because I said something about his immunity, but it felt like he was actually thinking about my lips, something about me and kissing. My breathing got a little bit shallow as he leaned closer.

"Dinner sounds great," I said in a slightly hysterical loud voice that made him step away from me.

"Good. Then you can meet my dad. You can wear something nice if you'd like."

Okay. What did that mean? In Flop's opinion it meant that Sean was really serious about me. That couldn't be it, but wearing something nice would be okay.

Flop's cousin had a skirt, long from when she'd gone through her goth stage that I wore with a turtleneck. Flop told me that I looked 'nice', which was good, and this time I wouldn't have to worry about plunging necklines.

I'd let my dad think I was at Flop's for movie night, so when Sean picked me up he wouldn't try to arm wrestle him or something fun like that.

When Sean pulled up, I was waiting inside the door so I could rush outside then climb into his car, giving him a nervous smile. "Hey, baby. You're looking hot."

He gave me a flat look with his chilling blue eyes that

made me want to giggle, just to see how cold his eyes could possibly get.

"You're looking rather warm yourself."

I felt ridiculous in my turtleneck and parka while he sat there, letting the engine idle while we stared at each other. He had a jacket on over his button up, which only emphasized his shoulders. Not that his shoulders weren't prominent no matter what he wore.

He turned his focus on the road and pulled out, sending me against the back of the seat.

"Nice jacket."

He made some sound that might have meant anything.

"So, what's for dinner? Not eels, right?"

He gave another non-answer. Wow. This conversation was amazing.

"Can I ask your dad about the lake and the monster?" I was sure that would get a reaction out of him, but he only shrugged.

"If you'd like."

"Are there any topics that I shouldn't discuss?"

"You're welcome to talk about anything, except..." He gave me a frown that made him look like one of those soap opera doctors right before they tell you that someone died. Also the same look they used to tell you that someone came back to life.

"No gills. I already promised."

He made that noise of non-communication, and I wished I dared turn on his radio, but if I messed up his music, I would never forgive myself.

We pulled into the driveway of the architectural wonder protruding from the hills, geometric glass walls jutting into the sky like a drawing. I stared at it while we waited for the garage door to open.

"I have this feeling," I said as I tugged on the suddenly too tight neck of my borrowed sweater.

"How fascinating. What feeling, exactly?"

We pulled in, letting the garage close behind us. He hadn't moved yet, staring at me like we were having a really deep conversation. "He's not going to like me."

He shook his head as he got out. I quickly followed suit.

"And why would you care?" he asked, shutting his door with a solid thump.

Why did I care? I made my own noncommittal noise as I followed him through the garage door that led into a hall right off the living room.

The pool looked weird without anyone in it. The whole place felt empty.

"Sean." The voice was warm, the man who came down the stairs the embodiment of graceful down-to-earth goodness with his sandy blond hair and warm blue eyes. He held out his hand to me and shook it warmly, glancing at Sean before smiling at me. "Hello. I don't remember seeing you at any of the swim meets. I'm Reeve Fielding."

It struck me as an accusation, although how I got that, when he sounded so warm and the words weren't particularly insulting, I didn't know. I stammered about how I didn't make it to meets because of work and choir, but felt more idiotic than usual. He had all of Sean's chiseled perfection, but his smile was more accessible and charming, like Oliver.

"This is Genevieve Castle," Sean said putting a hand on my shoulder. I thought I saw a slight frown flicker on Sean's dad face as he saw that slight physical contact. "We've been dating for some time now."

"Genevieve Castle," Sean's dad murmured while the grip on my hand he still held tightened. "Let me look at the remarkable girl who managed to turn my son's head."

He gave me a look that seemed to pass through all the layers of me, stripping me to the basically ordinary, except in my extraordinary idiocy, girl who would never match his own brilliant, perfect son. I felt like time stopped as I shriveled up under his gaze.

Sean put a hand around my arm. "Dinner smells done. Genevieve, would you help me..."

"Son," Mr. Fielding said, pulling me away from Sean. "You wouldn't ask a guest to serve herself. I'll give young Miss Castle a tour while you worry about dinner."

I opened my mouth to protest, but Mr. Fielding tucked my hand into his arm and led me up the stairs, back in the direction he'd come from. My backwards look at Sean showed him at the bottom of the stairs, frowning up at me.

Mr. Fielding lectured me about the art hanging on the walls, about the architect who'd built the house from that vantage point, about the difficulties of finding really capable housekeepers, and he talked about Sean. Sean went to museums and had picked out most of the brilliant pieces. Sean had a wonderful eye for design and architecture. Sean was going to design the most brilliant machinery ever imagined someday. I nodded in agreement but every word pressed home the point: I wasn't good enough for Sean. I wasn't brilliant. I wasn't an artist. I wasn't the captain of the swim team that the whole school respected. I wasn't going to be Valedictorian. I wasn't going to the college of my choice because of my perfect grades and all around brilliant accomplishments. I wasn't only a mere human; I was a lousy one at that.

I wasn't sure how he did it because his words were nothing but positive about Sean, and that was fine, but all the same, I felt smaller and smaller until by the time I heard Sean's low voice calling us for dinner, I was ready to run as far away from both of them as I could. Mr. Fielding dragged me to the dining room. Okay, he didn't drag me, I walked, but it took all of my notoriously small will not to bite his hand and make a run for it.

I stared at Sean, pleading wordlessly for him to end the pain, to give me food poisoning as quickly as possible so that I could leave. Unfortunately we hadn't worked very much on silent communication. He only raised his eyebrow as his father, perfect gentleman that he was, emphasis on perfect, held out my chair for me.

Dinner was beautiful, the glass plates and glasses a beautiful echo of the mirrored walls and the glass wall that was the opposite side of the aquarium I'd seen from the pool room. The food would have been better if I hadn't taken the wrong fork for my salad and had Sean's dad gently correct me with that wonderfully warm smile. It was like eating inside of a fishbowl beside two sharks with movement all around me, water, glass, it was enough to bring back some of my old water issues.

"Miss Castle, I've been trying to think," Sean's dad said with that smile. "What you have in common with my son."

I took a break from stirring the gorgeous noodles in exquisite white sauce around my plate to stare at him. What did I have in common with Sean? He was better in every way. Even when it came to music, which I considered my thing, he knew cooler and more obscure stuff than I did. It was time to get on with things. This pretending that Sean and I were actually together had to end. Sean had said that I could ask.

I shrugged. "Water. Sean fished me out of the pool the same way Oliver dragged me out of the lake. I find myself constantly drawn to liquid. The really weird thing isn't the way water sucks me in though, it's the monster I saw in Stinky Lake. Sean said you might know something about it."

He blinked, but the smile didn't twitch from his mouth. "You say that you saw a monster?"

"It was night, but the moon was out. It was like a big blob with fangs. Have you ever heard about anything like that before? It hissed and its eyes were enormous, but something about them reminded me of seal's eyes. You know how there's something human about them?"

Sean's dad wasn't smiling anymore, but the look that replaced his smile wasn't any better.

"You're saying that there's something in the lake where your mother was killed?"

I blinked. He was the second person who acted like her death was intentional, and he knew enough about me to know about her.

"Oliver thought there was something there. To humor him, I had the lake dragged. There was nothing. There is nothing," he said stressing every syllable. Then gave me a gentle smile. "Maybe whatever you thought you saw was something perfectly ordinary, but if you'd been drinking or were overtired…"

"It left a vicious gash on her friend's arm," Sean said in a cold voice that was refreshing compared to his father's. "It would be difficult for Genevieve to imagine that."

Sean's father frowned in concern. "We'll have to look into that then. I hope you're all right."

And that was it. We ate in silence for a few minutes while I felt stupid for asking him. Obviously, he wasn't going to tell me what he knew, if he knew anything, and in the meantime I'd gone from being an idiotic piece of trash to being a dangerous idiotic piece of trash.

When he asked me where I planned to go to college, I shook my head.

"You're not planning on college?"

"No, I'm just a junior. I have another year to think about it."

He blinked at me. "I see."

The two words didn't say much, but his tone said everything. I was even less motivated and more of a loser than he'd expected.

That was all the talking I did. I'd expected to get something out of him, either surprise, horror, or something, but that gentle concern and reassurance, 'we'll have to look into that,' stopped me dead. I didn't belong in that perfect house with those perfect men, both using their knives with amazing dexterity. Of course, the fact that they were such beautiful specimens of humanity when they weren't even human was hardly fair.

In the last few weeks Sean had become an extension of my life, more than an acquaintance or someone I liked to irritate, a friend. There at the table, he seemed like an alien. No, I was the alien. I felt like the one who didn't belong, the one who didn't fit and should leave before I put ripples in his world that messed up the perfection.

Sean's dad kept conversation going as I stirred the noodles on my plate. I felt smaller and smaller and smaller until at some point I was sure that I would disappear completely. It couldn't happen soon enough. By the time dinner was over, and we left Sean's dad to do the dishes, I was ready to drown myself in the pool.

"Do you want to do something?" Sean asked as we stood in the living room, by the beautiful blue water. Who had a pool in their living room? Oh, right. Gill people.

"I have this headache and this big thing I have to do. You should just take me home."

"Yeah?" He stood beside me with his arms crossed over his chest while he studied the pool as carefully as I did. "I thought you were spending the night at Flop's."

I blinked at him then looked away. "Um, yeah. Right. I'll do the thing with her."

"Gen," he said, grabbing my hand.

I had to look up at him, which was a mistake because he was so perfect for someone else.

"You could do the thing with me. Come on."

Did his eyes look slightly less icy than usual? My heart thumped as he squeezed my hand then dropped it. I followed him back into the garage. He opened his car door for me like we were on a real date, which was pretty weird, but whatever, and then he got in and turned on the engine.

Out in the night, he took his time driving. When he should have taken a right turn, he drove straight instead.

"Where are we going?" I asked, frowning at him.

"The lake. You were going to sneak out tonight, weren't you?"

I blinked at him. Was I? I hadn't thought that far, but honestly, yeah, I probably would somehow have found myself out there.

"No. Of course not. There's a dangerous monster in the lake."

He raised an eyebrow. "Do you really care about that? You're compelled to go there. The lake, the monster, something has a hold on you. It's not stupidity that drags you there, it's something else."

I scowled. It was my lake, my obsession, who was he to analyze it? "Awesome, so I'm a lake addict? You'll be my, what do they call it, enabler?"

"You shouldn't go there alone."

"What do you know about it? You've never seemed curious before. Oliver didn't see anything, there was no proof, but he still had your dad drag the lake."

He smiled, but it wasn't a nice smile. "You may not have noticed, but I'm not exactly like Oliver."

"If you don't care about whether it's real, why do you want to come with me?"

"To keep you safe."

I threw my hands up in the air. "You make no sense. Why would you care? Oh, that's right, because I'm the most broken thing you've seen and you're trying to fix me."

His jaw tightened, but he was still smiling. "Whatever you say. This is your compulsion, I'm only along for the ride."

"What's that supposed to mean?" I was breathing hard and gripped the seat as tightly as I could.

"It means we're here. I'm here. With you."

He braked the car with a jerk. His smile never quivered no matter how much I glared at him. I folded my arms over my chest. I hadn't told him I wanted to go to the lake. I did though. I could feel it eating at me around the edges of my mind. I had to sing. I had to get rid of the pain.

I stared ahead at where the headlights lit the weeds poking up from the white drifts of snow. I didn't have to sing if I didn't want to. Sean was wrong. So why was my hand inching towards the handle?

"Speaking of Oliver, did you have a nice vacation with all those gill people?"

"It was instructive."

"Could you be less specific, please? All those details kill me."

His smile tightened a notch then the headlights flickered off and I was left in the shadowy car with nothing but Sean and the wind as it whistled around us.

"It's not your world to understand."

I flinched. "No, it's not. So, the lake is my world. You don't belong here."

"I'm the one with gills."

"And I'm the one with the compulsion."

"Do you really want me to leave you out here in the dark, in the snow, without a bike or a car to get you home?"

I nodded. "Yes."

"If you think I'm leaving you here by yourself, you don't know me very well."

"Is that an invitation? Fine, Sean. Tell me all about yourself. What makes you tick? Oh, right. You can't, because it's none of my business. I don't belong in your world, human or otherwise, and I certainly don't belong with you." I was out of the car, stumbling up the bank in the dark without a clue where I was going, but it didn't matter so long as it was away from him.

The lake tugged at me, guiding my feet in the dark before a beam of light shone in front of me as Sean came behind me with a flashlight. I didn't say anything, because he'd made it clear that talking didn't make a difference. Maybe I'd shove him off the rock into the lake so I could sing in peace while he swam to shore. We crunched over the two inches of snow and frozen weeds to the water's edge. I stood there staring as Sean shone his flashlight on the surface of the slick, iced over water.

My stomach twisted as I closed my eyes. It wasn't my lake when it was frozen. I needed it, needed to sing, to forget about being too human for Sean and not human enough for the rest of the world. I needed the water to move, to sing back to me, to tell me all the things I had no words for, but instead there was nothing but ice.

I stepped out onto the slick surface while the wind whistled around me. I didn't feel the cold, not unless it was the cold inside of me. Sean's voice was carried away from me by the wind as I walked. I forgot about him, not caring if he followed me or if the ice was solid enough for my weight. My sob surprised me. I had no business crying over ice. I forced words out of my throat instead, a song about betrayal, loneliness, misery and pain. My voice came strong, loud, drowning out the wind until a sound like a gunshot cracked through the air.

I gasped and heard Sean's voice in the distance right before the ice beneath me split open to swallow me.

Chapter 30

I couldn't breathe. I tried to stay calm, to hold my breath, but it was hard not to thrash around in the icy water as my head became frozen solid. I tried to kick to the surface but my parka and the long skirt dragged me down. I was going to die in the dark, in the lake, because I was an idiot. I kicked harder, forcing my mind to focus, to hold onto my breath. I couldn't do it. I was going to die. The panic was so close to eating away my control, the scream that battled in my throat as my chest constricted from the cold, feeling like the breath in my lungs had frozen solid.

Something grabbed me under the arms in the dark death water then carried me up while I hung onto my not breathing. We exploded out into the night in a shower of ice close to the shore. I gasped in breaths, knowing that Sean must have rescued me, but then why was there a light bobbing towards me, and why was there hissing in my ears while something touched my cheek that burned, like a strand of fire?

I whimpered as I heard, "Gen?" from far away.

The monster shoved me across the ice, the surface scraping my hands and face until I came to a rest against the bank. I couldn't move, could barely shiver as Sean reached me. He pulled me up, off the ice and onto the snowy shore, touching my face, pushing my hair out of my eyes. I flinched when his thumb brushed the burn. I struggled to move, but my body felt so heavy, dragging me down and down back into the darkness, but at least this time there was air.

Things were fuzzy after that. I remembered Sean dragging me to my feet, making me move then carrying me to the car when I couldn't respond. He put me in then shoved my seat back so that when he climbed on top of me we'd both fit. He reached over to turn on the car, cranking up the heat before he stripped me out of my clothes.

I protested, but with limbs of ice, I had a hard time being assertive. I sat there, shivering in my underwear while he rubbed me down then wrapped me in his coat.

"Do you own any other underwear besides neon?" he demanded, sounding furious.

I shivered. He finally slid behind the wheel and peeled out, driving while he chewed on the inside of his cheek. Wow. I had no idea my underwear could disturb him so much.

"I n-n-never asked you to take off-f-f-f my clothes," I managed through chattering teeth.

"I'm sorry," he said, taking his hand off the stick shift to cover my knee. "Your love of pink and orange neon is fine. Don't listen to me. I thought I could handle it. I didn't think..." He tightened his jaw and I wondered if he was going to crack his teeth. "This one is all on me."

I was going to argue, but the shivering wasn't as bad, not when the numbness in my limbs was spreading through the rest of my body. Maybe that was a bad thing, maybe it would kill me, but I didn't seem to mind the idea of death very much, I mean, it was either die or gain feeling in my body, and that would hurt and I'd wish I were dead.

His parka was nice, soft and fluffy, the kind you wore on Arctic missions. I leaned against the door, thinking a few seconds of sleep wouldn't hurt, but then Sean pulled my face over, like it wasn't attached to my body, and scowled at me, so close I thought that maybe he lost his mind and was about to kiss me, but then he was driving, but with his hand against my neck so my head was against his shoulder instead of the door.

"Why would the monster save you?"

His voice came from inside of his chest where I could feel it through my forehead.

Why did the monster save me? It had burned me, but it hadn't seemed intentional.

"Doesn't like littering? My head hurts," I mumbled against his shirt.

He smelled good. Like wind and ice, and maybe a little bit like salt. I put my arms around his neck, sliding my face against his warm skin. It almost hurt to feel so much warmth against my non bloody cheek.

"All of you is going to hurt soon enough," he said as he pulled me onto his lap so that his arms could wrap around me as he drove.

It wasn't much longer before he pulled up to his house, waiting for the garage door to open before gunning the car up the drive. I shook my head, no way I was going to run into his father in my underwear, but I was hardly in fighting condition.

"Your dad…"

"He's gone away for the rest of the weekend to work. He's usually at work. No one's here except us." He already had me in his arms, so it wasn't much for him to carry me inside, hurrying, and then through a hall, up the stairs and into his bedroom, where I'd first discovered his gills. He flipped a switch and his bed folded up into the wall, revealing a tank full of dark water beneath it. He jumped in, carrying me down into the dark, warm, wet.

I was seriously sick of black water. I flailed then stopped because my arms weren't working right, and I was just going to die, but the water was really warm, so it would be drowning instead of freezing. Sean unzipped the parka underwater, giving me space to freak out, but with his hands on my skin, pushing me up so that my head broke the surface, I didn't need to panic. At least, not much.

His head came up a moment later, his eyes darker than usual while he held me up, pinned against the wall of the tank. I wasn't sure what to do, to think, what to freak out about first.

"You're going to be fine," he said, leaning his forehead against mine.

I made a seriously pathetic sound like a mewling kitten.

"I'm trying to warm you up slowly, keep you from going into shock." So, that was why his whole body pressed against mine. At least he had clothes on. I didn't, unless you counted neon underwear.

"Sean..." What to say? Where to begin? "You have a waterbed."

He laughed, the sound vibrating through his forehead into mine. "If you had gills you could see my real room. I read by phosphorescence."

"Doesn't it ruin your books?"

"There are different kinds of books." His eyes were really close to mine, okay, all of him was really close to me.

"Oh. So, your books have gills too?" That had to be the stupidest thing ever. "Nevermind. I'm sorry about the lake. Thanks for coming. I would be a solid block of ice if you hadn't been such a jerk."

"You're welcome. Being a jerk—it's what I do."

My thanks hadn't come out right, but I was still shivering.

"I didn't mean it that way."

I couldn't think straight, either from the shivering or the nearly naked with Sean pressing his whole body against mine while his forehead still rested on mine, like he was keeping me from facing it into his 'bed'. His mouth was too close, so close that I couldn't see it; I could just feel his breath on my lips.

"I meant, thanks for..."

"What happened?"

I stared into his eyes, watching them narrow as he waited for me to answer. "I fell through the ice."

"The ice split," he corrected, like there was a difference. "Like it wanted to eat you."

"Do we really have to give personality to a body of water? The whole thing's creepy enough as it is."

"As it is, I was sure the ice was thick enough to hold

you. Maybe the monster broke through, but…" He shook his head, no, which felt really weird against my skull. He should probably have backed off a little, but then, I had no idea how deep his 'bed' was, or if my limbs were capable of enough movement to keep me afloat on my own. Still, it was weird.

"But if it broke the ice, why did it bother to save me. It did save me, right? That's why my face hurts? The monster burned me while it was dragging me out of the lake?"

He nodded. He had to stop doing stuff like that when the movement brushed his nose against mine. Not that it meant anything, but it was so weird.

As feeling came into my body the weirdness escalated. I could feel the muscles under his t-shirt pressing against me. I felt soft, squishy all over compared to him. I really should have worked out more so that I could be a sleek athlete that matched him instead of whatever I was. What was I? Besides mostly naked. Maybe if I was less squishy the lake wouldn't want to eat me.

"Why does the lake want to eat me?"

"Why did the monster save you?"

"Why is your forehead still against mine?"

Silence, then he smiled a slow smile I'd never seen before. It was almost warm and made his eyes crinkle around the corners.

"I hadn't noticed."

"Really?"

That was depressing, but the depression didn't really hit as I stared at those crinkles. It was hardly fair that Sean could be even more… anyway. No point in going there. Maybe it wouldn't have mattered how toned my abs were, maybe he only noticed gills. Why did I care? It wasn't like he wasn't a complete jerk, albeit one who saved my life.

"No more than I notice anything else about you." What was that supposed to mean? "We could probably get you out now. You're not shaking so hard anymore."

"I'm not?"

"Are you ready?"

I opened my mouth to say, for what, but then he

pushed me up, his hands on my bare thighs until I sat
perched on the edge of the tank with only my ankles and
feet in the water. I fell over backwards onto the floor as
soon as he let go of me. I stared up at his ceiling feeling
particularly graceful while Sean made that sound, the
coughing snorting thing that he'd call laughter. It wasn't
attractive, except in its unattractiveness, which wasn't fair.
Nothing was fair, not when I had my feet in the air while
I flailed about, trying to get off the floor, but still not quite
capable of making my body respond the way it should.
Ugh.

I watched him roll over the edge to land beside me
dripping, while his grin was still that crinkle causing
thing. My heart pounded while he pulled me up, arm
wrapped around me while the bed descended, cutting off
the darkness of the tank.

He ran a towel over me then pushed me back into the
bed, beneath the blue duvet.

"Why does your blanket match your eyes?" Why did I
have to ask such stupid questions?

He blinked at me then shook his head. "I don't know.
Does it? I'm going to get you something hot to drink.
Chocolate?"

"Don't like chocolate," I said, snuggling deeper into the
blanket. My wet underwear was getting cold and uncomfortable. "If I take off my underwear will you make sure
the blanket stays on me?"

He frowned. "Right."

He took off his dripping shirt then moved onto his
pants, putting them into a hamper built into the wall while
I stared at the near nudity of him.

"Give me them," he said, holding out his hand.

Like I was going to give him my wet underwear.

"You do want your clothes dry when you put them
back on, right?"

I blinked at him.

"You're not really up to doing your own laundry."

Still, didn't move. He shrugged while I stared at his
body. When he offered me a clean shirt, a big shirt of

course because it fit him, I took it, at least I tried to, but he didn't let go.

"This is a trade. Nice, dry shirt for cold, wet underwear. Your choice."

I scowled at him but like I could rip the shirt out of his hand. I muttered fine as I got naked, but then the clasp on my bra got stuck, and I had the humiliation of him shoving me forward to unsnap the clasp for me leaving my back completely naked for five seconds before he pulled the blanket back over me. He had my underwear, I had his shirt, and I felt like he'd used me although it was kind of funny to see my neon orange panties and hot pink bra dangling from his hand.

"Put on my shirt. I'll be back with your herbal tea."

"Are you always such a bully?"

"The word is jerk. And, yes. I have my playlist to live up to."

With that, he was gone, still wearing wet dark blue underwear that I hadn't noticed at all, or the muscles in his thighs and... seriously. Had to stop.

Chapter 31

His room was too neat. I was glad that I got to see it messy because I'd hate him if I didn't know the other side, or the multiple other sides, like the dorky laugh and the messed up mother, the inability to hug and the way he ate my cookies. Crap. I was not going to think about the cookies, although why that would make me want to cry, I had no idea.

I was freezing, even under the duvet. I rolled up into a ball, and when you roll up into a ball it's nearly impossible not to cry. It's what you do, right? He found me like that, shivering, sniveling, but he didn't say anything, only pulled me upright and handed me the tea. I couldn't drink because I was too busy choking on tears, trying to be fine and stuff. With a long suffering sigh he sat on the edge of the bed.

"What's wrong?"

I glared at him. "I'm cold. My feet are freezing. You stole my underwear. Why do I have to go to the lake and almost die? I don't like almost dying. I don't like obsessing about jerks. What I hate the most is how I can't do anything about it. None of it. You want to be free, in control, well you're not the only one. You're just the only one who actually has a shot at it. Thanks for the tea," I mumbled, sticking my face inside the cup so I wouldn't have to look at perfect him and he wouldn't have to see snotty me with my red nose, red eyes, and hair that probably could take award for worst ever. And the cookies. I sniffed, but drank tea instead of letting out the sob.

"So, you're okay then."

I glared at him, but he only smiled.

"Yeah. I'm just… What are you doing?" I asked as he pulled back the blanket and climbed in. He was wearing clothes, baggy stuff that looked cozy so that was good, but still, when he wrapped his arms around me and pulled me against him, I had no idea what to do. His hand came around mine, steadying my tea.

"Try not to spill."

"Yeah, thanks. What are you doing?"

He sighed, and I could feel his breath on my neck. It was warm, but it made me shiver anyway. "It's called a hug. They make people feel better."

"Not in beds. In beds it's called snuggling."

"That's why it feels so much more natural for me. Closer to my puppy persona."

"Seriously, Sean, you can't cuddle me in your bed."

"Do you want to go back in the tank?" I hesitated. "Relax. It's just a cuddle, or was that snuggle? Don't you know how to…"

"No. I don't. I can't. Just…"

"Shhh," he whispered against my hair. "I'm not going to hurt you. I just want to warm you up. I feel responsible because I didn't stop you from going out onto the ice. I could have. I have at least a hundred pounds on you. I could have tackled you, dragged you to the car and tied you up, or worse, I could have told your father. I didn't. The least I can do is warm up your feet and make sure you don't catch pneumonia. Take a drink of tea. There, a little better? You're fine."

The idea of him telling my dad stopped the freaking out. That's what the sensible, responsible thing was to do. To tell my dad that I was obsessed with the lake after my mother's death and that I needed therapy. No. There was no way I was going to make him worry more than he already did. He worried about me. All the time. I couldn't just not tell him though; I had to be the person who didn't do stupid things, however much I wanted to.

I had to figure out ways to cope. Addicted people did it, stuff to make sure they didn't get swept up in their addictions, I could do that too. I leaned against him, sipping tea. I needed something to do, something like swimming only without the awkwardness of being in the swim team's space. Karate. I could do that instead, go to my dad's dojo and beat a board until I felt less like singing. It would also get me in shape.

The longer I sat in Sean's arms, the warmer and more contented I felt. He couldn't help but make the worries less, the issues I had sort of disappear. When I'd finished my tea, I turned so that I could curl around him, lying on his shoulder with my forehead against his throat.

"Sean, you smell like fresh laundry."

"Mmm," he said, sounding drowsy. "You smell like…" he mumbled something I didn't hear, but I was too comfortable to care.

When I woke up, it was weird because the light was on, and heavy even breathing was right above me. It was also weird because my leg was over his hip, and his hand was on my ankle, while his other arm cradled me against his chest. It was also weird because I was freaking sleeping with Captain Sean. Literally. Sleeping. I opened my mouth to freak out loud but coughed instead.

Sean tightened his hold on me, mumbling while he tucked my head under his chin. He was a mama hen. And I was his chick. Ugh. I had to pee. I had to freak out, but I kind of wanted to stay there and relax against him, to take advantage of him not being the perfect in-control person. I really wanted to. I snuggled my face against his chest, wrapping my leg tighter around him.

I inhaled him, felt his heart beat against mine and wanted to die. This was not good. This was the part where I stopped using the fact that he was an egotistical jerk to keep him out of that place in my chest that felt warm and squishy. Warm. Squishy. Pathetic. Giggling. Cookie baking. Just another idiot who wanted to wake up on a regular basis wrapped in his arms. It didn't matter. It was too late. I couldn't go back and wake up alone, I couldn't erase the way it felt to have someone unconsciously tighten their arms around me, that feeling of being exactly where I was supposed to be with the exact right person—the right person who wasn't my same species, who didn't want me in any actual way, who would always be on a completely separate plane than me. Awesome.

I should have pushed him away, I should have told him that I was awake and that he had to take me home, but instead I closed my eyes and listened to his heartbeat until I fell back asleep.

The next morning I woke up alone in his bed, but Sean wasn't far. He sat on the floor hunched over a pile of books. None of them were written in English.

"Good-morning," he said absently as he thumbed through a fat tome. "Good, you're awake." The back of his head looked ridiculously adorable as did the way his ears stuck out a little bit. Somebody shoot me.

"Hey." I looked around and saw my clothes, neatly folded on top of a dresser. They were easy to spot in the otherwise white and blue space as my neons dangled over the pile. I fingered my cheek where it throbbed slightly then felt my heart race as I remembered Cole.

"I treated your face last night," he said, still bent over the book. "It should be fine. We'll know I'm wrong if you turn blue. You can change in the bathroom then go to the kitchen. Everything's laid out on the counter for breakfast."

"Your dad still isn't here?"

He shook his head slightly.

"Oliver?"

He glanced up at me then. "No. Oliver hasn't been with us since he came back after the break. Disappointed?"

I shook my head. "Seeing him is always awkward. What are you reading?" I leaned over him until the blanket barely covered my bare legs. Being closer to a book written in a language I'd never seen before didn't exactly help, but being closer to Sean's ear... I pulled back while I felt my cheeks burn.

"I'm trying to find out what it was, not only that, what you are."

"What I am?"

His eyebrows were drawn over his blue eyes, making them look shadowy and mysterious. Gorgeous. Absolutely gorgeous.

"Someone who's bound to a body of water, someone who can cause the kiss of madness to herself, that sort of thing."

"Oh. So, what have you found out?"

He sighed and frowned at the book, no longer letting me feast on the sculpted symmetry of his face. I needed help. "I'll probably find more in the archives I keep in my…" he nodded to the bed, or beneath the bed to the mysterious watery depths it hid.

"Oh. I guess that makes sense." Not really. I still didn't get the 'there are different kinds of books' thing.

Finally, I made myself get out of bed. I really had to pee and then stare in the mirror at my reflection, studying the angry red line that crossed my cheek. Oh yeah. I was hot. My hair… wow, so bad. Half stuck to my head, half shooting out in different directions. Kind of amazing, really. I could have taken a shower but I felt like I'd had too much of that wet stuff already that week. I settled for leaving the bathroom for the kitchen where there were no mirrors.

The rest of the morning was awkward, me eating in Sean's huge kitchen while he read books, not really looking at me. Every time I thought of something to say, a question to ask, I'd fumble, feeling stupid and flustered. Later when Sean drove me to work, Sheila saw us together.

After waking up in Sean's bed, work was normal which was weird. Sheila kept asking about my boyfriend, like she still couldn't believe I'd managed to catch such a hottie. I wished she'd stop talking about it so I could stop thinking about it.

When I got home from work, my dad wasn't home, so I knew that he was in the studio, through the block from my house. Instead of crashing on my bed and drowning in music, I pulled on some leggings and a t-shirt under my parka to go break some boards.

I forgot how hard it was. I knew how to do this stuff in my head, but I couldn't do karate like I'd used to do it. Seriously frustrating. My dad seemed glad to see me, but he had his serious Sensei face on, so who knew.

I didn't have any lake effects other than a cough, well, and the welt on my cheek, thanks to Sean. For my dad, I came up with a lame story about skewering myself on Flop's antennae when I tried to get something that fell behind her radio. I wasn't sure if he believed me. The whole time he kept frowning at my cheek, like he couldn't stop looking at it. Seriously fun times.

Being obsessed with Oliver was one thing. I'd gotten used to it, accepted it, but this thing with Sean, wasn't the same. It didn't eat at me the same way, attacking my brain and nervous system, instead it took up residence in my stomach and chest. It made me mad. Sean didn't need another girl dizzy about him, one more cookie making adoring fan. Sean didn't need anything, anyone, and certainly not me. I had to do more karate, get serious about colleges and my future as a composer. My future as a composer. It was ridiculous and yet, I had to do something; I might as well shoot for something improbable yet incredible before settling down to be a CPA, or better yet, manager of the grocery store.

Monday morning, Sean pulled up at my house before I'd finished breakfast. My dad frowned at me but didn't say anything while I grabbed my books and shoved them into my bag.

"Hey, Sean," I said as cheerfully as was humanly possible, you know, without actually being cheerful. Luckily I had the advantage of being human.

"How are you?" he asked without pulling out. I knew my dad was watching out the window.

"Fine. Had a good weekend. You? I think you should drive before my dad comes outside and offers to show you his gun case."

He pulled out, but kept glancing at me with a frown. "Your breathing is raspy."

Unfortunately I took that moment to hack glamorously into my arm.

"I told you to call me if you got worse."

"Why? Is there something about your ability to fight colds that I don't know about? I can make myself herbal tea. How was your weekend?"

He frowned at me but didn't say anything. I wanted to ask him if he'd found anything, but I didn't want to talk to him any more than I had to, not when I had to fight from staring at his beautiful sculpted cheekbones and the profile of his nose. Ugh.

Finally we were in school and I practically vaulted out of his car as soon as he'd mostly come to a stop.

"Thanks for the ride, Sean. See you later."

I dashed into the school, sliding on ice which pulled my amazingly sore thighs from all the badly done karate I did. Torture. At my locker I had a mini mental breakdown while I let myself analyze our conversation. Had I sounded completely enraptured? I'd sounded normal, right? I hadn't thrown myself at him and confessed my love, or gone on about how I hadn't stopped thinking about him and listening to his album over and over again all weekend when he asked me how it had gone. Small victories.

"How's it going, Vee? I heard you were in the dojo Saturday," Cole said, draping an arm over my shoulder.

When I looked up at him he blinked a few times, pulling away from me then absently rubbed his arm where it had been bloodied from the monster.

"You went back to the lake?" He frowned.

I absently touched my cheek, feeling the welt. "Yeah. How's your arm?"

He shrugged, shoving his hands in his pockets and backing off.

"Fine. Later," he said, turning on his heels.

Did I look that bad? My welt didn't really hurt. Mostly felt numb and weird under my fingers.

"How was your weekend?" Flop asked beside me, yanking her locker door open with uncharacteristic force. "Don't tell me. If it was good, I don't want to hear it. If it was bad, I have no sympathy left for other people."

"What's up, Flop?"

She shook her head at her locker like it had caused her major disappointment. "I'm breaking up with Logan."

"What happened? What did he do? Did he hurt you?"

She raised her eyebrow at me. "Ha. I almost wish he'd done that, or something. All he does is whatever anyone else says, and he's all, 'yeah, awesome', instead of having his own opinion. The one thing we all have, is our opinions. Like Sean. He wouldn't think something because you told him to."

"Let's not talk about him."

"Why not? What's up, and what happened to your face?"

I shook my head, pushing away her hand. "Nothing."

She folded her arms over her chest and leaned on her locker. "Did he do that to you?"

"No! I fell scraped it on the ice or something, I don't really know because it was dark, and he..." I shook my head. "I think I might..."

She tapped her foot impatiently while I turned and grabbed all my books from my locker, not worrying about whether they were the right ones for my class.

"What?" she asked, grabbing my arm so I had to tow her along with me.

"You know that thing that's the opposite of hate? More than like? That thing at the end of all those beach movies?"

She gasped and let go of my arm before she hurried to catch up to me. "So, you're obsessed?"

I rolled my eyes. "Worse. In love."

"But, isn't that good?"

I slowed down my pace, not wanting to get to class that soon.

"No. It's exactly the same thing every other girl feels for him. It's exactly what he's trying to stay away from by dating me." I shook my head and took a deep breath, clutching my books to my chest. "I'll just ignore it. Maybe it will go away. I want to bake him cookies, Flop, the kind he likes. I want to look cute."

"You do look cute. You haven't worn a skirt to school since fall."

"My legs are cold, even in tights."

"Do you do layers? I think three layers of thin tights is warmer than one pair of regular leggings. Maybe he feels the same about you."

I shook my head. "Impossible. We're not even the same species."

I blinked at my lapse but she only looked sympathetic. "I guess I know what you mean, but still, maybe you should tell him how you feel and…"

I grabbed her arm in a death grip. "No."

"Okay, okay. You can let go of me," she said then rubbed her arm where I'd gripped her too tight.

"Sorry, just… Trust me. It's better if I keep all of this to myself. He's a senior, so he's going away to college anyway."

She looked at me and I felt queasy.

"Are you okay? You look kind of pale."

I nodded. "I'll be fine. I just need to sit down. Class is good for that, right? See you later."

When I passed out in class, no one noticed because we were watching a movie. I only noticed because of the panic when I couldn't breathe, when my lungs closed up and I started hyperventilating and then nothing until I woke to the droning of the guy onscreen. I might have fallen asleep like a normal person if it weren't for the panic.

It wasn't as bad as the headache when I stepped out of the dark room into the florescent lit hall. I closed my eyes, feeling dizzy and trying to stay on my feet. Maybe I wasn't as well after the lake thing as I'd thought. I squinted my way to the nurse's office, then spent the next two hours trying not to die from the agony every time light pierced my eyes and went straight into my brain.

By lunch everything was fine, normal enough that I didn't feel like I needed to tell Sean about any of it when he sat next to me.

"You don't have to sit by me," I said.

He ignored me as he bit into his bagel sandwich. "I don't have to do anything," he said after he'd finished his bite. I liked the way he didn't talk with food in his mouth. Tuba did that sometimes, which was fine because he was my friend, but still gross.

"So, Sean," Flop said from my other side. "Don't you

think Gen looks cute today?"

I stared at her. Her big, gray blue eyes looked innocent to the untrained observer.

"No. Gen's not a cute type."

Oh, thanks. I scowled at him. "No? And what type am I, exactly?" Wait. Maybe I didn't want to know.

He took his time looking at me while he ate, his brows lowering over his piercing blue eyes. "Gen's her own type." He said this to Flop in spite of still staring at me. "You're cute. She's more…distinctive."

Okay. I was officially going to die. I stabbed my salad with my fork, refusing to allow his words to affect me in any way even as my stomach twisted.

"I agree," Junie said, leaning forward. "Gen's beauty is sophisticated and subtle. What do you think, Tuba?"

Tuba shrugged and ate a fry. "I think Gen's cute."

I got up as my stomach twisted harder. I mumbled something as I left, bolting for the restroom. When I got there, I had trouble breathing normally. I couldn't let this happen to me just because I happened to talk to Sean. It wasn't like I'd expected a different answer. I stared at my reflection, hating the features that were not sophisticated, cute, or anything else. Distinctive, yeah, especially with the red line down my cheek.

I moaned and leaned against the porcelain, trying to breathe, to ignore the ache in my chest. When I was sure I wouldn't pass out, I stood up. In the mirror I thought I saw someone walk behind me. When I turned around, Sharky stood there with a furious expression on her face.

"You." Her voice was a flat, menacing sound that made me edge towards the door. "It's all your fault!"

"You shouldn't have tried to trip me. You know about karma; what goes around…"

"It was a stupid argument. I wanted him to stop talking to you, to go back to how it was when he pretended you didn't exist, but he said no. He wasn't going to let anyone else choose his friends. I broke up with him. I was sure he would change his mind, and then she took my place."

"Cole's with someone? Who?"

She glared at me as she shook her blond hair so it whacked herself in the face. "Don't pretend you don't know."

"I'm not pretending anything, but whatever. I don't care who Cole's hooking up with. His life is none of my business. We used to be friends, but we're not anymore. Not really. I'm sorry you guys didn't work out, but that happens."

"You're sorry?" She was in my face, looking pretty insane when a freshman walked in, completely oblivious to everything.

She smiled brightly at both of us and proceeded to carefully apply lipstick that was too dark for her pale skin tone. At least, that's what Flop would have said. With the witness, Sharky didn't have anything else to say, so I got out of there without it coming to violence.

Once out of the bathroom, I shook my head as I straightened my shirt and smoothed down the skirt that was cute, even if I wasn't. I couldn't let stuff make me crazy like Sharky, particularly when it was someone I'd never had any illusions about.

Over the next week, I had one other breathing episode, or not breathing anyway, and two massive headaches, but other than that, I'd come up with a formula. Stay busy, stay with people, talk to other people instead of Sean. That's how I managed it. I talked Sean into driving Flop to and from school with me. It was great. I kept the subjects on school stuff so that no one would get personal, and usually that worked. I started studying in the library with a group, so Sean and I weren't in the kitchen alone. Fridays, date nights I filled with exciting things, like group bowling or group ice skating, nothing alone, nothing where we could talk and get closer, nothing where I'd have to remember how to breathe again. The rest of my time I filled with school stuff and karate.

It worked because of Flop, because she wasn't with Logan, and I explained to Sean over and over again how hard it was to be single with a bunch of dating people, not that we were really dating. No, it didn't really make sense, but

I didn't want to stop seeing Sean, not when he still some-times gave me hugs, even with Flop there.

The only thing I allowed myself was going to the swim meets. I always had a tight excuse afterwards in case Sean caught me, so I wouldn't have to go somewhere alone with him, or worse, with the swim team.

Watching Sean swim was amazing, breathtaking. I wasn't the only one who went to the meets just to watch him. The other fan girls glared at me until it was obvious that I made no claim, that I was only there as an observer even if I did devour him as thoroughly as they did.

Days, weeks, winter passed, slowly as ice took to thaw. I avoided Oliver because every time I saw him I felt the obsession swallow me and then, closely following, this bizarre and irrational guilt. It was way worse than how I felt about lying to my dad. It was worse than pretty much everything. At the same time I struggled to balance love with obsession, the urge to go to the lake grew at the same rate the scar on my face disappeared. It astonished me how many things I could need simultaneously, well, it would have if I thought about it, but I made it a point to do my homework instead of thinking.

It was on the last swim meet, finals, whatever they called them when I sat high up on the bleachers behind a group that I could duck behind any time I felt like Sean or someone else might look up. While I waited for Sean to show up, one of his fans came up to me and sat down, star-ing at me curiously. The tips of her hair were dyed pink. Her shirt read, 'Keep Calm, Here comes Sean,' with an outline of a very buff swimmer at the top.

"I don't know what we're going to do now that it's over. Next season won't be nearly so good without The Captain." I nodded. "So, I wondered if you'd like a shirt." She changed from forlorn to perky in a scary short amount of time while she unslung her backpack and pulled out a stack of t-s.

I stared at the hello-kitty stickers on her nails before I read the slogan, 'Sean, Sean, he's all brawn'.

"Most people aren't interested in getting a shirt at the

very last meet, but I can tell that you're dedicated."

I blinked at her. "How much are they?"

Her beam increased twenty-five percent.

I glanced over at the pool while she told me the details and got a clear view of Sean diving off the side into the water. I inhaled sharply which shut up kitty-nails as she stared at him in a way that made me want to... something not nice.

He swam beautifully and was halfway through his laps when the people in front of me stood up so that I couldn't see. Kitty-nails grabbed my arm and stood up, pulling me with her. I watched, breathless as he swam, beating out the other swimmers, pushing hard, muscles straining, body arcing, until at last he made the final lap and came out of the water in a rush.

Kitty-nails was screaming his name beside me, jumping up and down while still gripping my arm. I sort-of had to jump up and down with her or risk tumbling down the bleachers. Honestly, I was screaming too, the rush of seeing him win totally swallowing the fear I had that he'd look up and see me. Naturally, he looked up and saw me.

He froze, staring blatantly up at me where I was still jumping and screaming with Kitty-nails.

"He's looking at me," she shrieked, kind of shredding my skin, but that was okay because I couldn't feel it, couldn't feel anything as my body went suddenly, solidly numb. Sean kind of blinked, then offered the audience a smiling wave before he grabbed a towel and sat down.

"This is the best meet ever! Do you think he'll sign my t-shirt?" she asked, dragging me back to sitting position. "So, which shirt did you want? I bet he'll sign yours too, if you're with me. I'm his biggest fan. He knows me."

"I'll take one of each. They're both such catchy slogans," I said while she looked ready to swoon from joy. It was ridiculously easy to make some people happy.

I shelled out the dough while she handed me two shirts that I stuffed into my backpack. Sean didn't look up again. Maybe he hadn't actually seen anything. I told myself I was an idiot for feeling disappointed, but it didn't make the feeling go away.

I was in the parking lot, nearly to my car when a shadow detached from the back, a huge, hulking shadow that was comfortably familiar.

"Sean. You startled me."

"Right," he said, edging towards me while his face was swathed in shadows, hiding the sarcastic tilt of his lips. "What would I be doing at a swim meet?"

"Haha." The laugh sucked. I'd have to do better, but I still felt the rush and euphoria, the kitty nails obsession that I'd been fighting so long. I wanted to ask him to auto-graph something and stare at him. "So, it was a great final. I wasn't sure if that other guy wouldn't take you. He was good, but you were better."

"You're beautiful."

I blinked at him, feeling my throat tighten and my stomach tangle into knots. "That's my line. Your swim-ming is perfect. You'd better watch out or your competition is going to poison you some day."

He reached for my hand, softly sliding his skin over mine. Tingling ran from my fingers up my arm while I tried to swallow normally.

"I'm really glad to see you here."

"You are?" I blinked in the darkness feeling like I couldn't breathe.

Maybe Sean would give me CPR. Maybe I could pre-tend to not breathe... pathetic.

"We're going out to celebrate. Will you come with me?" He tightened his hand on mine, pulling me a little bit closer to him. I fought the urge to melt against his chest and let the rest of the world disappear.

"Okay."

Wait, no, I couldn't do that, not when he pulled me even closer and his other arm came around me. I really was going to pass out. I fought the rising frustration and tears while I pulled back.

"Actually, I have to meet Junie and Flop for this thing."

"A thing?" His voice was flat, like I was off to obsess at the lake.

"No, not that thing: the soup kitchen. After that I'm going to be in the dojo until really late, so tonight doesn't really work for me."

He ran his thumb over the back of my hand, gentle, while he bent down, his lips centimeters from my ear. "I would like to celebrate with you. Tonight. I want to do something normal like watch a movie after your karate thing." His lips actually brushed my ear and I felt my world tilt upside down and dump me into a pool of my own jellified convictions.

"A movie would be good."

My lips touched his jaw when I said that. He was too close to think about things clearly, not when his thumb still moved against my skin, not when his jaw tasted like chlorine. Not that chlorine tasted good, but he tasted so good it made up for the chlorine. Pathetic. I had to say no, had to refuse, but instead I stayed there until I heard someone calling his name. Bernice.

I pulled away, hating every inch between us. "I'll see you later."

"Yes," he agreed, squeezing my hand once before letting go. "I'll pick you up at midnight."

I opened my mouth to protest, to backtrack, but he was gone, another shadow in the dark parking lot while I fumbled with my keys. It would be fine. I didn't need to get hysterical, I didn't need to lean my head against the steering wheel and try to breathe through my nose so I didn't pass out. It would be great. I'd get Flop and Junie to come with me.

"No," Flop said as she stood with the hairnet making her look ridiculous along with the oversize plastic cloves. "I'm not coming with you. You need to tell him how you feel. This is the perfect chance to be alone with him."

I turned from her to Junie where she stood over a steaming kettle, eyeing the contents with suspicion. "I'm with Flop. He deserves to know the truth."

I groaned as I grabbed a tray of cornbread and took it out of the kitchen to the dining room. I forced the smile for the unfortunates who frequented the soup kitchen until I returned, carrying empty bowls. "He'll hate me."

"If that happens, then you'll be free to find someone else," Flop said philosophically. "Or, he'll say that he loves you and wants you to have his babies. Can you imagine how gorgeous your kids would be?"

I rolled my eyes while Junie snorted. "Sean has goals, Flop. He's not going to throw away all his plans to make babies, however much he likes someone." Yeah, and he'd have to find someone with gills for all the baby making anyway. "He might want to include you in his plans, though," she said, gesturing for me to take the pot. "Like me and Tuba. There is room for love in a healthy, balanced life."

I groaned as I took the pot, careful not to spill. They were firm about leaving me to face Sean alone, no matter how pathetic I looked. Afterwards, in the dojo, I fought more aggressively than usual. My dad sent me home early, said I needed to meditate.

I sat in my room, 'meditating' to Sean's music, after my dad had long since gone to bed when I saw the dark car pull up to the curb outside my house. I watched through the window as Sean got out and leaned against the roof, staring up at me like he could see into my dark bedroom, right at me. I got up, pulled open the window, then climbed through, like he was the lake and I had no resistance to him. No, it wasn't like that. It was more like I was going to tell him that I couldn't go after all, but I had to tell him. I couldn't leave him standing there.

When I crossed the grass, he reached for me, pulling me against him in a hug that wiped away any words I'd had to protest. His lips against my forehead surprised me, making me freeze as the feel of his soft mouth against my hard head relaxed something inside my chest.

It wasn't very cold out, not cold at all when he had his arms around me, but we couldn't stand there forever. He opened his door, helping me in then closing it behind me, enveloping me in the sound of crashing waves and a deep underlying throbbing that made my heart beat faster. He was in, we were off, and then too soon, pulling up into his driveway, into the garage.

"Is your dad here?" For all my conviction, they were the first words I'd spoken.

"No. Is that all right?" Did he look nervous? Worried? Something other than cool, in control, typical captain Sean?

"It's fine. Um, so what movie did you want to watch?"

We walked into the house that felt even more enormous and empty than before. "I thought you'd like to see something from my world. I'll translate for you." We walked down stairs into space I hadn't gotten on the tour.

"Oh. That would be..." I stopped as he led me into a room with a theater, make that a room that was a theater. An enormous leather couch took up most of the space while a screen filled the wall. A table full of popcorn and various other junk food waited for us.

"Is this okay?" He definitely sounded nervous, but when I looked up at him, he seemed fine. I was beyond nervous, but I nodded anyway.

"Awesome." I settled on the couch, feeling like it swallowed me while he went and fiddled with the box at the back of the room. He turned off the light and I blinked at the screen, trying not to notice when he sat, his weight shifting me over against him until my leg rested against his.

The movie was weird, or maybe it was fine but being up against Sean while he whispered in my ear that was freaking me out. I ate popcorn, then mints, then nothing because I felt sick, but didn't know what to do with my hands. It was Sean's fault. His voice whispering in my ear, words he would never say to me in real life. The story was about a beautiful girl and boy who lived under the water inside a coral reef who had to fight the waves to be together. In the end they drifted apart, hands breaking as the last of their strength left them.

I laughed, okay, giggled at the end when the last confession of their love came from Sean's lips, trying not to hyperventilate. I was ready to leave, proud that I hadn't confessed my love, but then another movie filled the screen, this time without people, only about water and music.

I didn't feel ridiculous watching that. I felt right instead as the music spoke to me far deeper than the foreign words. I gripped his hand tighter then leaned against his shoulder as the waves crashed over me, around me, swallowing me in orchestral maneuvers that didn't need a plot.

I found my head against his chest, his arm around me as he sank down until we lay wrapped around each other, the beating of our hearts keeping time with the music. He wasn't Captain Sean, I wasn't Watergirl, there were no definitions, only emotions, and this sense of rightness, of belonging.

Chapter 32

I wasn't sure if I passed out or fell asleep, but when I woke up, head pressed against Sean's chest with his arms holding me tight against him, the movie was finished. I blinked against his chest until I pulled away, staring at his face, a face that wasn't beautiful because of its perfection, but because it belonged to him. I felt this ache in my chest that made me want to sing, not to the lake, but to him. I felt the song in my chest welling up, something that I'd never felt before, something that would show him how I felt. I couldn't hold it back, not anymore.

I brushed my fingers over his face, feeling the slickness of his skin before he jerked back, opening his eyes to stare at me, blinking rapidly while he shook away the disorientation.

"It's fine," I soothed, reaching again for him, but he sat up, sliding out from under me.

"It's morning." His voice was ice cold, his hands clenched when he crossed his arms over his chest. I didn't know how he could tell when there were no windows, no way to see outside in the room.

"Okay?"

"I think the plan was to watch a movie and then take you back home. I didn't think you'd last very long on the second one."

"It was amazing. I loved it. Sean, I..." I trailed off as he got up, running his hands through his hair as he walked away from me.

"Great. I need to take a swim. If you'd like to wait for me, there should be something in the fridge to eat. Don't eat anything in containers with red lids."

"Sean?"

My words echoed back to me from the bare walls. He had already gone. I blinked and then the room that had seemed perfectly visible became pitch black, only the distant light from the doorway visible. I banged my knees against the table knocking skittles or something like that across the floor.

"I love you," I said with a sigh as I made my way to the door. The song was stuck in my chest, leaving an ache that made it hurt to breathe.

I shook my head as I walked up the stairs, feeling weird to come out of the darkness into a bright sunshiny day that didn't exactly fit my mood. I wasn't about to hang around while he swam, not when he'd made it so clear… what had he made clear, exactly? He'd acted like it was a real date last night. He'd gotten junk food he didn't touch. He'd held me without me asking him to do it. He'd acted like… well, it was over today, whatever fluke that made him seem to like me. I blinked back tears as I walked out the front door then stopped to stare at Oliver in the doorway. The sight of him made me dizzy and my fingers tingle. Great.

"Answering Sean's door for him?"

He sounded jealous, but I only rolled my eyes. Even obsessed with me, Oliver wasn't really interested.

"I was just leaving. Sean's swimming."

He took a step towards me, brushing my hair behind my shoulder. "I didn't expect to see you here."

My scalp tingled in spite of there being no way that his touch could have traveled to my hair follicles.

"I suppose I shouldn't be surprised. I thought at first that maybe you were with him to help you stay away from me, but the way he looks at you…"

I laughed. It wasn't a good laugh. "Yeah, he's crazy about me." I shook my head and glared at him. "What's your deal? Flop says that you're stalking me. Is that true?"

He blinked and lost his smile for a second. "Ever since the kiss, I can't stop thinking about you."

I took a step closer to him, the ache in my chest growing with every second, a song that was closer to a scream at that point. "Thinking about what?" I wasn't sure what was with my voice, the way it came out like a purr as my hands slid up, over his chest and around his neck. The feel of him beneath my hands consumed rational thought. I trailed my fingers up the back of his neck to his scalp. There was buzzing in my head, dizziness that made me feel like a stranger, watching myself as I pressed him against the wall, touching my lips against his throat. I felt him swallow. He trembled against me as I pulled his head back, leaving an expanse of throat for me to completely ravage.

I did. Ravage, I mean. First his throat, then his shirt, ripping it down the back while my nails dug into his skin, drawing blood. I could smell it, the way I smelled him, the same scent on Sean that morning, a scent that made me want so much it consumed me. His skin was slippery, coated with something that tasted like salt, salt and some-thing indefinable I'd been able to taste on Sean beneath the chlorine the night before. I pushed against him harder, biting his mouth as I tried to think only of Oliver, to taste only Oliver, to drown out the memory of Sean, the ache I felt for Sean.

When Oliver finally broke, pulling me against him with a mindless intensity I hadn't expected, I let him, arch-ing against him like I could force my body to fit against his.

"If you'd close the door, I'd appreciate it." Sean's voice made me freeze, made the thing in my chest well up and then collapse as I fell away from Oliver. I blinked, staring at nothing while I tried to get my breathing under control.

"Lend me your shirt, Oliver," he said standing close enough to me that I could feel the movement as he stripped Oliver. "Genevieve, I'll drive you home."

He put his hand on my arm, pulling me away from the open door towards the garage while I refused to look at him, at Oliver, at anything or anyone who would make it all even worse.

I slid into the car, dropping my head onto my knees,

where I stayed while Sean got in and turned on the ignition. We sat there for a few minutes before he backed up, driving without any sign of emotion. It was like he hadn't even noticed that I'd been making out with Oliver, trying to consume him with a mindlessness that scared me.

"Sean," I said in a small voice that made me feel even worse.

"Mmm?"

"I can't do this anymore." I sat up and looked at him, drinking in every line and shadow, every speck in his blue eyes.

He glanced on me, his golden eyebrows slightly lowered. "Do what?"

"Pretend. I can't pretend to be your girlfriend."

"Who's pretending?" He gave me a slight smile. Why was he smiling? Couldn't he see that there was nothing to smile about?

"I know you want a girl who doesn't giggle, a girl who doesn't like you and won't act like an idiot around you, but I'm not that girl. I'm tired of pretending that I don't care, that I'm not interested."

He glanced at me again with an eyebrow raised but said nothing. This was it. I had to come clean, like Flop had told me to.

"I can't be with someone I like more than they like me. It was fine when we were mutual… whatever we were, but now…" I took a deep breath and stared out the windshield. "I love you." Silence. "So, I don't think we should see each other anymore. It's the only thing that makes sense."

"What do you want?" His voice was strange, his face when he pulled the car over so he could stare at me, glaring with those eyes that pierced through me.

I didn't care. I didn't have anything left to hide.

"I want you."

More silence while his expression grew darker with every second. "You want me. That's it? On a platter or stuffed and mounted on your wall?"

I sighed and looked down at my lap. Well, I hadn't expected this to go well. "You wouldn't fit very well on my wall, so I suppose that leaves the platter. I'm sorry, Sean. I didn't mean to like you. It's probably your fault for forgetting to be nasty to me all the time."

"You said love."

I winced. Well, nothing wrong with his memory. "Yeah. I didn't mean to love you. Maybe you'll forgive me someday."

"I…" he gripped his bare knees and I realized he was wearing nothing but jammers and Oliver's shredded button down.

I did not need to notice what he wasn't wearing. I groaned and covered my face with my hands.

My door was wrenched open and my dad was there. It was only then that I realized that Sean had pulled up in front of my house where I'd sat confessing my love while my dad watched.

"Genevieve, get in the house." His voice scared me.

I blinked up at him and reached instinctively for Sean, then stopped, instead getting out of the car, passing my dad where he stood, still, silent, staring at Sean like he could melt him with one glance. I stopped once I was past him, worried he'd do something to Sean, say something, but then again, what could he say? I'd already done it, destroyed whatever tentative friendship we had, all because I couldn't keep it bottled up inside. I felt so tired as I watched my dad lean in and say something to Sean too low for me to hear, then slam the door. He waited until Sean drove away before he turned and marched me into the house.

"Good morning," I muttered as he opened the door and pushed me down into a chair.

"I'm glad you noticed that it's morning," he said, his mouth a grim line.

"Yeah. Sorry if I made you worry." I was sorry but all the feelings seemed far away, inaccessible as I floated on this numb exhaustion. "We watched a movie and fell asleep."

"And that's why his shirt was ripped and your mouth

is bruised?"

I blinked. Right. Oliver. Well, I wasn't going to try and explain that to him. "That was this morning. It's not a big deal."

His glower deepened as he crossed his arms over his chest, standing over me like a drill sergeant. "You think getting serious with someone at your age isn't a big deal? You don't understand your emotions, the way that they can sweep you away into doing something you'll regret with permanent consequences."

Was he seriously talking about... no. He couldn't be. "I don't know. It doesn't matter. We broke up. That's what we were doing when you dragged me out of the car. You should be happy."

He blinked and didn't have anything to say for a second. "You broke up? Why?"

I shrugged. "Because it wouldn't work out. He's going to college. I'm going nowhere." My voice came out dead. "I'm tired. If you're going to ground me, get it over with, okay? I'm going to sleep until I have to go to work."

"Yes, you're grounded. I'll drive you to work and home. Flop and Junie can come over but other than that..." I zoned out while he went on, outlining the details of my grounding like he'd put a lot of thought into it. It made me wonder how long he'd been waiting for me to come home. I hoped he hadn't found me gone in the middle of the night. It was really hard for me to care though when I felt so tired.

Work was great. Yeah. Because I loved listening to Sheila talk about my boyfriend like I still had one.

That night, I lay in bed unable to sleep until I finally went to the window. I didn't plan to go to the lake, but I had to go, had to do something. That's when I found out that my dad had nailed the window shut and put an alarm on my door. At first I was furious. How dare he not trust me, then I sat down on my computer and tried to make music that expressed how I felt better than my words. The music came out as ugly as I felt.

Chapter 33

On Monday, I walked up to my locker and saw Flop talking to a guy with a serious expression on her face. She kept nodding like Junie did when someone mentioned conservation. He was a goth, biker hybrid. We didn't get any purists because we were in the middle of rural Ohio. Anyway, Flop talked to him while I waited, politely, until he gave her this half sneer and sauntered off.

"Isn't he Dean's friend?"

She jumped like I'd caught her doing something illicit. "No. Fred is completely solo. I don't think he's anybody's friend." She turned quickly to her locker to stuff something inside before I saw what it was.

"Flop, are you getting into drugs? If so, you probably should work on your sneakiness."

She sighed and turned, holding out a strip of leather. "He does his own leatherwork, you know, belts, boots, jackets, you must have noticed his incredible wardrobe."

I blinked at the leather where a lopsided flower looked like someone had squashed it. "So, he's giving you leather working tips? Nice."

"Anyway," she said, stuffing it back into her locker. "How did it go with Sean?"

Ugh. "We broke up."

"No! But, when you told him how you felt he must have…"

"He didn't. He made it clear that he found my emotional state a threat to his independence but didn't have time to really insult me because then my dad dragged me into the house. That was fun." I shook my head and slumped against my locker.

She frowned and looked uncomfortable. "It's all my fault. I'm the one who told you that... I couldn't believe that anyone would come to know you and not love you. You're great."

That made me laugh. "So glad someone thinks so. Let's forget about Sean. What do you want to do Friday?"

She blinked. "I was actually planning on leatherworking with Fred, but I can reschedule." She blushed and I had to look at her again.

"You like him. I mean, you really like the goth biker guy?"

She shrugged helplessly. "I had this thing in my head about what I wanted in a guy, and Logan was all those things but he didn't fit. Fred fits without being anything that I want. It probably won't work out long term, but in the meantime..." she blushed again.

"Have you kissed him?"

Her eyes blinked too much. "He kissed me."

"When? Flop, you can't be kissing guys and not tell me."

She shrugged. "It was kind of circumstantial. Every time I think it's not going to happen again, because, you know, we have nothing in common and he doesn't act like he wants a relationship, and then he gets close to me, and things sort of happen."

"Cool." I stood there nodding for a while until my protective streak overwhelmed me. "Well, I'll see you later. Got to get to class."

I found Fred in the shop room with a notebook, sketching. I sat down opposite him and stared at him until he looked up at me.

I didn't bother with introductions. "I think you should eat lunch with us today."

"No thanks. I prefer to consume in private." He said with a sneer made more moody from the darkness circling his eyes. The dude wore eyeliner. No wonder she wasn't entirely comfortable being seen with him.

"Then eat before you come. If you're going to be with

Flop, it should be out in the open."

He frowned at me. "Aren't you the swim guy's girl-friend?"

I shook my head. "We broke up. I got too emotionally attached. So, are you coming or what?"

"I'll think about it."

"Good," I said standing up. "I like your eyeliner."

"Maybe I can give you tips sometime."

I rolled my eyes and walked out into the hall. I'd taken two steps when I turned in the opposite direction. I wasn't fast enough. Sean put his hand on my shoulder, spinning me around.

"Um, hi..."

I started then trailed off as he pulled off his shirt, dropping it on the filthy hall floor while he flexed. I stood staring at him, at his half naked body as the muscles rippled beneath his perfect skin. I clenched my fist to keep from touching him.

"What's up?" I asked in a squeaky voice.

"I'm waiting for you to giggle," he said, giving me a slight scowl that only made him look sexier.

I tried to breathe, but... and... I leaned against the wall while black spots filled my vision.

When I blinked my eyes open, we were in the shop room while Fred pretended he didn't see us. Sean had laid me out on one of the counters. When I sat up, I realized I was covered in sawdust. Nice.

"You fainted," Sean accused. "Giggling I expected, not fainting."

I stared at him, at his arms folded across his now clothed body while his ice blue eyes pierced me.

"If you assault people with your bare chest you get whatever you get. Why did you want me to giggle, any-way?"

He lifted his chin a notch. "I didn't believe you'd do it. And you didn't."

"No. I fainted." I put my head down on my knees. He jerked my head up with my chin so I had to look at him, to stare at him while he stared back with those eyes I could gaze into forever.

"If you're serious about wanting me, why are you always ripping into Oliver?"

"You'd rather I rip into you?"

"Yes."

I blinked at him then frowned. There was no way he was serious. "Yeah right. Well if that was true, maybe you should have mentioned it at some point. It's hard enough to get you to hug me. With Oliver... that has nothing to do with what I want. I haven't... for so long... and you're always shoving me away. That's fine. But then Oliver showed up and... You certainly didn't seem to mind." I shook my head. He never had seemed bothered by anything I did with Oliver, except for the first kiss. That had made him pissed.

"I don't care. Of course that's what it is. I never care about anything, do I? I'm just an egotistical jerk who would rather push everyone away."

I rolled my eyes. "You've made it totally clear that your priorities are independence first, last and always. That's fine. I respect that. I just hate feeling guilty about liking you, and even being with Oliver when I know you don't care."

He stared at me, his eyes narrowing into slits. "Do you know what it was like to watch you lick slime off of him?"

I blinked. "Slime? I don't remember that part. With him it's always blurry. Maybe he was a little slippery, but I wouldn't call it slimy." The way he looked at me made me feel like an idiot, the kind who went around licking frogs. I felt suddenly exhausted. "What do you want, Sean? I don't feel like giggling. We broke up, okay? I'm kind of devastated about it."

"You told me it was over. You don't get to be devastated."

"Fine. I'm happy about it! Super happy. All the time!" I spun on the counter to get off but he stepped closer so that my knees were held on either side of him by his hands. The feeling in my chest, the song that had shifted into something else, grew harder and larger with every second.

"Do you honestly think that I'm indifferent to you? How could I be when you drive me insane? Every day you look at me and I know that you're seeing something inaccessible, someone that could never be part of your life until that moment when you wanted me. You ran away the second you thought I might be something worth fighting for. Threw yourself at Oliver. Breathe. You're not breathing again." He squeezed my knees, and I gasped a little bit, but breathing made the thing in my chest move up to my throat. "You tell yourself that you're respecting my space, but really, I think you're just afraid of caring about something that you think you'll lose."

"Maybe that's true. I lost Cole when he was my only friend, my mother, how could I survive to lose someone that took up that much of my heart, my life?" I stared at him. At perfect Sean who had made my heart bleed after he'd held me so close. "You're right. It's not worth the risk, not when I know that I'll never be what you really need."

His hands slid from my knees to my hips, squeezing my muscles and bones like he wanted to dig gills into me with his fingers. "I don't know what need is, if not this." His jaw was clenched so hard, I had to touch it, to trace his face with my fingers just to touch him.

"Sean, I'm not…"

His hands shifted, sliding up my sides, a hard grip that might bruise. He didn't stop at my ribs or the top of them until he got to my scars where they were puffy and sore. When his huge hands gripped me beneath my armpits, squeezing, digging into me, that thing in my throat exploded out in a scream of pain, shock, and something else that had me wrapping my arms around him. The scream left me feeling empty, like I had to hang onto him for dear life.

Sean's hands slid back down my sides while he pulled away, removing my hands from his neck. He stumbled back until he hit another counter, gripping the edge with white knuckles.

"Sean?" I felt so lost and alone without him. Why would he do that? Act like he wanted me and then throw me away as soon as I responded? "What are you doing? I told you that I'm not willing to be hurt, so you have to hurt me? Why can't you leave me alone? Why would you strip in public, make a scene when you and I both know that you don't want me in your life? Do you have to be the one who rejects me? Is that what this is? Fine. I love you, you don't love me, now we can both move on..."

I stopped yelling as he looked up at me, at the way his eyes didn't blink but the blue had retreated leaving mostly black enlarged pupils. It wasn't his eyes that stopped me though, it was the red that dripped from his jaw to his shirt.

I slid off the counter so I could reach up, feel the blood and see the trail from his ear, the other one as well. His ears were bleeding. Did he have a brain tumor? Did brain tumors make people's ears bleed? No, sometimes high sounds that pierced people's eardrums would cause...

I put my hand to my throat as I stumbled back.

"Dude, do you want some gauze?" I turned to stare at Fred who came forward with his backpack. "Man, girl, you've got some lungs. You're both complete freaks." He nodded like that wasn't an insult. "I'll be there at lunch. So I've got the gauze because fresh tattoos ooze sometimes. You've got to be prepared. Do you want to see them?"

I stared at him while he shrugged off his leather jacket and revealed skinny arms covered in swirls and designs.

"Er. Nice. The gauze?"

He nodded and dug around into his backpack before pulling out a baggie filled with antibiotic ointment and a roll of gauze along with tape. I took it and started for Sean. He still hadn't moved.

"Do you think you did brain damage?" Fred asked right before Sean grabbed Fred by the shirt and slammed him down on top of the counter.

"You are not going to have lunch with Genevieve." Sean sounded icy but furious at the same time. I felt chills run over my body like it was me he had beneath him.

"No, man, it's Flop I'm into. Not that your girlfriend's not hot, but Flop's more my speed."

Fred looked like a skinny black spider flailing around under Sean's enormous weight. Sean dropped him, pulling away while he looked around like a desperate animal. A very wild animal.

"Sean?" I asked, reaching out slowly to touch his arm. He turned his gaze on me, still looking hunted. "I have some gauze. Are you okay? You're bleeding."

"The bleeding stopped," he said, his expression shifting into a scowl as he took the gauze out of my hands then leaned against the counter, closing his eyes like he was dizzy. I hovered over him feeling like an idiot.

"Well, that's good. Do you need help getting to class?"

He opened his blue eyes to scowl at me again, his lips curling. "How exactly do you propose to help me to class? Would you like to carry me? I'm not in the mood for school anyway," he said, wiping the blood off his cheeks then shoving the baggie back at Fred. "Thanks," he said, but he didn't act grateful and he certainly didn't apologize for attacking him.

"No problem, man," Fred said, looking a little stunned but acting okay. "Any time you need some gauze..."

Sean had left by then, walking unsteadily, but with more purpose than anyone else at high school, except for Junie maybe, leaving us both behind.

I stared at Sean until he was gone while the emptiness inside of me grew and grew. I glanced at Fred, waiting for him to ask awkward questions, but he just pulled on his jacket and stuffed the baggie back in his backpack.

"I'm sorry about that."

He only shrugged like being slammed down wasn't a big deal. What world did he come from where that whole exchange wouldn't make him do more than blink?

"Do you do a lot of drugs?" I asked.

He glanced up. "If you're looking for a supplier you'll have to ask Dean. He keeps this school in a tight hold."

I shook my head. "I want you to be a good guy for Flop. She's..." I shook my head.

"I'm not really into that whole scene." He frowned at me and I nodded. He didn't like being questioned about that, defined by whether or not he did drugs.

"Sure. I just want her to be happy. That's all."

He nodded. "She's kind of happy without anyone else, you know? She's not the kind of person you have to make happy. I like that."

"Yeah." Awkward moment, then I smiled brightly and was about to leave when he told me that I might want to wipe the blood off my throat and hands.

"Because people talk."

There was a sink in the corner, where I hurried and cleaned up, getting a nod from Fred before I ducked back into the hall. My fingers still felt sticky from Sean's blood even if there wasn't anything on them I could see. I dodged a guy who hurtled through the hall as if monsters were after him.

My scream could make his ears bleed. I stopped moving, making people glare at me as they had to move around me.

My head pounded, my breathing came short, but I didn't pass out again. I headed to the library, but the lady behind the desk wouldn't let me go online to find out what the crap about making Sean's ears bleed until after school when there was a measly half hour open lab.

Chapter 34

At lunch, Fred was the first one at our table, opening up containers and looking comfortable. I sank into a chair across from him. Would I be able to eat anything or should I just go outside? It was almost warm at that point.

"Fred?" Flop's voice sounded incredulous.

He nodded at her but didn't give her any kind of really intense, 'I love you so much, I'm going to die,' look.

"I invited him," I said, sounding half dead. Really. It sucked.

"Yeah. She told me you liked me."

I glared at him but Flop only sat down beside me, cocking her head at him.

"So I thought maybe it would be cool for us to hang out more."

"Yeah," she said with a slight nod. "That would be cool."

Junie was slightly more skeptical than we were, but Fred didn't mind being disapproved of. He'd decided to eat with us, so that's what he was going to do. Perfect. For Flop.

As I sat there, I looked around the cafeteria, happening to glance over at the swimmer's table. It was pretty bare. Sean was obviously missing, but there was also no sign of Bernice.

I swallowed down a bite of sandwich but that was all that I could manage. Sean and Bernice. They made so much sense. Even if Bernice wasn't a gill girl, she fit in his world much better than I did. She would never make his ears bleed or make out with Oliver. Sean had almost convinced me that he liked me. And then I'd screamed. I could still feel the press of his hands down my sides, the ache of my armpits. I should tell him that. 'Sean, you make my armpits ache.' It would have been hilarious a few months earlier. We would have joked about the really pathetic t-shirt slogans. I would have ogled him for a second, but not felt like someone was rappelling with my intestines. Love. What a sucky thing. I realized that I was staring at Oliver when he glanced over and raised his eyebrows. I kept staring and eventually he came over, pulling a seat out to sit beside me.

My whole body woke up having him so close. My fingers tingled, my heart pounded, but none of it was real.

"Hey Oliver."

"Genevieve." He smiled at everyone else at the table too.

Sitting beside him was torture, particularly when I saw no point in holding back, not when I should be with someone else so that I didn't hurt Sean again, puncture his ears or whatever. I leaned against him and put my head on his shoulder. He stiffened up. He hadn't expected it. I didn't feel any better, not like with Sean. The only thing that happened was my heart pounded harder and my whole body started burning like I'd been in poison ivy. Awesome. I pulled away and stared at my lunch. Finally I got up, Oliver standing with me.

"So," I said as he walked beside me out of the cafeteria. "What do you want?"

He smiled sweetly, his emerald eyes twinkling. He really was gorgeous. "Besides you? I wanted to ask you to come to the lake with me."

I froze. "The lake? My lake? Why? It's dangerous. I've been using all of my willpower to stay away. Why would you want to go there?"

His gaze intensified and he stopped smiling. "I want to know what the creature is. I have this curiosity. I haven't even actually seen it, but I feel it there. It comes out for you."

"Yes, well, that's the reason I've been staying away. Not that it didn't save my life last time, but seriously, smart people stay away from monsters."

"It saved your life?" He looked so excited about that. "I wonder how much latent intelligence it possesses."

I shook my head and crossed my arms over my chest. "No. Every time I go to the lake, I almost die. It's stupid. I'm not going back just so that you can satisfy your twisted curiosity."

He stepped a little bit closer to me and traced my forearm with his finger. "You wouldn't like to spend some time alone with me?"

That made me laugh. "Oh, right. Because I'm obsessed that means that I have less self-control than you, right? You're obsessed too. That makes us even, or it would if you weren't the one who kissed me in the first place. What is it? The kiss of madness, or whatever you called it? How long will it last? Does it have anything to do with the thing in the lake?"

He frowned as he looked around the empty hall. "We could talk on the way."

I shook my head. "Not a chance. You're obsessed with the monster, fine. I'm obsessed with the lake. If you keep going you're going to get killed as much as I am."

He cocked his head, green gaze calculating. "I collect monsters. Where I'm from, there are games, one monster against another. It's a very important part of my culture. This thing, this creature is something I've never seen before. I have to have it. The danger is part of the fun." His smile was creepy, a little bit insane, but more genuine than most things I'd seen on his face.

"What kind of a person collects monsters?"

He smiled, leaning towards me to brush my face with the backs of his fingers. "The same kind of person whose kiss shouldn't affect anyone human. So, what kind of person are you that monsters save you?"

I shook my head, fighting off the tingling from the contact. "I don't know. For most of my life I haven't even been able to swim. Now..." I trailed off, refusing to talk about gills since I'd promised Sean. Sean. I felt a stab in my chest that made me grab Oliver's arm, gripping him tight. "Fine.

I'll go with you to the lake, but you have to promise not to hurt the thing. It saved me."

He raised his eyebrows while he studied me then nodded slowly. "It's probably nothing I haven't seen before, but different from living in freshwater. All I need is a closer look, to make sure."

I wasn't sure he was trying to fool but I nodded anyway.

His car wasn't the same. It was shinier than Sean's, paler, but as luxurious in its way.

"Where do you keep your monsters?" I asked as I settled into the cushy seat.

"Back home. There's an entire world you don't seem to know very much about, in spite of the kiss that shouldn't have affected you."

I swallowed. "Yeah. So, why did you kiss me? If you didn't mean to cause the obsession, why do it?"

He shrugged. "I took you for something you're not, something that would enjoy destroying my world and Sean's."

"I met his mother."

He turned his head quickly, fixing me with a frown before he turned his attention back to the road.

"So you think that I'd be something like her?" I'd said it without actually saying it.

He nodded. "What did you think of her?"

"If I were anything like her, I don't think that you'd want to kiss me, making you obsessed with me. That's just crazy." I shivered.

"But the kiss of madness is only supposed to go one way," he said quietly. "If it worked at all, the only one who was obsessed should have been you."

I blinked at him. "How is that fair?"

He shrugged. "Not fair. It's in the blood. My genetics are closer to pure... We won't talk about my genetics. Simply put, not a lot of people can hold power over me."

"But I did. Wow." I grinned at him. "That must have really messed you up, with your whole, 'I'm going to manipulate everybody to get what I want' thing. Whatever I am, you didn't see me coming."

He answered my smile with one of his own, apparently not resenting it, at least not much. "No, I didn't. So, what about you and Sean?"

I blinked, feeling the smile shrivel up and die. "I don't know. When I'm with him everything seems okay somehow. He makes all the crazy stuff go away. Maybe that's denial, and a bad thing, but I can't help needing it. Two obsessions in one life is more than anyone should have to deal with."

"Sean's immune."

I stared at him. "That's what he said when I got angry for him giving me CPR."

He frowned. "When did he give you CPR? After you fell into the pool?"

I shook my head. "Sometimes I can't get enough oxygen and I pass out. Usually when I'm singing, but sometimes, especially lately, just because."

He pulled over at the edge of the grass then turned to frown at me. "After you've been spending so much time in water. You didn't before, did you? You stayed out of water. What about baths? Do you have a bath tub at your house?"

It was kind of a personal question, but I shrugged. There was a huge tub in the bathroom upstairs that no one used. There were no windows and my dad said that if we used it without a fan too much mold would grow. Whatever. "Yeah, there's a tub, but I don't use it."

"Do you have any scars that are so old, you've forgotten how you got them?"

I blinked at him. This was not what we were talking about. "Sean already checked me. He was very thorough," I said, glaring at him. I barely kept from saying the word 'gills'.

He shrugged. "I'm just trying to understand you. I bet he enjoyed that." His smile turned sour.

"Oliver, you sound jealous."

He nodded. "I am. I tried to have a relationship with both of you, but you're right. I was trying to control everything, which didn't work out very well. I wanted Sean's

trust, your love, instead I have a monster, well, I have a
dream of a monster. Shall we get on with it?"

I blinked, trying to decide if Oliver was being sincere
or still trying to manipulate me. I really had no idea.

When I got out of the car, I could see my willow tree
in the distance covered in green fuzz. The mud was barely
covered by brush and weeds that were beginning to turn
green but not growing much yet.

"What's the plan?" I asked, shoving my hands in my
pockets.

"Do whatever you like. I'll stay back so it can't see me.
All right?"

It wasn't much of a plan, but whatever. I breathed deeply, loving the stench of decay and new growth as I walked
towards the water. It was fine. I'd been to Lake Stinky with
Oliver tons of times before when he'd taught me to swim.
There was nothing to worry about. Water didn't want to
drown you.

I stood in the grass a few feet from the water, staring
at the surface where it rippled gently in the wind, smelling
less vile than it would later in the summer, or maybe I'd
just missed it.

"What are you doing?" Sean's voice was so loud that
it was like it wasn't even inside my head. "Gen, get away
from the water!"

It was so real that I turned my head then felt myself
lose my balance, falling back, towards the lake where it
was almost like the water came up to swallow me. Sean
was there, angry, coming towards me at a run that showed
how beautiful he was in motion. Then he was gone, as
he and the rest of the world were swallowed by blue and
green.

I couldn't find my feet, couldn't stand, couldn't swim,
couldn't tell which direction was up as I was pulled down
by a current that I couldn't see. There wasn't as much panic
as before, not when it wasn't cold. I held onto my breath,
but it wasn't easy and it felt sort of pointless. The water
wouldn't let me go, and I didn't really want it to, except
then the pressure around me built and the water spun me

about more and more until I was dizzy, lost, confused, with nothing left inside my lungs to hold onto.

I kicked hard, struggling against the current that spun me. I didn't want to die. I didn't want to let the water decide my fate. The pressure built in my chest, pressure that I knew was something more, not a scream, but something. The sound emerged from my throat, sound that cut through water as easily as air, that made my ears shrink and for a moment split the water around me, an explosion of sound that cratered outward.

Unfortunately, I didn't have any oxygen left after that. I was lost to darkness until I felt claws sink into my flesh, ripping through my skin beneath my armpits. I opened my eyes, not sure if I was alive or dead, and saw the monster up close, eyes huge and glistening as it gazed at me. I opened my mouth to say something then closed it as water came in.

Darkness blocked out everything after that, at least until I found myself on the shore, on the hard ground with my shoulder on a rock while a very wet Sean pounded on my chest.

Water burned as it came from my nose and mouth as I gagged until coughing I rolled over, sinking into the mud as my body ejected the water. The pain in my lungs as I struggled to breathe competed with the growing awareness of the ache in my sides.

"Sean," I whispered, as he bent over me then my words were gone as his arms wrapped around me, dragging me to his chest where he held me next to his beating heart. I could have happily died there, but too soon he had me up as he stood, carrying me over the low brush to his car. He didn't put me down in the seat beside me, instead his arms tightened around me, making my chest and injuries ache as he drove one handed. It didn't matter when I could be safe for the first time in what felt like years. Funny how feeling safe had so little to do with actually being safe.

Chapter 35

The music in his car wrapped around my mind the same way he did, music that had been playing the first time I'd ridden in the car, sounds of violence and a struggle against forces, but now it wasn't two opposing forces, but creature against water, pounding waves that would rip you apart like it had a will of its own.

By the time we got to my house, I felt disoriented, like it was someone else's house, someone else's world, so far away from the struggle with the water, the constant struggle inside me to stay away from the waves and that world that threatened to drag me under.

Sean carried me inside, through the living room, up the stairs, and then fumbled a bit until he found the bathroom with its enormous tub that neither my father nor I used. I hated brown, so why was our whole house brown? Brown like the mud in the lake, brown like the monster's eyes when they weren't black holes that wanted to swallow you.

He set me down on the toilet, reluctantly letting go of me as he turned the water on in the tub then jerked on the laces of my wet, muddy boots. I saw blood staining his arms and shirt and felt frozen, unable to move or breathe.

"Gen?" he grabbed my shoulders and squeezed. "Breathe. Just breathe. Okay? I'm trying to get you out of your muddy stuff. You're bleeding. You're bleeding a lot." His hands were shaking as he struggled with the wet laces. Finally they pulled free and he took my feet out of them then the wet socks that stuck to the skin with blood stained edges.

When he moved on to my wet, muddy jeans I tried to stop him, but every time I moved my arms, it felt like I was ripping my chest open. It hurt so badly that I couldn't breathe, but I had to breathe. Sean told me to.

"Put your arms up," he said and I obeyed, unable to think past the red blurring around the edges of my vision. When he pulled up my shirt, where it was stuck to my sides with mud and blood, I screamed and pulled my knees up, wrapping my arms around my body. I inhaled, stuffing the sound back into my throat, staring at Sean, waiting for blood to trickle out of his ears, but he only frowned at me while he smoothed his hands over my shoulders and down my arms.

"Are you okay?" I whispered, my voice raspy and rough.

Sean grabbed my shoulders and shook his head glaring at me. "I should take you to a hospital. You're still bleeding. Not as much, but…" He took a shaky breath. "I'm afraid your beautiful neon underwear has had it."

I didn't care that I was wearing nothing but shredded underwear. "But your ears," I said reaching up, wincing as the movement triggered the agony in my chest, continuing anyway until I could touch his face. "Didn't I make them bleed before?"

He caught my hand in his, kissed it then shook his head. "That was nothing. Where do you keep your first aid kit?"

I told him and he left to go get it beneath the sink in the kitchen, coming back with the old box with a purple fish painted on top. He wasn't gone long, but my heart jumped when I saw him, like I could breathe a little bit better with him in the same room.

At least I breathed before he pulled out the bottle of rubbing alcohol. He took a deep breath through his nostrils and I knew something was about to hurt.

I gritted my teeth to keep from screaming as he cleaned the gashes, like he was handling my inner organs or something, pulling them like taffy. I bit back the scream until he moved to the other side, his teeth clenched while I whimpered. Fun for everybody.

I wanted to throw up but somehow I breathed through

it, even though breathing was difficult. It hurt so badly I didn't think I could stay conscious then the pain spread deeper through my chest, like the rubbing alcohol really was soaking into my inner organs.

He picked me up, wrapping his arms around my body before he perched on the edge of the ceramic monster with its clawed feet. He shifted me closer against him as the water swirled from the tap into the tub. He had his hand in my hair, pressing my head against his throat where I could feel every swallow.

"You went to the lake with Oliver."

I closed my eyes tightly. "Oliver collects monsters, and... it didn't seem to matter anymore." My voice sounded terrible. I supposed that's what happened after you drowned.

"I'm sorry, did I interrupt a suicide mission?"

His grip tightened and I cried out then bit my bottom lip, determined to keep my voice inside of me where it belonged.

"I'm sorry," he whispered against my hair. "I shouldn't have left you alone after you fainted. I could tell that you were in shock, maybe not as much as I was... I should have made sure that you were all right."

I laughed, well, it would have been a laugh if it hadn't been such a gurgle. "You're right. How could you leave me alone when your ears were bleeding?"

"I had to find out what I could," he explained, like I was seriously questioning his rationale. "I was at home triggering alarms I didn't know about, looking for answers."

I stared at the water, rising in the tub. The thing was so huge, it rose slowly. "What alarms?" It hurt to breathe. It hurt so much, I didn't care about alarms or the tub, or anything except that Sean still had his arms around me.

"I was looking up Sirens."

"That's ironic."

"Hmm?" he asked, still gripping me so tight.

I shifted against him, trying to loosen his grip beneath my arms without actually having him loosen his grip beneath my arms. He was probably trying to keep me from bleeding to death. He was thoughtful like that.

"You were looking up sirens and triggered an alarm. Was it a siren?"

He groaned. "You're being funny? You nearly died. Do you realize that you nearly died? Of course you do. You still can barely breathe. This tub has to be the slowest… I'm going to kill Oliver."

"What happened to him? He sort of disappeared after I got in the water. Is he okay?"

Sean snorted. "He's great, sitting at the lake checking the movement of the water for subtle disturbances that would be created by the creature, except that the creature itself hasn't shown itself to him. He's much better than he will be."

"Sean," I said, pulling back a little bit so I could look at him, but all I got was a low angle of his chiseled jaw before he tucked me back against him. "Are you going to fight Oliver for me?"

"No. I'm going to kill him. And it will be for me."

I frowned as I tried to gauge whether or not he was serious, but then I started coughing and didn't stop for a long time.

"Finally," Sean muttered then lowered me into the tub, so deep that water was all around me. I really felt mostly naked for the first time as I looked down and saw so much skin, so little neon, my bra straps holding on by a thread as wisps of red clouded around my body.

"Can I kiss you?" he asked, staring at me with his eyes while his thumb lightly traced over my cheek.

I stared at him.

"What?" I must have heard him wrong.

He wasn't going to kiss me now, while I bled in the tub wearing mostly nothing.

"Can I kiss you?" he repeated, leaning forward like a beautiful statue about to tip over on top of me, but when the end of his nose touched my cheek, it was warm, soft skin, alive and real.

I nodded as I felt his breath against my cheek, warm, a distraction from the pain, the difficulty of every breath.

His lips barely brushed mine when the door crashed open. My dad was there, grabbing Sean by the throat, pinning him against the wall while he stared at me, at the pile of wet and bloody clothes on the floor.

"You took her to the lake," he hissed at Sean, gripping his throat tighter. Sean was taller than my dad, but not by too much. He didn't fight my dad though, he simply stared back at him, denying nothing.

"He followed me and rescued me, again," I said reaching for my dad, then gasping as the movement pulled my sides. "Dad, let go of him," I whispered, feeling dizzier than before.

When my dad let go of Sean, it seemed more to come over to me than because he'd softened towards Sean. I expected something bad, a lecture or something. I didn't expect him to take his nice fatherly hands and shove my head under the water.

I struggled, panicking, trying to get up where I could breathe, but he had gravity and years of experience torturing his students. I stopped struggling, instead I stared up at him through the water while pressure built and built around me. Finally my mouth opened and bubbles floated up, because if my dad wanted to kill me I may as well get it over with.

He let me go and I surfaced with a scream in my mouth that I bit back, stuffing my fist in my mouth while I stared at Sean. I took huge gulps of air, sobbing between breaths. I turned to my dad, wondering where the person who loved me had gone, who this cold, cruel stranger was.

He shook his head and stepped away from me, frowning like I was a puzzle he'd put together wrong.

"It's going to be okay," he said before he grabbed Sean and left the room, leaving me alone to blink water out of my eyes and try to breathe.

I struggled to breathe, to stop sobbing and to think happy thoughts, but there were no happy thoughts when my dad was as crazy as my mother was dead. I closed my eyes and rested my head on the edge of the tub counting my breaths, drifting from consciousness, wishing I could be like Junie and take charge, or Flop and go with the flow, or someone else who didn't have psycho parents.

I heard a soft knock on the door and felt my body tense up as it slowly opened. I started breathing again when I saw Sean slip in giving me a slight smile, but his eyes seem a little bit big and dark like he wasn't sure what the crap was going on there, but who did?

"I'm not sure..." he began, with uncharacteristic uncertainty before he took a deep breath like he was focusing then pulled off his wet shirt.

I stared at him, feeling something in my throat that wasn't a giggle. I watched with this weird sensation of falling as he stripped down to orange underwear then sat on the edge of the tub, staring at me with an inscrutable expression on his face, like he was counting my breaths.

"We match," I whispered, trying not to stare at his underwear, not sure where to look at the massive gorgeousness that was his body.

A smile flickered over his mouth, but his eyes remained cold, ice blue even as he stepped into the tub and slid down beside me, raising the water from my stomach up to my chin.

"Um," I mumbled, as he wrapped his arms around me, sliding against me like my dad wasn't somewhere in the near proximity waiting to cut off his head and drown me. I sighed as he pulled me closer against him, ignoring the pain of movement while I wrapped my arms around him, forgetting about my dad when his mouth briefly slid against the skin of my jaw.

"Sean..." My voice was a slightly hysterical rasp that wasn't remotely attractive. So why did he tighten his hold on me, sliding his hands down the skin of my arms, resting for a moment on my hips before tracing up my sides to the gashes. I tensed, waiting for pain, but he stopped short of torture while his mouth continued to brush my neck, ear, throat.

"I have to kiss you," he whispered sounding desperate, the way I felt when he stopped touching me, when his mouth hovered away from my skin.

I turned my head and arched up, pressing against him while I wrapped my arms around his shoulders, pulling his mouth down, a mouth I'd only dreamed of tasting. It wasn't like Oliver. I tasted every centimeter of his lips, then deeper, drawing him in, unless he was drawing me in. Feeling him, not like it was a dream but like everything slowed down so I could experience every touch and taste individually in a way that made my heart pound and my chest tighten.

I pulled him down, deeper into the water, above me while I searched his skin with my hands, his hair, his shoulders, feeling the muscles flex beneath my touch as he held me against him, sliding his hands up and down my ribs, always stopping short of the gashes, until he didn't, instead spreading his hands wide to encompass the wounds, squeezing my ribs as he had in the shop room, causing pain that made me hold him down tighter, bruising his mouth with mine, taking his lips in my teeth, scraping while I tasted, drank and drowned in him.

The sound of his moan softened my kiss, made me pull back to see, to check that he hadn't changed his mind. His eyes were wide, pupils large and luminous with only a fingernail clipping of ice blue around them. He stared at me, struggling to hang back, to keep some of the distance between us even as his hands continued, like he was still searching for gills.

"I love you," I whispered, caressing his face with my fingertips until he turned and captured them with his mouth, biting, sucking, kissing with his eyes finally closed, the look on his face... I exhaled, sinking down, against him, feeling wrapped in safety, like even the pain could be sweetened by his touch. When he claimed my mouth, it was different, every kiss deeper, every touch truer as my heart beat faster and faster against his chest.

I couldn't breathe, I couldn't think, I didn't care. I was safe. Finally. Forever.

His grip tightened while the something grew in my

chest until it exploded, not quite pain, not quite ecstasy, maybe both at the same time. I could breathe. I felt oxygen swell in my chest as though his kiss were my breath, my oxygen, his touch filling me with more than I knew what to do with. I felt light, giddy, like laughing beneath his kiss, until his teeth fastened on my bottom lip and I felt his tongue tracing over my skin, leaving trails of fire and ice.

"Your water is probably getting cold." My dad's voice came from far away, the sound almost making me want to pull away, but Sean held me against him, ignoring my dad like if we kept our eyes shut he would leave us alone.

I felt a hand against my hair, a gentle touch this time instead of the other thing, the time when he'd tried to drown me. The anger flared up at me suddenly as I rolled over, shoving Sean down against the tub as I came up, dripping, hissing at my dad while my throat tightened and my whole body poised for attack. I moved, faster than I could think, twisting his wrist while the word came out.

"No!" Deep, rich, powerful enough that I felt the word strike the air and condense around me.

My father's face, his frown of worry stopped me from pressing out, from attacking him with the pressure that trembled in the air, like threads of sound I could use to cut him into pieces if I wanted.

Sean pulled me back, down against him, erasing the rest of the world with his arms while his mouth captured mine, scattering the sound like ripples across the top of the water.

The kiss was shorter as I pulled away, finding us alone in the bathroom my dad had left. The water really was getting cold. I felt awkward as I tried not to look at Sean, to not remember that I'd almost made my father's ears bleed the way I'd done to him. I'd actually hissed at my father. Even if he had tried to drown me... Only that made no sense.

"Sean?" I asked, but my voice wasn't weak anymore. It came out like a command.

He raised his eyebrows as I finally looked at him.

"Yes." It was an answer, not a question. It would have

been so annoying if his lips didn't quirk into a smile as he
absently stroked my side.

"Why did my father try to drown me? You didn't do
anything to stop him. Why?"

His eyes softened slightly while his hand came up to
trace an outline of my face. "Stop breathing."

I blinked at him. "What..."

His answer was a kiss, his movement sudden, the feel
of his mouth hard against mine. I blinked at him, both
of us looking while his mouth softened and his eyelids
drifted down. I fought the grip of the kiss, the sensation
that swirled through me, pulling me down as I tried to
think, to understand, to breathe.

Only I didn't need to breathe.

We were under the water, all of us except bits of knees
and arms, heads, mouths, noses, not breathing together.

I panicked, flailing around, at least trying, but his grip
was as unshakable as stone while he kissed me, not seeming to notice my struggles. I wasn't drowning. Eventually
I calmed down, staring at Sean, past him to the water's
surface and above that, the edges of the tub.

Something about his kiss could make me not need to
breathe under water.

Finally, he relaxed his arms and pulled away to rise
to the surface while I stayed, watching his face distort as
it split the surface, waiting for my lungs to burn as I held
onto my oxygen, but I could still breathe. Under the water.
Without him.

He put his face down staring at me with something in
his eyes, something so sharp and hot that I felt afraid. Not
of drowning, of him.

"Watergirl," he said, the sound echoing strangely beneath the water, the words like a hiss in my ears.

"Sean," I said, hearing my own voice loud, like a shout
that made him blink and pull back for a second, like it had
surprised him as much as me.

He smiled though as he lowered his body, his face, eyes
caught on my mouth.

"Stop." I hadn't meant to shout, but he flinched again

before he continued. I braced against his chest, rolling over as I pushed him down until I broke through the surface, seeing him beneath me, as I must have looked to him. I blinked as I continued up until I sat on the edge of the tub. Suddenly, breathing wasn't so easy. I instinctively grabbed my ribs, feeling the fluttering as the gashes moved under my fingers, still raw, throbbing, but moving, functioning, part of me.

"I have gills," I whispered right before everything went dark.

Chapter 36

I woke up underwater. It was everything I'd ever had nightmares about, but breathing was not the problem. The problem was the rest of it. What was I? Was I Soremni, like Sean's dad, Vashni like his mom, or something else, something with gills in the wrong place, something water wanted to kill?

The biggest problem right away was the breathing. So... breathing isn't something you're supposed to learn when you're seventeen. It took me a week before I consistently stopped passing out when I wasn't in the tub. I was so sick of that tub by the end of the week. Multiple lungs were a complication in my life that I didn't need, but whatever.

The worst thing, or the most disgusting was the slime, mucous, whatever. It came out of my skin all over my body leaving huge strings like boogers when I tried to pull it off. Sean told me that the mucous secretion would calm down after a little while, well, he told my dad that because I wasn't allowed to talk to him.

The first time I'd seen him, after I'd found myself in the dark in the tub and had climbed out, shaking and freaking out, I'd managed to fall down the stairs and into Sean before I'd passed out. Meeting him like that, knocking him off his feet while I struggled to breathe and see, because seeing was easier for me in the dark... Not good.

It was worse the next time I woke up my dad was there, in the dark of the bathroom, a face I could see as easily as if we were in the bright sun. He knew what I was, and worse, what my mother was.

"A long time ago, in the ages of myths and dreams..."

"Dad, I have freaking gills! Just tell me what's going on with me? Why is mucous coming out of my elbows?"

"There was a world where dragons ruled the sky, the water people ruled the sea, and man ruled the land."

"Thanks for listening. It shows me that you really care. Where's Sean? Is he okay from when I knocked him down the stairs?"

"I majored in mythology in College," my dad answered with a hurt look, like this was the time for me to humor him. "I want you to understand the scope…"

"Long time ago there were sea people. Yeah. Please don't tell me about dragons unless they're relevant. If I start breathing fire I'm going to seriously kill myself."

He shook his head slightly. "There was an island called 'The Soul of the Siren', and on that island there lived a race of those not quite sea, not quite land. They were both and neither at the same time."

"Right. So people with gills. I know all about that."

He shook his head suddenly furious. "No. The sea people like Sean are nothing like you. The son of the traitor has no heart, no honor. They could survive on land if they had to, but could never hesitate to slaughter a human, much less have children with one of us. The Sirens, the women were the link between sea and land, song and story, human and monster…"

"Wait. Siren? Sean said something about Sirens. Like the women who lure men to their deaths and drink their blood or something?"

I stared at my dad while he shrugged like that wasn't the craziest thing he'd ever heard.

He sighed. "You sing. You're linked to music, to water, with a voice powerful enough to rip the air to shreds. When you're submerged in the water your gills supplying you with oxygen that makes your other lungs a tool to harness that power…"

"Power? You call making people's ears bleed a power? Wait. That was before I was breathing under water. What now?" My voice was growing louder, shriller, and my father winced, covering his ears with his hands while I struggled to get it together.

"Yes. Destructive power might not be something you've ever craved, but you certainly have the potential. Not only can you destroy, you can protect. Power can be used for many causes."

"Thanks, dad. I feel much better now. So, I'm a Siren? That's what mom was before she died? How did she drown if she had gills? Hers worked, right?"

He sighed. "Can I tell you the story?"

I shook my head before I shrugged helplessly. I crossed my arms over the towel that I'd been wrapped in when I woke up. At least it covered most of my body and ripped underwear while I sat in the tub with my arms against the edge, listening to my dad's 'explanation'.

"As I was saying," he continued and then told me a really long story about this island and the people on it who were torn apart by the war between the land and sea until there was nothing left of them but myths and legends, only it turned out that they'd simply learned how to hide, with humans or gill folk, whichever they preferred. Master's of disguise, or something. I listened to the mythology until I couldn't help but break in.

"So, if my mother had gills, how was it possible for her to drown?" I didn't see how the story really had anything to do with the important stuff.

My dad's frown made me feel cold and sick, but I refused to look away. "She didn't."

I nodded and finally looked down, staring at the blanket over my lap.

"So, she was murdered."

"No, she's not dead. She's still in the lake. Someone hired people to kill her, but they didn't do it, only crushed her upper lungs so that she's trapped there in the lake without the ability to speak, sing, or be your mother."

"She's in the lake?" I stared at him while my mouth went dry and I had this weird idea I knew exactly what he was going to say next.

"Yes. She ripped your gills open. She must have thought you were drowning or that there wasn't a chance to hide you anymore, that you had to be able to protect yourself. It didn't help to have that traitor's son hanging around you all the time. I tried to keep you away from that world, from the lake, watching you suffer after we sewed your gills shut… I'm sorry you had to find out about it like this. If he hadn't dragged you into that world…" His jaw became tight while the fury burned in his eyes.

I blinked. That was about all I could do for twenty-four hours. My mother wasn't dead, oh no, instead, she was a monster in the lake that had ripped me open. Awesome. All that time when I'd been singing to her, she'd been listening. My dad didn't understand all the technicalities that went along with being a Siren, but being compelled to sing, scream was part of the description. More awesome.

On the positive side, I could breed with Sean. Of course, our children would be Sirens, like me, compelled to shatter people's eardrums if they were girls, and if they were boys, they'd be something else. My dad hadn't enjoyed talking about it. He kept referring to the 'traitor's son', until I got out another explanation. The kind that made everything else sound practically insane.

"Sean's mother, queen of the Vashni, and Sean's father, the Soremni king's brother betrayed the king…"

"Sean's dad is the Soremni king's brother?"

My dad nodded. "I talked to the traitor's son," I rolled my eyes, "And it turns out, Oliver is the prince, trying to convince the traitor's son to return with him and build up the kingdom. Apparently there are problems with their world."

"Oliver is the prince? So, why is he collecting monsters?" I sat up, splashing my dad. "He thinks my mother is a monster? He's going to put her in some gladiator thing?"

"Your mother can protect herself, Gen. Calm down."

I took a deep breath and nodded, then shook my head. "How can my mother be the monster? I remember her. She was beautiful and good. So gentle and…" I started sobbing and didn't stop for a long time while my dad patted me awkwardly on my head. I was a freak of the freaks and my mother had been hunted and broken, like my dad was afraid I would be if anyone discovered what I was.

Sean had mentioned something about sirens. Sirens. I'd made a joke. I should have jumped out of the window instead, only there were no windows in the soundproof bathroom. Now it all made sense—having a gigantic bathtub in a room without any windows, the only room in the house that wasn't audible a block away.

Being able to see in the dark was kind of cool, at least when I didn't try to see when it was light and get one of those killer headaches. My dad said that I'd be able to control it along with the urges I had to scream/sing if I kept practicing.

So, that's what I did. I practiced breathing, practiced singing, practiced controlling the fear and emotions.

I could do more than make people's ears bleed; I could make the water in the tub swirl around me with my voice, my will. When I really pushed it, I could get waves splashing over the side to pool onto the towel covered floor. At first I thought it was a coincidence, but gradually I could control how high the waves leapt using my voice.

I wanted to see Sean, of course I did, and I argued with my dad about it at first, but until I could control my voice, keep from accidentally hurting him, it was best if he stayed away. I couldn't have cared less if he was 'the traitor's son'. If he could deal with whatever I was, I could deal with him having psycho parents. I hated it in the bathtub with nothing to do in the dark bathroom besides practice breathing and trying not to miss Sean while I did my best to ignore the obnoxious Oliver obsession.

One thing that bothered me all the time was the kissing. At the time, it had felt like we were the only people in the world, that everything was finally completely fine, but afterwards, maybe it was like my dad shoving my head under water only more pleasant.

What if he'd only kissed me to distract me, using my stupidly in love to get my gills to work? But why would he bother unless he cared about me, unless he had some motive I didn't know about, wanted to collect me the way

Oliver wanted to collect my mother... anyway. Those were the kinds of things I thought about while I rolled around in the tub, hating the ceramic confines with all of my soul.

I was like my mother, trapped in the lake, even though it was bigger than the tub, still too small, too lonely.

I was half way through my second week at home with most of the basics figured out, when I heard a pounding on the door downstairs. I sank deeper into the darkness of the bathroom, darkness that I could clearly do my homework in if I'd wanted to, but the knocking kept going until I finally got out of the tub, wrapped a wet towel around my body, then one of my dad's sweatshirts and pants over that.

Glamorous. Yeah. My heart pounded as I walked down the stairs on shaky legs. Was it Sean? Had he come while my dad was gone to sneak me out or something?

When I finally got to the front door, I deflated when I saw Bernice, eyes big and scared while she pounded. Her fist should have been black and blue. I almost turned around, but the sight of another human... well, a human anyway since I wasn't one so she couldn't be another... at any rate, I was sick of being alone in my tub, so I opened the door.

"Gen, thank-you for opening the door. Are you okay? You've been out forever. So, I guess you're wondering why I'm here." She swallowed nervously while she twisted her hands.

I felt sorry for her. I mean, she had been my friend and spent all those unholy early mornings teaching me how to swim.

"Yeah, I guess I am," I whispered. The whisper wasn't intentional, it was the voice of someone who was used to having an extra set of lungs.

"It's Sean."

"What about Sean?" I stepped back, letting her inside.

"I've been with Cole, you know? We haven't been public, but I really like him. I know that I liked Ben and would look like an idiot but sometimes these things happen," she said shrugging helplessly while I stared at her. Bernice and Cole? Bernice when Cole had warned me specifically against her? Weird. "While Cole is great, I feel like Sean is family. He's been a mess. When he comes to school, he's not really there. He's almost as bad as you," she said gesturing to my super cute outfit. "Cole told me about the thing…" Her bottom lip trembled and her eyes got all big. "That's when it made sense. Something attacked you, didn't it? Today when I saw Sean, he was talking crazy, said he was going to kill it once and for all. He's at the lake now…" I left her to shove my feet in a pair of hiking boots still caked in mud from who knew when, without bothering with socks.

Sean was going to try and kill my mother? What would happen in that stand-off? I should have seen him. I should have made sure that he wasn't freaking out as much as I was. I should have… I ran across the lawn towards the curb.

"We can take my car," Bernice said, leading the way.

I got in, feeling weird in my wet, squishy layers as I pulled the seatbelt across my chest.

I didn't have to give her any instructions as we drove. It made me wonder how many times she'd gone there. I felt a twinge of irrational possessiveness. Maybe not so irrational because it was my mother who lived there, like it was her house or something.

When we got the lake, Bernice drove around to the side where there was a low muddy place boats went in and got stuck. I could see, long before we got there, the large, red vessel with nets, hooks, pulleys, and other things that made me cringe when I thought of my mother.

As soon as Bernice parked, I was out of the car, thumping across the squishy ground. It felt weird to be so active after sitting in my tub in the dark, but good, particularly if I stopped something bad from happening. I had to tell Sean what I was, or what I could be, anyway, keep him from taking on my mother. She wouldn't be so worried about hurting him as me, and she'd ripped me open.

I felt like I was running towards home as I sloshed through the knee deep water to the ladder and climbed. I'd missed him so much, and my mother? Seeing her would be different now, knowing who she was, that she'd been listening to me all those years. Maybe he'd give me a hug before I had to tell him that my mother was the monster he wanted to kill. Maybe I could think of another way to stop him without mentioning my genetics. No. I didn't care if my dad didn't trust him. He had to know. I loved him too much to pretend to be something else, something less dangerous.

At the top of the ladder, I put my leg over, then the other one. One the deck, I took a moment to adjust the towel beneath my dad's sweatshirt before I started forward, peering into the window of the steering house, or whatever it was called, then to the wide open deck with rigging piled up. Everything felt so… empty.

"Wondering where he is?" Bernice asked, her voice loud in the air, making me spin around. I stared at her, at the object in her hand. It was a cell phone, small, silver, harmless. So why was her face like that, like she was holding a weapon?

"Yeah. Maybe they're duking it out at the bottom of the lake."

No. They weren't. I could see by that smile, the gloating little smug look that she'd known he wasn't here all along.

"Let me explain something," she hissed, taking two steps towards me, narrowing her eyes at me so that she was suddenly threatening.

"By all means."

"There are greater things in this world than individuals. Forces at work that are more important than the little things, like friendships, love, or even loyalty."

"Yeah. Like pedicures. What's going on with you?" She looked different, wild, sort of in control of the situation but not of herself, if that made any sense.

"It didn't have to be like this. You gave me no choice. Seven years I've been waiting for Sean to notice me. The first girl he sees is you. Why?" Her face turned livid for a moment before she shook her head letting the emotion drain, leaving nothing but ice. "I'm not going to stay here forever. I won't. I can't. The world out there, it's mine. I belong there, not here. Do you understand?"

"Um, sure." I smiled helpfully while I edged back the way I had come. "Sean feels the same way. You guys are perfect for each other. I didn't mean to mess that up for you. Why don't we go and tell him that." Hopefully I was saying the sort of things a psycho girl would want to hear. Bernice had clearly flipped.

She frowned at me, clutching her phone tighter. "I just want you to know that your sacrifice serves the greater good."

"What sacrifice would that be, specifically?"

She flipped open the phone and dialed. "Hi. It's me. Is she awake yet? Good. Now remember what I showed you? Only do it to the count of five. That should be long enough. We don't want to really hurt her."

My heart pounded as she pushed speaker phone and I listened intently until I heard the scream going on and on for the count of five until she began sobbing and gasping, begging someone... Bernice clicked speaker off and I was left to stare at her while horror, disbelieving horror clouded my vision. I barely heard the rest of her words in the phone.

"You know what I said. If I don't call back in five minutes, you'll have to do the rest of it. I know you don't want to, but it's the only way to keep me safe. I love you so much." Then Bernice snapped the phone shut and put her hands on her hips.

I stared at her, reeling. "Did you just... Who was that?"

"Flop. Your sweet, stupid friend."

"Flop was your friend! You tortured your own friend? For what?" I started towards her, hands like claws, wanting to rip it away from her and take out her hair while I was at it.

"Now you understand that I'm serious," she said taking a step back and holding up the phone so that I stopped.

"You're psychotic. What do you want, you twisted..." I bit my lip, trying to control my voice, the pressure that built in my chest.

She smiled brightly, like she was going to go on in detail about how cute Ben was. "If I can't have Sean, convince him that he needs me then I must have the monster. That's my key out of this place, this world. So, you're going to sacrifice yourself, luring the monster to me, so that I can give it to the lady, even if I can't do anything about that arrogant imbecile." Even as she said the words, I heard the longing in her voice. Whatever she called him, she still wanted him. I could relate.

I swallowed, trying to think before I said something that might send her over the edge. Who was I kidding? She already sounded completely unstable. "I'm sure that's a good plan, except for the part where you, all by yourself, capture a very dangerous, terrifying creature. I'm thinking that you want me to call the monster, let it eat me then ask it to climb into your net? It doesn't really work that way. It's a force of nature not my pet."

"I want you to stand over there at the bow and sing to it. That's what Cole says you do. So do it. Call it and I'll worry about everything else.

I closed my eyes, fighting the headache, trying to balance my breathing. When I opened them I was still on the boat with Bernice too far away from me to kick. "That's very reassuring. What guarantee do I have that you won't hurt Flop even after you use me as bait?"

She rolled her eyes. "I don't want to hurt her. I have nothing against Flop. It's only her stupidity that she'd choose to be friends with you. She should have been my friend instead of yours all those years ago."

"Right. She'd be way better off with someone who tortures people to catch some monster. You're worse than Oliver. Fine. I'll do it, but I'm warning you, every time I've come here bad things have happened. I can't control the lake or the monster; I just call it."

Her eyes were cold as I walked over to the front of the deck where the two sides came together in a point. I couldn't see what Bernice would use to capture my mother, didn't understand how she could possibly be stupid enough to think that this would be a good idea. Sure, she'd about announced herself as a Vashni who wanted to control Sean, but gills did not give you the power to keep

a monster from eating you, particularly when you threatened that monster's only offspring.

It was all so stupid. She was hurting Flop for no reason.
There was no way she could actually capture… I noticed
movement behind the steering house I hadn't seen before.
We weren't alone on the ship as I'd thought. Bernice wasn't
as naïve and stupid as I'd given her credit for. Crap.

I bit my lip as I stood at the bow, trying to think my
way through the tangle. What if I really were luring my
mother into a trap? How could I sacrifice her for Flop?
What kind of a choice was that?

The panic in my chest grew, spreading to my throat. I
clenched my teeth as I gripped the railing, trying to think
past the panic. I had five minutes. What could I do in five
minutes? I looked out over the water that was already tossing and curling eagerly, like it could tell that I was there.

I took a deep breath, well, as deep as I could take out of
water then threw myself overboard.

The water swirled around me, the darkness taking a
few blinks to get into focus. Almost immediately, I saw
Bernice above me, her teeth bared at me as she screamed,
a sound of pure rage as she came out me, nails extended
like claws. I twisted away from her, but it was ridiculous.
I'd barely learned to swim and could do nearly nothing as
she gripped me around the throat and dragged me to the
surface.

"You don't want to sing?" she whispered in my ear as
water dripped into my eyes. "Then you'll scream."

I didn't see the knife, but I felt it, the pain in my back
sharp as the scream that split the air.

The waves roiled around us, like an ocean in a storm,
while Bernice gripped me tighter, pushing the blade
deeper into me.

The pain was so sharp, the feel of her clinging to me
as unbearable as life without Sean. I tried to shake her off,
then begged the water, the waves for help, not with words
but with sounds like the ones I'd heard in Sean's music.

The water came, dragging me down at the same time it
ripped her away, spinning me into the depths while I sang.

The song was like a force of nature, a gale that shredded the water, spinning everything around me into whorls and waves.

For a moment I saw my mother, saw her eyes through the distorting layers of mucous that she hadn't scraped off her face for a decade. She opened her mouth, but only hissing came out. The water bucked her up, then spun me away and out of sight.

I saw the ship, broken in half, coming at me through the murky water before my mother grabbed me, pulling me away from the jagged edges of the metal beast. My mother pulled me up, on the surface and for a moment the water followed me, clinging to me. There was a hole in the spinning water where I could see the bottom of the lake, far, far below, waiting to swallow me, the ship, the world. Gills were not made for storms like this, not when the pull of the water seemed to twist the knife in my back.

I closed my eyes as I arched my back to let the song spread, like a bird, soaring across the waves, full of pain, and anger as I hovered on the edge of the turbulent cliff.

My mother dragged me back, the hiss seeming to plead with me as she carried me, ever so slowly away from the awful drop. The waves plunged and fell sending us down to the murky, muddy depths of the lake. The song came less powerfully as her hands wrapped around my throat. Finally, I closed my mouth, exhausted and aching.

The water swirled around me even after my song had ended, still pounding me apart, intent to consume me until I was finally part of it, a piece of the lake. My mother clung to me as the water swirled around us, throwing us against the bottom, then up above the surface again. I saw the shore before the water swallowed us again. My mother moved towards it, the whole of her body moving as one unit that slid through the water, dragging me with her. The next time the water surged up, my mother took that moment to shove me out in the mud. I clung to broken weeds as I gasped, hanging onto earth while the water tugging my feet, ankles until I dragged myself further ashore. I coughed, breathing in mud before I struggled to my feet, further from the murderous waves. I gasped as I breathed, feeling the pain in my back, reaching behind me while I jerked out the blade, no longer than my index finger, dripping with my blood. I looked up from the small knife at what used to be my lake.

The water wasn't as wild as it had been before but it still moved like something alive thrashed right beneath the surface. The shoreline had moved, shifted further than it had been, the grasses washed down to mud. My rock, where I'd fallen into the lake was gone while my tree lay with roots sticking up, water bubbled around it. Stuff from the lake was sticking up in the mud, old metal rods, a fishing pole and old boots scattered the ground.

I felt a wave of dizziness. I forced myself to stay standing, to breathe and get a grip instead of letting the hysteria, the hyperventilation take over, drowning me in darkness to take away the reality of this...this horror that I'd created, that I was.

I clenched my teeth and forced myself to turn, putting my back on the lake while I stumbled through the weeds to the road with only one hiking boot on. The boat was gone, along with Bernice.

I couldn't think about that or the pain in my back. I had to focus on Flop, figure out where she was and save her before it was too late. The question was whether I'd go straight home or to Sean's house. My house was closer. I'd have to call him and hope he'd answer.

I shook my head and forced myself into a jog that made my back ache with every step. Sean would find Flop and fix the mess I couldn't think about, not if I didn't want to give in to the hysteria waiting for me to think too much.

Chapter 37

It took forever to make it those two miles in one boot until I finally crashed through my front door to the kitchen, dropping into a chair while I dialed Sean's number. I'd never called him before. I tried not to feel nervous since none of that mattered, but still, when he answered it took me a second to respond.

"Hello?" he said the second time, sounding more irritated than usual.

"Sean," I whispered, still trying to catch my breath. "Can you come over?"

There was a silence that felt like a gulf between us. I tapped the chipped formica table, waiting before he said, "I could do that. Now?"

"Please."

"I'll be there soon." He hung up leaving me to grip the phone like it was a lifeline before I yanked off my stupid boot and stripped out of the soaked, stinky, filthy sweats. I'd lost the towel at some point, but my black underwear was intact. The bra straps were a little lower than my other ones so they were beneath my gills—a good thing when my gills were still healing. I grabbed the first aid kit beneath the sink, but I couldn't quite reach where she'd stabbed me, literally, in the back.

My hands shook as I tried to think, to know who to call, what to do, but there was too much struggle just to breathe. Finally I forced myself to dial Junie's number. I let it ring for hours, well, at least a dozen times before I hung up. I didn't have a directory unless I climbed all the way up the stairs to my room. I put my head down on the table and tried to keep from sobbing. Now was not the time to lose it, with Sean about to come over.

I lifted my head as the someone politely knocked on the door, a decisive, knock that knew what it wanted, where it was going, and wouldn't wait very long for an answer.

I dragged myself to my feet, stepping over the pile of ripped and muddy clothes as I went to the door.

I jerked it open, fast so I wouldn't have to think about it.

Sean stood there in his shirt, the one the color of his eyes. It looked freshly ironed. His face had no expression at first, but the longer I stood there staring at him, the narrower his eyes got until he shook his head and stepped forward, forcing me backwards then closing the door behind him.

"Thanks for coming," I said, leaning against the door and letting my hair fall across my face. "You came faster than I thought you would."

"Did I?" He walked into the kitchen.

I dragged myself after him, noticing the backpack right before he unslung it onto the table.

"How are you doing?" His voice was empty of everything, not even ice coated his words as he opened the first aid kit and ran his hands over the contents, like they were familiar to him.

I opened my mouth then shut it, fighting back the tears that suddenly clogged my throat. He hadn't hugged me. I bit my lip because it didn't matter when Flop was in danger.

"Great other than killing Bernice and being responsible for Flop's kidnapping." I took a shaky breath while he frowned at the first aid kit.

"Are you bleeding?" When he turned around, scowling at me, I jerked back, pulling the hole in my back.

"I don't know. Not much. It was a little knife, but I can't quite reach…"

He grabbed me and a chair at the same time, pushing it against my knees so I collapsed on it, then proceeded to prod my back with his hands while I leaned on the table.

"It doesn't matter, Sean," I protested, trying to push against him, but he didn't even notice. "We have to save Flop. She's being tortured and…"

I stopped talking when I heard his voice. He wasn't talking to me.

"Hey, Leslie. I'm looking to recruit Flop for next year. She might be with Fred, the loner. Do you think you could track her down for me? Thanks. You're going to be an excellent captain next year."

I heard his phone flip shut then gasped as he poured the nasty anti-bacterial into my new wound.

"Did you try calling Flop's house?"

I blinked then shook my head. "She's not there. Bernice kidnapped her."

"Do you have proof? I have proof that you're bleeding, bruised and near hysteria. So, I'll take care of you before I run out into the street looking for Flop." I whimpered as he irrigated my wound.

"Have you called anyone besides me? The police?" I shook my head no. "Junie?"

"She didn't answer her phone," I mumbled as I closed my eyes. I couldn't stay there, with my head back on the table, feeling like my body was far away from me while the pain in my back went far away. I had to get up, had to do something. I had to save Flop. But I couldn't move. The jogging home had been on pure adrenaline, now that I stopped moving, I couldn't start again.

"You need stitches," Sean said, pulling me up by my arms. I didn't fight him, not when I could almost lean against him, smell his laundry detergent and the other non-human smell that I found so freakishly awesome. "Then you need a bath, a nice, calm bath to keep you from going into shock. Although it looks like we might be too late for that."

"I can't," I said, sort of struggling, then giving up since fighting against Sean wasn't possible for me at that point.

"Leslie will find either confirm or deny that Flop is missing. Until then, you're coming with me," he said as he kept me moving towards the front door.

I barely noticed when he wrapped a shirt around me, but then I realized that he didn't have one on. It took me that long to blush about him seeing me in my underwear.

"So, what happened?"

I sighed and wished that for just five seconds I wouldn't have to say anything while he held me. He didn't give me a chance to stop as he kept urging me forward, through the front door, onto the porch, then crossing the yard to his car.

I started after he'd urged me into my seat, pulling the seatbelt over me carefully so I didn't have to lean against the back with my knife wound.

"Bernice convinced me that I had to go and save you from my mother, you know, the monster in the lake. She's my mother." I stared at him while he stood there, watched him close my door and come around to the driver's side.

"Where are we going again? I have to save Flop."

He frowned at me. "I'm taking you to my house. Oliver is there. He'll be able to sew you up. I could do it, but it would be good for him to see this."

I blinked at him. "You want Oliver to see me in my underwear?"

A near smile touched his mouth for a moment before it disappeared and his eyes became cold again, cold and hard.

His phone rang and he flipped it open.

"Yes?" He said, then listened, nodding slowly.

I clenched my hands into fists while I waited.

"Don't worry about it. We have all summer to change her mind. Good work Leslie."

He flipped the phone closed then shifted gears, taking off so fast that the force pressed me against my seat. I yelped at the contact and he eased off the gas.

"What did she say?"

"Flop doesn't want to be on the team next year, but she's flattered that we thought of her," he said drily. "Bernice played you."

I waited for him to continue, to tell me what an idiot I was, but instead he put a hand on my bare knee and brushed his thumb across the skin, skin that was slick with mucous. Sexy. I collapsed against the seat, taking in deep gulps of air as I tried not to lose it, to cry, or something destructive to Sean's eardrums.

"She's okay." I wrapped my arms around myself and realized how cold I felt.

"Yeah," Sean said, his voice soft as he squeezed my knee before shifting his hand back to the steering wheel.

"Bernice wanted to use me as bait, to catch the… monster in the lake. Oh, and I sank your dad's boat."

He raised his eyebrows, flicking his gaze to me. "That was clever of you. Not everyone can sink one of those. Luckily for you, Oliver's the one who borrowed it, and he'll have no trouble repaying my father. Otherwise you'd be forced to iron my shirts for the rest of your life."

"Right, Oliver's a prince. I guess princes have money." I shrugged. "I don't know how to iron."

He sighed. "Then I'll have to iron your shirts for the rest of your life." He shrugged his massive shoulders while his grip tightened on the wheel. "So, Bernice was using you as bait…"

"Anyway, she called someone who was torturing Flop, making her scream, only I guess it wasn't Flop after all. She wanted me to sing to call my… the monster. Cole told her about it, about the way I sing to the lake. I kind of hate him for that."

"He probably couldn't help it. Bernice's kind can get secrets out of almost anybody."

"Not you. You're immune."

He shrugged. "You were singing to the lake?"

I shook my head. "I had this idea that if I got into the water, away from her, that I could control the waves, make them hurt her while I saved Flop. It wasn't a very good plan."

He sighed as he pulled into his driveway, waiting for the garage door to open before pulling inside. "The water tried to eat you again."

I shuddered as I remembered the way it had come to life. "It's really annoying the way that nothing seems to surprise you."

"I've been doing research," he said as he opened the door, coming around to my side. "The history of Sirens is very convoluted. No one thinks it would be possible for someone to sing water to life. I've seen it, though. It heard you through ice. That definitely surprised me. I'll try to recreate that face for you if you'd like." I glared at him as he pulled me out of the car, making me gasp from the stab wound. "No? Well, I offered. What annoys me is the way that you..." He frowned as he ran his hands over my hair, surprisingly gentle considering the frown on his face.

"What?" I asked, noticing that his bare chest was awfully close to mine, and nobody had thought to button up his shirt. Not that it was a big deal. Bra and underwear were practically the same as bikini.

"It took near death, murder and a kidnapping for you to call me," he said in a quiet voice, gazing down at me with his blue eyes burning into me. "My number isn't only for emergencies."

I bit my lip as I swayed against him. "I'm sorry. My dad didn't want... I thought you... No. I didn't want to tell you that my mother's the monster in the lake. I wanted to have it all together when I saw you again, you know, not secreting insane amounts of mucous, or accidentally making your ears bleed, that kind of thing. It didn't help that I figured the only reason that you kissed me was to make me breathe underwater. I wanted you to like me irrationally, to want to kiss me just because. I want you to love me, but how could you when I'm..."

I swallowed hard as I looked down, avoiding his gaze. The silence in the garage grew heavier with every breath between us.

"I knew about your mother," he said, breaking the silence.

I stopped breathing while I searched his face for signs of disgust and horror. I couldn't see any emotion at all.

"When did you find out?"

"I told you, I researched Sirens. There's a story about how one Siren went from woman to monster. It sounded too much like our creature in the lake to be a coincidence."

I blinked at him. "When did you read that?"

He stared back at me. "After you made my ears bleed. That surprised me too, but I don't think you liked that face very much. Your voice can be a weapon, but you can control it. You're already learning to control it. You're not a monster." He smoothed my hair back, my filthy, muddy, monstrous hair.

"Why didn't you say anything?"

He shrugged and brushed his fingers against my cheek. "There wasn't a lot of time. When I saw you at the lake I didn't exactly have time to explain my research. After that, it was trying to get you to breathe before your gills became infected. You never called me, and your father changed your number. I couldn't call you. Every time I stopped by, you dad told me that you didn't want to see me, that it was my fault that you'd started the process, taking you into water so often that your other instincts would surface, that you'd be in danger. I thought that maybe he was right. I still think that maybe he was right. I'm the one who showed you my gills."

"That's true," I said with a wry smile. "It was kind of a stupid thing to do."

As I smiled up at him something changed, shifted, and the world was suddenly all right.

He raised an eyebrow. "So now I'm a stupid, egotistical jerk?"

I shook my head and reached up to brush my fingers across the softness of his mouth. "You wish. No, I think you're stuck with wriggling puppy. I made a playlist."

He smiled, leaning down, holding me carefully against him, his arms wrapped beneath the wound. "I missed you."

My heart pounded as I leaned against his chest, wrapping my arms around his neck. "No one to destroy your perfectly nice shirts?"

I felt his breath against the top of my head. "If bleeding ears and ripped shirts are the price for kissing you, I'll take it."

I leaned back to ask him what he meant by that, but stopped as his mouth covered mine, soft, warm, careful as his lips explored mine until he pulled away.

He exhaled as he touched his forehead to mine. "I love you, Watergirl. I love every inch and part of you."

I grabbed him, pulling him against me, drowning out the words that filled me with bright hope, euphoria that made my heart beat hard, but then I was gasping, unable to find enough oxygen.

Things got spotty, but I was there enough to realize that Sean had his arms around me as he carried me into the house.

He put me into a tub, a normal tub that regular non gill people would find comforting, except that it was see-through.

When Oliver came in carrying a big dark green bag, it was interesting to see the look on Sean's face. He glared at Oliver while he held me closer to him, on his lap in the tub as the water filled over our legs.

"I smelled the blood," Oliver said pleasantly as he opened the bag, rummaging around in the contents.

"Thanks," I said, giving Sean a puzzled glance. "Sean brought me here so that you could give me stitches." I leaned forward, pulling Sean's shirt up so Oliver could see my back.

Sean held me against him, stroking my hair while Oliver brushed his fingers along my spine. The tingling that followed made me want to punch someone. Seriously, so awkward to want Oliver when I didn't want him at all.

"You're secreting mucous," he said quietly.

"So are you," I said, turning my head to glare at him. "I wouldn't hold it against me."

He raised his black eyebrows while he studied me. "Who did this to you?"

I took a deep breath. "Bernice. Since she couldn't have Sean, she wanted the monster. She tried to use me to lure the monster. It didn't work very well for anybody. I think she works for Sean's mother, at least she wanted to."

"Where is she now?"

I shook my head and looked down, resting my head against Sean's shoulder. "I left her at the bottom of the lake. I…" I took a shaky breath. "I don't think she made it."

Oliver sighed and I felt a slight tug on my skin, but nothing very painful. "I'm sorry to hear that. She was a friend of yours."

"And yours."

"And mine," Sean put in, holding my head against his shoulder possessively. "She was very good. I didn't realize how close I let her come to me. She's the one who told Gen to stop the fight."

"And she's the one who was always whispering to me about the way Gen was controlling you, manipulating you, changing you. She fed my jealousy." Oliver sounded more thoughtful than angry about it, but Sean's voice was hard.

"Without Bernice, you wouldn't have kissed Gen."

I winced as Oliver pulled stretched my skin.

"I don't know. I might have done it anyway. The draw was always there, the same for me as it is for you. How could I help it when faced with a Siren?"

The bathroom was silent for a long time, only the rushing of water breaking up the sound of breathing.

"You know what I am?" I asked, feeling small.

"It took me a little bit longer than Sean, but I should have known the first time she commanded me to leave, and I had to do it. Nothing short of a Siren could have done that."

Sean stared at Oliver, his gaze filled with so much ice that I shivered and he wasn't staring at me.

"Do you consider a Siren eligible for the games?"

Oliver frowned thoughtfully before he shook his head. "No. I don't. And, I don't consider the creature in the lake worth pursuing, either. Your secret is safe with me, although whatever Bernice knows…"

He shrugged and started putting away the rolls of gauze and packets of needles.

"You already stitched me up? I didn't feel anything."

"He's good at what he does," Sean said, pulling my borrowed shirt back down over me. "Thank you," he said, stretching a hand out to Oliver who looked down at it before he took it slowly, the expression on his face not exactly pleasant, but not anything I could pin down.

"She's my true love's kiss," he said quietly, squeezing Sean's hand. "It pleases me to find that I'm obsessed with such a worthy object."

"I'm not an object," I said, but neither guy seemed to hear me. They still stared at each other, gripping hands.

"You take care of her," Oliver finally said, staring directly at Sean.

Sean's jaw tightened. "I'll do that."

Oliver flashed a smile then stood, dropping Sean's hand.

"It seems like I'm in the way here. Watch your tub, it's about to overflow," he said, winking at me before he left the room, closing the door behind him.

"What was that?" I asked as Sean turned off the water then leaned against the side like he was tired.

"I wish I knew," he said in a voice more uncertain than I'd ever heard him sound before.

"But, you love me?"

He looked at me, pushing my hair away from my face, fingers lingering on the skin of my cheek. "I like you wearing my shirt."

"You said love."

"Are you sure?"

I nodded.

"Then that explains why you've been driving me crazy ever since that stupid baseball game."

I blinked at him. "The baseball game?"

"Sixth grade. You took a ball to the eye instead of ducking."

I frowned at him. I'd played baseball in sixth grade, and come to think of it, I'd gotten a beautiful black eye. "But I caught the ball. You saw that?"

"Oh, yes," he said, nodding as he rubbed the tip of his nose against my cheek. "You couldn't see for a week. I've never seen such a colorful black eye."

"Huh." I tentatively put my hand on his knee, feeling

the solid flesh and bone beneath his wet jeans. "That's a long time to think someone's an idiot."

"It is," he agreed, brushing my hair away from my face. "If it hasn't gone away by now, it might be permanent."

I swallowed, leaning against him while his hands smoothed down to my neck to my shoulders.

"What about your whole, 'I don't need anyone to tell me how to live my life' thing?"

He smiled as he leaned close to me, his breath swirling across my skin.

"You're welcome to try."

Juliann was born and raised in South Central Utah-the desert-and currently lives in Southeastern Ohio-the jungle. She studied, among more than a few other things, Creative Writing and Fine Art at the University of Utah. She also enjoys gardening, sewing, painting, sculpture, and in all things combining the magic of imagination with the magic of the world around her.

Discover other titles by Juliann Whicker at Smash-words.com:
House of Slide- Hybrid
Also on Amazon: House of Slide; Hotblood
Connect with the author online:
Twitter: https://twitter.com/JuliannWhicker
Facebook: https://www.facebook.com/juliann.whicker
Smashwords: https://www.smashwords.com/profile/view/JlnnWhicker
Blog: http://juliacrow.blogspot.com/

If you're interested in Dark Paranormal Fantasy, read on for a look at House of Slide: Hotblood, Book one in Juliann Whicker's House of Slide series.

House of Slide; Hotblood
Chapter 1~Lewis

"It's been too long, boy," Old Peter said, looking up at me. I stood on the worn wooden floor of the hall and let the screen door snap shut behind me. I glanced around the small house purposefully avoiding his gaze, focusing instead on the faded wallpaper peeling behind the door. Calling me boy was one of his favorite ways to irritate me.

In one of Old Peter's large, gnarled hands he held a knotted brown cane. I gritted my teeth as I studied the cane, the way he clung to it as he sat at the table off the kitchen. The cane was a part of Old Peter, but usually it was leaning against a wall, a warning, not ready in his hand. I looked around the room again, more carefully this time but I saw the same dull brown paper, the small adjoining kitchen with its ancient appliances, then the table. I took a deep, even breath as I stared at the table and the deck of creased, well-used cards spread across the warped wooden surface. I ignored the knot developing in my stomach even as those huge hands gathered them up, clumsy as he shuffled them into a pile.

"Nice hand," I said, sounding casual however much I wanted to raise my voice. Old Peter had trained me, had treated me like a son of sorts. I respected him, loved him even, but I did not trust him. In my world, trust is the last thing you do with the people you love. The cards were obsolete, showing the four suits like they still existed. Obsolete, but my profile had been painted on one of them.

"Practically apocalyptic," he said as he shuffled the cards into the pocket of his worn brown trench coat that didn't fit him anymore. He was dressed for going; he'd only been waiting for me.

I edged towards the fridge around him, the sudden need for sustenance occurring at the same time I broke into a sweat. "Do you have anything to eat?"

The chair groaned as he lurched to his feet and straightened slowly "Grab something then come along, boy. We've got places to go."

"Yes, sir," I said as I rummaged through the fridge coming up with a couple of chicken legs and some sausage rolls. It looked like he'd been stocking up for me; apparently we were right back where we'd left off: him feeding me, me saying yes, sir. Yeah. Like old times. "Where are we going? To feed the animals?" I asked as I followed him out to the porch where he stood bouncing slightly to get the circulation going. Of course he didn't need my help with that, he hadn't asked me to come but he'd been expecting me, and not for help with his small, town farm, however ancient he was.

He shook his head as he handed me a soft gray hoodie, like he'd had it in his lap all along, just for me. "Funeral," he said, slowly moving down the steps.

"Funeral? Is it anyone I know?" I shrugged on the old zip sweatshirt, trying not to notice how hot I was already, how little I needed any extra layers on a nicely overcast spring day. I followed him as he ambled down the gravel drive with the inevitable rolling gait of someone who would get there, however long it took.

"The corpse is not the interesting one—well, not anymore," Old Peter muttered as he walked past my beautiful restored Mustang, a dark purple color that looked practically edible. When I'd brought it down from the city, I was certain Old Peter would say something, knowing his love for fast cars, but he didn't give it a second glance.

"Why don't we drive?" I asked hesitating by the door, wishing that he would get in and let me drive instead of having to keep with his slow pace.

"Keep walking," he said shortly. "What kind of accent is that anyway?"

I took my time answering as I finished chewing. "South African. Do you like it?"

"Hmmph. Won't go over too well around here."

"I didn't think much of me would," I muttered then more loudly, "What would you suggest?" I thought for a moment before quoting; "A thing of beauty is a joy for ever; It's loveliness increases, it will never pass into nothingness, but still will..." From the look on his face my crisp British accent wasn't going over well either.

"No! Not that one. Suppose someone were to hear you?"

I looked around at the unimpressive low-slung building that gazed back at me dully. The green lawn was as dull as the suburban housing. Not a soul was in sight—not any bodies either. "How terrible the need for solitude: that appetite for life so ravenous a man's a beast in his own house, a beast with fangs, and out for his own blood..." I took a breath, mildly surprised he hadn't cut me off yet. Old Peter was not a fan of Roethke. "Dream of a woman, and a dream of death;" I finished but the words left a bitter taste in my mouth. My accent was a flat American that could have come from anywhere and nowhere. Old Peter looked at me for a moment and nodded.

"Now that's the right one. Tell me what you know about Sanders?"

Sanders was the town he'd retired to, a town that was as dull as it was avoided at all costs. For Old Peter to leave the action and find a nice quiet spot like Sanders had seemed strange to me since he'd never seemed too old for the game. I shrugged as I gave another look at the quiet houses crouched beneath the trees, the woods omnipresent in the background. In the distance a towering gothic relic from another world stood out from the rest of the place. It was just a little town based on the pharmaceuticals company that had moved here two decades ago. There was not much interesting to see, not when everything had been painted thoroughly normal, but I could feel the wildness of the woods on the other side of the river that used to cover most of what was now residential housing.

I finally said, "Sanders is a new name for an old place; it used to be called Hollow Haven. What used to be the cathedral is the only thing left from Haven. This area is highly defensible, surrounded by the rivers and the woods. The woods across the river are old. They're a refuge for some of the most dangerous creatures known and unknown to man. It's a very good hunting ground." This town used to be good hunting and would be again if given the chance. It felt like the neat lawns and shrubbery would be swallowed by the tangled vines if you didn't keep constant vigilance.

"Get that smile off your face. We're not here for fun and games," he snapped, his tone crusty.

"No?" I studied him for a moment while he walked. He was old, age creased every inch of his skin, and he seemed to move by sheer will, well, will and momentum. He moved with confidence experience gave him, experience and the knowledge that he had in his hands a leveling tool that would work on any playing field. The cane was as innocuous looking as he was. So much for appearances. There was no one like Old Peter; it was almost good to be back. Almost. "You could tell me why we are here," I suggested, looking up at the sky where low lying clouds scudded, ominous, ready to break at any second.

"Me?" He blinked at me with blue eyes, eyes so intense that I forgot about the age, the stooped frame and the paper thin skin. "How would I know?" he asked with a shrug.

I sighed only once before I shrugged back. "Oh I don't know. You seem to be pretty well informed for an old guy. If you wanted an escort to a funeral, I could have worn a suit." I glanced down at my jeans with my hands firmly in the pockets of the hoodie.

"Put up the hood, and you'll be fine. Shut up now, and listen closely." He frowned at me to make sure I was paying attention. "Sanders was established twenty years ago or so by Alex Sanders and his wife Helen. Helen is the daughter of the House of Slide. Keep up, boy." I glanced up at the sky and thought I knew why the clouds looked so ominous.

"I've never heard of Sanders House. Is he a normal warm blood?" It wouldn't be entirely unheard of for a prestigious daughter of a House to marry a nice normal man who didn't know that his wife was the daughter of one of the most notorious Wild Houses, probably raised knowing all the most interesting ways to kill someone. It wasn't impossible, but the chances of a daughter of any House, particularly an elitist House like Slide giving up her birthright was hardly likely.

Old Peter looked irritated at the interruption. "No. He's Cool." I stopped walking again and then took a few strides to catch up when the implications had set in.

"Wilds don't marry Cools. It's illegal." It was obvious but had to be said, particularly when Slide was White, a code follower, the kind that minded if something was illegal.

"Usually, but this isn't just any Cool. Besides that, they're soul mates." I snorted. I couldn't help it. The idea of a daughter of any House, least of all The House of Slide, giving up her birthright for love was ridiculous.

"You're telling me that the Daughter of Slide married a Cool, and that they weren't destroyed by every Wild House on this continent? Really?" He shook his head, not bothering to turn around and look at me as he kept walking. Apparently this wasn't news to him. Maybe he'd found an interesting place to retire after all.

"He didn't used to be Alex Sanders. That's a nice new name that makes people a little less nervous around him." Old Peter chuckled like he was looking forward to the time when people got nervous again. He sounded less and less retired all the time.

"Oh? Do you know him?" Old Peter knew practically every dangerous bloodworker, Hotblood, Hunter, and anyone else you should avoid.

Old Peter chuckled. "Know him? He thought he killed me a few times." Old Peter was not easy to kill. "He's even harder to kill than I am," he said almost reading my mind.

"He's an interesting man. I can't quite make out what he's got going on right now. You need to stay far away from him at the funeral. Shouldn't be a problem though since he's likely to be otherwise occupied."

"You're taking me to a funeral so I can avoid the people who are there? That sounds like your idea of a good time. Why don't you tell me exactly what I am doing here, Old Peter? Oh that's right, because then you'd have to explain things instead of just leaving me to blindly wade into all kinds of fun. Wouldn't want to spoil your fun by turning on the light every now and then." All right, I did sound a little bit irritated, but with Old Peter I had to stay on my toes, and I was already getting a headache from trying to keep my temper.

"You're not still bitter about that time in upstate New York?" He chuckled. "You handled yourself very well, boy."

Boy. He'd called me boy three times already, reminding me of my place and his. The boy and the reminder of the time in upstate New York did not help with my temper or the heat behind my eyes. "Thanks. The compliment makes me all warm inside." I wouldn't have had to handle myself well if Old Peter hadn't dragged me into the middle of a Hotblood war, a war that we could not afford any Wilds knowing about. I grinned at him, and he raised his hairy eyebrows as he took in the unmistakable signs of my fury. I wasn't kidding when I said I felt warm, not when I could feel my heart race, beating faster as my entire body heated up. The fury was controllable, of course. I'd been working on it for some time, but the headache was something I could live without. The terrible migraines were the worst part of having a fury—unless it was waking up covered in blood, unable to remember the events in the previous 24 hours; that took getting used to.

"You came here fast, boy, faster than you should have if you've been loafing in South Africa. What brings you to the area? Good hunting?"

I gave him a level gaze before I shrugged. "For somebody." He knew I would come—he'd been waiting for me.

If I were patient and didn't lose my temper first, he might tell me why.

Old Peter glanced at me, a quick darting glance with those sharp blue eyes that made me feel like the rabbit instead of the hawk. My temperature rose a little bit more.

"I'm here. You don't have to play games with me," I said, keeping my voice level with a ridiculous amount of effort. Apparently I'd spent too much time with rational people if I was already edgy.

"But you're so good at playing games. Listen, Lewis…" I jerked my head up when he said that name, a name no one else would have dared call me, a name worse than boy, a reminder of someone I tried hard to forget.

"Lewis? I haven't heard that name for a while." It brought back the kind of memories that spread the heat in my chest through my limbs. I had to force my shoulders down and to relax hands that wanted to clench into fists. Being a Hotblood got rather tedious some days. Maybe it was being a disciplined Hotblood that was so annoying. If I ripped off Old Peter's head like I wanted to, then it would be more fun. He was testing me, seeing how far he could push me. Like old times.

"It's Lewis now, or it will be soon. Listen Lewis, the cemetery's getting close. Can you smell the rain and feel the electricity in the air? This is going to be some storm. Who knows when it's going to end? Whatever happens, stay with me. Do you hear me, boy?"

I nodded and closed my eyes trying to slow the beating of my heart. I hadn't had trouble with a fury for years. It wasn't simply that Old Peter knew how to get under my skin when he wanted to. For the past few months, I'd been tracking but it felt more like a scavenger hunt that led me from one clue to the next, returning me to places I'd tried to forget. The sense of being manipulated by an unknown hand had me nervous, but walking along with Old Peter, whatever he said, shouldn't trigger a fury.

I let the fury build up until my head pounded in time to my pumping heart. I concentrated on the heat and let go of my will, becoming lost as I submitted to the consuming rage. For an instant there was that feeling that my body would fly apart under the strain, but with the next breath the anger was gone leaving me a little light headed. Submitting doesn't come naturally to a Hotblood, even when submitting to the fury.

As we got closer to the cemetery, I noted the long line of parked cars that stretched out as far as I could see. People hurried through the windy May morning towards the iron gate that clanged against an ivy covered wall with each gust of wind. At the end of the wall to the right was a slope dotted with headstones, and dead center was the coffin where people gathered, pale faces and hands in stark contrast to their black clothing. There were countless faces, each wearing an expression of deepest sorrow as they gazed at the coffin.

We slowed down when we reached the fringe of the crowd. I still had no idea what I was doing there. All I really wanted was to get the names from him I needed to continue my hunt then get out of Sanders. Getting the names would take persuasion though, patience, and a ridiculous lack of dignity.

"We are gathered together," began the quavering of the priest. In spite of his weak voice we heard him clearly; his voice carried to us on the wind.

I let my eyes and attention wander to take in the crowd. It looked like the entire town and then some had turned out for the event. I saw a few high schoolers standing around the coffin. One girl had white blond hair that stood in sharp contrast to the requisite black. When I looked past the coffin, a flash of lightning illuminated a line of men with umbrellas. It took that flash of light for me to see them in the growing darkness. I sighed at the heat and rush of adrenaline as my body prepared to fight. I inhaled deeply trying to contain the fury as my senses filled with the smell of their Wild blood.

If I didn't contain my irrational anger they would kill me, or worse. For a moment I contemplated how many I could take out first then shook off the thought. I'd put a great deal of effort into convincing Wilds that I was already dead. The dead were the only souls they didn't try to manipulate. Wilds had a tenacious belief that whatever they were doing was morally justified, which was annoying enough, but when you add their abilities to manipulate the elements of nature, it was better to avoid them at all costs. House of Slide was different though—trained to kill. All of them had fought hand to hand in real battles. The big one, the one called Satan had taken out more Hotbloods than I cared to think about. He actually liked fighting, whatever your blood. Most Wilds thought that was beneath them when they could control things without getting their hands dirty, one reason Hotbloods were so often called in to do their fighting for them.

I felt assaulted by their Wild blood but struggled almost successfully to smother out the heat in my eyes. Old Peter had warned me about the father, but he hadn't said that every one of the legendary House of Slide brothers would be in attendance. It was the kind of thing he would have known.

The black-haired woman in the center shared their blood—I could smell it. She must be Helen, former daughter to the House of Slide who had given up her birthright for love. I held my breath as I studied the Wild woman. She looked as calculating and icy as any Wild I'd known. The whole thing made my head ache. Why was Slide making such a big show for someone who had been disowned? The man to her side opened an umbrella and covered her and the slumped figure between them. I shifted trying to make out who that was, but it was impossible.

The wind began to pick up, and I could smell the sorrow in waves and gusts as the grieving people looked yearningly towards the coffin. I'd known more than enough Wilds in my time, but I'd never been to a packed funeral where everyone felt real regret at the loss.

"Who's in the box?" I whispered.

"Devlin, Son of Helen and Alex Sanders."

Devlin, I had heard of. I studied the gray umbrella over the central group and felt a wave of heat as I looked at the umbrella the man held. "It's not even raining yet.

What does he think the umbrella is going to protect them from?" It wasn't the umbrella that irritated me, how could it be, and yet, I wanted to personally destroy the umbrella and see those people, the ones who'd created someone like Devlin, a foreteller, someone who could see the future, who could have told Old Peter when I'd be coming by. Being known, being seen by a Wild, even a dead one made me really, really want to hurt someone.

Old Peter glanced over at me, and I tried to shake it off. I had more important things to worry about than a group of people under an umbrella.

"Who's the other one?" I asked, aware of how irritated I sounded. The third figure, the one that Old Peter hadn't even mentioned, worried me. He had a nasty habit of overlooking the things I'd find most helpful and dangerous.

"Daughter," he said, short and to the point without actually giving me any information. If she was anything like Devlin, like her mother and the rest of the House, she was beautiful, gifted, dangerous—the kind of girl I'd spent the better part of my life actively avoiding. It was fine though, hardly something to worry about, only Devlin's family, I thought. I breathed deeply and tried to focus on her scent, the scent I'd been unable to pick up before. It would give me something to distract me from the Wilds who made it so difficult to stay cool. It was something to do, to trace a scent while the wind blew hundreds of different smells at me. I had the strong odor of the woman Helen to guide me. I caught a flash of something enticing from the mystery girl just before the subtle scent of the man holding the umbrella struck me like a physical blow.

I exhaled and closed my eyes as the first spattering drops fell from the sky. I let my senses become blind in the smell of ozone. When I thought I had myself under control, I opened my eyes and studied the threesome closest to the casket. The man's silver hair trailed down the back of his black suit, as much as I could see for the umbrella. His scent was difficult to pick up like all Cool ones, but he was much more than simply Cool; he had an especially high dose of Nether blood—the blood that created all of us and our gifts.

As a rule I stayed away from Cools, because I didn't like the way that they could manipulate people. While most of them were willing to relax and embrace nature they weren't anything like helpless. A recent infusion of Netherblood like this Cool had would make his traits stronger, his powers greater, and bring out his aggressive side. If the Cool was who I thought he was, you couldn't let him get inside your head or he would never get out, controlling what you thought, felt, and did. Some people thought Wilds knew how to play games and scheme, but they were nothing compared to motivated Cools. Happily, most Cools were content to let things go. This one was not.

Old Peter hadn't mentioned why he was so dangerous; if he had, there was no way I would have come. He was tall and slender like all Nether. I couldn't be certain at this distance, but I had a strong suspicion that his face was on the deck of cards in Old Peter's pocket. Cools lived a very long time even without the Nether blood. Did the woman beside him know what he was? She watched nothing and everything like a Wild, but she always kept her body between the slight figure beside her and everyone else. I realized that every individual was centered, not on the coffin as I'd first thought but on that threesome and the single person in the center. The daughter.

The crowd began shifting as the wind picked up speed, flapping dresses against legs. The sound of rain beating its way across the hills triggered a running exodus towards the cars. Not a lot of people had brought umbrellas and this wasn't going to be your run-of-the-mill May shower. Old Peter didn't flinch as we were pelted with rain that stung my cheeks. It felt good. I would have found it refreshing if I weren't still preoccupied with the brothers of the House of Slide, a Nether Cool, and her, the unseen daughter. When the hail began, I shifted to block Old Peter from most of it, wishing I could run away or fight something. Another flash of lightning illuminated the seven Wild brothers of the House of Slide as they gathered near the grave. It grated that it was nearly impossible to see them in their nondescript trench coats even with my eyes. The largest of the brothers motioned, and two others lowered the casket.

I flinched as a hailstone struck me on the neck through my hood. I could hear the steady slopping sound as they shoveled mud onto the coffin. The seven of them made quick work of the job until there was a mound. The other guests would be disappointed when they emerged from their cars and found the service finished. Helen stepped forward, and I kept my eyes trained on her, waiting for the moment I would finally get a clear view of the girl. It was no use; she moved with Helen. I clenched my fists as waves of fury rose inside of me.

I felt electricity gather the moment before the bright flash that exploded into the earth. Helen kept her feet but the girl fell to her knees. For a moment I saw an outline of her but then the uncles and Helen blocked me as they helped her to her feet. Alex Sanders, the Nether Cool, walked with her towards his car. At the last second the girl held back and turned to take one last look at the grave.

I stopped breathing when I saw her face.

Seeing her was so unbalancing that I reached out to that other sense, the one I avoided using if I possibly could. The world around me disappeared into a blurry melding of inanimate and animate as everything was reduced to its basic spiritual structure. The brothers and Helen were darkly burning sparks with red lines twining where their bodies would have been. Where the girl had been was nothing.

I stared blindly in front of me, hardly noting the flashing silver fire of Alex before he ducked into the car. I turned to Old Peter and stared at him dumbly as the sparkling of his soul faded and I could see him with my eyes.

"Huh." I couldn't think of anything else to say, so I stared into the distance instead. When I looked at the world through that sense, I could see people's souls. It wasn't something I was proud of however useful it could be. Every living person has a soul, well, everyone except for this one girl, apparently.

Old Peter turned and started walking back home. "Well?"

I started after him and felt a building fury that would no doubt leave me with a headache. "Well, what? Not that it wasn't an enjoyable afternoon, but I have no idea what I was supposed to learn from that sermon. I feel like I'm dealing with Wilds again. I've successfully avoided Wilds for how long, and now I have to go right back to the beginning. Do you know how frustrating that is? I don't even know who she is. I don't know why I care. Every time I run into you, things get complicated." I realized that I was pointing a finger at him, and I shoved my hands in my pockets and focused on my steps across the unstable graveyard. Water streamed beneath my feet towards the road, but at least the hail had quit.

Old Peter shuffled along with me and put his hand on my arm when he slipped in the mud. "You didn't see it. No, you're not losing your mind. You didn't see it because it wasn't there. So the question now would be where is it?"

No one liked to talk about this kind of thing. It was brave of Old Peter to bring it up, and I should appreciate his efforts at clarity. I should not want to pound him into... I slumped slightly and tried to submit but the fury wasn't hot enough. It was burning steady just below submission, the most dangerous levels of heat. Irritating. "It was not just a trick of the light? She really doesn't have a soul?"

Old Peter shook his head sadly. "Dariana Sanders was the younger sister of Devlin Sanders who you've heard of, daughter to Helen and Alex Sanders, and current Daughter of the House of Slide."

I looked at him waiting for more, then impatiently prodded him. "And she's missing her soul? Did anyone check the lost and found?" I winced when the words came out of my mouth while he scowled at me. I had a tendency to make bad jokes under stress. "Sorry. Did she lose it when her brother died?"

He shook his head. "She's been soulless for a decade or so."

I stared at him then looked forward through the driving rain. Impossible. I knew souls. For as long as I could remember, I'd been able to see people, know what they really were. Good people, bad people—one thing they all had in common was that they had a soul. Some people's souls were barely alive, some people fed their souls to demons, but there was always something. People couldn't live without their souls, at least not long. I recalled the image of her face, burned indelibly in my mind. I pushed past the impression of shocking beauty and recalled the sunken eyes, the pallor of her skin, and the way she'd trembled as she moved. It was possible to survive a few days without a soul, a few weeks if someone knew what he was doing, but anything longer than that was impossible.

"Huh." We walked along in silence while I considered my options. Old Peter was usually right about things, but he couldn't be right about this. There was absolutely nothing right about a girl, who looked to be about seventeen or eighteen, to have had no soul for a decade. I realized that I was rubbing the scar across my chest and forced my hand back to my pockets. I glanced at Old Peter and his lowered head covered in sodden white hair, his scalp visible beneath the thin strands. He moved slowly, more slowly than I'd ever seen. For a moment I felt concerned that he might catch a chill in the rain before I reminded myself what he was capable of.

"Aren't you going to ask how she lost her soul?" Old Peter finally said.

"What happened?" It surprised me that he knew, and if he knew that he'd tell me.

"Her brother took it." He looked at me and gave me a gummy smile. "Yep. Her brother took it and kept her alive. I don't think she's had any human contact besides him since then. Not that she'd care," he finished glumly.

I slowed and let him get ahead of me while I struggled to understand why I was anything other than vaguely interested with a clinical detachment that would be thinking how you would be able to keep someone alive without a soul, instead of what I wanted to do with the person who had. I burned with a fury that made clear thinking next to impossible, but I tried. I had an irrational urge to turn around and do something with the grave; what exactly, I had no idea, but I was sure I could come up with something. I wasn't used to digging up graves and messing around with corpses, but I had a few friends… I took a deep breath and let the fury fill me and dissipate. It would do no good to bring someone back from the dead just so I could kill him again.

"Do you want dinner before you head back to the city?" Old Peter asked sounding almost sympathetic.

"Yeah. I'd like that." My head was pounding, and although I could handle it, Old Peter made something that helped Hotbloods and the aftereffects of the furies we dealt with. "I may hang around for a few days. I'm a little bit curious." That was an understatement. I also hadn't gotten the information I'd come for, but now it seemed less important. "It's not something I've ever seen before." I tried to justify myself as Old Peter gave me a wry look that seemed to understand my motives better than I did. "She has no soul?"

Old Peter shook his head then shrugged. "We'll slaughter something. What are you in the mood for?"

Old Peter liked his dinner to go from kicking to the table in an hour. Keeping fresh meat meant that it bleated at you when you walked up with a knife. Three hours after we got back to the house I was still in the yard packaging meat when Old Peter leaned out of the screen door to see if I'd lost the fight with the goat. It wasn't like me to be so slow, but I was in a careful mood. The fury lurked right behind my eyes, and I couldn't get the idea of visiting the gravesite out of my head. It wasn't a good idea. It was one of the worst ideas I'd ever had, and I'd had some bad ones. The girl's uncles would be hanging around for at least twenty-four hours. They had sealed the grave with lightning. That wasn't an ordinary precaution most people took to keep a dead body in its grave. Of course, they were Wilds with traditions that were actually relevant. It was in everyone's best interest that a body with those capacities stayed where it was.

I'd heard of Hybrids like Devlin and been aware of his reputation, one of the best foretellers of his time, but I'd never imagined he had any ability with souls. Who would think a Wild son would mess around with souls, particularly his sister's, someone he should be sworn to protect? After I'd seen his father firsthand, I shouldn't have been shocked about Devlin's abilities since not only did his Wild blood give him foretelling, but his father, Cool and extra Nether, would have given him the ability to bend people to his will. I still couldn't understand about the soul. Cools were in the realm of the soul, but that meant they did soul flight, not that they stole souls from someone else. Hollows were the ones who borrowed souls, or had before they'd been wiped out.

It didn't make sense. Puzzle it over as I might, it seemed impossible that a soulless daughter of the House of Slide would be acceptable. Helen might be disinherited, but her blood was still precious to the House, and the son had been working with the uncles. He'd made a splash in the year he'd been one of Slide's boys. He'd moved up the ranks until no one in the House was as feared as Devlin. I'd heard about his abilities to manipulate situations and always be in the right place at the right time and had wondered how any Wild could be that powerful, that good at what he did. Now I knew. Of course, having his abilities hadn't kept him from getting killed.

For the next few days, I woke up in the small spare bedroom of Old Peter's house determined that it would be the last day I saw Sanders, but every evening I was still there, waiting. When I saw Old Peter he'd say, "Well?" In that gruff voice of his, and I'd find a reason to get out of the room without admitting that I'd spent all night camped outside the Sanders residence. Of course, he knew, and I could see the intense amusement he got out of the situation. I was not amused. I had better things to do than watch her die. She was dying. Every glimpse of her verified that fact. No one seemed to be doing anything, but what could you do with someone who had no soul? The Nether blood was keeping her alive, but not even that would keep her for much longer.

Days of lurking went on until one evening I sighed as I pushed a branch away so I could get a clearer view into the house. I sat perched forty feet off the ground, spring growth exploding around me thoroughly camouflaging me but making spying on the Sanders' mansion difficult. It wasn't really a mansion, not in Wild terms, but it stuck out from the modest housing of the rest of Sanders. The lights were coming on one by one, and I could see through the glass doors as the uncles gathered in the white modern living room.

Helen stared out the window oblivious to her brothers. It didn't seem possible that all those men could fit into one room, however large it was, but eventually they took seats leaving the couch empty. Satan, the biggest brother, came in wearing his slouchy hat but not the trench coat. He prodded the slight figure of Dariana Sanders, dressed in gray sweats and a black hoodie, ahead of him. Her eyes looked enormous in her lifeless face. Even at that distance I wondered how she had lasted so long.

She sat curled around a cup of tea, looking like it was the only warmth she'd ever known. Eventually it cooled, and the cup fell limply from her fingers as she stared at nothing.

Hours passed, and a thick fog clouded my view. I minded more than I should have. Nothing was happening besides the brothers talking and gesturing while Satan sat and watched Dariana. The mother never looked away from the window. Suddenly Dariana jerked twice and stumbled to her feet. She said something and walked from the room. The discussion went on without her, and I closed my eyes and felt sick.

It was wrong.

I slipped out of the tree and started walking in the direction of Old Peter's, determined to leave the town for good. I hesitated when I heard raised voices for a moment before the sound cut off. Someone had opened a door or window of the Sanders' residence.

I was grateful for the fog as I slipped out the backyard

and through the gate that led to the front. I couldn't see anything but heard the sound of something dragging in the road. I nearly ran into her when she stopped to stare at the bare feet that poked out of the bottom of the worn trench coat. After a slight shrug she kept going, not noticing me where I stood two short steps away from her. I stopped breathing until she was at a safe distance. For days she'd been in the house surrounded by the Slide Brothers. The idea that if I wanted I could reach forward and lift a strand of hair off her shoulder made me tremble. She was so close. She was not close enough.

I waited until she was far enough I could only hear the coat dragging on the pavement before I continued after her.

She followed the road through the town, seeming oblivious to everything around her until she stopped outside of town near the bridge. She stood still then took a step off the road and into the woods. I hurried to catch up with her. She was nearly invisible in the uncle's coat, and the fog didn't help. She walked forward without looking to the left or right. I began to get nervous. This girl was going to be missed at some point, and I would have more uncles than I wanted to deal with coming down on me. While nothing like the darkness that inhabited the other side of the river, the woods were probably hiding things that wouldn't do Dariana any good. Some would argue that you couldn't do anything to her that wouldn't be a mercy. Some would say that she needed to be put out of her misery. It bothered me that I would have been that someone a week before.

As I followed her, I knew where her direct route would take her. There was a ledge that hung over the river where the drop was fast and far to the cold waters below. It was a nice grassy ledge where some people liked to picnic. It was also where a few notables had taken that final leap. However lifeless she was, I couldn't stand the idea of her committing suicide. I winced at the thought that you could call death after soullessness a suicide.

When I smelled the scavengers, I shook off the thoughts of the girl, the realization of the danger she was in bringing an edge to my fury. I saw a face, tinged green with a gaping mouth in an approximation to a smile, dimly through the fog. They should never have made it to this side of the river, not when the runes were laid so thick, so heavy on the other side, keeping the monsters and nightmares at bay, safely away from the people who lived in Sanders, unaware of the terrors that lurked across the river. Scavengers weren't the worst out there, in fact they were practically harmless against anyone who would fight back; they didn't like losing their loosely attached body parts, but Dariana wouldn't fight. I broke into a run, glad for the coat that camouflaged her. If she could stay hidden for a few minutes then she'd never know how close she'd come to danger.

One of them held a torch high above his head, waving it back and forth in his loosely jointed hands. There were others; scavengers never hunted alone, but their leader with the torch would be the only one I needed to convince. I didn't have time to try and reason with them—reason not being the strongest talent of scavengers—not when I had to find Dari, to save her from herself. My knife, the nondescript knife that I'd managed to keep track of for months, cut through the tendons of his knees before he saw me. It gave a staccato-like shriek before it tumbled over. I didn't even need to bring out my lighter, not when the torch lit his ragged shirt, setting him on fire. The others didn't run like I'd expected, instead turning on me with hisses and curses that were almost intelligible. One of them managed to wrap her hand, with the talon at the end of it, around my arm, slicing through my shirt before I grabbed her throat and burned, letting the fury consume me as she struggled, the fury driving my metabolism, building up the proteins until the cut was gone, and so was she, burned out from the inside. Most of them ran then, the few left were quick work to undo; a fury is good for some things.

When the scavengers were disassembled, I turned back to Dari. I searched the woods as the panic grew inside of me. The Scavengers shouldn't have been on this side of the river, and they hadn't acted right, slowing me down more than they should have with their unexpected tenacity. Maybe the scavengers were a diversion for something worse, something that wanted the girl as much as I did. I inhaled deeply smelling the wet woods but nothing human. I began to move faster towards the clearing hoping that she hadn't changed direction. When I reached the end of the woods before the clearing, I let out a breath I hadn't noticed I'd been holding.

She sat still, perched on the ledge to look up at the moon; it had broken through the mist enough to light her pale face. I slowed, knowing that even if she did fall, I would manage to pull her out of the river in time.

I heard an ear-shattering scream from the other side of the river. A certifiable nightmare wanted some company. I should get Dariana back home, but how could I get her attention without startling her? I could grab her and carry her home. She couldn't have weighed a hundred pounds, not that weight mattered when I was burning fury, but it seemed like it would make a bad first impression to pick her up and carry her off. The first impression seemed important, particularly considering the fact that there likely wouldn't be a second.

I stared at her, watching through the fog, and wondered if I'd been mistaken the first time. Did she really have no soul? I concentrated, and through the fog could make out the life that flickered from the plants and across the river the red brand of the eager nightmare. Everything else, all the life in the world disappeared when I saw her soul hovering around her. She had a soul, or at least she'd had it at one time, but it was outside of her now, a quivering iridescence of perfect purity and breathtaking beauty. I stepped forward without thinking and snapped a stick. I blinked her back into focus and saw her staring in my direction as if she could see me in the dark. I took a few steps forward until she could see my outline.

"What are you doing here?" I asked and realized how gruff I sounded. She opened her mouth but nothing came out. "It's probably not the best idea for you to wander around in the woods at night." She looked down and hunched deeper into the trench coat. "You look cold. Maybe I can make a fire for you." A fire was a terrible idea but I couldn't stand to watch her shiver. A fire would draw her uncles. It would draw all sorts of unwanted attention but in the meantime it would get her warm. It seemed like the least I could do.

She nodded, and I started moving, gathering sticks and putting them in a pile, all while trying hard not to stare at her. In a few minutes I was crouched over some pine needles blowing on a spark. When I looked up, her hair brushed my cheek she was so close. Why hadn't I heard her? I looked down and realized I'd dropped my lighter. What was wrong with me? I couldn't help but look up for a glimpse of the soul hovering above her. I forced myself to focus on the fire and finally got it lit. As I fed twigs to the flames, I noticed how heavy the silence felt between us.

"Do you come up here often?" I wasn't sure if she could even answer questions.

"With my brother Devlin." Her voice surprised me. It was a little like hearing a corpse talk, only corpses probably didn't have such nice voices. It was husky but sweet. When I looked up at her she looked confused like her voice had surprised her as well.

"Good. It's good to have family. At least that's what they say. So do you go to high school here? It's a beautiful building. It's always nice to see old architecture so well preserved." I paused for a moment then kept talking, mostly to distract myself from her soul. "I love woods. I love to walk around in the darkness never knowing what kind of dangerous thing I'm going to run into. I like fast cars too. Do you… never mind. I saw you at the funeral; that was quite a storm." Even as I said those last words I realized what I should have already noticed. The wind had picked up, and the fog was thinning out. I heard lightning from the direction of Dariana's house. Her mother had found out that she was gone. We probably had some time since she would not be easy to track, as I knew from experience. Of course, I had a bright fire that would draw them right to me.

I hesitated to douse the fire, caught in her gaze. Flickers of firelight reflected in her eyes as she stared at me, her hands over the flames. I realized with a start that she was going to burn herself and reached forward without thinking. When I caught her hands in mine to pull them away from the fire she gasped, and I had trouble breathing myself. Her soul slid between the skin of our hands, and I could taste it through that touch. She leaned over the fire never dropping her eyes from my face. I pulled my hand away and felt a bitter taste in my mouth when the sweetness of her soul disappeared. I moved quickly to put out the fire while she watched me with a desperate hunger that matched how I felt. Her soul was the most beautiful, sweet thing I'd ever seen and now tasted. It would take all the willpower I had to leave without it. I had built up a remarkable reservoir of willpower but it was vanishing the longer she looked at me, strands of her hair standing out dark against her pale skin, her lifeless eyes begging me.

"You're warm." It was half whisper as she made a helpless gesture towards me with her hand. I sat for a moment trying to think what could possibly make a situation like this right.

"I'm sorry about the fire but it looks like rain. I think I'd better take you home now."

"Oh." She sat there staring at me looking even more dejected until I reached a hand to help her up. She took it quickly, grasping it with both hands as I pulled her to her feet. I stood for a moment trying to ignore the taste of her soul while she clung to me, then turned and started through the woods. I tried to block out the taste, the sight of the dispossessed soul hovering between us, but with every step her hands crept higher up my arm, until at some point she put her freezing cold hand on my back. I think I kept my manly calm, but I may have yelped. She had one arm wrapped around me, and the other hand clung to mine. Her head rested on my upper arm while we walked. She moved her legs, but mostly, I pulled her along. I felt a rush of anger at the stupidity of it all. Here I was dragging her home so she could be cold and die there slowly instead of out here quickly. I slowed then stopped and turned to her so I could look down at her face. She had more color to her cheeks. She almost smiled as she leaned towards me rising on her tiptoes. What was she waiting for? I was no prince charming, and she was no princess. Her soul hovered between us, and I could hear it making a sound of indefinable sweetness. A soul had never sung to me before. In a few days it would fade, her life would snap, and her soul would disappear. Her eyelids drifted shut, and her cold breath touched the skin of my neck. I realized my hands were tightening on her arms, I felt the heat in me soak into her.

I felt her soul, sweet and tantalizing around the edges, but the real brightness and beauty was deeper. I didn't make a decision to kiss her. One moment I was a breath away, and then her mouth was on mine, her breath became mine, and her soul was even sweeter than I'd imagined. I felt it wrap around me along with her arms, tangling fingers in my hair, and then something changed. The sweetness became too sweet, an ache that grew along with the coldness, as I tasted her. I realized that it wasn't me who was doing the tasting. She was taking my warmth. I began to pull away but she held on and ripped all the heat, rage, and life out of me. I lost the feeling in my legs and slid down her, feeling the buttons of her coat scrape my cheek. I tried to hold onto something, but everything disintegrated as I slid into darkness.

Made in the USA
Lexington, KY
22 June 2014